F. Scott Fitzgerald

This Side of Paradise

Flappers and Philosophers

F. Scott Fitzgerald

This Side of Paradise

Flappers and Philosophers

GRAMERCY BOOKS

New York • Avenel

Introduction and compilation © 1996
by Random House Value Publishing, Inc.
All right reserved.

This 1996 edition is published by Gramercy Books,
distributed by Random House Value Publishing, Inc.,
40 Engelhard Avenue, Avenel, New Jersey 07001.

Printed and bound in the United States of America

Library of Congress Cataloging-in-Publication Data
Fitzgerald, F. Scott (Francis Scott), 1896–1940.
[Selections. 1996]
F. Scott Fitzgerald : selected works / F. Scott Fitzgerald.
p.   cm.—Gramercy modern classics)
Contents: This side of paradise—Flappers and philosophers.
ISBN 0-517-14882-X (HC)
I. Fitzgerald, F. Scott (Francis Scott), 1896–1940. This side of paradise.   II. Fitzgerald, F. Scott (Francis Scott), 1896–1940. Flappers and philosophers.   III. Title.   IV. Title: This side of paradise.   V. Title: Flappers and philosophers.   VI. Series.
PS3511.I9A6   1996

813'.52—dc20   95-48822
                                                                                                           CIP

10 9 8 7 6 5 4 3 2 1

F. Scott Fitzgerald

Introduction

———————◆———————

"My whole theory of writing I can sum up in one sentence. An author ought to write for the youth of his own generation, the critics of the next, and the schoolmasters of ever afterward." These were the exuberant words of the young F. Scott Fitzgerald experiencing the glow of success following the publication of his first novel, **This Side of Paradise**. It was a self-fulfilling prophecy. Though in his all-too brief career—a dozen years of success, then years of disappointments—Fitzgerald wrote only five novels (but some 160 published stories), these works did indeed speak to his generation. Today they continue to fascinate and arouse readers, critics and scholars alike while being discovered by many new to the Fitzgerald table.

Born in 1896 in St. Paul, Minnesota, Francis Scott Key Fitzgerald was educated at St. Paul Academy, the Newman School, and Princeton University. His was not a distinguished academic career and he almost flunked out of Princeton in January 1917. Though he dreamed of triumph and fame as a writer, he was hardly prepared to starve for the privilege. It was America's entrance into World War I that solved the immediate problem of where his future lay and, temporarily forsaking his dreams of becoming a writer, he entered the infantry as a second lieutenant in October of 1917. This period marked two significant events that would alter the course of his life: he began writing the novel that would become **This Side of Paradise**, and he met the woman whose influence would be felt throughout most of his writing, the southern belle Zelda Sayre. Beautiful, reckless and impulsive, Zelda would become the model for several of the alluring, flighty, capricious women of his novels and stories. She was, however, eminently practical on the subject of marriage to a soldier and unpublished writer. Zelda recognized that love could hardly flourish on a budget, an attitude that would be reborn in the character of Rosalind in **This Side of Paradise**. Until success came, marriage would have to wait.

In 1918, while still in the army, Fitzgerald submitted his novel, then titled "The Romantic Egoist," to Charles Scribner's Sons. Actually, the book was sent in by Scott's mentor and friend, the writer and lecturer Shane Leslie, who had been published by Scribner's. Leslie included a cover letter which stated: "Though Scott Fitzgerald is still alive it has literary value. Of course, when he is killed, it will also have a commercial value." A rather modern view of marketing possibilities. The novel was promptly rejected; while editor Maxwell Perkins (who was not then the legend he would become) thought the book had merit, he was overridden by senior editors. The following year, Fitzgerald was discharged from the Army and went to work for an advertising agency in New York. During the spring of 1919, Scott wrote nineteen stories but sold only one, "Babes In the Woods," to the magazine *Smart Set*, edited by H.L. Mencken and George Jean Nathan. In June, Zelda broke off their engagement and Fitzgerald went on an alcoholic bender that lasted until July 1, when the country went dry; prohibition was now the law. Quitting his job, he went home to St. Paul. "After that," he would relate later, "I dug in and wrote my first book."

In September of 1919, Fitzgerald completed the second version of his novel and sent it back to Scribner's. This time Maxwell Perkins prevailed, threatening to resign and commenting, "My feeling is that a publisher's first allegiance is to talent. If we're going to turn down the likes of Fitzgerald, I will lose all interest in publishing books." On September 16, Perkins accepted **This Side of Paradise**. It marked the beginning of a career that would run the gamut from glittering success to never-filmed movie scripts.

This Side of Paradise was published in 1920 when F. Scott Fitzgerald was just twenty-three. The novel was greeted with reviews that would have been the envy of more accomplished, less successful authors. Wrote Robert Benchley in the *New York Morning World*, "He tells a story in a new way, without regard to rules or convention . . . I should be inclined to hail as a genius any twenty-three-year-old author who can think up something new and say it in a new way so that it will be interesting to a great many people." "The glorious spirit of abounding youth glows through this fascinating tale . . ." enthused *The New York Times Book Review*. "As a picture of the daily existence of what we call loosely college men, this book is as nearly perfect as such a work could be," it went on. **This Side of Paradise**, the first chronicle of flaming youth and the '20s jazz babies, was published on March 26, 1920. With his success assured, Zelda finally acquiesced to Scott; the couple married on April 3, 1920.

Strongly autobiographical, F. Scott Fitzgerald's **This Side of Paradise** follows the fortunes of Amory Blaine, born to wealth, possessed of a certainty that his was to be a great destiny, though the nature of that destiny is not clear. Reared by an eccentric and indulgent mother, Amory attends prep schools, the right parties and, ultimately, Princeton. Amory has chosen Princeton, rather than Yale or Harvard, because he sees it as "lazy and goodlooking and aristocratic" in addition to the important attribute of having an "alluring reputation as the pleasantest country club in America."

This Side of Paradise is a chronicle of youth. Regarded as the first realistic American college novel, it revealed what Princeton was like during a period when the school was exclusive and glamorous. It depicts all of the fury, fancy and folly of the time just before World War I—the Great War. In his vivid picture of campus life, Fitzgerald captures the manic spirit of wild girls, wilder boys, alcohol-soaked parties, and fast cars in a style that still enchants the reader today. It also offers a startling look at the sexuality of the day's young women that caught the attention of the public. The daring of **This Side of Paradise** was that it acknowledged that the young men and women of the time celebrated, even as Prohibition was enacted, both drinking and sex. It is particularly interesting to observe the attitudes and thoughts of the young women of the day. This was the era of the jazz babies, the flappers (a term popularized by Fitzgerald); these were liberated American women, still bound by some convention, but making up their own rules. As Fitzgerald writes, "Amory saw girls doing things that even in his memory would have been impossible: eating three-o'clock, after-dance suppers in impossible cafes, talking of every side of life with an air half of earnestness, half of mockery, yet with a furtive excitement that Amory considered stood for a real moral letdown. But he never realized how widespread it was until he saw the cities between New York and Chicago as one vast juvenile intrigue." Then, at a party, Amory is smitten by a girl he remembers only slightly from his childhood. Isabelle Borge is a sixteen-year-old quite taken with her own charms. She's most certainly been kissed and has been called by some, a "Speed." Isabelle also know exactly how to keep her men on a string, eager for her smallest favor. And her social skills are quite considerable: for conversation, "a humorous reference to the past was all she needed. The things Isabelle coud do socially with one idea were remarkable."

In his novel, Fitzgerald charted the progress of these girls from "belle" to "flirt" to "baby vamp." And while college boys were delighted to find vamps, many still thought casual kissing morally wrong and that a serious kiss was not possible without a proposal of marriage. Kissing was serious "coin of the realm" in the relationship between young men and women, and these jazz babies knew quite well how to dangle the possibilities of a kiss and (though highly unlikely) more provocative favors. When Isabelle, in a fit of pique over an imagined lack of sympathy from Amory, refuses to be kissed any longer, he realizes that he has no real affection for her. On the other hand, he is irritated by the feeling that it isn't "dignified to come off second best, *pleading*, with a doughty warrior like Isabelle."

But it is the beautiful, selfish and spoiled Rosalind with whom Amory falls desperately in love after his Princeton days. Rosalind has her own modern and highly liberated view of kissing: "There used to be two kinds of kisses. First when girls were kissed and deserted; second when they were engaged. Now there's a third kind, where the man is kissed and deserted. . . . Given a decent start any girl can beat a man nowadays." She is also sufficiently self-aware to realize that, because Amory's family fortunes have dwindled and he has only the income from his job as an advertising copywriter, he cannot possibly keep her in the highly expensive style she has always known. "I can't be cooped up in a little flat, waiting for you. You'd hate me in a narrow atmosphere. I'd make you hate me."

One more girl makes a mark on Amory. Eleanor Savage, "a witch of perhaps nineteen, alert and dreamy," is unlike any girl he has met before. She announces quite grandly that she doesn't believe in God or immortality and characterizes herself as "a romantic little materialist." But she is also furious at the world's inequity. "Rotten, rotten old world and the wretchedest thing of all is me—oh *why* am I a girl? You can play around with girls without being involved in meshes of sentiment, and you can do anything and be justified—and here am I with the brains to do everything, yet tied to the sinking ship of future matrimony. If I were born a hundred years from now, well, and good, but now what's in store for me—I have to marry, that goes without saying. Who? I'm too bright for most men, and yet I have to descend to their level and let them patronize my intellect in order to get their attention." The more things change. . . .

Following **This Side of Paradise**, Scribner's, as was their custom, published a volume of Fitzgerald's short stories, **Flappers and Philosophers**. This collection of eight stories was dedicated to Zelda and included "Bernice Bobs Her Hair," "The Ice Palace," and "The Offshore Pirate." While it appeared in 1920 to capitalize on the success of **This Side of Paradise**, reviewers were lukewarm in their praise of these stories and perplexed by what they felt was the uneven quality of the work. Still, the *Chicago Tribune* called its author the laureate of the high-spirited younger generation. "There is something far more important than his popularity about Scott Fitzgerald. It is youth, uncompromising, unclothed, but not, as youth often is, dour and morbid. It is youth conscious of its powers and joyous in them." Responding to critic H.L. Mencken, who had commented upon the diffence between Fitzgerald the entertainer and Fitzgerald the serious novelist, Scott sent a copy of **Flappers and Philosophers**, rating the stories: *Worth reading:* "The Ice Palace," "The Cut-Glass Bowl," "Benediction," "Dalyrimple Goes Wrong"; *Amusing:* "The Offshore Pirate"; *Trash:* "Head and Shoulders," "The Four Fists," "Bernice Bobs Her Hair." Modern readers will wish to draw their own conclusions.

This Side of Paradise and **Flappers and Philosophers** were the books that were to give F. Scott Fitzgerald his first, most intoxicating, taste of the pleasures that accrue to those with fame and the money to enjoy it. Scott and Zelda learned to enjoy a luxurious lifestyle, but making enough money to maintain their style of living required that Scott work at an accelerated pace. His second novel, **The Beautiful and the Damned**, and another collection of short stories, **Tales of the Jazz Age**, appeared only two years later, in 1922.

Along the way, the couple, often seen as the evocation of many of Scott's characters, achieved a certain notoriety as they danced and drank their way through New York, Paris, the Riviera, and Rome. When they moved to Europe in 1924, the Fitzgeralds counted among their friends other American expatriates including Gertrude Stein, Ernest Hemingway, John Dos Passos, and other writers who came of age immediately after World War I. They became known as the "Lost

Generation," stemming from a remark by Stein that their generation was "lost" in the sense that its inherited values were no longer relevant in the postwar world; they were alienated from a United States that seemed to them hopelessly provincial, materialistic, and emotionally barren.

It was in the south of France, in the village of St. Raphaël, that Fitzgerald wrote **The Great Gatsby**. Its publication in 1925 marked the pinnacle of his success, a height he would never quite reach again. Zelda's institutionalization after a nervous breakdown in the same year, as well as his own drinking problems, added to the difficulties he experienced during the writing of **Tender Is the Night**. When the novel failed to sell, Scott felt the sting of defeat. Faced with supporting the expensive lifestyle to which he was accustomed and Zelda's expenses, Fitzgerald turned more frequently to short story writing for *The Saturday Evening Post, Scribner's Magazine,* and *Esquire.* He moved to Hollywood where his attempts as a screenwriter brought little success, and his years there were marked by alcoholic excess. When F. Scott Fitgerald died of a heart attack in 1940 at the age of forty-four, he was working on the novel he hoped would return his name to its former luster, a tale of Hollywood, **The Last Tycoon**.

The mere mention of F. Scott Fitzgerald's name evokes a time and place; jazz babies, college boys with flasks in their back pockets, women whose hearts could harden in a moment, men obsessed by unfulfilled dreams. He has been seen by some as a man who managed to eke out masterpieces while looking through the bottom of a martini glass. But to see him in this light only diminishes his gift. As Zelda Fitzgerald observed after his death, "I do not know that a personality *can* be divorced from the times which evoke it. . . . I feel that Scott's greatest contribution was the dramatization of a heart-broken and despairing era, giving it a new *raison d'être* in the sense of tragic courage with which he endowed it."

At the time of his death, many believed his books were out of print—which was not the case. Nearly a half century after his death, noted his publisher, Charles Scribner III, more copies of Fitzgerald's books were being ordered each year than were sold during his lifetime.

KAROLE LINDELL

New York City
1996

This Side
of Paradise

. . . Well this side of Paradise! . . .
There's little comfort in the wise.

—RUPERT BROOKE

Experience is the name so many people
give to their mistakes.

—OSCAR WILDE

To Sigourney Fay

Contents

BOOK ONE

The
Romantic
Egotist

One

Amory,

Son of Beatrice

AMORY BLAINE INHERITED FROM HIS MOTHER every trait, except the stray inexpressible few, that made him worth while. His father, an ineffectual, inarticulate man with a taste for Byron and a habit of drowsing over the *Encyclopædia Britannica*, grew wealthy at thirty through the death of two elder brothers, successful Chicago brokers, and in the first flush of feeling that the world was his, went to Bar Harbor and met Beatrice O'Hara. In consequence, Stephen Blaine handed down to posterity his height of just under six feet and his tendency to waver at crucial moments, these two abstractions appearing in his son, Amory. For many years he hovered in the background of his family's life, an unassertive figure with a face half-obliterated by lifeless, silky hair continually occupied in "taking care" of his wife, continually harassed by the idea that he didn't and couldn't understand her.

But Beatrice Blaine! There was a woman! Early pictures taken on her father's estate at Lake Geneva, Wisconsin, or in Rome at the Sacred Heart Convent—an educational extravagance that in her youth was only for the daughters of the exceptionally wealthy—showed the exquisite delicacy of her features, the consummate art and simplicity of her clothes. A brilliant education she had—her youth passed in renaissance glory, she was versed in the latest gossip of the Older Roman Families; known by name as a fabulously wealthy American girl to Cardinal Vitori and Queen Margherita and more subtle celebrities that one must have had some culture even to have heard of. She learned in England to prefer whiskey and soda to wine, and her small talk was broadened in two senses during a winter in Vienna. All in all Beatrice O'Hara absorbed the sort of education that will be quite impossible ever again; a tutelage measured by the number of things and people one could be contemptuous of and charming about; a culture rich in all arts and traditions, barren of all ideas, in the last of those days when the great gardener clipped the inferior roses to produce one perfect bud.

In her less important moments she returned to America, met Stephen Blaine and married him—this almost entirely because she was a little bit weary, a little bit sad. Her only child was carried through a tiresome season and brought into the world on a spring day in ninety-six.

When Amory was five he was already a delightful companion for her. He was an auburn-haired boy, with great, handsome eyes which he would grow up to in time, a facile imaginative mind and a taste for fancy dress. From his fourth to his tenth year he *did* the country with his mother in her father's private car, from Coronado, where his mother became so bored that she had a nervous breakdown in a fashionable hotel, down to Mexico City, where she took a mild, almost epidemic consumption. This trouble pleased her, and later she made use of it as an intrinsic part of her atmosphere—especially after several astounding bracers.

So, while more or less fortunate little rich boys were defying governesses on the beach at Newport, or being spanked or tutored or read to from "Do and Dare," or "Frank on the Lower Mississippi," Amory was biting acquiescent bell-boys in the Waldorf, outgrowing a natural repugnance to chamber music and symphonies, and deriving a highly specialized education from his mother.

"Amory."

"Yes, Beatrice." (Such a quaint name for his mother; she encouraged it.)

"Dear, don't *think* of getting out of bed yet. I've always suspected that early rising in early life makes one nervous. Clothilde is having your breakfast brought up."

"All right."

"I am feeling very old today, Amory," she would sigh, her face a rare cameo of pathos, her voice exquistely modulated, her hands as facile as Bernhardt's. "My nerves are on edge—on edge. We must leave this terrifying place tomorrow and go searching for sunshine."

Amory's penetrating green eyes would look out through tangled hair at his mother. Even at this age he had no illusions about her.

"Amory."

"Oh, *yes.*"

"I want you to take a red-hot bath—as hot as you can bear it, and just relax your nerves. You can read in the tub if you wish."

She fed him sections of the "Fêtes Galantes" before he was ten; at eleven he could talk glibly, if rather reminiscently, of Brahms and Mozart and Beethoven. One afternoon, when left alone in the hotel at Hot Springs, he sampled his mother's apricot cordial, and as the taste pleased him, he became quite tipsy. This was fun for a while, but he essayed a cigarette in his exaltation, and succumbed to a vulgar, plebeian reaction. Though this incident horrified Beatrice, it also secretly amused her and became part of what in a later generation would have been termed her "line."

"This son of mine," he heard her tell a room full of awestruck, admiring women one day, "is entirely sophisticated and quite charming—but delicate—we're all delicate; *here*, you know." Her hand was radiantly outlined against her beautiful bosom; then sinking her voice to a whisper, she told them of the apricot cordial. They rejoiced, for she was a brave raconteuse, but many were the keys turned in sideboard locks that night against the possible defection of little Bobby or Barbara. . . .

These domestic pilgrimages were invariably in state; two maids, the private car, or Mr. Blaine when available, and very often a physician. When Amory had the whooping-cough four disgusted specialists glared at each other hunched around his bed; when he took scarlet fever the number of attendants, including physicians and nurses, totalled fourteen. However, blood being thicker than broth, he was pulled through.

The Blaines were attached to no city. They were the Blaines of Lake Geneva; they had quite enough relatives to serve in place of friends, and an enviable standing from Pasadena to Cape Cod. But Beatrice grew more and more prone to like only new acquaintances, as there were certain stories, such as the history of her constitution and its many amendments and her memories of her years abroad, that it was necessary for her to repeat at regular intervals. Like Freudian dreams, they must be thrown off, else they would sweep in and lay seige to her nerves. But Beatrice was critical about American women, especially the floating population of ex-Westerners.

"They have accents, my dear," she told Amory, "not Southern accents or Boston accents, not an accent attached to any locality, just an accent"—she became dreamy. "They pick up old, moth-eaten London accents that are down on their luck and have to be used by some one. They talk as an English butler might after several years in a Chicago grand opera company." She became almost incoherent— "Suppose— time in every Western woman's life—she feels her husband is prosperous enough for her to have—accent—they try to impress *me*, my dear—"

Though she thought of her body as a mass of frailties, she considered her soul quite as ill, and therefore important in her life. She had once been a Catholic, but discovering that priests were infinitely more attentive when she was in process of losing or regaining faith in Mother Church, she maintained an enchantingly wavering attitude. Often she deplored the bourgeois quality of the American Catholic clergy, and was quite sure that had she lived in the shadow of the great Continental cathedrals her soul would still be a thin flame on the mighty altar of Rome. Still, next to doctors, priests were her favorite sport.

"Ah, Bishop Wiston," she would declare, "I do not *want* to talk of myself. I can imagine the stream of hysterical women fluttering at your doors, beseeching you to be sim*pat*ico"—then after an interlude filled by the clergyman—"but my mood—is—oddly dissimilar."

Only to bishops and above did she divulge her clerical romance. When she had first returned to her country there had been a pagan, Swinburnian young man in Asheville, for whose passionate kisses and unsentimental conversations she had taken a decided penchant—they had discussed the matter pro and con with an intellectual romancing quite devoid of soppiness. Eventually she had decided to marry for background, and the young pagan from Asheville had gone through a spiritual crisis, joined the Catholic Church, and was now—Monsignor Darcy.

"Indeed, Mrs. Blaine, he is still delightful company—quite the cardinal's right-hand man."

"Amory will go to him one day, I know," breathed the beautiful lady, "and Monsignor Darcy will understand him as he understood me."

Amory became thirteen, rather tall and slender, and more than ever on to his Celtic mother. He had tutored occasionally—the idea being that he was to "keep up," at each place "taking up the work where he left off," yet as no tutor ever found the place he left off, his mind was still in very good shape. What a few more years of this life would have made of him is problematical. However, four hours out from land, Italy bound, with Beatrice, his appendix burst, probably from too many meals in bed, and after a series of frantic telegrams to Europe and America, to the amazement of the passengers the great ship slowly wheeled around and returned to New York to deposit Amory at the pier. You will admit that if it was not life it was magnificent.

After the operation Beatrice had a nervous breakdown that bore a suspicious resemblance to delirium tremens, and Amory was left in Minneapolis, destined to spend the ensuing two years with his aunt and uncle. There the crude, vulgar air of Western civilization first catches him—in his underwear, so to speak.

A KISS FOR AMORY

His lip curled when he read it.

I am going to have a bobbing party, it said, *on Thursday, December the seventeenth, at five o'clock, and I would like it very much if you could come.*

Yours truly,
R.S.V.P.   *Myra St. Claire.*

He had been two months in Minneapolis, and his chief struggle had been the concealing from "the other guys at school" how particularly superior he felt himself to be, yet this conviction was built upon shifting sands. He had shown off one day in French class (he was in senior French class) to the utter confusion of Mr. Reardon, whose accent Amory damned contemptuously, and to the delight of the class. Mr. Reardon, who had spent several weeks in Paris ten years before, took his revenge on the verbs, whenever he had his book open. But another time Amory showed off in history class, with quite disastrous results, for the boys there were his own age, and they shrilled innuendoes at each other all the following week:

"Aw—I b'lieve, doncherknow, the Umuricun revolution was *lawgely* an affair of the middul *clawses,*" or

"Washington came of very good blood—aw, quite good—I b'lieve."

Amory ingeniously tried to retrieve himself by blundering on purpose. Two years before he had commenced a history of the United
States which, though it only got as far as the Colonial Wars, had been
pronounced by his mother completely enchanting.

His chief disadvantage lay in athletics, but as soon as he discovered
that it was the touchstone of power and popularity at school, he began
to make furious, persistent efforts to excel in the winter sports, and
with his ankles aching and bending in spite of his efforts, he skated
valiantly around the Lorelei rink every afternoon, wondering how soon
he would be able to carry a hockey stick without getting it inexplicably
tangled in his skates.

The invitation to Miss Myra St. Claire's bobbing party spent the
morning in his coat pocket, where it had an intense physical affair with
a dusty piece of peanut brittle. During the afternoon he brought it to
light with a sigh, and after some consideration and a preliminary draft
in the back of Collar and Daniell's "First Year Latin," composed an
answer:

My dear Miss St. Claire:
Your truly charming envitation for the evening of next Thursday evening
was truly delightful to receive this morning. I will be charm and inchanted
indeed to present my compliments on next Thursday evening.

Faithfully,
Amory Blaine.

On Thursday, therefore, he walked pensively along the slippery,
shovel-scraped sidewalks, and came in sight of Myra's house, on the
half-hour after five, a lateness which he fancied his mother would have
favored. He waited on the doorstep with his eyes nonchalantly half-
closed, and planned his entrance with precision. He would cross the
floor, not too hastily, to Mrs. St. Claire, and say with exactly the
correct modulation:

"My *dear* Mrs. St. Claire, I'm *frightfully* sorry to be late, but my
maid"—he paused there and realized he would be quoting—"but my
uncle and I had to see a fella— Yes, I've met your enchanting daughter
at dancing-school."

Then he would shake hands, using that slight, half-foreign bow,
with all the starchy little females, and nod to the fellas who would be
standing 'round, paralyzed into rigid groups for mutual protection.

A butler (one of the three in Minneapolis) swung open the door.
Amory stepped inside and divested himself of cap and coat. He was

mildly surprised not to hear the shrill squawk of conversation from the next room, and he decided it must be quite formal. He approved of that—as he approved of the butler.

"Miss Myra," he said.

To his surprise the butler grinned horribly.

"Oh, yeah," he declared, "she's here." He was unaware that his failure to be cockney was ruining his standing. Amory considered him coldly.

"But," continued the butler, his voice rising unnecessarily, "she's the only one what *is* here. The party's gone."

Amory gasped in sudden horror.

"What?"

"She's been waitin' for Amory Blaine. That's you, ain't it? Her mother says that if you showed up by five-thirty you two was to go after 'em in the Packard."

Amory's despair was crystallized by the appearance of Myra herself, bundled to the ears in a polo coat, her face plainly sulky, her voice pleasant only with difficulty.

" 'Lo, Amory."

" 'Lo, Myra." He had described the state of his vitality.

"Well—you *got* here, *any*ways."

"Well—I'll tell you. I guess you don't know about the auto accident," he romanced.

Myra's eyes opened wide.

"Who was it to?"

"Well," he continued desperately, "uncle'n aunt'n I."

"Was anyone *killed?*"

Amory paused and then nodded.

"Your uncle?"—alarm.

"Oh, no—just a horse—a sorta gray horse."

At this point the Erse butler snickered.

"Probably killed the engine," he suggested. Amory would have put him on the rack without a scruple.

"We'll go now," said Myra coolly. "You see, Amory, the bobs were ordered for five and everybody was here, so we couldn't wait—"

"Well, I couldn't help it, could I?"

"So mama said for me to wait till ha'past five. We'll catch the bob before it gets to the Minnehaha Club, Amory."

Amory's shredded poise dropped from him. He pictured the happy party jingling along snowy streets, the appearance of the limousine, the horrible public descent of him and Myra before sixty reproachful eyes, his apology—a real one this time. He sighed aloud.

"What?" inquired Myra.

"Nothing. I was just yawning. Are we going to *surely* catch up with 'em before they get there?" He was encouraging a faint hope that they might slip into the Minnehaha Club and meet the others there, be found in blasé seclusion before the fire and quite regain his lost attitude.

"Oh, sure Mike, we'll catch 'em all right—let's hurry."

He became conscious of his stomach. As they stepped into the machine he hurriedly slapped the paint of diplomacy over a rather box-like plan he had conceived. It was based upon some "trade-lasts" gleaned at dancing-school, to the effect that he was "awful good-looking and *English,* sort of."

"Myra," he said, lowering his voice and choosing his words carefully, "I beg a thousand pardons. Can you ever forgive me?"

She regarded him gravely, his intent green eyes, his mouth, that to her thirteen-year-old, arrow-collar taste was the quintessence of romance. Yes, Myra could forgive him very easily.

"Why—yes—sure."

He looked at her again, and then dropped his eyes. He had lashes.

"I'm awful," he said sadly. "I'm diff'runt. I don't know why I make faux pas. 'Cause I don't care, I s'pose." Then, recklessly: "I been smoking too much. I've got t'bacca heart."

Myra pictured an all-night tobacco debauch, with Amory pale and reeling from the effect of nicotined lungs. She gave a little gasp.

"Oh, *Amory,* don't smoke. You'll stunt your *growth!*"

"I don't care," he persisted gloomily. "I gotta. I got the habit. I've done a lot of things that if my family knew"—he hesitated, giving her imagination time to picture dark horrors—"I went to the burlesque show last week."

Myra was quite overcome. He turned the green eyes on her again.

"You're the only girl in town I like much," he exclaimed in a rush of sentiment. "You're simpatico."

Myra was not sure that she was, but it sounded stylish though vaguely improper.

Thick dusk had descended outside, and as the limousine made a sudden turn she was jolted against him; their hands touched.

"You shouldn't smoke, Amory," she whispered. "Don't you know that?"

He shook his head.

"Nobody cares."

Myra hesitated.

"*I* care."

Something stirred within Amory.

"Oh, yes, you do! You got a crush on Froggy Parker. I guess everybody knows that."

"No, I haven't," very slowly.

A silence, while Amory thrilled. There was something fascinating about Myra, shut away here cosily from the dim, chill air. Myra, a little bundle of clothes, with strands of yellow hair curling out from under her skating cap.

"Because I've got a crush, too—" He paused, for he heard in the distance the sound of young laughter and, peering through the frosted glass along the lamp-lit street, he made out the dark outline of the bobbing party. He must act quickly. He reached over with a violent, jerky effort, and clutched Myra's hand—her thumb, to be exact.

"Tell him to go to the Minnehaha straight," he whispered. "I wanta talk to you—I *got* to talk to you."

Myra made out the party ahead, had an instant vision of her mother, and then—alas for convention—glanced into the eyes beside.

"Turn down this side street, Richard, and drive straight to the Minnehaha Club!" she cried through the speaking tube. Amory sank back against the cushions with a sigh of relief.

"I can kiss her," he thought. "I'll bet I can. I'll *bet* I can!"

Overhead the sky was half crystaline, half misty, and the night around was chill and vibrant with rich tension. From the Country Club steps the roads stretched away, dark creases on the white blanket; huge heaps of snow lining the sides like the tracks of giant moles. They lingered for a moment on the steps, and watched the white holiday moon.

"Pale moons like that one"—Amory made a vague gesture—"make people mysterieuse. You look like a young witch with her cap off and her hair sorta mussed"—her hands clutched at her hair—"Oh, leave it, it looks *good*."

They drifted up the stairs and Myra led the way into the little den of his dreams, where a cosy fire was burning before a big sink-down couch. A few years later this was to be a great stage for Amory, a cradle for many an emotional crisis. Now they talked for a moment about bobbing parties.

"There's always a bunch of shy fellas," he commented, "sitting at the tail of the bob, sorta lurkin' an' whisperin' an' pushin' each other off. Then there's always some crazy cross-eyed girl"—he gave a terrifying imitation—"she's always talkin' *hard*, sorta, to the chaperon."

"You're such a funny boy," puzzled Myra.

"How d'y' mean?" Amory gave immediate attention, on his own ground at last.

"Oh—always talking about crazy things. Why don't you come skiing with Marylyn and I tomorrow?"

"I don't like girls in the daytime," he said shortly, and then, thinking this a bit abrupt, he added: "But I like you." He cleared his throat.
"I like you first and second and third."

Myra's eyes became dreamy. What a story this would make to tell
Marylyn! Here on the couch with this *wonderful*-looking boy—the little
fire—the sense that they were alone in the great building——

Myra capitulated. The atmosphere was too appropriate.

"I like you the first twenty-five," she confessed, her voice trembling, "and Froggy Parker twenty-sixth."

Froggy had fallen twenty-five places in one hour. As yet he had not
even noticed it.

But Amory, being on the spot, leaned over quickly and kissed
Myra's cheek. He had never kissed a girl before, and he tasted his lips
curiously, as if he had munched some new fruit. Then their lips
brushed like young wild flowers in the wind.

"We're awful," rejoiced Myra gently. She slipped her hand into his,
her head drooped against his shoulder. Sudden revulsion seized
Amory, disgust, loathing for the whole incident. He desired frantically
to be away, never to see Myra again, never to kiss any one; he became
conscious of his face and hers, of their clinging hands, and he wanted
to creep out of his body and hide somewhere safe out of sight, up in the
corner of his mind.

"Kiss me again." Her voice came out of a great void.

"I don't want to," he heard himself saying. There was another
pause.

"I don't want to!" he repeated passionately.

Myra sprang up, her cheeks pink with bruised vanity, the great
bow on the back of her head trembling sympathetically.

"I hate you!" she cried. "Don't you ever dare to speak to me
again!"

"What?" stammered Amory.

"I'll tell mama you kissed me! I will too! I will too! I'll tell mama,
and she won't let me play with you!"

Amory rose and stared at her helplessly, as though she were a new
animal of whose presence on the earth he had not heretofore been
aware.

The door opened suddenly, and Myra's mother appeared on the
threshold, fumbling with her lorgnette.

"Well," she began, adjusting it benignantly, "the man at the desk
told me you two children were up here—How do you do, Amory."

Amory watched Myra and waited for the crash—but none came.

The pout faded, the high pink subsided, and Myra's voice was placid as a summer lake when she answered her mother.

"Oh, we started so late, mama, that I thought we might as well — — "

He heard from below the shrieks of laughter, and smelled the vapid odor of hot chocolate and tea-cakes as he silently followed mother and daughter downstairs. The sound of the graphophone mingled with the voices of many girls humming the air, and a faint glow was born and spread over him:

> "*Casey-Jones — mounted to the cab-un*
> *Casey-Jones — 'th his orders in his hand.*
> *Casey-Jones — mounted to the cab-un*
> *Took his farewell journey to the prom-ised land.*"

SNAPSHOTS OF THE YOUNG EGOTIST

Amory spent nearly two years in Minneapolis. The first winter he wore moccasins that were born yellow, but after many applications of oil and dirt assumed their mature color, a dirty, greenish brown; he wore a gray plaid mackinaw coat, and a red toboggan cap. His dog, Count Del Monte, ate the red cap, so his uncle gave him a gray one that pulled down over his face. The trouble with this one was that you breathed into it and your breath froze; one day the darn thing froze his cheek. He rubbed snow on his cheek, but it turned bluish-black just the same.

The Count Del Monte ate a box of bluing once, but it didn't hurt him. Later, however, he lost his mind and ran madly up the street, bumping into fences, rolling in gutters, and pursuing his eccentric course out of Amory's life. Amory cried on his bed.

"Poor little Count," he cried. "Oh, *poor* little *Count!*"

After several months he suspected Count of a fine piece of emotional acting.

Amory and Frog Parker considered that the greatest line in literature occurred in Act III of "Arsene Lupin."

They sat in the first row at the Wednesday and Saturday matinées. The line was:

"If one can't be a great artist or a great soldier, the next best thing is to be a great criminal."

✤ ✤ ✤

Amory fell in love again, and wrote a poem. This was it:

Marylyn and Sallee,
Those are the girls for me.
Marylyn stands above
Sallee in that sweet, deep love.

He was interested in whether McGovern of Minnesota would make the first or second All-American, how to do the card-pass, how to do the coin-pass, chameleon ties, how babies were born, and whether Three-finger Brown was really a better pitcher than Christy Mathewson.

Among other things he read: "For the Honor of the School," "Little Women" (twice), "Common Law," "Sapho," "Dangerous Dan Mc-Grew," "The Broad Highway" (three times), "The Fall of the House of Usher," "Three Weeks," "Mary Ware, the Little Colonel's Chum," "Gunga Din," *the Police Gazette,* and *Jim-Jam Jems.*

He had all the Henty biasses in history, and was particularly fond of the cheerful murder stories of Mary Roberts Rinehart.

School ruined his French and gave him a distaste for standard authors. His masters considered him idle, unreliable and superficially clever.

He collected locks of hair from many girls. He wore the rings of several. Finally he could borrow no more rings, owing to his nervous habit of chewing them out of shape. This, it seemed, usually aroused the jealous suspicions of the next borrower.

All through the summer months Amory and Frog Parker went each week to the Stock Company. Afterward they would stroll home in the balmy air of August night, dreaming along Hennepin and Nicollet Avenues, through the gay crowd. Amory wondered how people could fail to notice that he was a boy marked for glory, and when faces of the throng turned toward him and ambiguous eyes stared into his, he assumed the most romantic of expressions and walked on the air cushions that lie on the asphalts of fourteen.

Always, after he was in bed, there were voices—indefinite, fading, enchanting—just outside his window, and before he fell asleep he would dream one of his favorite waking dreams, the one about becoming a great halfback, or the one about the Japanese invasion, when he was rewarded by being made the youngest general in the world. It was always the becoming he dreamed of, never the being. This, too, was quite characteristic of Amory.

CODE OF THE YOUNG EGOTIST

Before he was summoned back to Lake Geneva, he had appeared, shy but inwardly glowing, in his first long trousers, set off by a purple accordian tie and a "Belmont" collar with the edges unassailably meeting, purple socks, and handkerchief with a purple border peeping from his breast pocket. But more than that, he had formulated his first philosophy, a code to live by, which, as near as it can be named, was a sort of aristocratic egotism.

He had realized that his best interests were bound up with those of a certain variant, changing person, whose label, in order that his past might always be identified with him, was Amory Blaine. Amory marked himself a fortunate youth, capable of infinite expansion for good or evil. He did not consider himself a "strong char'c'ter," but relied on his facility (learn things sorta quick) and his superior mentality (read a lotta deep books). He was proud of the fact that he could never become a mechanical or scientific genius. From no other heights was he debarred.

Physically.—Amory thought that he was exceedingly handsome. He was. He fancied himself an athlete of possibilities and a supple dancer.

Socially.—Here his condition was, perhaps, most dangerous. He granted himself personality, charm, magnetism, poise, the power of dominating all contemporary males, the gift of fascinating all women.

Mentally.—Complete, unquestioned superiority.

Now a confession will have to be made. Amory had rather a Puritan conscience. Not that he yielded to it—later in life he almost completely slew it—but at fifteen it made him consider himself a great deal worse than other boys . . . unscrupulousness . . . the desire to influence people in almost every way, even for evil . . . a certain coldness and lack of affection, amounting sometimes to cruelty . . . a shifting sense of honor . . . an unholy selfishness . . . a puzzled, furtive interest in everything concerning sex.

There was, also, a curious strain of weakness running crosswise through his make-up . . . . a harsh phrase from the lips of an older boy (older boys usually detested him) was liable to sweep him off his poise into surly sensitiveness, or timid stupidity . . . he was a slave to his own moods and he felt that though he was capable of recklessness and audacity, he possessed neither courage, perseverance, nor self-respect.

Vanity, tempered with self-suspicion if not self-knowledge, a sense of people as automatons to his will, a desire to "pass" as many boys as possible and get to a vague top of the world . . . with this background did Amory drift into adolescence.

PREPARATORY TO THE GREAT ADVENTURE

The train slowed up with midsummer languor at Lake Geneva, and Amory caught sight of his mother waiting in her electric on the gravelled station drive. It was an ancient electric, one of the early types, and painted gray. The sight of her sitting there, slenderly erect, and of her face, where beauty and dignity combined, melting to a dreamy recollected smile, filled him with a sudden great pride of her. As they kissed coolly and he stepped into the electric, he felt a quick fear lest he had lost the requisite charm to measure up to her.

"Dear boy—you're *so* tall . . . look behind and see if there's anything coming . . ."

She looked left and right, she slipped cautiously into a speed of two miles an hour, beseeching Amory to act as sentinel; and at one busy crossing she made him get out and run ahead to signal her forward like a traffic policeman. Beatrice was what might be termed a careful driver.

"You *are* tall—but you're still very handsome—you've skipped the awkward age, or is that sixteen; perhaps it's fourteen or fifteen; I can never remember; but you've skipped it."

"Don't embarrass me," murmured Amory.

"But, my dear boy, what odd clothes! They look as if they were a *set*—don't they? Is your underwear purple, too?"

Amory grunted impolitely.

"You must go to Brooks' and get some really nice suits. Oh, we'll have a talk tonight or perhaps tomorrow night. I want to tell you about your heart—you've probably been neglecting your heart—and you don't *know*."

Amory thought how superficial was the recent overlay of his own generation. Aside from a minute shyness, he felt that the old cynical kinship with his mother had not been one bit broken. Yet for the first few days he wandered about the gardens and along the shore in a state of superloneliness, finding a lethargic content in smoking "Bull" at the garage with one of the chauffeurs.

The sixty acres of the estate were dotted with old and new summer houses and many fountains and white benches that came suddenly into sight from foliage-hung hiding-places; there was a great and constantly increasing family of white cats that prowled the many flower-beds and were silhouetted suddenly at night against the darkening trees. It was on one of the shadowy paths that Beatrice at last captured Amory, after Mr. Blaine had, as usual, retired for the evening to his private library. After reproving him for avoiding her, she took him for a long tête-à-tête in the moonlight. He could not reconcile himself to her beauty, that was mother to his own, the exquisite neck and shoulders, the grace of a fortunate woman of thirty.

"Amory, dear," she crooned softly, "I had such a strange, weird time after I left you."

"Did you, Beatrice?"

"When I had my last breakdown"—she spoke of it as a sturdy, gallant feat.

"The doctors told me"—her voice sang on a confidential note—"that if any man alive had done the consistent drinking that I have, he would have been physically *shattered*, my dear, and in his *grave*—long in his grave."

Amory winced, and wondered how this would have sounded to Froggy Parker.

"Yes," continued Beatrice tragically, "I had dreams—wonderful visions." She pressed the palms of her hands into her eyes. "I saw bronze rivers lapping marble shores, and great birds that soared through the air, parti-colored birds with iridescent plumage. I heard strange music and the flare of barbaric trumpets—what?"

Amory had snickered.

"What, Amory?"

"I said go on, Beatrice."

"That was all—it merely recurred and recurred—gardens that flaunted coloring against which this would be quite dull, moons that whirled and swayed, paler than winter moons, more golden than harvest moons——"

"Are you quite well now, Beatrice?"

"Quite well—as well as I will ever be. I am not understood, Amory. I know that can't express it to you, Amory, but—I am not understood."

"Amory was quite moved. He put his arm around his mother, rubbing his head gently against her shoulder.

"Poor Beatrice—poor Beatrice."

"Tell me about *you*, Amory. Did you have two *horrible* years?"

Amory considered lying, and then decided against it.

"No, Beatrice. I enjoyed them. I adapted myself to the bourgeoisie. I became conventional." He surprised himself by saying that, and he pictured how Froggy would have gaped.

"Beatrice," he said suddenly, "I want to go away to school. Everybody in Minneapolis is going to go away to school."

Beatrice showed some alarm.

"But you're only fifteen."

"Yes, but everybody goes away to school at fifteen, and I *want* to, Beatrice."

On Beatrice's suggestion the subject was dropped for the rest of the walk, but a week later she delighted him by saying:

"Amory, I have decided to let you have your way. If you still want to, you can go to school."

"Yes?"

"To St. Regis' in Connecticut."

Amory felt a quick excitement.

"It's being arranged," continued Beatrice. "It's better that you should go away. I'd have preferred you to have gone to Eton, and then to Christ Church, Oxford, but it seems impracticable now—and for the present we'll let the university question take care of itself."

"What are you going to do, Beatrice?"

"Heaven knows. It seems my fate to fret away my years in this country. Not for a second do I regret being American—indeed, I think that a regret typical of very vulgar people, and I feel sure we are the great coming nation—yet"—and she sighed—"I feel my life should have drowsed away close to an older, mellower civilization, a land of greens and autumnal browns——"

Amory did not answer, so his mother continued:

"My regret is that you haven't been abroad, but still, as you are a man, it's better that you should grow up here under the snarling eagle—is that the right term?"

Amory agreed that it was. She would not have appreciated the Japanese invasion.

"When do I go to school?"

"Next month. You'll have to start East a little early to take your examinations. After that you'll have a free week, so I want you to go up the Hudson and pay a visit."

"To who?"

"To Monsignor Darcy, Amory. He wants to see you. He went to Harrow and then to Yale—became a Catholic. I want him to talk to you—I feel he can be such a help—" She stroked his auburn hair gently. "Dear Amory, dear Amory——"

"Dear Beatrice——"

So early in September Amory, provided with "six suits summer underwear, six suits winter underwear, one sweater or T shirt, one jersey, one overcoat, winter, etc.," set out for New England, the land of schools.

There were Andover and Exeter with their memories of New England dead—large, college-like democracies; St. Mark's, Groton, St. Regis'—recruited from Boston and the Knickerbocker families of New York; St. Paul's, with its great rinks; Pomfret and St. George's, prosperous and well-dressed; Taft and Hotchkiss, which prepared the wealth of the Middle West for social success at Yale; Pawling, Westminster, Choate, Kent, and a hundred others; all milling out their well-set-up, conventional, impressive type, year after year; their mental stimulus the college entrance exams; their vague purpose set forth in a hundred circulars as "To impart a Thorough Mental, Moral, and Physical Training as a Christian Gentleman, to fit the boy *for meeting the problems of his day and generation,* and to give a solid foundation in the Arts and Sciences."

At St. Regis' Amory stayed three days and took his exams with a scoffing confidence, then doubling back to New York to pay his tutelary visit. The metropolis, barely glimpsed, made little impression on him, except for the sense of cleanliness he drew from the tall white buildings seen from a Hudson River steamboat in the early morning. Indeed, his mind was so crowded with dreams of athletic prowess at school that he considered this visit only as a rather tiresome prelude to the great adventure. This, however, it did not prove to be.

Monsignor Darcy's house was an ancient, rambling structure set on a hill overlooking the river, and there lived its owner, between his trips to all parts of the Roman Catholic world, rather like an exiled Stuart king waiting to be called to the rule of his land. Monsignor was forty-four then, and bustling—a trifle too stout for symmetry, with hair the color of spun gold, and a brilliant, enveloping personality. When he came into a room clad in his full purple regalia from thatch to toe, he resembled a Turner sunset, and attracted both admiration and attention. He had written two novels: one of them violently anti-Catholic, just before his conversion, and five years later another, in which he had attempted to turn all his clever jibes against Catholics into even cleverer innuendoes against Episcopalians. He was intensely ritualistic, startlingly dramatic, loved the idea of God enough to be a celibate, and rather liked his neighbor.

Children adored him because he was like a child; youth revelled in his company because he was still a youth, and couldn't be shocked. In the proper land and century he might have been a Richelieu—at present he was a very moral, very religious (if not particularly pious) clergyman, making a great mystery about pulling rusty wires, and appreciating life to the fullest, if not entirely enjoying it.

He and Amory took to each other at first sight—the jovial, impressive prelate who could dazzle an embassy ball, and the green-eyed, intent youth, in his first long trousers, accepted in their own minds a relation of father and son within a half-hour's conversation.

"My dear boy, I've been waiting to see you for years. Take a big chair and we'll have a chat."

"I've just come from school—St. Regis', you know."

"So your mother says—a remarkable woman; have a cigarette— I'm sure you smoke. Well, if you're like me, you loathe all science and mathematics——"

Amory nodded vehemently.

"Hate 'em all. Like English and history."

"Of course. You'll hate school for a while, too, but I'm glad you're going to St. Regis'."

"Why?"

"Because it's a gentleman's school, and democracy won't hit you so early. You'll find plenty of that in college."

"I want to go to Princeton," said Amory. "I don't know why, but I think of all Harvard men as sissies, like I used to be, and all Yale men as wearing big blue sweaters and smoking pipes."

Monsignor chuckled.

"I'm one, you know."

"Oh, you're different—I think of Princeton as being lazy and good-looking and aristocratic—you know, like a spring day. Harvard seems sort of indoors——"

"And Yale is November, crisp and energetic," finished Monsignor.

"That's it."

They slipped briskly into an intimacy from which they never recovered.

"I was for Bonnie Prince Charlie," announced Amory.

"Of course you were—and for Hannibal——"

"Yes, and for the Southern Confederacy." He was rather skeptical about being an Irish patriot—he suspected that being Irish was being somewhat common—but Monsignor assured him that Ireland was a romantic lost cause and Irish people quite charming, and that it should, by all means, be one of his principal biasses.

After a crowded hour which included several more cigarettes, and during which Monsignor learned, to his surprise but not to his horror, that Amory had not been brought up a Catholic, he announced that he had another guest. This turned out to be the Honorable Thornton Hancock, of Boston, ex-minister to The Hague, author of an erudite history of the Middle Ages and the last of a distinguished, patriotic, and brilliant family.

"He comes here for a rest," said Monsignor confidentially, treating Amory as a contemporary. "I act as an escape from the weariness of agnosticism, and I think I'm the only man who knows how his staid old mind is really at sea and longs for a sturdy spar like the Church to cling to."

Their first luncheon was one of the memorable events of Amory's early life. He was quite radiant and gave off a peculiar brightness and charm. Monsignor called out the best that he had thought by question and suggestion, and Amory talked with an ingenious brilliance of a thousand impulses and desires and repulsions and faiths and fears. He and Monsignor held the floor, and the older man, with his less receptive, less accepting, yet certainly not colder mentality, seemed content to listen and bask in the mellow sunshine that played between these two. Monsignor gave the effect of sunlight to many people; Amory gave it in his youth and, to some extent, when he was very much older, but never again was it quite so mutually spontaneous.

"He's a radiant boy," thought Thornton Hancock, who had seen the splendor of two continents and talked with Parnell and Gladstone and Bismarck—and afterward he added to Monsignor: "But his education ought not to be intrusted to a school or college."

But for the next four years the best of Amory's intellect was concentrated on matters of popularity, the intricacies of a university social system and American Society as represented by Biltmore Teas and Hot Springs golf links.

. . . In all, a wonderful week, that saw Amory's mind turned inside out, a hundred of his theories confirmed, and his joy of life crystallized to a thousand ambitions. Not that the conversation was scholastic—heaven forbid! Amory had only the vaguest idea as to what Bernard Shaw was—but Monsignor made quite as much out of "The Beloved Vagabond" and "Sir Nigel," taking good care that Amory never once felt out of his depth.

But the trumpets were sounding for Amory's preliminary skirmish with his own generation.

"You're not sorry to go, of course. With people like us our home is where we are not," said Monsignor.

"I *am* sorry——"

"No, you're not. No one person in the world is necessary to you or to me."

"Well——"

"Good-by."

THE EGOTIST DOWN

Amory's two years at St. Regis', though in turn painful and triumphant, had as little real significance in his own life as the American "prep" school, crushed as it is under the heel of the universities, has to American life in general. We have no Eton to create the self-consciousness of a governing class; we have, instead, clean, flaccid and innocuous preparatory schools.

He went all wrong at the start, was generally considered both conceited and arrogant, and universally detested. He played football intensely, alternating a reckless brilliancy with a tendency to keep himself as safe from hazard as decency would permit. In a wild panic he backed out of a fight with a boy his own size, to a chorus of scorn, and a week later, in desperation, picked a battle with another boy very much bigger, from which he emerged badly beaten, but rather proud of himself.

He was resentful against all those in authority over him, and this, combined with a lazy indifference toward his work, exasperated every master in school. He grew discouraged and imagined himself a pariah; took to sulking in corners and reading after lights. With a dread of being alone he attached a few friends, but since they were not among the élite of the school, he used them simply as mirrors of himself, audiences before which he might do that posing absolutely essential to him. He was unbearably lonely, desperately unhappy.

There were some few grains of comfort. Whenever Amory was submerged, his vanity was the last part to go below the surface, so he could still enjoy a comfortable glow when "Wookey-wookey," the deaf old housekeeper, told him that he was the best-looking boy she had ever seen. It had pleased him to be the lightest and youngest man on the first football squad; it pleased him when Doctor Dougall told him at the end of a heated conference that he could, if he wished, get the best marks in school. But Doctor Dougall was wrong. It was tempermentally impossible for Amory to get the best marks in school.

Miserable, confined to bounds, unpopular with both faculty and students—that was Amory's first term. But at Christmas he had returned to Minneapolis, tight-lipped and strangely jubilant.

"Oh, I was sort of fresh at first," he told Frog Parker patronizingly, "but I got along fine—lightest man on the squad. You ought to go away to school, Froggy. It's great stuff."

INCIDENT OF THE WELL-MEANING PROFESSOR

On the last night of his first term, Mr. Margotson, the senior master, sent word to study hall that Amory was to come to his room at nine. Amory suspected that advice was forthcoming, but he determined to be courteous, because this Mr. Margotson had been kindly disposed toward him.

His summoner received him gravely, and motioned him to a chair. He hemmed several times and looked consciously kind, as a man will when he knows he's on delicate ground.

"Amory," he began. "I've sent for you on a personal matter."

"Yes, sir."

"I've noticed you this year and I—I like you. I think you have in you the makings of a—a very good man."

"Yes, sir," Amory managed to articulate. He hated having people talk as if he were an admitted failure.

"But I've noticed," continued the older man blindly, "that you're not very popular with the boys."

"No, sir." Amory licked his lips.

"Ah—I thought you might not understand exactly what it was they—ah—objected to. I'm going to tell you, because I believe—ah— that when a boy knows his difficulties he's better able to cope with them—to conform to what others expect of him." He a-hemmed again with delicate reticence, and continued: "They seem to think that you're—ah—rather too fresh——"

Amory could stand no more. He rose from his chair, scarcely controlling his voice when he spoke.

"I know—oh, *don't* you s'pose I know." His voice rose. "I know what they think; do you s'pose you have to *tell* me." He paused. "I'm— I've got to go back now—hope I'm not rude——"

He left the room hurriedly. In the cool air outside, as he walked to his house, he exulted in his refusal to be helped.

"That *damn* old fool!" he cried wildly. "As if I didn't *know!*"

He decided, however, that this was a good excuse not to go back to study hall that night, so, comfortably couched up in his room, he munched Nabiscos and finished "The White Company."

INCIDENT OF THE WONDERFUL GIRL

There was a bright star in February. New York burst upon him on Washington's Birthday with the brilliance of a long-anticipated event. His glimpse of it as a vivid whiteness against a deep blue sky had left a picture of splendor that rivalled the dream cities in the Arabian Nights; but this time he saw it by electric light, and romance gleamed from the chariot-race sign on Broadway and from the women's eyes at the Astor, where he and young Paskert from St. Regis' had dinner. When they walked down the aisle of the theatre, greeted by the nervous twanging and discord of untuned violins and the sensuous, heavy fragrance of paint and powder, he moved in a sphere of epicurean delight. Everything enchanted him. The play was "The Little Millionaire," with George M. Cohan, and there was one stunning young brunette who made him sit with brimming eyes in the ecstasy of watching her dance.

> "Oh—you—wonderful girl,
> What a wonderful girl you are—"

sang the tenor, and Amory agreed silently, but passionately.

> "All—your—wonderful words
> Thrill me through— —"

The violins swelled and quavered on the last notes, the girl sank to a crumpled butterfly on the stage, a great burst of clapping filled the house. Oh, to fall in love like that, to the languorous magic melody of such a tune!

The last scene was laid on a roof-garden, and the 'cellos sighed to the musical moon, while light adventure and facile froth-like comedy flitted back and forth in the calcium. Amory was on fire to be an habitué of roof-gardens, to meet a girl who should look like that— better, that very girl; whose hair would be drenched with golden moonlight, while at his elbow sparkling wine was poured by an unintelligible waiter. When the curtain fell for the last time he gave such a long sigh that the people in front of him twisted around and stared and said loud enough for him to hear:

"What a *remarkable*-looking boy!"

This took his mind off the play, and he wondered if he really did seem handsome to the population of New York.

Paskert and he walked in silence toward their hotel. The former was the first to speak. His uncertain fifteen-year-old voice broke in in a melancholy strain on Amory's musings:

"I'd marry that girl tonight."

There was no need to ask what girl he referred to.

"I'd be proud to take her home and introduce her to my people," continued Paskert.

Amory was distinctly impressed. He wished he had said it instead of Paskert. It sounded so mature.

"I wonder about actresses; are they all pretty bad?"

"No, *sir*, not by a darn sight," said the worldly youth with emphasis, "and I know that girl's as good as gold. I can tell."

They wandered on, mixing in the Broadway crowd, dreaming on the music that eddied out of the cafés. New faces flashed on and off like myriad lights, pale or rouged faces, tired, yet sustained by a weary excitement. Amory watched them in fascination. He was planning his life. He was going to live in New York, and be known at every restaurant and café, wearing a dress suit from early evening to early morning, sleeping away the dull hours of the forenoon.

"Yes, *sir*, I'd marry that girl tonight!"

HEROIC IN GENERAL TONE

October of his second and last year at St. Regis' was a high point in Amory's memory. The game with Groton was played from three of a snappy, exhilarating afternoon far into the crisp autumnal twilight, and Amory at quarterback, exhorting in wild despair, making impossible tackles, calling signals in a voice that had diminished to a hoarse, furious whisper, yet found time to revel in the blood-stained bandage around his head, and the straining, glorious heroism of plunging, crashing bodies and aching limbs. For those minutes courage flowed like wine out of dusk, and he was the eternal hero, one with the sea-rover on the prow of a Norse galley, one with Roland and Horatius, Sir Nigel and Ted Coy, scraped and stripped into trim and then flung by his own will into the breach, beating back the tide, hearing from afar the thunder of cheers . . . finally bruised and weary, but still elusive, circling an end, twisting, changing pace, straight-arming . . . falling behind the Groton goal with two men on his legs, in the only touchdown of the game.

THE PHILOSOPHY OF THE SLICKER

From the scoffing superiority of sixth-form year and success Amory looked back with cynical wonder on his status of the year before. He was changed as completely as Amory Blaine could ever be changed. Amory plus Beatrice plus two years in Minneapolis—these had been his ingredients when he entered St. Regis'. But the Minneapolis years were not a thick enough overlay to conceal the "Amory plus Beatrice" from the ferreting eyes of a boarding school, so St. Regis' had very painfully drilled Beatrice out of him, and had begun to lay down new and more conventional planking on the fundamental Amory. But both St. Regis' and Amory were unconscious of the fact that this fundamental Amory had not in himself changed. Those qualities for which he had suffered, his moodiness, his tendency to pose, his laziness, and his love of playing the fool, were now taken as a matter of course, recognized eccentricities in a star quarterback, a clever actor, and the editor of the *St. Regis' Tattler:* it puzzled him to see impressionable small boys imitating the very vanities that had not long ago been contemptible weaknesses.

After the football season he slumped into dreamy content. The night of the pre-holiday dance he slipped away and went early to bed for the pleasure of hearing the violin music cross the grass and come surging in at his window. Many nights he lay there dreaming awake of secret cafés in Montmartre, where ivory women delved in romantic mysteries with diplomats and soldiers of fortune, while orchestras played Hungarian waltzes and the air was thick and exotic with intrigue and moonlight and adventure. In the spring he read "L'Allegro," by request, and was inspired to lyrical outpourings on the subject of Arcady and the pipes of Pan. He moved his bed so that the sun would wake him at dawn, that he might dress and go out to the archaic swing that hung from an apple tree near the sixth-form house. Seating himself in this he would pump higher and higher until he got the effect of swinging into the wide air, into a fairyland of piping satyrs and nymphs with the faces of fair-haired girls he passed in the streets of Eastchester. As the swing reached its highest point, Arcady really lay just over the brow of a certain hill, where the brown road dwindled out of sight in a golden dot.

He read voluminously all spring, the beginning of his eighteenth year: "The Gentleman from Indiana," "The New Arabian Nights," "The Morals of Marcus Ordeyne," "The Man Who Was Thursday," which he liked without understanding; "Stover at Yale," that became somewhat of a textbook; "Dombey and Son," because he thought he really should read better stuff; Robert Chambers, David Graham Phillips, and E. Phillips Oppenheim complete, and a scattering of Tennyson and Kipling. Of all his class work only "L'Allegro" and some quality of rigid clarity in solid geometry stirred his languid interest.

As June drew near, he felt the need of conversation to formulate his own ideas, and, to his surprise, found a co-philosopher in Rahill, the president of the sixth form. In many a talk, on the highroad or lying belly-down along the edge of the baseball diamond, or late at night with their cigarettes glowing in the dark, they threshed out the questions of school, and there was developed the term "slicker."

"Got tobacco?" whispered Rahill one night, putting his head inside the door five minutes after lights.

"Sure."

"I'm coming in."

"Take a couple of pillows and lie in the window-seat, why don't you."

Amory sat up in bed and lit a cigarette while Rahill settled for a conversation. Rahill's favorite subject was the respective futures of the sixth form, and Amory never tired of outlining them for his benefit.

"Ted Converse? 'At's easy. He'll fail his exams, tutor all summer at Harstrum's, get into Sheff with about four conditions, and flunk out in the middle of the freshman year. Then he'll go back West and raise hell for a year or so; finally his father will make him go into the paint business. He'll marry and have four sons, all bone heads. He'll always think St. Regis' spoiled him, so he'll send his sons to day school in Portland. He'll die of locomotor ataxia when he's forty-one, and his wife will give a baptizing stand or whatever you call it to the Presbyterian Church, with his name on it — —"

"Hold up, Amory. That's too darned gloomy. How about yourself?"

"I'm in a superior class. You are, too. We're philosophers."

"I'm not."

"Sure you are. You've got a darn good head on you." But Amory knew that nothing in the abstract, no theory or generality, ever moved Rahill until he stubbed his toe upon the concrete minutiæ of it.

"Haven't," insisted Rahill. "I let people impose on me here and don't get anything out of it. I'm the prey of my friends, damn it — do their lessons, get 'em out of trouble, pay 'em stupid summer visits, and always entertain their kid sisters; keep my temper when they get selfish and *then* they think they pay me back by voting for me and telling me

I'm the 'big man' of St. Regis'. I want to get where everybody does their own work and I can tell people where to go. I'm tired of being nice to every poor fish in school."

"You're not a slicker," said Amory suddenly.

"A what?"

"A slicker."

"What the devil's that?"

"Well, it's something that—that—there's a lot of them. You're not one, and neither am I, though I am more than you are."

"Who is one? What makes you one?"

Amory considered.

"Why—why, I suppose that the *sign* of it is when a fellow slicks his hair back with water."

"Like Carstairs?"

"Yes—sure. He's a slicker."

They spent two evenings getting an exact definition. The slicker was good-looking or *clean*-looking; he had brains, social brains, that is, and he used all means on the broad path of honesty to get ahead, be popular, admired, and never in trouble. He dressed well, was particularly neat in appearance, and derived his name from the fact that his hair was inevitably worn short, soaked in water or tonic, parted in the middle, and slicked back as the current of fashion dictated. The slickers of that year had adopted tortoise-shell spectacles as badges of their slickerhood, and this made them so easy to recognize that Amory and Rahill never missed one. The slicker seemed distributed through school, always a little wiser and shrewder than his contemporaries, managing some team or other, and keeping his cleverness carefully concealed.

Amory found the slicker a most valuable classification until his junior year in college, when the outline became so blurred and indeterminate that it had to be subdivided many times, and became only a quality. Amory's secret ideal had all the slicker qualifications, but, in addition, courage and tremendous brains and talents—also Amory conceded him a bizarre streak that was quite irreconcilable to the slicker proper.

This was a first real break from the hypocrisy of school tradition. The slicker was a definite element of success, differing intrinsically from the prep school "big man."

The Slicker	*The Big Man*
1. Clever sense of social values.	1. Inclined to stupidity and unconscious of social values.

2. Dresses well. Pretends that dress is superficial—but knows that it isn't.
3. Goes into such activities as he can shine in.
4. Gets to college and is, in a worldly way, successful.

5. Hair slicked.

2. Thinks dress is superficial, and is inclined to be careless about it.
3. Goes out for everything from a sense of duty.
4. Gets to college and has a problematical future. Feels lost without his circle, and always says that school days were happiest, after all. Goes back to school and makes speeches about what St. Regis' boys are doing.

5. Hair not slicked.

Amory had decided definitely on Princeton, even though he would be the only boy entering that year from St. Regis'. Yale had a romance and glamour from the tales of Minneapolis, and St. Regis' men who had been "tapped for Skull and Bones," but Princeton drew him most, with its atmosphere of bright colors and its alluring reputation as the pleasantest country club in America. Dwarfed by the menacing college exams, Amory's school days drifted into the past. Years afterward, when he went back to St. Regis', he seemed to have forgotten the successes of sixth-form year, and to be able to picture himself only as the unadjustable boy who had hurried down corridors, jeered at by his rabid contemporaries mad with common sense.

Two

Spires and

Gargoyles

At FIRST AMORY NOTICED ONLY THE WEALTH of sunshine creeping across the long greenswards, dancing on the leaded windowpanes, and swimming around the tops of spires and towers and battlemented walls. Gradually he realized that he was really walking up University Place, self-conscious about his suitcase, developing a new tendency to glare straight ahead when he passed any one. Several times he could have sworn that men turned to look at him critically. He wondered vaguely if there was something the matter with his clothes, and wished he had shaved that morning on the train. He felt unnecessarily stiff and awkward among these white-flannelled, bareheaded youths, who must be juniors and seniors, judging from the savoir faire with which they strolled.

He found that 12 University Place was a large, dilapidated mansion, at present apparently uninhabited, though he knew it housed usually a dozen freshmen. After a hurried skirmish with his landlady he sallied out on a tour of exploration, but he had gone scarcely a block when he became horribly conscious that he must be the only man in town who was wearing a hat. He returned hurriedly to 12 University, left his derby, and, emerging bareheaded, loitered down Nassau Street, stopping to investigate a display of athletic photographs in a store window, including a large one of Allenby, the football captain, and next attracted by the sign "Jigger Shop" over a confectionery window. This sounded familiar, so he sauntered in and took a seat on a high stool.

"Chocolate sundae," he told a colored person.

"Double chocolate jiggah? Anything else?"

"Why—yes."

"Bacon bun?"

"Why—yes."

He munched four of these, finding them of pleasing savor, and then consumed another double-chocolate jigger before ease descended upon him. After a cursory inspection of the pillowcases, leather pennants, and Gibson Girls that lined the walls, he left, and continued along Nassau Street with his hands in his pockets. Gradually he was learning to distinguish between upper classmen and entering men, even though the freshman cap would not appear until the following Monday. Those who were too obviously, too nervously at home were freshmen, for as each train brought a new contingent it was immediately absorbed into the hatless, white-shod, book-laden throng, whose function seemed to be to drift endlessly up and down the street, emitting great clouds of smoke from brand-new pipes. By afternoon Amory realized that now the newest arrivals were taking him for an upper classman, and he tried conscientiously to look both pleasantly blasé and casually critical, which was as near as he could analyze the prevalent facial expression.

At five o'clock he felt the need of hearing his own voice, so he retreated to his house to see if any one else had arrived. Having climbed the rickety stairs he scrutinized his room resignedly, concluding that it was hopeless to attempt any more inspired decoration than class banners and tiger pictures. There was a tap at the door.

"Come in!"

A slim face with gray eyes and a humorous smile appeared in the doorway.

"Got a hammer?"

"No—sorry. Maybe Mrs. Twelve, or whatever she goes by, has one."

The stranger advanced into the room.

"You an inmate of this asylum?"

Amory nodded.

"Awful barn for the rent we pay."

Amory had to agree that it was.

"I thought of the campus," he said, "but they say there's so few freshmen that they're lost. Have to sit around and study for something to do."

The gray-eyed man decided to introduce himself.

"My name's Holiday."

"Blaine's my name."

They shook hands with the fashionable low swoop. Amory grinned.

"Where'd you prep?"

"Andover—where did you?"

"St. Regis'."

"Oh, did you? I had a cousin there."

They discussed the cousin thoroughly, and then Holiday announced that he was to meet his brother for dinner at six.

"Come along and have a bite with us."

"All right."

At the Kenilworth Amory met Burne Holiday—he of the gray eyes was Kerry—and during a limpid meal of thin soup and anæmic vegetables they stared at the other freshmen, who sat either in small groups looking very ill at ease, or in large groups seeming very much at home.

"I hear Commons is pretty bad," said Amory.

"That's the rumor. But you've got to eat there—or pay anyways."

"Crime!"

"Imposition!"

"Oh, at Princeton you've got to swallow everything the first year. It's like a damned prep school."

Amory agreed.

"Lot of pep, though," he insisted. "I wouldn't have gone to Yale for a million."

"Me either."

"You going out for anything?" inquired Amory of the elder brother.

"Not me—Burne here is going out for *The Prince—The Daily Princetonian*, you know."

"Yes, I know."

"You going out for anything?"

"Why—yes. I'm going to take a whack at freshman football."

"Play at St. Regis'?"

"Some," admitted Amory depreciatingly, "but I'm getting so damned thin."

"You're not thin."

"Well, I used to be stocky last fall."

"Oh!"

After supper they attended the movies, where Amory was fascinated by the glib comments of a man in front of him, as well as by the wild yelling and shouting.

"*Yoho!*"

"Oh, honey-*baby*—you're so big and strong, but oh, so *gentle!*"

"Clinch!"

"Oh, *Clinch!*"

"Kiss her, kiss 'at lady, *quick!*"

"Oh-h-h—!"

A group began whistling "By the Sea," and the audience took it up noisily. This was followed by an indistinguishable song that included much stamping and then by an endless, incoherent dirge.

> "Oh-h-h-h-h
> She works in a Jam Factoree
> And—that-may-be-all-right
> But you can't-fool-me
> For I know—DAMN—WELL
> That she DON'T-make-jam-all-night!
> Oh-h-h-h!"

As they pushed out, giving and receiving curious impersonal glances, Amory decided that he liked the movies, wanted to enjoy them as the row of upper classmen in front had enjoyed them, with their arms along the backs of the seats, their comments Gaelic and caustic, their attitude a mixture of critical wit and tolerant amusement.

"Want a sundae—I mean a jigger?" asked Kerry.

"Sure."

They suppered heavily and then, still sauntering, eased back to 12.

"Wonderful night."

"It's a whiz."

"You men going to unpack?"

"Guess so. Come on, Burne."

Amory decided to sit for a while on the front steps, so he bade them good night.

The great tapestries of trees had darkened to ghosts back at the last edge of twilight. The early moon had drenched the arches with pale blue, and, weaving over the night, in and out of the gossamer rifts of moon, swept a song, a song with more than a hint of sadness, infinitely transient, infinitely regretful.

He remembered that an alumnus of the nineties had told him of one of Booth Tarkington's amusements: standing in mid-campus in the small hours and singing tenor songs to the stars, arousing mingled emotions in the couched undergraduates according to the sentiment of their moods.

Now, far down the shadowy line of University Place a white-clad phalanx broke the gloom, and marching figures, white-shirted, white-trousered, swung rhythmically up the street, with linked arms and heads thrown back:

> "Going back—going back,
> Going—back—to—Nas-sau—Hall,
> Going back—going back—
> To the—Best—Old—Place—of—All
> Going back—going back,
> From all—this—earth-ly—ball,
> We'll—clear—the—track—as—we—go—back—
> Going—back—to—Nas-sau—Hall!"

Amory closed his eyes as the ghostly procession drew near. The song soared so high that all dropped out except the tenors, who bore the melody triumphantly past the danger-point and relinquished it to the fantastic chorus. Then Amory opened his eyes, half afraid that sight would spoil the rich illusion of harmony.

He sighed eagerly. There at the head of the white platoon marched Allenby, the football captain, slim and defiant, as if aware that this year the hopes of the college rested on him, that his hundred-and-sixty pounds were expected to dodge to victory through the heavy blue and crimson lines.

Fascinated, Amory watched each rank of linked arms as it came abreast, the faces indistinct above the polo shirts, the voices blent in a pæan of triumph—and then the procession passed through shadowy Campbell Arch, and the voices grew fainter as it wound eastward over the campus.

The minutes passed and Amory sat there very quietly. He regretted the rule that would forbid freshmen to be outdoors after curfew, for he wanted to ramble through the shadowy scented lanes, where Witherspoon brooded like a dark mother over Whig and Clio, her Attic children, where the black Gothic snake of Little curled down to Cuyler and Patton, these in turn flinging the mystery out over the placid slope rolling to the lake.

Princeton of the daytime filtered slowly into his consciousness—West and Reunion, redolent of the sixties, Seventy-nine Hall, brick-red and arrogant, Upper and Lower Pyne, aristocratic Elizabethan ladies not quite content to live among shopkeepers, and, topping all, climbing with clear blue aspiration, the great dreaming spires of Holder and Cleveland towers.

From the first he loved Princeton—its lazy beauty, its half-grasped significance, the wild moonlight revel of the rushes, the handsome, prosperous big-game crowds, and under it all the air of struggle that pervaded his class. From the day when, wild-eyed and exhausted, the jerseyed freshmen sat in the gymnasium and elected some one from Hill School class president, a Lawrenceville celebrity vice-president, a hockey star from St. Paul's secretary, up until the end of sophomore year it never ceased, that breathless social system, that worship, seldom named, never really admitted, of the bogey "Big Man."

First it was schools, and Amory, alone from St. Regis', watched the crowds form and widen and form again; St. Paul's, Hill, Pomfret, eating at certain tacitly reserved tables in Commons, dressing in their own corners of the gymnasium, and drawing unconsciously about them a barrier of the slightly less important but socially ambitious to protect them from the friendly, rather puzzled high school element. From the moment he realized this Amory resented social barriers as artificial distinctions made by the strong to bolster up their weak retainers and keep out the almost strong.

Having decided to be one of the gods of the class, he reported for freshman football practice, but in the second week, playing quarterback, already paragraphed in corners of the *Princetonian*, he wrenched his knee seriously enough to put him out for the rest of the season. This forced him to retire and consider the situation.

"12 Univee" housed a dozen miscellaneous question marks. There were three or four inconspicuous and quite startled boys from Lawrenceville, two amateur wild men from a New York private school (Kerry Holiday christened them the "plebian drunks"), a Jewish youth, also from New York, and, as compensation for Amory, the two Holidays, to whom he took an instant fancy.

The Holidays were rumored twins, but really the dark-haired one, Kerry, was a year older than his blond brother, Burne. Kerry was tall, with humorous gray eyes, and a sudden, attractive smile; he became at once the mentor of the house, reaper of ears that grew too high, censor of conceit, vendor of rare, satirical humor. Amory spread the table of their future friendship with all his ideas of what college should and did mean. Kerry, not inclined as yet to take things seriously, chided him gently for being curious at this inopportune time about the intricacies of the social system, but liked him and was both interested and amused.

Burne, fair-haired, silent, and intent, appeared in the house only as a busy apparition, gliding in quietly at night and off again in the early morning to get up his work in the library—he was out for the *Princetonian*, competing furiously against forty others for the coveted first place. In December he came down with diphtheria, and someone else won the competition, but, returning to college in February, he dauntlessly went after the prize again. Necessarily, Amory's acquaintance with him was in the way of three-minute chats, walking to and from lectures, so he failed to penetrate Burne's one absorbing interest and find what lay beneath it.

Amory was far from contented. He missed the place he had won at St. Regis', the being known and admired, yet Princeton stimulated him, and there were many things ahead calculated to arouse the Machiavelli latent in him, could he but insert a wedge. The upper-class clubs, concerning which he had pumped a reluctant graduate during the previous summer, excited his curiosity: Ivy, detached and breathlessly aristocratic; Cottage, an impressive mélange of brilliant adventurers and well-dressed philanderers; Tiger Inn, broad-shouldered and athletic, vitalized by an honest elaboration of prep-school standards; Cap and Gown, anti-alcoholic, faintly religious and politically powerful; flamboyant Colonial; literary Quadrangle; and the dozen others, varying in age and position.

Anything which brought an under classman into too glaring a light was labelled with the damning brand of "running it out." The movies thrived on caustic comments, but the men who made them were generally running it out; talking of clubs was running it out; standing for anything very strongly, as, for instance, drinking parties or teetotalling, was running it out; in short, being personally conspicuous was not tolerated, and the influential man was the non-committal man, until at club elections in sophomore year every one should be sewed up in some bag for the rest of his college career.

Amory found that writing for the *Nassau Literary Magazine* would get him nothing, but that being on the board of the *Daily Princetonian* would get any one a good deal. His vague desire to do immortal acting with the English Dramatic Association faded out when he found that the most ingenious brains and talents were concentrated upon the Triangle Club, a musical comedy organization that every year took a great Christmas trip. In the meanwhile, feeling strangely alone and restless in Commons, with new desires and ambitions stirring in his mind, he let the first term go by between an envy of the embryo successes and a puzzled fretting with Kerry as to why they were not accepted immediately among the élite of the class.

Many afternoons they lounged in the windows of 12 Univee and watched the class pass to and from Commons, noting satellites already attaching themselves to the more prominent, watching the lonely grind with his hurried step and downcast eye, envying the happy security of the big school groups.

"We're the damned middle class, that's what!" he complained to Kerry one day as he lay stretched out on the sofa, consuming a family of Fatimas with contemplative precision.

"Well, why not? We came to Princeton so we could feel that way toward the small colleges—have it on 'em, more self-confidence, dress better, cut a swath—"

"Oh, it isn't that I mind the glittering caste system," admitted Amory. "I like having a bunch of hot cats on top, but gosh, Kerry, I've got to be one of them."

"But just now, Amory, you're only a sweaty bourgeois."

Amory lay for a moment without speaking.

"I won't be—long," he said finally. "But I hate to get anywhere by working for it. I'll show the marks, don't you know."

"Honorable scars." Kerry craned his neck suddenly at the street. "There's Langueduc, if you want to see what he looks like—and Humbird just behind."

Amory rose dynamically and sought the windows.

"Oh," he said, scrutinizing these worthies, "Humbird looks like a knockout, but this Langueduc—he's the rugged type, isn't he? I distrust that sort. All diamonds look big in the rough."

"Well," said Kerry, as the excitement subsided, "you're a literary genius. It's up to you."

"I wonder"—Amory paused—"if I could be. I honestly think so sometimes. That sounds like the devil, and I wouldn't say it to anybody except you."

"Well—go ahead. Let your hair grow and write poems like this guy D'Invilliers in the Lit."

Amory reached lazily at a pile of magazines on the table.

"Read his latest effort?"

"Never miss 'em. They're rare."

Amory glanced through the issue.

"Hello!" he said in surprise, "he's a freshman, isn't he?"

"Yeah."

"Listen to this! My God!

A serving lady speaks:
Black velvet trails its folds over the day,
White tapers, prisoned in their silver frames,
Wave their thin flames like shadows in the wind,
Pia, Pompia, come—come away—

"Now, what the devil does that mean?"

"It's a pantry scene."

Her toes are stiffened like a stork's in flight;
She's laid upon her bed, on the white sheets,
Her hands pressed on her smooth bust like a saint,
Bella Cunizza, come into the light!

"My gosh, Kerry, what in hell is it all about? I swear I don't get him at all, and I'm a literary bird myself."

"It's pretty tricky," said Kerry, "only you've got to think of hearses and stale milk when you read it. That isn't as pash as some of them."

Amory tossed the magazine on the table.

"Well," he sighed, "I sure am up in the air. I know I'm not a regular fellow, yet I loathe anybody else that isn't. I can't decide whether to cultivate my mind and be a great dramatist, or to thumb my nose at the Golden Treasury and be a Princeton slicker."

"Why decide?" suggested Kerry. "Better drift, like me. I'm going to sail into prominence on Burne's coattails."

"I can't drift—I want to be interested. I want to pull strings, even for somebody else, or be *Princetonian* chairman or Triangle president. I want to be admired, Kerry."

"You're thinking too much about yourself."

Amory sat up at this.

"No. I'm thinking about you, too. We've got to get out and mix around the class right now, when it's fun to be a snob. I'd like to bring a sardine to the prom in June, for instance, but I wouldn't do it unless I could be damn debonaire about it—introduce her to all the prize parlor-snakes, and the football captain, and all that simple stuff."

"Amory," said Kerry impatiently, "you're just going around in a circle. If you want to be prominent, get out and try for something; if you don't, just take it easy." He yawned. "Come on, let's let the smoke drift off. We'll go down and watch football practice."

Amory gradually accepted this point of view, decided that next fall would inaugurate his career, and relinquished himself to watching Kerry extract joy from 12 Univee.

They filled the Jewish youth's bed with lemon pie; they put out the gas all over the house every night by blowing into the jet in Amory's room, to the bewilderment of Mrs. Twelve and the local plumber; they set up the effects of the plebeian drunks—pictures, books, and furniture—in the bathroom, to the confusion of the pair, who hazily discovered the transposition on their return from a Trenton spree; they were disappointed beyond measure when the plebeian drunks decided to take it as a joke; they played red-dog and twenty-one and jackpot from dinner to dawn, and on the occasion of one man's birthday persuaded him to buy sufficient champagne for a hilarious celebration. The donor of the party having remained sober, Kerry and Amory accidently dropped him down two flights of stairs and called, shame-faced and penitent, at the infirmary all the following week.

"Say, who are all these women?" demanded Kerry one day, protesting at the size of Amory's mail. "I've been looking at the postmarks lately—Farmington and Dobbs and Westover and Dana Hall—what's the idea?"

Amory grinned.

"All from the Twin Cities." He named them off. "There's Marylyn De Witt—she's pretty, got a car of her own and that's damn convenient; there's Sally Weatherby—she's getting too fat; there's Myra St. Claire, she's an old flame, easy to kiss if you like it— —"

"What line do you throw 'em?" demanded Kerry. "I've tried everything, and the mad wags aren't even afraid of me."

"You're the 'nice boy' type," suggested Amory.

"That's just it. Mother always feels the girl is safe if she's with me. Honestly, it's annoying. If I start to hold somebody's hand, they laugh at me, and *let* me, just as if it wasn't part of them. As soon as I get hold of a hand they sort of disconnect if from the rest of them."

"Sulk," suggested Amory. "Tell 'em you're wild and have 'em reform you—go home furious—come back in half an hour—startle 'em."

Kerry shook his head.

"No chance. I wrote a St. Timothy girl a really loving letter last year. In one place I got rattled and said: 'My God, how I love you!' She took a nail scissors, clipped out the 'My God' and showed the rest of the letter all over school. Doesn't work at all. I'm just 'good old Kerry' and all that rot."

Amory smiled and tried to picture himself as "good old Amory." He failed completely.

February dripped snow and rain, the cyclonic freshman mid-years passed, and life in 12 Univee continued interesting if not purposeful. Once a day Amory indulged in a club sandwich, cornflakes, and Julienne potatoes at "Joe's," accompanied usually by Kerry or Alec Connage. The latter was a quiet, rather aloof slicker from Hotchkiss, who lived next door and shared the same enforced singleness as Amory, due to the fact that his entire class had gone to Yale. "Joe's" was unæsthetic and faintly unsanitary, but a limitless charge account could be opened there, a convenience that Amory appreciated. His father had been experimenting with mining stocks and, in consequence, his allowance, while liberal, was not at all what he had expected.

"Joe's" had the additional advantage of seclusion from curious upper-class eyes, so at four each afternoon Amory, accompanied by friend or book, went up to experiment with his digestion. One day in March, finding that all the tables were occupied, he slipped into a chair opposite a freshman who bent intently over a book at the last table. They nodded briefly. For twenty minutes Amory sat consuming bacon buns and reading "Mrs. Warren's Profession" (he had discovered Shaw quite by accident while browsing in the library during midyears); the other freshman, also intent on his volume, meanwhile did away with a trio of chocolate malted milks.

By and by Amory's eyes wandered curiously to his fellow-luncher's book. He spelled out the name and title upside down—"Marpessa," by Stephen Phillips. This meant nothing to him, his metrical education having been confined to such Sunday classics as "Come into the Garden, Maud," and what morsels of Shakespeare and Milton had been recently forced upon him.

Moved to address his vis-à-vis, he simulated interest in his book for a moment, and then exclaimed aloud as if involuntarily:

"Ha! Great stuff!"

The other freshman looked up and Amory registered artificial embarrassment.

"Are you referring to your bacon buns?" His cracked, kindly voice went well with the large spectacles and the impression of a voluminous keenness that he gave.

"No," Amory answered. "I was referring to Bernard Shaw." He turned the book around in explanation.

"I've never read any Shaw. I've always meant to." The boy paused and then continued: "Did you ever read Stephen Phillips, or do you like poetry?"

"Yes, indeed," Amory affirmed eagerly. "I've never read much of Phillips, though." (He had never heard of any Phillips except the late David Graham.)

"It's pretty fair, I think. Of course he's a Victorian." They sallied into a discussion of poetry, in the course of which they introduced themselves, and Amory's companion proved to be none other than "that awful highbrow, Thomas Parke D'Invilliers," who signed the passionate love-poems in the *Lit.* He was, perhaps, nineteen, with stooped shoulders, pale blue eyes, and, as Amory could tell from his general appearance, without much conception of social competition and such phenomena of absorbing interest. Still, he liked books, and it seemed forever since Amory had met any one who did; if only that St. Paul's crowd at the next table would not mistake *him* for a bird, too, he would enjoy the encounter tremendously. They didn't seem to be noticing, so he let himself go, discussed books by the dozens—books he had read, read about, books he had never heard of, rattling off lists of titles with the facility of a Brentano's clerk. D'Invilliers was partially taken in and wholly delighted. In a good-natured way he had almost decided that Princeton was one part deadly Philistines and one part deadly grinds, and to find a person who could mention Keats without stammering, yet evidently washed his hands, was rather a treat.

"Ever read any Oscar Wilde?" he asked.

"No. Who wrote it?"

"It's a man—don't you know?"

"Oh, surely." A faint chord was struck in Amory's memory. "Wasn't the comic opera, 'Patience,' written about him?"

"Yes, that's the fella. I've just finished a book of his, 'The Picture of Dorian Gray,' and I certainly wish you'd read it. You'd like it. You can borrow it if you want to."

"Why, I'd like it a lot—thanks."

"Don't you want to come up to the room? I've got a few other books."

Amory hesitated, glanced at the St. Paul's group—one of them was the magnificent, exquisite Humbird—and he considered how determinate the addition of this friend would be. He never got to the stage of making them and getting rid of them—he was not hard enough for that—so he measured Thomas Parke D'Invilliers' undoubted attractions and value against the menace of cold eyes behind tortoise-rimmed spectacles that he fancied glared from the next table.

"Yes, I'll go."

So he found "Dorian Gray" and the "Mystic and Somber Dolores" and the "Belle Dame sans Merci"; for a month was keen on naught else. The world became pale and interesting, and he tried hard to look at Princeton through the satiated eyes of Oscar Wilde and Swinburne—or "Fingal O'Flaherty" and "Algernon Charles," as he called them in précieuse jest. He read enormously every night—Shaw, Chesterton, Barrie, Pinero, Yeats, Synge, Ernest Dowson, Arthur Symons, Keats, Sudermann, Robert Hugh Benson, the Savoy Operas—just a heterogeneous mixture, for he suddenly discovered that he had read nothing for years.

Tom D'Invilliers became at first an occasion rather than a friend. Amory saw him about once a week, and together they gilded the ceiling of Tom's room and decorated the walls with imitation tapestry, bought at an auction, tall candlesticks and figured curtains. Amory liked him for being clever and literary without effeminacy or affectation. In fact, Amory did most of the strutting and tried painfully to make every remark an epigram, than which, if one is content with ostensible epigrams, there are many feats harder. 12 Univee was amused. Kerry read "Dorian Gray" and simulated Lord Henry, following Amory about, addressing him as "Dorian" and pretending to encourage in him wicked fancies and attenuated tendencies to ennui. When he carried it into Commons, to the amazement of the others at table, Amory became furiously embarrassed, and after that made epigrams only before D'Invilliers or a convenient mirror.

One day Tom and Amory tried reciting their own and Lord Dunsany's poems to the music of Kerry's graphophone.

"Chant!" cried Tom. "Don't recite. *Chant!*"

Amory, who was performing, looked annoyed, and claimed that he needed a record with less piano in it. Kerry thereupon rolled on the floor in stifled laughter.

"Put on 'Hearts and Flowers'!" he howled. "Oh, my Lord, I'm going to cast a kitten."

"Shut off the damn graphophone," Amory cried, rather red in the face. "I'm not giving an exhibition."

In the meanwhile Amory delicately kept trying to awaken a sense of the social system in D'Invilliers, for he knew that this poet was really more conventional than he, and needed merely watered hair, a smaller range of conversation, and a darker brown hat to become quite regular. But the liturgy of Livingstone collars and dark ties fell on heedless ears; in fact D'Invilliers faintly resented his efforts; so Amory confined himself to calls once a week, and brought him occasionaly to 12 Univee. This caused mild titters among the other freshmen, who called them "Doctor Johnson and Boswell."

Alec Connage, another frequent visitor, liked him in a vague way, but was afraid of him as a highbrow. Kerry, who saw through his poetic patter to the solid, almost respectable depths within, was immensely amused and would have him recite poetry by the hour, while he lay with closed eyes on Amory's sofa and listened:

> *Asleep or waking is it? for her neck,*
> *Kissed over close, wears yet a purple speck*
> *Wherein the pained blood falters and goes out;*
> *Soft, and stung softly—fairer for a fleck.*

"That's good," Kerry would say softly. "It pleases the elder Holiday. That's a great poet, I guess." Tom, delighted at an audience, would ramble through the "Poems and Ballads" until Kerry and Amory knew them almost as well as he.

Amory took to writing poetry on spring afternoons, in the gardens of the big estates near Princeton, while swans made effective atmosphere in the artificial pools, and slow clouds sailed harmoniously above the willows. May came too soon, and suddenly unable to bear walls, he wandered the campus at all hours through starlight and rain.

A DAMP SYMBOLIC INTERLUDE

The night mist fell. From the moon it rolled, clustered about the spires and towers, and then settled below them, so that the dreaming peaks were still in lofty aspiration toward the sky. Figures that dotted the day like ants now brushed along as shadowy ghosts, in and out of the foreground. The Gothic halls and cloisters were infinitely more mysterious as they loomed suddenly out of the darkness, outlined each by myriad faint squares of yellow light. Indefinitely from somewhere a bell boomed the quarter-hour, and Amory, pausing by the sundial, stretched himself out full length on the damp grass. The cool bathed his eyes and slowed the flight of time—time that had crept so insidiously through the lazy April afternoons, seemed so intangible in the long spring twilights. Evening after evening the senior singing had drifted over the campus in melancholy beauty, and through the shell of his undergraduate consciousness had broken a deep and reverent devotion to the gray walls and Gothic peaks and all they symbolized as warehouses of dead ages.

The tower that in view of his window sprang upward, grew into a spire, yearning higher until its uppermost tip was half invisible against the morning skies, gave him the first sense of the transiency and unimportance of the campus figures except as holders of the apostolic succession. He liked knowing that Gothic architecture, with its upward trend, was peculiarly appropriate to universities, and the idea became personal to him. The silent stretches of green, the quiet halls with an occasional late-burning scholastic light held his imagination in a strong grasp, and the chastity of the spire became a symbol of this perception.

"Damn it all," he whispered aloud, wetting his hands in the damp and running them through his hair. "Next year I work!" Yet he knew that where now the spirit of spires and towers made him dreamily acquiescent, it would then overawe him. Where now he realized only his own inconsequence, effort would make him aware of his own impotency and insufficiency.

The college dreamed on—awake. He felt a nervous excitement that might have been the very throb of its slow heart. It was a stream where he was to throw a stone whose faint ripple would be vanishing almost as it left his hand. As yet he had given nothing, he had taken nothing.

A belated freshman, his oilskin slicker rasping loudly, slushed along the soft path. A voice from somewhere called the inevitable formula, "Stick out your head!" below an unseen window. A hundred little sounds of the current drifting on under the fog pressed in finally on his consciousness.

"Oh, *God!*" he cried suddenly, and started at the sound of his voice in the stillness. The rain dripped on. A minute longer he lay without moving, his hands clinched. Then he sprang to his feet and gave his clothes a tentative pat.

"I'm very damn wet!" he said aloud to the sundial.

HISTORICAL

The war began in the summer following his freshman year. Beyond a sporting interest in the German dash for Paris the whole affair failed either to thrill or interest him. With the attitude he might have held toward an amusing melodrama he hoped it would be long and bloody. If it had not continued he would have felt like an irate ticket holder at a prizefight where the principals refused to mix it up.

That was his total reaction.

"HA-HA HORTENSE!"

"All right, po*nies!*"

"Shake it up!"

"Hey, ponies—how about easing up on that crap game and shaking a mean hip?"

"Hey, *ponies!*"

The coach fumed helplessly, the Triangle Club president, glowering with anxiety, varied between furious bursts of authority and fits of temperamental lassitude, when he sat spiritless and wondered how the devil the show was ever going on tour by Christmas.

"All right. We'll take the pirate song."

The ponies took last drags at their cigarettes and slumped into place; the leading lady rushed into the foreground, setting his hands and feet in an atmospheric mince; and as the coach clapped and stamped and tumped and da-da'd, they hashed out a dance.

A great, seething anthill was the Triangle Club. It gave a musical comedy every year, travelling with cast, chorus, orchestra, and scenery all through Christmas vacation. The play and music were the work of undergraduates, and the club itself was the most influential of institutions, over three hundred men competing for it every year.

Amory, after an easy victory in the first sophomore *Princetonian* competition, stepped into a vacancy of the cast as *Boiling Oil, a Pirate Lieutenant.* Every night for the last week they had rehearsed "Ha-Ha Hortense!" in the Casino, from two in the afternoon until eight in the morning, sustained by dark and powerful coffee, and sleeping in lectures through the interim. A rare scene, the Casino. A big, barnlike auditorium, dotted with boys as girls, boys as pirates, boys as babies; the scenery in the course of being violently set up; the spotlight man rehearsing by throwing weird shafts into angry eyes; over all the constant tuning of the orchestra or the cheerful tumpty-tump of a Triangle tune. The boy who writes the lyrics stands in the corner, biting a pencil, with twenty minutes to think of an encore; the business manager argues with the secretary as to how much money can be spent on "those damn milkmaid costumes"; the old graduate, president in ninety-eight, perches on a box and thinks how much simpler it was in his day.

How a Triangle show ever got off was a mystery, but it was a riotous mystery, anyway, whether or not one did enough service to wear a little gold Triangle on his watch-chain. "Ha-Ha Hortense!" was written over six times and had the names of nine collaborators on the programme. All Triangle shows started by being "something different—not just a regular musical comedy," but when the several authors, the president, the coach and the faculty committee finished with it, there remained just the old reliable Triangle show with the old reliable jokes and the star comedian who got expelled or sick or something just before the trip, and the dark-whiskered man in the pony ballet, who "absolutely won't shave twice a day, doggone it!"

There was one brilliant place in "Ha-Ha Hortense!" It is a Princeton tradition that whenever a Yale man who is a member of the widely advertised "Skull and Bones" hears the sacred name mentioned, he must leave the room. It is also a tradition that the members are invariably successful in later life, amassing fortunes or votes or coupons or whatever they choose to amass. Therefore, at each performance of "Ha-Ha Hortense!" half-a-dozen seats were kept from sale and occupied by six of the worst-looking vagabonds that could be hired from the streets, further touched up by the Triangle make-up man. At the moment in the show where *Firebrand, the Pirate Chief,* pointed at his black flag and said, "I am a Yale graduate—note my Skull and Bones!"—at this very moment the six vagabonds were instructed to rise *conspicuously* and leave the theatre with looks of deep melancholy and an injured dignity. It was claimed though never proved that on one occasion the hired Elis were swelled by one of the real thing.

They played through vacation to the fashionable of eight cities. Amory liked Louisville and Memphis best: these knew how to meet strangers, furnished extraordinary punch, and flaunted an astonishing array of feminine beauty. Chicago he approved for a certain verve that transcended its loud accent—however, it was a Yale town, and as the Yale Glee Club was expected in a week the Triangle received only divided homage. In Baltimore, Princeton was at home, and every one fell in love. There was a proper consumption of strong waters all along the line; one man invariably went on the stage highly stimulated, claiming that his particular interpretation of the part required it. There were three private cars; however, no one slept except in the third car, which was called the "animal car," and where were herded the spectacled wind-jammers of the orchestra. Everything was so hurried that there was no time to be bored, but when they arrived in Philadelphia, with vacation nearly over, there was rest in getting out of the heavy atmosphere of flowers and grease paint, and the ponies took off their corsets with abdominal pains and sighs of relief.

When the disbanding came, Amory set out post haste for Minneapolis, for Sally Weatherby's cousin, Isabelle Borgé, was coming to spend the winter in Minneapolis while her parents went abroad. He remembered Isabelle only as a little girl with whom had played sometimes when he first went to Minneapolis. She had gone to Baltimore to live—but since then she had developed a past.

Amory was in full stride, confident, nervous, and jubilant. Scurrying back to Minneapolis to see a girl he had known as a child seemed the interesting and romantic thing to do, so without compunction he wired his mother not to expect him . . . sat in the train, and thought about himself for thirty-six hours.

"PETTING"

On the Triangle trip Amory had come into constant contact with that great current American phenomenon, the "petting party."

None of the Victorian mothers—and most of the mothers were Victorian—had any idea how casually their daughters were accustomed to be kissed. *"Servant*-girls are that way," says Mrs. Huston-

Carmelite to her popular daughter. "They are kissed first and proposed to afterward."

But the Popular Daughter becomes engaged every six months between sixteen and twenty-two, when she arranges a match with young Hambell, of Cambell & Hambell, who fatuously considers himself her first love, and between engagements the P.D. (she is selected by the cut-in system at dances, which favors the survival of the fittest) has other sentimental last kisses in the moonlight, or the firelight, or the outer darkness.

Amory saw girls doing things that even in his memory would have been impossible: eating three-o'clock, after-dance suppers in impossible cafés, talking of every side of life with an air half of earnestness, half of mockery, yet with a furtive excitement that Amory considered stood for a real moral letdown. But he never realized how widespread it was until he saw the cities between New York and Chicago as one vast juvenile intrigue.

Afternoon at the Plaza, with winter twilight hovering outside and faint drums downstairs . . . they strut and fret in the lobby, taking another cocktail, scrupulously attired and waiting. Then the swinging doors revolve and three bundles of fur mince in. The theatre comes afterward; then a table at the Midnight Frolic—of course, mother will be along there, but she will serve only to make things more secretive and brilliant as she sits in solitary state at the deserted table and thinks such entertainments as this are not half so bad as they are painted, only rather wearying. But the P.D. is in love again . . . it was odd, wasn't it?—that though there was so much room left in the taxi the P.D. and the boy from Williams were somehow crowded out and had to go in a separate car. Odd! Didn't you notice how flushed the P.D. was when she arrived just seven minutes late? But the P.D. "gets away with it."

The "belle" had become the "flirt," the "flirt" had become the "baby vamp." The "belle" had five or six callers every afternoon. If the P.D., by some strange accident, has two, it is made pretty uncomfortable for the one who hasn't a date with her. The "belle" was surrounded by a dozen men in the intermissions between dances. Try to find the P.D. between dances, just *try* to find her.

The same girl . . . deep in an atmosphere of jungle music and the questioning of moral codes. Amory found it rather fascinating to feel that any popular girl he met before eight he might quite possibly kiss before twelve.

"Why on earth are we here?" he asked the girl with the green combs one night as they sat in some one's limousine, outside the Country Club in Louisville.

"I don't know. I'm just full of the devil."

"Let's be frank—we'll never see each other again. I wanted to come out here with you because I thought you were the best-looking girl in sight. You really don't care whether you ever see me again, do you?"

"No—but is this your line for every girl? What have I done to deserve it?"

"And you didn't feel tired dancing or want a cigarette or any of the things you said? You just wanted to be— —"

"Oh, let's go in," she interrupted, "if you want to *analyze*. Let's not *talk* about it."

When the hand-knit, sleeveless jerseys were stylish, Amory, in a burst of inspiration, named them "petting shirts." The name travelled from coast to coast on the lips of parlor-snakes and P.D.'s.

DESCRIPTIVE

Amory was now eighteen years old, just under six feet tall and exceptionally, but not conventionally, handsome. He had rather a young face, the ingenuousness of which was marred by the penetrating green eyes, fringed with long dark eyelashes. He lacked somehow that intense animal magnetism that so often accompanies beauty in men or women; his personality seemed rather a mental thing, and it was not in his power to turn it on and off like a water faucet. But people never forgot his face.

ISABELLE

She paused at the top of the staircase. The sensations attributed to divers on spring-boards, leading ladies on opening nights, and lumpy, husky young men on the day of the Big Game, crowded through her. She should have descended to a burst of drums or a discordant blend of themes from "Thais" and "Carmen." She had never been so curious about her appearance, she had never been so satisfied with it. She had been sixteen years old for six months.

"Isabelle!" called her cousin Sally from the doorway of the dressing-room.

"I'm ready." She caught a slight lump of nervousness in her throat.

"I had to send back to the house for another pair of slippers. It'll be just a minute."

Isabelle started toward the dressing room for a last peek in the mirror, but something decided her to stand there and gaze down the broad stairs of the Minnehaha Club. They curved tantalizingly, and she could catch just a glimpse of two pairs of masculine feet in the hall below. Pump-shod in uniform black, they gave no hint of identity, but she wondered eagerly if one pair were attached to Amory Blaine. This young man, not as yet encountered, had nevertheless taken up a considerable part of her day—the first day of her arrival. Coming up in the machine from the station, Sally had volunteered, amid a rain of question, comment, revelation, and exaggeration:

"You remember Amory Blaine, of *course*. Well, he's simply mad to see you again. He's stayed over a day from college, and he's coming tonight. He's heard so much about you—says he remembers your eyes."

This had pleased Isabelle. It put them on equal terms, although she was quite capable of staging her own romances, with or without advance advertising. But following her happy tremble of anticipation, came a sinking sensation that made her ask:

"How do you mean he's heard about me? What sort of things?"

Sally smiled. She felt rather in the capacity of a showman with her more exotic cousin.

"He knows you're—you're considered beautiful and all that"—she paused—"and I guess he knows you've been kissed."

At this Isabelle's little fist had clinched suddenly under the fur robe. She was accustomed to be thus followed by her desperate past, and it never failed to rouse in her the same feeling of resentment; yet— in a strange town it was an advantageous reputation. She was a "Speed," was she? Well—let them find out.

Out of the window Isabelle watched the snow glide by in the frosty morning. It was ever so much colder here than in Baltimore; she had not remembered; the glass of the side door was iced, the windows were shirred with snow in the corners. Her mind played still with one subject. Did *he* dress like that boy there, who walked calmly down a bustling business street, in moccasins and winter-carnival costume? How very *Western!* Of course he wasn't that way: he went to Princeton, was a sophomore or something. Really she had no distinct idea of him. An ancient snapshot she had preserved in an old kodak book had impressed her by the big eyes (which he had probably grown up to by now). However, in the last month, when her winter visit to Sally had been decided on, he had assumed the proportions of a worthy adversary. Children, most astute of matchmakers, plot their campaigns quickly, and Sally had played a clever correspondence sonata to Isabelle's excitable temperament. Isabelle had been for some time capable of very strong, if very transient emotions. . . .

They drew up at a spreading, white-stone building, set back from the snowy street. Mrs. Weatherby greeted her warmly and her various younger cousins were produced from the corners where they skulked politely. Isabelle met them tactfully. At her best she allied all with whom she came in contact—except older girls and some women. All the impressions she made were conscious. The half-dozen girls she renewed acquaintance with that morning were all rather impressed and as much by her direct personality as by her reputation. Amory Blaine was an open subject. Evidently a bit light of love, neither popular nor unpopular—every girl there seemed to have had an affair with him at some time or other, but no one volunteered any really useful information. He was going to fall for her. . . . Sally had published that information to her young set and they were retailing it back to Sally as fast as they set eyes on Isabelle. Isabelle resolved secretly that she would, if necessary, *force* herself to like him—she owed it to Sally. Suppose she were terribly disappointed. Sally had painted him in such glowing colors—he was good-looking, "sort of distinguished, when he wants to be," had a line, and was properly inconstant. In fact, he summed up all the romance that her age and environment led her to desire. She wondered if those were his dancing shoes that fox-trotted tentatively around the soft rug below.

All impressions and, in fact, all ideas were extremely kaleidoscopic to Isabelle. She had that curious mixture of the social and the artistic temperaments found often in two classes, society women and actresses. Her education, or rather, her sophistication, had been absorbed from the boys who had dangled on her favor; her tact was instinctive, and her capacity for love-affairs was limited only by the number of the susceptible within telephone distance. Flirt smiled from her large black-brown eyes and shone through her intense physical magnetism.

So she waited at the head of the stairs that evening while slippers were fetched. Just as she was growing impatient, Sally came out of the dressing-room, beaming with her accustomed good nature and high spirits, and together they descended to the floor below, while the shifting searchlight of Isabelle's mind flashed on two ideas: she was glad she had high color tonight, and she wondered if he danced well.

Downstairs, in the club's great room, she was surrounded for a moment by the girls she had met in the afternoon, then she heard Sally's voice repeating a cycle of names, and found herself bowing to a sextet of black and white, terribly stiff, vaguely familiar figures. The name Blaine figured somewhere, but at first she could not place him. A very confused, very juvenile moment of awkward backings and bumpings followed, and everyone found himself talking to the person he least desired to. Isabelle manoeuvered herself and Froggy Parker, freshman at Harvard, with whom she had once played hopscotch, to a seat on the stairs. A humorous reference to the past was all she needed. The things

Isabelle could do socially with one idea were remarkable. First, she repeated it rapturously in an enthusiastic contralto with a soupçon of Southern accent; then she held it off at a distance and smiled at it—her wonderful smile; then she delivered it in variations and played a sort of mental catch with it, all this in the nominal form of dialogue. Froggy was fascinated and quite unconscious that this was being done, not for him, but for the green eyes that glistened under the shining carefully watered hair, a little to her left, for Isabelle had discovered Amory. As an actress even in the fullest flush of her own conscious magnetism gets a deep impression of most of the people in the front row, so Isabelle sized up her antagonist. First, he had auburn hair, and from her feeling of disappointment she knew that she had expected him to be dark and of garter-advertisement slenderness. . . . For the rest, a faint flush and a straight, romantic profile; the effect set off by a close-fitting dress suit and a silk ruffled shirt of the kind that women still delight to see men wear, but men were just beginning to get tired of.

During this inspection Amory was quietly watching.

"Don't *you* think so?" she said suddenly, turning to him, innocent-eyed.

There was a stir, and Sally led the way over to their table. Amory struggled to Isabelle's side, and whispered:

"You're my dinner partner, you know. We're all coached for each other."

Isabelle gasped—this was rather right in line. But really she felt as if a good speech had been taken from the star and given to a minor character. . . . She mustn't lose the leadership a bit. The dinner-table glittered with laughter at the confusion of getting places and then curious eyes were turned on her, sitting near the head. She was enjoying this immensely, and Froggy Parker was so engrossed with the added sparkle of her rising color that he forgot to pull out Sally's chair, and fell into a dim confusion. Amory was on the other side, full of confidence and vanity, gazing at her in open admiration. He began directly, and so did Froggy:

"I've heard a lot about you since you wore braids— —"

"Wasn't it funny this afternoon— —"

Both stopped. Isabelle turned to Amory shyly. Her face was always enough answer for any one, but she decided to speak.

"How—from whom?"

"From everybody—for all the years since you've been away." She blushed appropriately. On her right Froggy was *hors de combat* already, although he hadn't quite realized it.

"I'll tell you what I remembered about you all these years," Amory continued. She leaned slightly toward him and looked modestly at the celery before her. Froggy sighed—he knew Amory, and the situations that Amory seemed born to handle. He turned to Sally and asked her if she was going away to school next year. Amory opened with grape-shot.

"I've got an adjective that just fits you." This was one of his favorite starts—he seldom had a word in mind, but it was a curiosity provoker, and he could always produce something complimentary if he got in a tight corner.

"Oh—what?" Isabelle's face was a study in enraptured curiosity.

Amory shook his head.

"I don't know you very well yet."

"Will you tell me—afterward?" she half whispered.

He nodded.

"We'll sit out."

Isabelle nodded.

"Did any one ever tell you, you have keen eyes?" she said.

Amory attempted to make them look even keener. He fancied, but he was not sure, that her foot had just touched his under the table. But it might possibly have been only the table leg. It was so hard to tell. Still it thrilled him. He wondered quickly if there would be any difficulty in securing the little den upstairs.

BABES IN THE WOODS

Isabelle and Amory were distinctly not innocent, nor were they particularly brazen. Moreover, amateur standing had very little value in the game they were playing, a game that would presumably be her principal study for years to come. She had begun as he had, with good looks and an excitable temperament, and the rest was the result of accessible popular novels and dressing room conversation culled from a slightly older set. Isabelle had walked with an artificial gait at nine and a half, and when her eyes, wide and starry, proclaimed the ingenue most. Amory was proportionately less deceived. He waited for the mask to drop off, but at the same time he did not question her right to wear it. She, on her part, was not impressed by his studied air of blasé sophistication. She had lived in a larger city and had slightly an advantage in range. But she accepted his pose—it was one of the dozen little conventions of this kind of affair. He was aware that he was getting this particular favor now because she had been coached; he knew that he stood for merely the best game in sight, and that he would have to improve his opportunity before he lost his advantage. So they proceeded with an infinite guile that would have horrified her parents.

After the dinner the dance began . . . smoothly. Smoothly?— boys cut in on Isabelle every few feet and then squabbled in the corners with: "You might let me get more than an inch!" and "She didn't like it either—she told me so next time I cut in." It was true—she told every one so, and gave every hand a parting pressure that said: "You know that your dances are *making* my evening."

But time passed, two hours of it, and the less subtle beaux had better learned to focus their pseudo-passionate glances elsewhere, for eleven o'clock found Isabelle and Amory sitting on the couch in the little den off the reading-room upstairs. She was conscious that they were a handsome pair, and seemed to belong distinctively in this seclusion, while lesser lights fluttered and chattered downstairs.

Boys who passed the door looked in enviously—girls who passed only laughed and frowned and grew wise within themselves.

They had now reached a very definite stage. They had traded accounts of their progress since they had met last, and she had listened to much she had heard before. He was a sophomore, was on the *Princetonian* board, hoped to be chairman in senior year. He learned that some of the boys she went with in Baltimore were "terrible speeds" and came to dances in states of artificial stimulation; most of them were twenty or so, and drove alluring red Stutzes. A good half seemed to have already flunked out of various schools and colleges, but some of them bore athletic names that made him look at her admiringly. As a matter of fact, Isabelle's closer acquaintance with the universities was just commencing. She had bowing acquaintance with a lot of young men who thought she was a "pretty kid—worth keeping an eye on." But Isabelle strung the names into a fabrication of gayety that would have dazzled a Viennese nobleman. Such is the power of young contralto voices on sink-down sofas.

He asked her if she thought he was conceited. She said there was a difference between conceit and self-confidence. She adored self-confidence in men.

"Is Froggy a good friend of yours?" she asked.

"Rather—why?"

"He's a bum dancer."

Amory laughed.

"He dances as if the girl were on his back instead of in his arms."

She appreciated this.

"You're awfully good at sizing people up."

Amory denied this painfully. However, he sized up several people for her. Then they talked about hands.

"You've got awfully nice hands," she said. "They look as if you played the piano. Do you?"

I have said they had reached a very definite stage—nay, more, a very critical stage. Amory had stayed over a day to see her, and his train left at twelve-eighteen that night. His trunk and suitcase awaited him at the station; his watch was beginning to hang heavy in his pocket.

"Isabelle," he said suddenly, "I want to tell you something." They had been talking lightly about "that funny look in her eyes," and Isabelle knew from the change in his manner what was coming—indeed, she had been wondering how soon it would come. Amory reached above their heads and turned out the electric light, so that they were in the dark, except for the red glow that fell through the door from the reading-room lamps. Then he began:

"I don't know whether or not you know what you—what I'm going to say. Lordy, Isabelle—this *sounds* like a line, but it isn't."

"I know," said Isabelle softly.

"Maybe we'll never meet again like this—I have darned hard luck sometimes." He was leaning away from her on the other arm of the lounge, but she could see his eyes plainly in the dark.

"You'll meet me again—silly." There was just the slightest emphasis on the last word—so that it became almost a term of endearment. He continued a bit huskily:

"I've fallen for a lot of people—girls—and I guess you have, too—boys, I mean, but, honestly, you—" he broke off suddenly and leaned forward, chin on his hands: "Oh, what's the use—you'll go your way and I suppose I'll go mine."

Silence for a moment. Isabelle was quite stirred; she wound her handkerchief into a tight ball, and by the faint light that streamed over her, dropped it deliberately on the floor. Their hands touched for an instant, but neither spoke. Silences were becoming more frequent and more delicious. Outside another stray couple had come up and were experimenting on the piano in the next room. After the usual preliminary of "chopsticks," one of them started "Babes in the Woods" and a light tenor carried the words into the den:

> "Give me your hand—
> I'll understand
> We're off to slumberland."

Isabelle hummed it softly and trembled as she felt Amory's hand close over hers.

"Isabelle," he whispered. "You know I'm mad about you. You *do* give a darn about me."

"Yes."

"How much do you care—do you like any one better?"

"No." He could scarcely hear her, although he bent so near that he felt her breath against his cheek.

"Isabelle, I'm going back to college for six long months, and why shouldn't we—if I could only just have one thing to remember you by——"

"Close the door. . . ." Her voice had just stirred so that he half wondered whether she had spoken at all. As he swung the door softly shut, the music seemed quivering just outside.

> "Moonlight is bright,
> Kiss me good night."

What a wonderful song, she thought—everything was wonderful tonight, most of all this romantic scene in the den, with their hands clinging and the inevitable looming charmingly close. The future vista of her life seemed an unending succession of scenes like this: under moonlight and pale starlight, and in the backs of warm limousines and in low, cosey roadsters stopped under sheltering trees—only the boy might change, and this one was *so* nice. He took her hand softly. With a sudden movement he turned it and, holding it to his lips, kissed the palm.

"Isabelle!" His whisper blended in the music, and they seemed to float nearer together. Her breath came faster. "Can't I kiss you, Isabelle—Isabelle?" Lips half parted, she turned her head to him in the dark. Suddenly the ring of voices, the sound of running footsteps surged toward them. Quick as a flash Amory reached up and turned on the light, and when the door opened and three boys, the wrathy and dance-craving Froggy among them, rushed in, he was turning over the magazines on the table, while she sat without moving, serene and unembarrassed, and even greeted them with a welcoming smile. But her heart was beating wildly, and she felt somehow as if she had been deprived.

It was evidently over. There was a clamor for a dance, there was a glance that passed between them—on his side despair, on hers regret, and then the evening went on, with the reassured beaux and the eternal cutting in.

At quarter to twelve Amory shook hands with her gravely, in the midst of a small crowd assembled to wish him good-speed. For an instant he lost his poise, and she felt a bit rattled when a satirical voice from a concealed wit cried:

"Take her outside, Amory!" As he took her hand he pressed it a little, and she returned the pressure as she had done to twenty hands that evening—that was all.

At two o'clock back at the Weatherbys' Sally asked her if she and Amory had had a "time" in the den. Isabelle turned to her quietly. In her eyes was the light of the idealist, the inviolate dreamer of Joan-like dreams.

"No," she answered. "I don't do that sort of thing any more; he asked me to, but I said no."

As she crept in bed she wondered what he'd say in his special delivery tomorrow. He had such a good-looking mouth—would she ever——?

"Fourteen angels were watching o'er them," sang Sally sleepily from the next room.

"Damn!" muttered Isabelle, punching the pillow into a luxurious lump and exploring the cold sheets cautiously. "Damn!"

CARNIVAL

Amory, by way of the *Princetonian*, had arrived. The minor snobs, finely balanced thermometers of success, warmed to him as the club elections grew nigh, and he and Tom were visited by groups of upper classmen who arrived awkwardly, balanced on the edge of the furniture and talked of all subjects except the one of absorbing interest. Amory was amused at the intent eyes upon him, and, in case the visitors represented some club in which he was not interested, took great pleasure in shocking them with unorthodox remarks.

"Oh, let me see—" he said one night to a flabbergasted delegation, "what club do you represent?"

With visitors from Ivy and Cottage and Tiger Inn he played the "nice, unspoilt, ingenuous boy" very much at ease and quite unaware of the object of the call.

When the fatal morning arrived, early in March, and the campus became a document in hysteria, he slid smoothly into Cottage with Alec Connage and watched his suddenly neurotic class with much wonder.

There were fickle groups that jumped from club to club; there were friends of two or three days who announced tearfully and wildly that they must join the same club, nothing should separate them; there were snarling disclosures of long-hidden grudges as the Suddenly Prominent remembered snubs of freshman year. Unknown men were elevated into importance when they received certain coverted bids; others who were considered "all set" found that they had made unexpected enemies, felt themselves stranded and deserted, talked wildly of leaving college.

In his own crowd Amory saw men kept out for wearing green hats, for being "a damn tailor's dummy," for having "too much pull in heaven," for getting drunk one night "not like a gentleman, by God," or for unfathomable secret reasons known to no one but the wielders of the black balls.

This orgy of sociability culminated in a gigantic party at the Nassau Inn, where punch was dispensed from immense bowls, and the whole downstairs became a delirious, circulating, shouting pattern of faces and voices.

"Hi, Dibby—'gratulations!"

"Goo' boy, Tom, you got a good bunch in Cap."

"Say, Kerry——"

"Oh, Kerry—I hear you went Tiger with all the weight-lifters!"

"Well, I didn't go Cottage—the parlor-snakes' delight."

"They say Overton fainted when he got his Ivy bid—Did he sign up the first day?—oh, no. Tore over to Murray-Dodge on a bicycle—afraid it was a mistake."

"How'd you get into Cap—you old roué?"

"'Gratulations!"

"'Gratulations yourself. Hear you got a good crowd."

When the bar closed, the party broke up into groups and streamed, singing, over the snow-clad campus, in a weird delusion that snobbishness and strain were over at last, and that they could do what they pleased for the next two years.

Long afterward Amory thought of sophomore spring as the happiest time of his life. His ideas were in tune with life as he found it; he wanted no more than to drift and dream and enjoy a dozen new-found friendships through the April afternoons.

Alec Connage came into his room one morning and woke him up into the sunshine and peculiar glory of Campbell Hall shining in the window.

"Wake up, Original Sin, and scrape yourself together. Be in front of Renwick's in half an hour. Somebody's got a car." He took the bureau cover and carefully deposited it, with its load of small articles, upon the bed.

"Where'd you get the car?" demanded Amory cynically.

"Sacred trust, but don't be a critical goopher or you can't go!"

"I think I'll sleep," Amory said calmly, resettling himself and reaching beside the bed for a cigarette.

"Sleep!"

"Why not? I've got a class at eleven-thirty."

"You damned gloom! Of course, if you don't want to go to the coast——"

With a bound Amory was out of bed, scattering the bureau cover's burden on the floor. The coast . . . he hadn't seen it for years, since he and his mother were on their pilgrimage.

"Who's going?" he demanded as he wiggled into his B. V. D.'s.

"Oh, Dick Humbird and Kerry Holiday and Jesse Ferrenby and—oh about five or six. Speed it up, kid!"

In ten minutes Amory was devouring cornflakes in Renwick's, and at nine-thirty they bowled happily out of town, headed for the sands of Deal Beach.

"You see," said Kerry, "the car belongs down there. In fact, it was stolen from Asbury Park by persons unknown, who deserted it in Princeton and left for the West. Heartless Humbird here got permission from the city council to deliver it."

"Anybody got any money?" suggested Ferrenby, turning around from the front seat.

There was an emphatic negative chorus.

"That makes it interesting."

"Money—what's money? We can sell the car."

"Charge him salvage or something."

"How're we going to get food?" asked Amory.

"Honestly," answered Kerry, eying him reprovingly, "do you doubt Kerry's ability for three short days? Some people have lived on nothing for years at a time. Read the Boy Scout Monthly."

"Three days," Amory mused, "and I've got classes."

"One of the days is the Sabbath."

"Just the same, I can only cut six more classes, with over a month and a half to go."

"Throw him out!"

"It's a long walk back."

"Amory, you're running it out, if I may coin a new phrase."

"Hadn't you better get some dope on yourself, Amory?"

Amory subsided resignedly and drooped into a contemplation of the scenery. Swinburne seemed to fit in somehow.

> For, winter's rains and ruins are over,
>   And all the season of snows and sins;
> The days dividing lover and lover,
>   The light that loses, the night that wins;
> And time remembered is grief forgotten,
> And frosts are slain and flowers begotten,
> And in green underwood and cover
>   Blossom by blossom the spring begins.
>
> The full streams feed on flower of— —

"What's the matter, Amory? Amory's thinking about poetry, about the pretty birds and flowers. I can see it in his eye."

"No, I'm not," he lied. "I'm thinking about the *Princetonian*. I ought to make up tonight; but I can telephone back, I suppose."

"Oh," said Kerry respectfully, "these important men——"

Amory flushed and it seemed to him that Ferrenby, a defeated competitor, winced a little. Of course, Kerry was only kidding, but he really mustn't mention the *Princetonian*.

It was a halcyon day, and as they neared the shore and the salt breezes scurried by, he began to picture the ocean and long, level stretches of sand and red roofs over blue sea. Then they hurried through the little town and it all flashed upon his consciousness to a mighty pæan of emotion. . . .

"Oh, good Lord! *Look* at it!" he cried.

"What?"

"Let me out, quick—I haven't seen it for eight years! Oh, gentlefolk, stop the car!"

"What an odd child!" remarked Alec.

"I do believe he's a bit eccentric."

The car was obligingly drawn up at a curb, and Amory ran for the boardwalk. First, he realized that the sea was blue and that there was an enormous quantity of it, and that it roared and roared—really all the banalities about the ocean that one could realize, but if any one had told him then that these things were banalities, he would have gaped in wonder.

"Now we'll get lunch," ordered Kerry, wandering up with the crowd. "Come on, Amory, tear yourself away and get practical."

"We'll try the best hotel first," he went on, "and thence and so forth."

They strolled along the boardwalk to the most imposing hostelry in sight, and, entering the dining-room, scattered about a table.

"Eight Bronxes," commanded Alec, "and a club sandwich and Juliennes. The food for one. Hand the rest around."

Amory ate little, having seized a chair where he could watch the sea and feel the rock of it. When luncheon was over they sat and smoked quietly.

"What's the bill?"

Some one scanned it.

"Eight twenty-five."

"Rotten overcharge. We'll give them two dollars and one for the waiter. Kerry, collect the small change."

The waiter approached, and Kerry gravely handed him a dollar, tossed two dollars on the check, and turned away. They sauntered leisurely toward the door, pursued in a moment by the suspicious Ganymede.

"Some mistake, sir."

Kerry took the bill and examined it critically.

"No mistake!" he said, shaking his head gravely, and, tearing it into four pieces, he handed the scraps to the waiter, who was so dumfounded that he stood motionless and expressionless while they walked out.

"Won't he send after us?"

"No," said Kerry; "for a minute he'll think we're the proprietor's sons or something; then he'll look at the check again and call the manager, and in the meantime——"

They left the car at Asbury and street-car'd to Allenhurst, where they investigated the crowded pavilions for beauty. At four there were refreshments in a lunchroom, and this time they paid an even smaller per cent on the total cost; something about the appearance and savoir faire of the crowd made the thing go, and they were not pursued.

"You see, Amory, we're Marxian Socialists," explained Kerry. "We don't believe in property and we're putting it to the great test."

"Night will descend," Amory suggested.

"Watch, and put your trust in Holiday."

They became jovial about five-thirty and, linking arms, strolled up and down the boardwalk in a row, chanting a monotonous ditty about the sad sea waves. Then Kerry saw a face in the crowd that attracted him and, rushing off, reappeared in a moment with one of the homeliest girls Amory had ever set eyes on. Her pale mouth extended from ear to ear, her teeth projected in a solid wedge, and she had little, squinty eyes that peeped ingratiatingly over the side sweep of her nose. Kerry presented them formally.

"Name of Kaluka, Hawaiian queen! Let me present Messrs. Connage, Sloane, Humbird, Ferrenby, and Blaine."

The girl bobbed courtesies all around. Poor creature; Amory supposed she had never before been noticed in her life—possibly she was half-witted. While she accompanied them (Kerry had invited her to supper) she said nothing which could discountenance such a belief.

"She prefers her native dishes," said Alec gravely to the waiter, "but any coarse food will do."

All through supper he addressed her in the most respectful language, while Kerry made idiotic love to her on the other side, and she giggled and grinned. Amory was content to sit and watch the by-play, thinking what a light touch Kerry had, and how he could transform the barest incident into a thing of curve and contour. They all seemed to have the spirit of it more or less, and it was a relaxation to be with them. Amory usually liked men individually, yet feared them in crowds unless the crowd was around *him.* He wondered how much each one contributed to the party, for there was somewhat of a spiritual tax levied. Alec and Kerry were the life of it, but not quite the centre. Somehow the quiet Humbird, and Sloane, with his impatient supercil-iousness, were the centre.

Dick Humbird had, ever since freshman year, seemed to Amory a perfect type of aristocrat. He was slender but well-built—black curly hair, straight features, and rather a dark skin. Everything he said sounded intangibly appropriate. He possessed infinite courage, an av-eragely good mind, and a sense of honor with a clear charm and *no-blesse oblige* that varied it from righteousness. He could dissipate without going to pieces, and even his most bohemian adventures never seemed "running it out." People dressed like him, tried to talk as he did. . . . Amory decided that he probably held the world back, but he wouldn't have changed him. . . .

He differed from the healthy type that was essentially middle class—he never seemed to perspire. Some people couldn't be familiar with a chauffeur without having it returned; Humbird could have lunched at Sherry's with a colored man, yet people would have some-how known that it was all right. He was not a snob, though he knew only half his class. His friends ranged from the highest to the lowest, but it was impossible to "cultivate" him. Servants worshipped him, and treated him like a god. He seemed the eternal example of what the upper class tries to be.

"He's like those pictures in the Illustrated London News of the English officers who have been killed," Amory had said to Alec.

"Well," Alec had answered, "if you want to know the shocking truth, his father was a grocery clerk who made a fortune in Tacoma real estate and came to New York ten years ago."

Amory had felt a curious sinking sensation.

This present type of party was made possible by the surging to-gether of the class after club elections—as if to make a last desperate attempt to know itself, to keep together, to fight off the tightening spirit of the clubs. It was a letdown from the conventional heights they had all walked so rigidly.

After supper they saw Kaluka to the boardwalk, and then strolled back along the beach to Asbury. The evening sea was a new sensation, for all its color and mellow age was gone, and it seemed the bleak waste that made the Norse sagas sad; Amory thought of Kipling's

The Beaches of Lukannon—before the sealers came!

It was still a music, though, infinitely sorrowful.

Ten o'clock found them penniless. They had suppered greatly on their last eleven cents and, singing, strolled up through the casinos and lighted arches on the boardwalk, stopping to listen approvingly to all band concerts. In one place Kerry took up a collection for the French War Orphans which netted a dollar and twenty cents, and with this they bought some brandy in case they caught cold in the night. They finished the day in a moving-picture show and went into solemn systematic roars of laughter at an ancient comedy, to the startled annoyance of the rest of the audience. Their entrance was distinctly strategic, for each man as he entered pointed reproachfully at the one just behind him. Sloane, bringing up the rear, disclaimed all knowledge and responsibility as soon as the others were scattered inside; then as the irate ticket-taker rushed in he followed nonchalantly.

They reassembled later by the Casino and made arrangements for the night. Kerry wormed permission from the watchman to sleep on the platform and, having collected a huge pile of rugs from the booths to serve as mattresses and blankets, they talked until midnight, and then fell into a dreamless sleep, though Amory tried hard to stay awake and watch that marvelous moon settle on the sea.

So they progressed for two happy days, up and down the shore by streetcar or machine, or by shoe-leather on the crowded boardwalk; sometimes eating with the wealthy, more frequently dining frugally at the expense of an unsuspecting restaurateur. They had their photos taken, eight poses, in a quick-development store. Kerry insisted on grouping them as a "varsity" football team, and then as a tough gang from the East Side, with their coats inside out, and himself sitting in the middle on a cardboard moon. The photographer probably has them yet—at least they never called for them. The weather was perfect, and again they slept outside, and again Amory fell unwillingly asleep.

Sunday broke stolid and respectable, and even the sea seemed to mumble and complain, so they returned to Princeton via Fords of transient farmers, and broke up with colds in their heads, but otherwise none the worse for wandering.

Even more than in the year before, Amory neglected his work, not deliberately but lazily and through a multitude of other interests. Coordinate geometry and the melancholy hexameters of Corneille and Racine held forth small allurements, and even psychology, which he had eagerly awaited, proved to be a dull subject full of muscular reactions and biological phrases rather than the study of personality and influence. That was a noon class, and it always sent him dozing. Having found that "subjective and objective, sir," answered most of the questions, he used the phrase on all occasions, and it became the class joke when, a query being levelled at him, he was nudged awake by Ferrenby or Sloane to gasp it out.

Mostly there were parties—to Orange or the Shore, more rarely to New York and Philadelphia, though one night they marshalled fourteen waitresses out of Childs' and took them to ride down Fifth Avenue on top of an autobus. They all cut more classes than were allowed, which meant an additional course the following year, but spring was too rare to let anything interfere with their colorful ramblings. In May Amory was elected to the Sophomore Prom Committee, and when after a long evening's discussion with Alec they made out a tentative list of class probabilities for the senior council, they placed themselves among the surest. The senior council was composed presumably of the eighteen most representative seniors, and in view of Alec's football mangership and Amory's chance of nosing out Burne Holiday as *Princetonian* chairman, they seemed fairly justified in this presumption. Oddly enough, they both placed D'Invilliers as among the possibilities, a guess that a year before the class would have gaped at.

All through the spring Amory had kept up an intermittent correspondence with Isabelle Borgé, punctuated by violent squabbles and chiefly enlivened by his attempts to find new words for love. He discovered Isabelle to be discreetly and aggravatingly unsentimental in letters, but he hoped against hope that she would prove not too exotic a bloom to fit the large spaces of spring as she had fitted the den in the Minnehaha Club. During May he wrote thirty-page documents almost nightly, and sent them to her in bulky envelopes exteriorly labelled "Part I" and "Part II."

"Oh, Alec, I believe I'm tired of college," he said sadly, as they walked the dusk together.

"I think I am, too, in a way."

"All I'd like would be a little home in the country, some warm country, and a wife, and just enough to do to keep from rotting."

"Me, too."

"I'd like to quit."

"What does your girl say?"

"Oh!" Amory gasped in horror. "She wouldn't *think* of marrying . . . that is, not now. I mean the future, you know."

"My girl would. I'm engaged."

"Are you really?"

"Yes. Don't say a word to anybody, please, but I am. I may not come back next year."

"But you're only twenty! Give up college?"

"Why, Amory, you were saying a minute ago——"

"Yes," Amory interrupted, "but I was just wishing. I wouldn't think of leaving college. It's just that I feel so sad these wonderful nights. I sort of feel they're never coming again, and I'm not really getting all I could out of them. I wish my girl lived here. But marry—not a chance. Especially as father says the money isn't forthcoming as it used to be."

"What a waste these nights are!" agreed Alec.

But Amory sighed and made use of the nights. He had a snapshot of Isabelle, enshrined in an old watch, and at eight almost every night he would turn off all the lights except the desk lamp and, sitting by the open windows with the picture before him, write her rapturous letters.

> . . . Oh, it's so hard to write you what I really feel when I think about you so much; you've gotten to mean to me a dream that I can't put on paper any more. Your last letter came and it was wonderful! I read it over about six times, especially the last part, but I do wish, sometimes, you'd be more frank and tell me what you really do think of me, yet your last letter was too good to be true, and I can hardly wait until June! Be sure and be able to come to the prom. It'll be fine, I think, and I want to bring you just at the end of a wonderful year. I often think over what you said on that night and wonder how much you meant. If it were any one but you—but you see I thought you were fickle the first time I saw you and you are so popular and everything that I can't imagine your really liking me best.
>
> Oh, Isabelle, dear—it's a wonderful night. Somebody is playing "Love Moon" on a mandolin far across the campus, and the music seems to bring you into the window. Now he's playing "Good-by, Boys, I'm Through," and how well it suits me. For I am through with everything. I have decided never to take a cocktail again, and I know I'll never again fall in love—I couldn't—you've been too much a part of my days and nights to ever let me think of another girl. I meet them all the time and they don't interest me. I'm not pretending to be blasé, because it's not that. It's just that I'm in love. Oh, dearest Isabelle (somehow I can't call you just Isabelle, and I'm afraid I'll come out with the "dearest" before your family this June), you've got to come to the prom, and then I'll come up to your house for a day and everything'll be perfect. . . .

And so on in an eternal monotone that seemed to both of them infinitely charming, infinitely new.

June came and the days grew so hot and lazy that they could not worry even about exams, but spent dreamy evenings on the court of Cottage, talking of long subjects until the sweep of country toward Stony Brook became a blue haze and the lilacs were white around tennis courts, and words gave way to silent cigarettes. . . . Then down deserted Prospect and along McCosh with song everywhere around them, up to the hot joviality of Nassau Street.

Tom D'Invilliers and Amory walked late in those days. A gambling fever swept through the sophomore class and they bent over the bones till three o'clock many a sultry night. After one session they came out of Sloane's room to find the dew fallen and the stars old in the sky.

"Let's borrow bicycles and take a ride," Amory suggested.

"All right. I'm not a bit tired and this is almost the last night of the year, really, because the prom stuff starts Monday."

They found two unlocked bicycles in Holder Court and rode out about half-past three along the Lawrenceville Road.

"What are you going to do this summer, Amory?"

"Don't ask me—same old things, I suppose. A month or two in Lake Geneva—I'm counting on you to be there in July, you know—then there'll be Minneapolis, and that means hundreds of summer hops, parlor-snaking, getting bored—But oh, Tom," he added suddenly, "hasn't this year been slick!"

"No," declared Tom emphatically, a new Tom, clothed by Brooks, shod by Franks, "I've won this game, but I feel as if I never want to play another. You're all right—you're a rubber ball, and somehow it suits you, but I'm sick of adapting myself to the local snobbishness of this corner of the world. I want to go where people aren't barred because of the color of their neckties and the roll of their coats."

"You can't, Tom," argued Amory, as they rolled along through the scattering night; "wherever you go now you'll always unconsciously apply these standards of 'having it' or 'lacking it.' For better or worse we've stamped you; you're a Princeton type!"

"Well, then," complained Tom, his cracked voice rising plaintively, "why do I have to come back at all? I've learned all that Princeton has to offer. Two years more of mere pedantry and lying around a club aren't going to help. They're just going to disorganize me, conventionalize me completely. Even now I'm so spineless that I wonder how I get away with it."

"Oh, but you're missing the real point, Tom," Amory interrupted. "You've just had your eyes opened to the snobbishness of the world in a rather abrupt manner. Princeton invariably gives the thoughtful man a social sense."

"You consider you taught me that, don't you?" he asked quizzically, eying Amory in the half dark.

Amory laughed quietly.

"Didn't I?"

"Sometimes," he said slowly, "I think you're my bad angel. I might have been a pretty fair poet."

"Come on, that's rather hard. You chose to come to an Eastern college. Either your eyes were opened to the mean scrambling quality of people, or you'd have gone through blind, and you'd hate to have done that—been like Marty Kaye."

"Yes," he agreed, "you're right. I wouldn't have liked it. Still, it's hard to be made a cynic at twenty."

"I was born one," Amory murmured. "I'm a cynical idealist." He paused and wondered if that meant anything.

They reached the sleeping school of Lawrenceville, and turned to ride back.

"It's good, this ride, isn't it?" Tom said presently.

"Yes; it's a good finish, it's knock-out; everything's good tonight. Oh, for a hot, languorous summer and Isabelle!"

"Oh, you and your Isabelle! I'll bet she's a simple one . . . let's say some poetry."

So Amory declaimed "The Ode to a Nightingale" to the bushes they passed.

"I'll never be a poet," said Amory as he finished. "I'm not enough of a sensualist really; there are only a few obvious things that I notice as primarily beautiful: women, spring evenings, music at night, the sea; I don't catch the subtle things like 'silver-snarling trumpets.' I may turn out an intellectual, but I'll never write anything but mediocre poetry."

They rode into Princeton as the sun was making colored maps of the sky behind the graduate school, and hurried to the refreshment of a shower that would have to serve in place of sleep. By noon the bright-costumed alumni crowded the streets with their bands and choruses, and in the tents there was great reunion under the orange and black banners that curled and strained in the wind. Amory looked long at one house which bore the legend "Sixty-nine." There a few gray-haired men sat and talked quietly while the classes swept by in panorama of life.

UNDER THE ARC-LIGHT

Then tragedy's emerald eyes glared suddenly at Amory over the edge of June. On the night after his ride to Lawrenceville a crowd sallied to New York in quest of adventure, and started back to Princeton about twelve o'clock in two machines. It had been a gay party and different stages of sobriety were represented. Amory was in the car behind; they had taken the wrong road and lost the way, and so were hurrying to catch up.

It was a clear night and the exhilaration of the road went to Amory's head. He had the ghost of two stanzas of a poem forming in his mind. . . .

So the gray car crept nightward in the dark and there was no life stirred as it went by. . . . As the still ocean paths before the shark in starred and glittering waterways, beauty-high, the moon-swathed trees divided, pair on pair, while flapping nightbirds cried across the air. . . .

A moment by an inn of lamps and shades, a yellow inn under a yellow moon—then silence, where crescendo laughter fades . . . the car swung out again to the winds of June, mellowed the shadows where the distance grew, then crushed the yellow shadows into blue. . . .

They jolted to a stop, and Amory peered up, startled. A woman was standing beside the road, talking to Alec at the wheel. Afterward he remembered the harpy effect that her old kimono gave her, and the cracked hollowness of her voice as she spoke:

"You Princeton boys?"

"Yes."

"Well, there's one of you killed here, and two others about dead."

"My God!"

"Look!" She pointed and they gazed in horror. Under the full light of a roadside arc-light lay a form, face downward in a widening circle of blood.

They sprang from the car. Amory thought of the back of that head—that hair—that hair . . . and then they turned the form over.

"It's Dick—Dick Humbird!"

"Oh, Christ!"

"Feel his heart!"

Then the insistent voice of the old crone in a sort of croaking triumph:

"He's quite dead, all right. The car turned over. Two of the men that weren't hurt just carried the others in, but this one's no use."

Amory rushed into the house and the rest followed with a limp mass that they laid on the sofa in the shoddy little front parlor. Sloane, with his shoulder punctured, was on another lounge. He was half delirious, and kept calling something about a chemistry lecture at 8:10.

"I don't know what happened," said Ferrenby in a strained voice. "Dick was driving and he wouldn't give up the wheel; we told him he'd been drinking too much—then there was this damn curve—oh, my *God!* . . ." He threw himself face downward on the floor and broke into dry sobs.

The doctor had arrived, and Amory went over to the couch, where some one handed him a sheet to put over the body. With a sudden hardness, he raised one of the hands and let it fall back inertly. The brow was cold but the face not expressionless. He looked at the shoe-laces—Dick had tied them that morning. *He* had tied them—and now he was this heavy white mass. All that remained of the charm and personality of the Dick Humbird he had known—oh, it was all so horrible and unaristocratic and close to the earth. All tragedy has that strain of the grotesque and squalid—so useless, futile . . . the way animals die. . . . Amory was reminded of a cat that had lain horribly mangled in some alley of his childhood.

"Some one go to Princeton with Ferrenby"

Amory stepped outside the door and shivered slightly at the late night wind—a wind that stirred a broken fender on the mass of bent metal to a plaintive, tinny sound.

CRESCENDO!

The next day, by a merciful chance, passed in a whirl. When Amory was by himself his thoughts zigzagged inevitably to the picture of that red mouth yawning incongruously in the white face, but with a determined effort he piled present excitement upon the memory of it and shut it coldly away from his mind.

Isabelle and her mother drove into town at four, and they rode up smiling Prospect Avenue, through the gay crowd, to have tea at Cottage. The clubs had their annual dinners that night, so at seven he loaned her to a freshman and arranged to meet her in the gymnasium at eleven, when the upper classmen were admitted to the freshman dance. She was all he had expected, and he was happy and eager to make that night the center of every dream. At nine the upper classes stood in front of the clubs as the freshman torchlight parade rioted past, and Amory wondered if the dress-suited groups against the dark, stately backgrounds and under the flare of the torches made the night as brilliant to the staring, cheering freshman as it had been to him the year before.

The next day was another whirl. They lunched in a gay party of six in a private dining-room at the club, while Isabelle and Amory looked at each other tenderly over the fried chicken and knew that their love was to be eternal. They danced away the prom until five, and the stags cut in on Isabelle with joyous abandon, which grew more and more enthusiastic as the hour grew late, and their wines, stored in overcoat pockets in the coat room, made old weariness wait until another day. The stag line is a most homogeneous mass of men. It fairly sways with a single soul. A dark-haired beauty dances by and there is a half-gasping sound as the ripple surges forward and some one sleeker than the rest darts out and cuts in. Then when the six-foot girl (brought by Kaye in your class, and to whom he has been trying to introduce you all evening) gallops by, the line surges back and the groups face about and become intent on far corners of the hall, for Kaye, anxious and perspiring, appears, elbowing through the crowd in search of familiar faces.

"I say, old man, I've got an awfully nice—"

"Sorry, Kaye, but I'm set for this one. I've got to cut in on a fella."

"Well, the next one?"

"What—ah—er—I swear I've got to go cut in—look me up when she's got a dance free."

It delighted Amory when Isabelle suggested that they leave for a while and drive around in her car. For a delicious hour that passed too soon they glided the silent roads about Princeton and talked from the surface of their hearts in shy excitement. Amory felt strangely ingenuous and made no attempt to kiss her.

Next day they rode up through the Jersey country, had luncheon in New York, and in the afternoon went to see a problem play at which Isabelle wept all through the second act, rather to Amory's embarrassment—though it filled him with tenderness to watch her. He was tempted to lean over and kiss away her tears, and she slipped her hand into his under cover of darkness to be pressed softly.

Then at six they arrived at the Borgés' summer place on Long Island, and Amory rushed upstairs to change into a dinner coat. As he put in his studs he realized that he was enjoying life as he would probably never enjoy it again. Everything was hallowed by the haze of his own youth. He had arrived, abreast of the best in his generation at Princeton. He was in love and his love was returned. Turning on all the lights, he looked at himself in the mirror, trying to find in his own face the qualities that made him see more clearly than the great crowd of people, that made him decide firmly, and able to influence and follow his own will. There was little in his life now that he would have changed. . . . Oxford might have been a bigger field.

Silently he admired himself. How conveniently well he looked, and how well a dinner coat became him. He stepped into the hall and then waited at the top of the stairs, for he heard footsteps coming. It was Isabelle, and from the top of her shining hair to her little golden slippers she had never seemed so beautiful.

"Isabelle!" he cried, half involuntarily, and held out his arms. As in the story-books, she ran into them, and on that half-minute, as their lips first touched, rested the high point of vanity, the crest of his young egotism.

Three

The Egotist

Considers

"OUCH! LET ME GO!"

He dropped his arms to his sides.

"What's the matter?"

"Your shirt stud—it hurt me—look!" She was looking down at her neck, where a little blue spot about the size of a pea marred its pallor.

"Oh, Isabelle," he reproached himself, "I'm a goopher. Really, I'm sorry—I shouldn't have held you so close."

She looked up impatiently.

"Oh, Amory, of course you couldn't help it, and it didn't hurt much; but what *are* we going to do about it?"

"*Do* about it?" he asked. "Oh—that spot; it'll disappear in a second."

"It isn't," she said, after a moment of concentrated gazing, "it's still there—and it looks like Old Nick—oh, Amory, what'll we do! It's *just* the height of your shoulder."

"Massage it," he suggested, repressing the faintest inclination to laugh.

She rubbed it delicately with the tips of her fingers, and then a tear gathered in the corner of her eye, and slid down her cheek.

"Oh, Amory," she said despairingly, lifting up a most pathetic face, "I'll just make my whole neck *flame* if I rub it. What'll I do?"

A quotation sailed into his head and he couldn't resist repeating it aloud.

All the perfumes of Arabia will not whiten this little hand.

She looked up and the sparkle of the tear in her eye was like ice.

"You're not very sympathetic."

Amory mistook her meaning.

"Isabelle, darling, I think it'll——"

"Don't touch me!" she cried. "Haven't I enough on my mind and you stand there and *laugh!*"

Then he slipped again.

"Well, it *is* funny, Isabelle, and we were talking the other day about a sense of humor being——"

She was looking at him with something that was not a smile, rather the faint, mirthless echo of a smile, in the corners of her mouth.

"Oh, shut up!" she cried suddenly, and fled down the hallway toward her room. Amory stood there, covered with remorseful confusion.

"Damn!"

When Isabelle reappeared she had thrown a light wrap about her shoulders, and they descended the stairs in a silence that endured through dinner.

"Isabelle," he began rather testily, as they arranged themselves in the car, bound for a dance at the Greenwich Country Club, "you're angry, and I'll be, too, in a minute. Let's kiss and make up."

Isabelle considered glumly.

"I hate to be laughed at," she said finally.

"I won't laugh any more. I'm not laughing now, am I?"

"You did."

"Oh, don't be so darned feminine."

Her lips curled slightly.

"I'll be anything I want."

Amory kept his temper with difficulty. He became aware that he had not an ounce of real affection for Isabelle, but her coldness piqued him. He wanted to kiss her, kiss her a lot, because then he knew he could leave in the morning and not care. On the contrary, if he didn't kiss her, it would worry him. . . . It would interfere vaguely with his idea of himself as a conqueror. It wasn't dignified to come off second best, *pleading*, with a doughty warrior like Isabelle.

Perhaps she suspected this. At any rate, Amory watched the night that should have been the consummation of romance glide by with great moths overhead and the heavy fragrance of roadside gardens, but without those broken words, those little sighs. . . .

Afterward they supped on ginger ale and devil's food in the pantry, and Amory announced a decision.

"I'm leaving early in the morning."

"Why?"

"Why not?" he countered.

"There's no need."

"However, I'm going."

"Well, if you insist on being ridiculous—"

"Oh, don't put it that way," he objected.

"—just because I won't let you kiss me. Do you think——"

"Now, Isabelle," he interrupted, "you know it's not that—even suppose it is. We've reached the stage where we either ought to kiss—or—or—nothing. It isn't as if you were refusing on moral grounds."

She hesitated.

"I really don't know what to think about you," she began, in a feeble, perverse attempt at conciliation. "You're so funny."

"How?"

"Well, I thought you had a lot of self-confidence and all that; remember you told me the other day that you could do anything you wanted, or get anything you wanted?"

Amory flushed. He *had* told her a lot of things.

"Yes."

"Well, you didn't seem to feel so self-confident tonight. Maybe you're just plain conceited."

"No, I'm not," he hesitated. "At Princeton——"

"Oh, you and Princeton! You'd think that was the world, the way you talk! Perhaps you *can* write better than anybody else on your old *Princetonian;* maybe the freshmen *do* think you're important——"

"You don't understand——"

"Yes, I do," she interrupted. "I *do*, because you're always talking about yourself and I used to like it; now I don't."

"Have I tonight?"

"That's just the point," insisted Isabelle. "You got all upset tonight. You just sat and watched my eyes. Besides, I have to think all the time I'm talking to you—you're so critical."

"I make you think, do I?" Amory repeated with a touch of vanity.

"You're a nervous strain"—this emphatically—"and when you analyze every little emotion and instinct I just don't have 'em."

"I know." Amory admitted her point and shook his head helplessly.

"Let's go." She stood up.

He rose abstractedly and they walked to the foot of the stairs.

"What train can I get?"

"There's one about 9:11 if you really must go."

"Yes, I've got to go, really. Good night."

"Good night."

They were at the head of the stairs, and as Amory turned into his
room he thought he caught just the faintest cloud of discontent in her
face. He lay awake in the darkness and wondered how much he
cared—how much of his sudden unhappiness was hurt vanity—
whether he was, after all, temperamentally unfitted for romance.

When he awoke, it was with a glad flood of consciousness. The
early wind stirred the chintz curtains at the windows and he was idly
puzzled not to be in his room at Princeton with his school football
picture over the bureau and the Triangle Club on the wall opposite.
Then the grandfather's clock in the hall outside struck eight, and the
memory of the night before came to him. He was out of bed, dressing,
like the wind; he must get out of the house before he saw Isabelle.
What had seemed a melancholy happening now seemed a tiresome
anticlimax. He was dressed at half past, so he sat down by the window;
felt that the sinews of his heart were twisted somewhat more than he
had thought. What an ironic mockery the morning seemed!—bright
and sunny, and full of the smell of the garden; hearing Mrs. Borgé's
voice in the sun-parlor below, he wondered where was Isabelle.

There was a knock at the door.

"The car will be around at ten minutes of nine, sir."

He returned to his contemplation of the outdoors, and began repeating over and over, mechanically, a verse from Browning, which he
had once quoted to Isabelle in a letter:

> *Each life unfulfilled, you see;*
> *It hangs still, patchy and scrappy:*
> *We have not sighed deep, laughed free,*
> *Starved, feasted, despaired,—been happy.*

But his life would not be unfulfilled. He took a sombre satisfaction
in thinking that perhaps all along she had been nothing except what he
had read into her; that this was her high point, that no one else would

ever make her think. Yet that was what she had objected to in him; and Amory was suddenly tired of thinking, thinking!

"Damn her!" he said bitterly, "she's spoiled my year!"

THE SUPERMAN GROWS CARELESS

On a dusty day in September Amory arrived in Princeton and joined the sweltering crowd of conditioned men who thronged the streets. It seemed a stupid way to commence his upper-class years, to spend four hours a morning in the stuffy room of a tutoring school, imbibing the infinite boredom of conic sections. Mr. Rooney, pander to the dull, conducted the class and smoked innumerable Pall Malls as he drew diagrams and worked equations from six in the morning until midnight.

"Now, Langueduc, if I used that formula, where would my 'A' point be?"

Langueduc lazily shifts his six-foot-three of football material and tries to concentrate.

"Oh—ah—I'm damned if I know, Mr. Rooney."

"Oh, why of course, of course you can't *use* that formula. *That's* what I wanted you to say."

"Why, sure, of course."

"Do you see why?"

"You bet—I suppose so."

"If you don't see, tell me. I'm here to show you."

"Well, Mr. Rooney, if you don't mind, I wish you'd go over that again."

"Gladly. Now here's 'A' . . ."

The room was a study in stupidity—two huge stands for paper, Mr. Rooney in his shirt-sleeves in front of them, and slouched around on chairs, a dozen men: Fred Sloane, the pitcher, who absolutely *had* to get eligible; "Slim" Langueduc, who would beat Yale this fall, if only he could muster a poor fifty per cent; McDowell, gay young sophomore, who thought it was quite a sporting thing to be tutoring here with all these prominent athletes.

"Those poor birds who haven't a cent to tutor, and have to study during the term are the ones I pity," he announced to Amory one day, with a flaccid camaraderie in the droop of the cigarette from his pale lips. "I should think it would be such a bore, there's so much else to do in New York during the term. I suppose they don't know what they miss, anyhow." There was such an air of "you and I" about Mr. McDowell that Amory very nearly pushed him out of the open window when he said this. . . . Next February his mother would wonder why he didn't make a club and increase his allowance . . . simple little nut. . . .

Through the smoke and the air of solemn, dense earnestness that filled the room would come the inevitable helpless cry:

"I don't get it! Repeat that, Mr. Rooney!" Most of them were so stupid or careless that they wouldn't admit when they didn't understand, and Amory was of the latter. He found it impossible to study conic sections; something in their calm and tantalizing respectability breathing defiantly through Mr. Rooney's fetid parlors distorted their equations into insoluble anagrams. He made a last night's effort with the proverbial wet towel, and then blissfully took the exam, wondering unhappily why all the color and ambition of the spring before had faded out. Somehow, with the defection of Isabelle the idea of undergraduate success had loosed its grasp on his imagination, and he contemplated a possible failure to pass off his condition with equanimity, even though it would arbitrarily mean his removal from the *Princetonian* board and the slaughter of his chances for the Senior Council.

There was always luck.

He yawned, scribbled his honor pledge on the cover, and sauntered from the room.

"If you don't pass it," said the newly arrived Alec as they sat on the window-seat of Amory's room and mused upon a scheme of wall decoration, "you're the world's worst goopher. Your stock will go down like an elevator at the club and on the campus."

"Oh, hell, I know it. Why rub it in?"

"'Cause you deserve it. Anybody that'd risk what you were in line for *ought* to be ineligible for *Princetonian* chairman."

"Oh, drop the subject," Amory protested. "Watch and wait and shut up. I don't want every one at the club asking me about it, as if I were a prize potato being fattened for a vegetable show."

One evening a week later Amory stopped below his own window on the way to Renwick's, and, seeing a light, called up:

"Oh, Tom, any mail?"

Alec's head appeared against the yellow square of light.

"Yes, your result's here."

His heart clamored violently.

"What is it, blue or pink?"

"Don't know. Better come up."

He walked into the room and straight over to the table, and then suddenly noticed that there were other people in the room.

"'Lo, Kerry." He was most polite. "Ah, men of Princeton." They seemed to be mostly friends, so he picked up the envelope marked "Registrar's Office," and weighed it nervously.

"We have here quite a slip of paper."

"Open it, Amory."

"Just to be dramatic, I'll let you know that if it's blue, my name is withdrawn from the editorial board of the *Prince*, and my short career is over."

He paused, and then saw for the first time Ferrenby's eyes, wearing a hungry look and watching him eagerly. Amory returned the gaze pointedly.

"Watch my face, gentlemen, for the primitive emotions."

He tore it open and held the slip up to the light.

"Well?"

"Pink or blue?"

"Say what it is."

"We're all ears, Amory."

"Smile or swear—or something."

There was a pause . . . a small crowd of seconds swept by . . . then he looked again and another crowd went on into time.

"Blue as the sky, gentlemen. . . ."

AFTERMATH

What Amory did that year from early September to late in the spring was so purposeless and inconsecutive that it seems scarcely worth recording. He was, of course, immediately sorry for what he had lost. His philosophy of success had tumbled down upon him, and he looked for the reasons.

"Your own laziness," said Alec later.

"No—something deeper than that. I've begun to feel that I was meant to lose this chance."

"They're rather off you at the club, you know; every man that doesn't come through makes our crowd just so much weaker."

"I hate that point of view."

"Of course, with a little effort you could still stage a comeback."

"No—I'm through—as far as ever being a power in college is concerned."

"But, Amory, honestly, what makes me the angriest isn't the fact that you won't be chairman of the *Prince* and on the Senior Council, but just that you didn't get down and pass that exam."

"Not me," said Amory slowly; "I'm mad at the concrete thing. My own idleness was quite in accord with my system, but the luck broke."

"Your system broke, you mean."

"Maybe."

"Well, what are you going to do? Get a better one quick, or just bum around for two more years as a has-been?"

"I don't know yet . . ."

"Oh, Amory, buck up!"

"Maybe."

Amory's point of view, though dangerous, was not far from the true one. If his reactions to his environment could be tabulated, the chart would have appeared like this, beginning with his earliest years:

1. The fundamental Amory.
2. Amory plus Beatrice.
3. Amory plus Beatrice plus Minneapolis.

Then St. Regis' had pulled him to pieces and started him over again:

4. Amory plus St. Regis'.
5. Amory plus St. Regis' plus Princeton.

That had been his nearest approach to success through conformity. The fundamental Amory, idle, imaginative, rebellious, had been nearly snowed under. He had conformed, he had succeeded, but as his imagination was neither satisfied nor grasped by his own success, he had listlessly, half-accidentally chucked the whole thing and become again:

6. The fundamental Amory.

FINANCIAL

His father died quietly and inconspicuously at Thanksgiving. The incongruity of death with either the beauties of Lake Geneva or with his mother's dignified, reticent attitude diverted him, and he looked at the funeral with an amused tolerance. He decided that burial was after all preferable to cremation, and he smiled at his old boyhood choice, slow oxidation in the top of a tree. The day after the ceremony he was amusing himself in the great library by sinking back on a couch in graceful mortuary attitudes, trying to determine whether he would, when his day came, be found with his arms crossed piously over his chest (Monsignor Darcy had once advocated this posture as being the most distinguished), or with his hands clasped behind his head, a more pagan and Byronic attitude.

What interested him much more than the final departure of his father from things mundane was a tricornered conversation among Beatrice, Mr. Barton, of Barton and Krogman, their lawyers, and himself, that took place several days after the funeral. For the first time he came into actual cognizance of the family finances, and realized what a tidy fortune had once been under his father's management. He took a ledger labelled "1906" and ran through it rather carefully. The total expenditure that year had come to something over one hundred and ten thousand dollars. Forty thousand of this had been Beatrice's own income, and there had been no attempt to account for it: it was all under the heading, "Drafts, checks, and letters of credit forwarded to Beatrice Blaine." The dispersal of the rest was rather minutely itemized: the taxes and improvements on the Lake Geneva estate had come to almost nine thousand dollars; the general up-keep, including Beatrice's electric and a French car, bought that year, was over thirty-five thousand dollars. The rest was fully taken care of, and there were invariably items which failed to balance on the right side of the ledger.

In the volume for 1912 Amory was shocked to discover the decrease in the number of bond holdings and the great drop in the income. In the case of Beatrice's money this was not so pronounced, but it was obvious that his father had devoted the previous year to several unfortunate gambles in oil. Very little of the oil had been burned, but Stephen Blaine had been rather badly singed. The next year and the next and the next showed similar desreases, and Beatrice had for the first time begun using her own money for keeping up the house. Yet her doctor's bill for 1913 had been over nine thousand dollars.

About the exact state of things Mr. Barton was quite vague and confused. There had been recent investments, the outcome of which was for the present problematical, and he had an idea there were further speculations and exchanges concerning which he had not been consulted.

It was not for several months that Beatrice wrote Amory the full situation. The entire residue of the Blaine and O'Hara fortunes consisted of the place at Lake Geneva and approximately a half million dollars, invested now in fairly conservative six-per-cent holdings. In face, Beatrice wrote that she was putting the money into railroad and street-car bonds as fast as she could conveniently transfer it.

I am quite sure, she wrote to Amory, *that if there is one thing we can be positive of, it is that people will not stay in one place. This Ford person has certainly made the most of that idea. So I am instructing Mr. Barton to specialize on such things as Northern Pacific and these Rapid Transit Companies, as they call the street-cars. I shall never forgive myself for not buying Bethlehem Steel. I've heard the most fascinating stories. You must go into finance, Amory. I'm sure you would revel in it. You start as a messenger or a teller, I believe, and from that you go up—almost indefinitely. I'm sure if I were a man I'd love the handling of money; it has become quite a senile passion with me. Before I get any farther I want to discuss something. A Mrs. Bispam, an overcordial little lady whom I met at a tea the other day, told me that her son, he is at Yale, wrote her that all the boys there wore their summer underwear all during the winter, and also went about with their heads wet and in low shoes on the coldest days. Now, Amory, I don't know whether that is a fad at Princeton too, but I don't want you to be so foolish. It not only inclines a young man to pneumonia and infantile paralysis, but to all forms of lung trouble, to which you are particularly inclined. You cannot experiment with your health. I have found that out. I will not make myself ridiculous as some mothers no doubt do, by insisting that you wear overshoes, though I remember one Christmas you wore them around constantly without a single buckle latched, making such a curious swishing sound, and you refused to buckle them because it was not the thing to do. The very next Christmas you would not wear even rubbers, though I begged you. You are nearly twenty years old now, dear, and I can't be with you constantly to find whether you are doing the sensible thing.*

This has been a very practical letter. I warned you in my last that the lack of money to do the things one wants to makes one quite prosy and domestic, but there is still plenty for everything if we are not too extravagant. Take care of yourself, my dear boy, and do try to write as least once a week, because I imagine all sorts of horrible things if I don't hear from you.

Affectionately,
Mother.

FIRST APPEARANCE OF THE TERM "PERSONAGE"

Monsignor Darcy invited Amory up to the Stuart palace on the Hudson for a week at Christmas, and they had enormous conversations around the open fire. Monsignor was growing a trifle stouter and his personality had expanded even with that, and Amory felt both rest and security in sinking into a squat, cushioned chair and joining him in the middle-aged sanity of a cigar.

"I've felt like leaving college, Monsignor."

"Why?"

"All my career's gone up in smoke; you think it's petty and all that, but——"

"Not at all petty. I think it's most important. I want to hear the whole thing. Everything you've been doing since I saw you last."

Amory talked; he went thoroughly into the destruction of his egotistic highways, and in a half-hour the listless quality had left his voice.

"What would you do if you left college?" asked Monsignor.

"Don't know. I'd like to travel, but of course this tiresome war prevents that. Anyways, mother would hate not having me graduate. I'm just at sea. Kerry Holiday wants me to go over with him and join the Lafayette Escadrille."

"You know you wouldn't like to go."

"Sometimes I would—tonight I'd go in a second."

"Well, you'd have to be very much more tired of life than I think you are. I know you."

"I'm afraid you do," agreed Amory reluctantly. "It just seemed an easy way out of everything—when I think of another useless, draggy year."

"Yes, I know; but to tell you the truth, I'm not worried about you; you seem to me to be progressing perfectly naturally."

"No," Amory objected. "I've lost half my personality in a year."

"Not a bit of it!" scoffed Monsignor. "You've lost a great amount of vanity and that's all."

"Lordy! I feel, anyway, as if I'd gone through another fifth form at St. Regis'."

"No." Monsignor shook his head. "That was a misfortune; this has been a good thing. Whatever worth while comes to you won't be through the channels you were searching last year."

"What could be more unprofitable than my present lack of pep?"

"Perhaps in itself . . . but you're developing. This has given you time to think and you're casting off a lot of your old luggage about success and the superman and all. People like us can't adopt whole theories, as you did. If we can do the next thing, and have an hour a day to think in, we can accomplish marvels, but as far as any high-handed scheme of blind dominance is concerned—we'd just make asses of ourselves."

"But, Monsignor, I can't do the next thing."

"Amory, between you and me, I have only just learned to do it myself. I can do the one hundred things beyond the next thing, but I stub my toe on that, just as you stubbed your toe on mathematics this fall."

"Why do we have to do the next thing? It never seems the sort of thing I should do."

"We have to do it because we're not personalities, but personages."

"That's a good line—what do you mean?"

"A personality is what you thought you were, what this Kerry and Sloane you tell me of evidently are. Personality is a physical matter almost entirely; it lowers the people it acts on—I've seen it vanish in a long sickness. But while a personality is active, it overrides 'the next thing.' Now a personage, on the other hand, gathers. He is never thought of apart from what he's done. He's a bar on which a thousand things have been hung—glittering things sometimes, as ours are, but he uses those things with a cold mentality back of them."

"And several of my most glittering possessions had fallen off when I needed them." Amory continued the simile eagerly.

"Yes, that's it; when you feel that your garnered prestige and talents and all that are hung out, you need never bother about anybody; you can cope with them without difficulty."

"But, on the other hand, if I haven't my possessions, I'm helpless!"

"Absolutely."

"That's certainly an idea."

"Now you've a clean start—a start Kerry or Sloane can constitutionally never have. You brushed three or four ornaments down, and, in a fit of pique, knocked off the rest of them. The thing now is to collect some new ones, and the farther you look ahead in the collecting the better. But remember, do the next thing!"

"How clear you can make things!"

So they talked, often about themselves, sometimes of philosophy and religion, and life as respectively a game or a mystery. The priest seemed to guess Amory's thoughts before they were clear in his own head, so closely related were their minds in form and groove.

"Why do I make lists?" Amory asked him one night. "Lists of all sorts of things?"

"Because you're a mediævalist," Monsignor answered. "We both are. It's the passion for classifying and finding a type."

"It's a desire to get something definite."

"It's the nucleus of scholastic philosophy."

"I was beginning to think I was growing eccentric 'till I came up here. It was a pose, I guess."

"Don't worry about that; for you not posing may be the biggest pose of all. Pose——"

"Yes?"

"But do the next thing."

After Amory returned to college he received several letters from Monsignor which gave him more egotistic food for consumption.

I am afraid that I gave you too much assurance of your inevitable safety, and you must remember that I did that through faith in your springs of effort; not in the silly conviction that you will arrive without struggle. Some nuances of character you will have to take for granted in yourself, though you must be careful in confessing them to others. You are unsentimental, almost incapable of affection, astute without being cunning and vain without being proud.

Don't let yourself feel worthless; often through life you will really be at your worst when you seem to think best of yourself; and don't worry about losing your "personality," as you persist in calling it; at fifteen you had the radiance of early morning, at twenty you will begin to have the melancholy brilliance of the moon, and when you are my age you will give out, as I do, the genial golden warmth of 4 P.M.

If you write me letters, please let them be natural ones. Your last, that dissertation on architecture, was perfectly awful—so "highbrow" that I picture you living in an intellectual and emotional vacuum; and beware of trying to classify people too definitely into types; you will find that all through their youth they will persist annoyingly in jumping from class to class, and by pasting a supercilious label on every one you meet you are merely packing a Jack-in-the-box that will spring up and leer at you when you begin to come into really antagonistic contact with the world. An idealization of some such a man as Leonardo da Vinci would be a more valuable beacon to you at present.

You are bound to go up and down, just as I did in my youth, but do keep your clarity of mind, and if fools or sages dare to criticise don't blame yourself too much.

You say that convention is all that really keeps you straight in this "woman proposition"; but it's more than that, Amory; it's the fear that what you begin you can't stop; you would run amuck, and I know whereof I speak; it's that half-miraculous sixth sense by which you detect evil, it's the half-realized fear of God in your heart.

Whatever your metier proves to be—religion, architecture, literature— I'm sure you would be much safer anchored to the Church, but I won't risk my influence by arguing with you even though I am secretly sure that the "black chasm of Romanism" yawns beneath you. Do write me soon.

With affectionate regards,
Thayer Darcy.

Even Amory's reading paled during this period; he delved further into the misty side streets of literature: Huysmans, Walter Pater, Theophile Gautier, and the racier sections of Rabelais, Boccaccio, Petronius, and Suetonius. One week, through general curiosity, he inspected the private libraries of his classmates and found Sloane's as typical as any: sets of Kipling, O. Henry, John Fox, Jr., and Richard Harding Davis; "What Every Middle-Aged Woman Ought to Know," "The Spell of the Yukon"; a "gift" copy of James Whitcomb Riley, an assortment of battered, annotated schoolbooks, and, finally, to his surprise, one of his own late discoveries, the collected poems of Rupert Brooke.

Together with Tom D'Invilliers, he sought among the lights of Princeton for some one who might found the Great American Poetic Tradition.

The undergraduate body itself was rather more interesting that year than had been the entirely Philistine Princeton of two years before. Things had livened surprisingly, though at the sacrifice of much of the spontaneous charm of freshman year. In the old Princeton they would never have discovered Tanaduke Wylie. Tanaduke was a sophomore, with tremendous ears and a way of saying, "The earth swirls down through the ominous moons of preconsidered generations!" that made them vaguely wonder why it did not sound quite clear, but never question that it was the utterance of a supersoul. At least so Tom and Amory took him. They told him in all earnestness that he had a mind like Shelley's, and featured his ultrafree free verse and prose poetry in the *Nassau Literary Magazine.* But Tanaduke's genius absorbed the many colors of the age, and he took to the Bohemian life, to their great disappointment. He talked of Greenwich Village now instead of "noon-swirled moons," and met winter muses, unacademic, and cloistered by Forty-second Street and Broadway, instead of the Shelleyan dream-children with whom he had regaled their expectant appreciation. So they surrendered Tanaduke to the futurists, deciding that he and his flaming ties would do better there. Tom gave him the final advice that he should stop writing for two years and read the complete works of Alexander Pope four times, but on Amory's suggestion that Pope for Tanaduke was like foot-ease for stomach trouble, they withdrew in laughter, and called it a coin's toss whether this genius was too big or too petty for them.

Amory rather scornfully avoided the popular professors who dispensed easy epigrams and thimblefuls of Chartreuse to groups of admirers every night. He was disappointed, too, at the air of general uncertainty on every subject that seemed linked with the pedantic temperament; his opinions took shape in a miniature satire called "In a Lecture-Room," which he persuaded Tom to print in the *Nassau Lit.*

> *Good-morning, Fool . . .*
>> *Three times a week*
> *You hold us helpless while you speak,*
> *Teasing our thirsty souls with the*
> *Sleek 'yeas' of your philosophy . . .*
> *Well, here we are, your hundred sheep,*
> *Tune up, play on, pour forth . . . we sleep . . .*
> *You are a student, so they say;*
> *You hammered out the other day*

A syllabus, from what we know
Of some forgotten folio;
You'd sniffled through an era's must,
Filling your nostrils up with dust,
And then, arising from your knees,
Published, in one gigantic sneeze . . .
But here's a neighbor on my right,
An Eager Ass, considered bright;
Asker of questions. . . . How he'll stand,
With earnest air and fidgy hand,
After this hour, telling you
He sat all night and burrowed through
Your book. . . . Oh, you'll be coy and he
Will simulate precosity,
And pedants both, you'll smile and smirk,
And leer and hasten back to work. . . .

'Twas this day week, sir, you returned
A theme of mine, from which I learned
(Through various comment on the side
Which you had scrawled) that I defied
The highest rules of criticism
For cheap and careless witticism. . . .
        'Are you quite sure that this could be?'
And
        'Shaw is no authority!'
But Eager Ass, with what he's sent,
Plays havoc with your best per cent.
Still—still I meet you here and there . . .
When Shakespeare's played you hold a chair,
And some defunct, moth-eaten star
Enchants the mental prig you are . . .
A radical comes down and shocks
The atheistic orthodox?—
You're representing Common Sense,
Mouth open, in the audience.
And, sometimes, even chapel lures
That conscious tolerance of yours,
That broad and beaming view of truth
(Including Kant and General Booth . . .)
And so from shock to shock you live,
A hollow, pale affirmative . . .

The hour's up . . . and roused from rest
One hundred children of the blest
Cheat you a word or two with feet
That down the noisy aisle-ways beat . . .
Forget on narrow-minded earth
The Mighty Yawn that gave you birth.

In April, Kerry Holiday left college and sailed for France to enroll in the Lafayette Escadrille. Amory's envy and admiration of this step was drowned in an experience of his own to which he never succeeded in giving an appropriate value, but which, nevertheless, haunted him for three years afterward.

THE DEVIL

Healy's they left at twelve and taxied to Bistolary's. There were Axia Marlowe and Phœbe Column, from the Summer Garden show, Fred Sloane and Amory. The evening was so very young that they felt ridiculous with surplus energy, and burst into the café like Dionysian revellers.

"Table for four in the middle of the floor," yelled Phœbe. "Hurry, old dear, tell 'em we're here!"

"Tell 'em to play 'Admiration'!" shouted Sloane. "You two order; Phœbe and I are going to shake a wicked calf," and they sailed off in the muddled crowd. Axia and Amory, acquaintances of an hour, jostled behind a waiter to a table at a point of vantage; there they took seats and watched.

"There's Findle Marbotson, from New Haven!" she cried above the uproar. "'Lo, Findle! Whoo-ee!"

"Oh, Axia!" he shouted in salutation. "C'mon over to our table."

"No!" Amory whispered.

"Can't do it, Findle; I'm with somebody else! Call me up tomorrow about one o'clock!"

Findle, a nondescript man-about-Bisty's, answered incoherently and turned back to the brilliant blonde whom he was endeavoring to steer around the room.

"There's a natural damn fool," commented Amory.

"Oh, he's all right. Here's the old jitney waiter. If you ask me, I want a double Daiquiri."

"Make it four."

The crowd whirled and changed and shifted. They were mostly from the colleges, with a scattering of the male refuse of Broadway, and women of two types, the higher of which was the chorus girl. On the whole it was a typical crowd, and their party as typical as any. About three-fourths of the whole business was for effect and therefore harmless, ended at the door of the café, soon enough for the five-o'clock train back to Yale or Princeton; about one-fourth continued on into the dimmer hours and gathered strange dust from strange places. Their party was scheduled to be one of the harmless kind. Fred Sloane and Phœbe Column were old friends; Axia and Amory new ones. But strange things are prepared even in the dead of night, and the unusual, which lurks least in the café, home of the prosaic and inevitable, was preparing to spoil for him the waning romance of Broadway. The way it took was so inexpressibly terrible, so unbelievable, that afterward he never thought of it as experience; but it was a scene from a misty tragedy, played far behind the veil, and that it meant something definite he knew.

About one o'clock they moved to Maxim's, and two found them in Devinière's. Sloane had been drinking consecutively and was in a state of unsteady exhilaration, but Amory was quite tiresomely sober; they had run across none of those ancient, corrupt buyers of champagne who usually assisted their New York parties.

They were just through dancing and were making their way back to their chairs when Amory became aware that someone at a nearby table was looking at him. He turned and glanced casually . . . a middle-aged man dressed in a brown sack suit, it was, sitting a little apart at a table by himself and watching their party intently. At Amory's glance he smiled faintly. Amory turned to Fred, who was just sitting down.

"Who's that pale fool watching us?" he complained indignantly.

"Where?" cried Sloane. "We'll have him thrown out!" He rose to his feet and swayed back and forth, clinging to his chair. "Where is he?"

Axia and Phœbe suddenly leaned and whispered to each other across the table, and before Amory realized it they found themselves on their way to the door.

"Where now?"

"Up to the flat," suggested Phœbe. "We've got brandy and fizz — and everything's slow down here tonight."

Amory considered quickly. He hadn't been drinking, and decided that if he took no more, it would be reasonably discreet for him to trot along in the party. In fact, it would be, perhaps, the thing to do in order to keep an eye on Sloane, who was not in a state to do his own thinking. So he took Axia's arm and, piling intimately into a taxicab, they drove out over the hundreds and drew up at a tall, white-stone apartment-house. . . . Never would he forget that street. . . . It was a broad street, lined on both sides with just such tall, white-stone buildings, dotted with dark windows; they stretched along as far as the eye could see, flooded with a bright moonlight that gave them a calcium pallor. He imagined each one to have an elevator and a colored hall-boy and a key-rack; each one to be eight stories high and full of three and four room suites. He was rather glad to walk into the cheeriness of Phœbe's living-room and sink onto a sofa, while the girls went rummaging for food.

"Phœbe's great stuff," confided Sloane, sotto voce.

"I'm only going to stay half an hour," Amory said sternly. He wondered if it sounded priggish.

"Hell y' say," protested Sloane. "We're here now—don't le's rush."

"I don't like this place," Amory said sulkily, "and I don't want any food."

Phœbe reappeared with sandwiches, brandy bottle, siphon, and four glasses.

"Amory, pour 'em out," she said, "and we'll drink to Fred Sloane, who has a rare, distinguished edge."

"Yes," said Axia, coming in, "and Amory. I like Amory." She sat down beside him and laid her yellow head on his shoulder.

"I'll pour," said Sloane; "you use siphon, Phœbe."

They filled the tray with glasses.

"Ready, here she goes!"

Amory hesitated, glass in hand.

There was a minute while temptation crept over him like a warm wind, and his imagination turned to fire, and he took the glass from Phœbe's hand. That was all; for at the second that his decision came, he looked up and saw, ten yards from him, the man who had been in the café, and with his jump of astonishment the glass fell from his uplifted hand. There the man half sat, half leaned against a pile of pillows on the corner divan. His face was cast in the same yellow wax as in the café, neither the dull, pasty color of a dead man—rather a sort of virile pallor—nor unhealthy, you'd have called it; but like a strong man who'd worked in a mine or done night shifts in a damp climate. Amory looked him over carefully and later he could have drawn him after a fashion, down to the merest details. His mouth was the kind that is called frank, and he had steady gray eyes that moved slowly from one to the other of their group, with just the shade of a questioning expression. Amory noticed his hands; they weren't fine at all, but they had versatility and a tenuous strength . . . they were nervous hands that sat lightly along the cushions and moved constantly with little jerky openings and closings. Then, suddenly, Amory perceived the feet, and with a rush of blood to the head he realized he was afraid. The feet were all wrong . . . with a sort of wrongness that he felt rather than knew. . . . It was like weakness in a good woman, or blood on satin; one of those terrible incongruities that shake little things in the back of the brain. He wore no shoes, but, instead, a sort of half moccasin, pointed, though, like the shoes they wore in the fourteenth century, and with the little ends curling up. They were a darkish brown and his toes seemed to fill them to the end. . . . They were unutterably terrible. . . .

He must have said something, or looked something, for Axia's voice came out of the void with a strange goodness.

"Well, look at Amory! Poor old Amory's sick—old head going 'round?"

"Look at that man!" cried Amory, pointing toward the corner divan.

"You mean that purple zebra!" shrieked Axia facetiously. "Ooo-ee! Amory's got a purple zebra watching him!"

Sloane laughed vacantly.

"Ole zebra gotcha, Amory?"

There was a silence. . . . The man regarded Amory quizzically. . . . Then the human voices fell faintly on his ear:

"Thought you weren't drinking," remarked Axia sardonically, but her voice was good to hear; the whole divan that held the man was alive; alive like heat waves over asphalt, like wriggling worms. . . .

"Come back! Come back!" Axia's arm fell on his. "Amory, dear, you aren't going, Amory!" He was half-way to the door.

"Come on, Amory, stick 'th us!"

"Sick, are you?"

"Sit down a second!"

"Take some water."

"Take a little brandy. . . ."

The elevator was close, and the colored boy was half asleep, paled to a livid bronze . . . Axia's beseeching voice floated down the shaft. Those feet . . . those feet . . .

As they settled to the lower floor the feet came into view in the sickly electric light of the paved hall.

IN THE ALLEY

Down the long street came the moon, and Amory turned his back on it and walked. Ten, fifteen steps away sounded the footsteps. They were like a slow dripping, with just the slightest insistence in their fall.

Amory's shadow lay, perhaps, ten feet ahead of him, and soft shoes was presumably that far behind. With the instinct of a child Amory edged in under the blue darkness of the white buildings, cleaving the moonlight for haggard seconds, once bursting into a slow run with clumsy stumblings. After that he stopped suddenly; he must keep hold, he thought. His lips were dry and he licked them.

If he met any one good—were there any good people left in the world or did they all live in white apartment-houses now? Was every one followed in the moonlight? But if he met some one good who'd know what he meant and hear this damned scuffle . . . then the scuffling grew suddenly nearer, and a black cloud settled over the moon. When again the pale sheen skimmed the cornices, it was almost beside him, and Amory thought he heard a quiet breathing. Suddenly he realized that the footsteps were not behind, had never been behind, they were ahead and he was not eluding but following . . . following. He began to run, blindly, his heart knocking heavily, his hands clinched. Far ahead a black dot showed itself, resolved slowly into a human shape. But Amory was beyond that now; he turned off the street and darted into an alley, narrow and dark and smelling of old rottenness. He twisted down a long, sinuous blackness, where the moonlight was shut away except for tiny glints and patches . . . then suddenly sank panting into a corner by a fence, exhausted. The steps ahead stopped, and he could hear them shift slightly with a continuous motion, like waves around a dock.

He put his face in his hands and covered eyes and ears as well as he could. During all this time it never occurred to him that he was delirious or drunk. He had a sense of reality such as material things could never give him. His intellectual content seemed to submit passively to it, and it fitted like a glove everything that had ever preceded it in his life. It did not muddle him. It was like a problem whose answer he knew on paper, yet whose solution he was unable to grasp. He was far beyond horror. He had sunk through the thin surface of that, now moved in a region where the feet and the fear of white walls were real, living things, things he must accept. Only far inside his soul a little fire leaped and cried that something was pulling him down, trying to get him inside a door and slam it behind him. After that door was slammed there would be only footfalls and white buildings in the moonlight, and perhaps he would be one of the footfalls.

During the five or ten minutes he waited in the shadow of the fence, there was somehow this fire . . . that was as near as he could name it afterward. He remembered calling aloud:

"I want someone stupid. Oh, send someone stupid!" This to the black fence opposite him, in whose shadows the footsteps shuffled

. . . shuffled. He supposed "stupid" and "good" had become some- how intermingled through previous association. When he called thus it was not an act of will at all—will had turned him away from the moving figure in the street; it was almost instinct that called, just the pile on pile of inherent tradition or some wild prayer from way over the night. Then something clanged like a low gong struck at a distance, and before his eyes a face flashed over the two feet, a face pale and distorted with a sort of infinite evil that twisted it like flame in the wind; *but he knew, for the half instant that the gong tanged and hummed, that it was the face of Dick Humbird.*

Minutes later he sprang to his feet, realizing dimly that there was no more sound, and that he was alone in the graying alley. It was cold, and he started on a steady run for the light that showed the street at the other end.

AT THE WINDOW

It was late morning when he woke and found the telephone beside his bed in the hotel tolling frantically, and remembered that he had left word to be called at eleven. Sloane was snoring heavily, his clothes in a pile by his bed. They dressed and ate breakfast in silence, and then sauntered out to get some air. Amory's mind was working slowly, trying to assimilate what had happened and separate from the chaotic imagery that stacked his memory the bare shreds of truth. If the morn- ing had been cold and gray he could have grasped the reins of the past in an instant, but it was one of those days that New York gets some- times in May, when the air of Fifth Avenue is a soft, light wine. How much or how little Sloane remembered Amory did not care to know; he apparently had none of the nervous tension that was gripping Amory and forcing his mind back and forth like a shrieking saw.

Then Broadway broke upon them, and with the babel of noise and the painted faces a sudden sickness rushed over Amory.

"For God's sake, let's go back! Let's get off of this—this place!"

Sloane looked at him in amazement.

"What do you mean?"

"This street, it's ghastly! Come on! let's get back to the Avenue!"

"Do you mean to say," said Sloane stolidly, "that 'cause you had some sort of indigestion that made you act like a maniac last night, you're never coming on Broadway again?"

Simultaneously Amory classed him with the crowd, and he seemed no longer Sloane of the debonair humor and the happy personality, but only one of the evil faces that whirled along the turbid stream.

"Man!" he shouted so loud that the people on the corner turned and followed them with their eyes, "it's filthy, and if you can't see it, you're filthy, too!"

"I can't help it," said Sloane doggedly. "What's the matter with you? Old remorse getting you? You'd be in a fine state if you'd gone through with our little party."

"I'm going, Fred," said Amory slowly. His knees were shaking under him, and he knew that if he stayed another minute on this street he would keel over where he stood. "I'll be at the Vanderbilt for lunch." And he strode rapidly off and turned over to Fifth Avenue. Back at the hotel he felt better, but as he walked into the barber-shop, intending to get a head massage, the smell of the powders and tonics brought back Axia's sidelong, suggestive smile, and he left hurriedly. In the doorway of his room a sudden blackness flowed around him like a divided river.

When he came to himself he knew that several hours had passed. He pitched onto the bed and rolled over on his face with a deadly fear that he was going mad. He wanted people, people, some one sane and stupid and good. He lay for he knew not how long without moving. He could feel the little hot veins on his forehead standing out, and his terror had hardened on him like plaster. He felt he was passing up again through the thin crust of horror, and now only could he distinguish the shadowy twilight he was leaving. He must have fallen asleep again, for when he next recollected himself he had paid the hotel bill and was stepping into a taxi at the door. It was raining torrents.

On the train for Princeton he saw no one he knew, only a crowd of fagged-looking Philadelphians. The presence of a painted woman across the aisle filled him with a fresh burst of sickness and he changed to another car, tried to concentrate on an article in a popular magazine. He found himself reading the same paragraphs over and over, so he abandoned this attempt and leaning over wearily pressed his hot forehead against the damp window-pane. The car, a smoker, was hot and stuffy with most of the smells of the state's alien population; he opened a window and shivered against the cloud of fog that drifted in over him. The two hours' ride were like days, and he nearly cried aloud with joy when the towers of Princeton loomed up beside him and the yellow squares of light filtered through the blue rain.

Tom was standing in the centre of the room, pensively relighting a cigar-stub. Amory fancied he looked rather relieved on seeing him.

"Had a hell of a dream about you last night," came in the cracked voice through the cigar smoke. "I had an idea you were in some trouble."

"Don't tell me about it!" Amory almost shrieked. "Don't say a word; I'm tired and pepped out."

Tom looked at him queerly and then sank into a chair and opened his Italian notebook. Amory threw his coat and hat on the floor, loosened his collar, and took a Wells novel at random from the shelf. "Wells is sane," he thought, "and if he won't do I'll read Rupert Brooke."

Half an hour passed. Outside the wind came up, and Amory started as the wet branches moved and clawed with their fingernails at the window-pane. Tom was deep in his work, and inside the room only the occasional scratch of a match or the rustle of leather as they shifted in their chairs broke the stillness. Then like a zigzag of lightning came the change. Amory sat bolt upright, frozen cold in his chair. Tom was looking at him with his mouth drooping, eyes fixed.

"God help us!" Amory cried.

"Oh, my heavens!" shouted Tom, "look behind!" Quick as a flash Amory whirled around. He saw nothing but the dark window-pane.

"It's gone now," came Tom's voice after a second in a still terror. "Something was looking at you."

Trembling violently, Amory dropped into his chair again.

"I've got to tell you," he said. "I've had one hell of an experience. I think I've—I've seen the devil or—something like him. What face did you just see?—or no," he added quickly, "don't tell me!"

And he gave Tom the story. It was midnight when he finished, and after that, with all lights burning, two sleepy, shivering boys read to each other from "The New Machiavelli," until dawn came up out of Witherspoon Hall, and the *Princetonian* fell against the door, and the May birds hailed the sun on last night's rain.

Four

Narcissus

Off Duty

DURING PRINCETON'S TRANSITION PERIOD, that is, during Amory's last two years there, while he saw it change and broaden and live up to its Gothic beauty by better means than night parades, certain individuals arrived who stirred it to its plethoric depths. Some of them had been freshmen, and wild freshmen, with Amory; some were in the class below; and it was in the beginning of his last year and around small tables at the Nassau Inn that they began questioning aloud the institutions that Amory and countless others before him had questioned so long in secret. First, and partly by accident, they struck on certain books, a definite type of biographical novel that Amory christened "quest" books. In the "quest" book the hero set off in life armed with the best weapons and avowedly intending to use them as such weapons are usually used, to push their possessors ahead as selfishly and blindly as possible, but the heroes of the "quest" books discovered that there might be a more magnificent use for them. "None Other Gods," "Sinister Street," and "The Research Magnificent" were examples of such books; it was the last of these three that gripped Burne Holiday and made him wonder in the beginning of senior year how much it was worth while being a diplomatic autocrat around his club on Prospect Avenue and basking in the high lights of class office. It was distinctly through the channels of aristocracy that Burne found his way. Amory, through Kerry, had had a vague drifting acquaintance with him, but not until January of senior year did their friendship commence.

"Heard the latest?" said Tom, coming in late one drizzly evening with that triumphant air he always wore after a successful conversational bout.

"No. Somebody flunked out? Or another ship sunk?"

"Worse than that. About one-third of the junior class are going to resign from their clubs."

"What!"

"Actual fact!"

"Why!"

"Spirit of reform and all that. Burne Holiday is behind it. The club presidents are holding a meeting tonight to see if they can find a joint means of combating it."

"Well, what's the idea of the thing?"

"Oh, clubs injurious to Princeton democracy; cost a lot; draw social lines, take time; the regular line you get sometimes from disappointed sophomores. Woodrow thought they should be abolished and all that."

"But this is the real thing?"

"Absolutely. I think it'll go through."

"For Pete's sake, tell me more about it."

"Well," began Tom, "it seems that the idea developed simultaneously in several heads. I was talking to Burne awhile ago, and he claims that it's a logical result if an intelligent person thinks long enough about the social system. They had a 'discussion crowd' and the point of abolishing the clubs was brought up by some one—everybody there leaped at it—it had been in each one's mind, more or less, and it just needed a spark to bring it out."

"Fine! I swear I think it'll be most entertaining. How do they feel up at Cap and Gown?"

"Wild, of course. Every one's been sitting and arguing and swearing and getting mad and getting sentimental and getting brutal. It's the same at all the clubs; I've been the rounds. They get one of the radicals in the corner and fire questions at him."

"How do the radicals stand up?"

"Oh, moderately well. Burne's a damn good talker, and so obviously sincere that you can't get anywhere with him. It's so evident that resigning from his club means so much more to him than preventing it does to us that I felt futile when I argued; finally took a position that was brilliantly neutral. In fact, I believe Burne thought for a while that he'd converted me."

"And you say almost a third of the junior class are going to resign?"

"Call it a fourth and be safe."

"Lord—who'd have thought it possible!"

There was a brisk knock at the door, and Burne himself came in.

"Hello, Amory—hello, Tom."

Amory rose.

"'Evening, Burne. Don't mind if I seem to rush; I'm going to Renwick's."

Burne turned to him quickly.

"You probably know what I want to talk to Tom about, and it isn't a bit private. I wish you'd stay."

"I'd be glad to." Amory sat down again, and as Burne perched on a table and launched into argument with Tom, he looked at this revolutionary more carefully than he ever had before. Broad-browed and strong-chinned, with a fineness in the honest gray eyes that were like Kerry's, Burne was a man who gave an immediate impression of bigness and security—stubborn, that was evident, but his stubbornness wore no stolidity, and when he had talked for five minutes Amory knew that this keen enthusiasm had in it no quality of diletantism.

The intense power Amory felt later in Burne Holiday differed from the admiration he had had for Humbird. This time it began as purely a mental interest. With other men whom he had thought as primarily first-class, he had been attracted first by their personalities, and in Burne he missed that immediate magnetism to which he usually swore allegiance. But that night Amory was struck by Burne's intense earnestness, a quality he was accustomed to associate only with the dread stupidity, and by the great enthusiasm that struck dead chords in his heart. Burne stood vaguely for a land Amory hoped he was drifting toward—and it was almost time that land was in sight. Tom and Amory and Alec had reached an impasse; never did they seem to have new experiences in common, for Tom and Alec had been as blindly busy with their committees and boards as Amory had been blindly idling, and the things they had for dissection—college, contemporary personality and the like—they had hashed and rehashed for many a frugal conversational meal.

That night they discussed the clubs until twelve, and, in the main, they agreed with Burne. To the roommates it did not seem such a vital subject as it had in the two years before, but the logic of Burne's objections to the social system dovetailed so completely with everything they had thought, that they questioned rather than argued, and envied the sanity that enabled this man to stand out so against all traditions.

Then Amory branched off and found that Burne was deep in other things as well. Economics had interested him and he was turning socialist. Pacifism played in the back of his mind, and he read *The Masses* and Lyof Tolstoi faithfully.

"How about religion?" Amory asked him.

"Don't know. I'm in a muddle about a lot of things—I've just discovered that I've a mind, and I'm starting to read."

"Read what?"

"Everything. I have to pick and choose, of course, but mostly things to make me think. I'm reading the four gospels now, and the 'Varieties of Religious Experience.'"

"What chiefly started you?"

"Wells, I guess, and Tolstoi, and a man named Edward Carpenter. I've been reading for over a year now—on a few lines, on what I consider the essential lines."

"Poetry?"

"Well, frankly, not what you call poetry, or for your reasons—you two write, of course, and look at things differently. Whitman is the man that attracts me."

"Whitman?"

"Yes; he's a definite ethical force."

"Well, I'm ashamed to say that I'm a blank on the subject of Whitman. How about you, Tom?"

Tom nodded sheepishly.

"Well," continued Burne, "you may strike a few poems that are tiresome, but I mean the mass of his work. He's tremendous—like Tolstoi. They both look things in the face, and, somehow, different as they are, stand for somewhat the same things."

"You have me stumped, Burne," Amory admitted. "I've read 'Anna Karénina' and the 'Kreutzer Sonata' of course, but Tolstoi is mostly in the original Russian as far as I'm concerned."

"He's the greatest man in hundreds of years," cried Burne enthusiastically. "Did you ever see a picture of that shaggy old head of his?"

They talked until three, from biology to organized religion, and when Amory crept shivering into bed it was with his mind aglow with ideas and a sense of shock that some one else had discovered the path he might have followed. Burne Holiday was so evidently developing—and Amory had considered that he was doing the same. He had fallen into a deep cynicism over what had crossed his path, plotted the imperfectability of man and read Shaw and Chesterton enough to keep his mind from the edges of decadence—now suddenly all his mental processes of the last year and a half seemed stale and futile—a petty consummation of himself . . . and like a sombre background lay that incident of the spring before, that filled half his nights with a dreary terror and made him unable to pray. He was not even a Catholic, yet that was the only ghost of a code that he had, the gaudy, ritualistic, paradoxical Catholicism whose prophet was Chesterton, whose claqueurs were such reformed rakes of literature as Huysmans and Bourget, whose American sponsor was Ralph Adams Cram, with his adulation of thirteenth-century cathedrals—a Catholicism which Amory found convenient and ready-made, without priest or sacraments or sacrifice.

He could not sleep, so he turned on his reading-lamp and, taking down the "Kreutzer Sonata," searched it carefully for the germs of Burne's enthusiasm. Being Burne was suddenly so much realler than being clever. Yet he sighed . . . here were other possible clay feet.

He thought back through two years, of Burne as a hurried, nervous freshman, quite submerged in his brother's personality. Then he remembered an incident of sophomore year, in which Burne had been suspected of the leading role.

Dean Hollister had been heard by a large group arguing with a taxi-driver, who had driven him from the junction. In the course of the altercation the dean remarked that he "might as well buy the taxicab." He paid and walked off, but next morning he entered his private office to find the taxicab itself in the space usually occupied by his desk, bearing a sign which read "Property of Dean Hollister. Bought and Paid for." . . . It took two expert mechanics half a day to dissemble it into its minutest parts and remove it, which only goes to prove the rare energy of sophomore humor under efficient leadership.

Then again, that very fall, Burne had caused a sensation. A certain Phyllis Styles, an intercollegiate prom-trotter, had failed to get her yearly invitation to the Harvard-Princeton game.

Jesse Ferrenby had brought her to a smaller game a few weeks before, and had pressed Burne into service—to the ruination of the latter's misogyny.

"Are you coming to the Harvard game?" Burne had asked indiscreetly, merely to make conversation.

"If you ask me," cried Phyllis quickly.

"Of course I do," said Burne feebly. He was unversed in the arts of

Phyllis, and was sure that this was merely a vapid form of kidding. Before an hour had passed he knew that he was indeed involved. Phyllis had pinned him down and served him up, informed him the train she was arriving by, and depressed him thoroughly. Aside from loathing Phyllis, he had particularly wanted to stag that game and entertain some Harvard friends.

"She'll see," he informed a delegation who arrived in his room to josh him. "This will be the last game she ever persuades any young innocent to take her to!"

"But, Burne—why did you *invite* her if you didn't want her?"

"Burne, you *know* you're secretly mad about her—that's the *real* trouble."

"What can *you* do, Burne? What can *you* do against Phyllis?"

But Burne only shook his head and muttered threats which consisted largely of the phrase: "She'll see, she'll see!"

The blithesome Phyllis bore her twenty-five summers gayly from the train, but on the platform a ghastly sight met her eyes. There were Burne and Fred Sloane arrayed to the last dot like the lurid figures on college posters. They had bought flaring suits with huge peg-top trousers and gigantic padded shoulders. On their heads were rakish college hats, pinned up in front and sporting bright orange-and-black bands, while from their celluloid collars blossomed flaming orange ties. They wore black arm-bands with orange "P's," and carried canes flying Princeton pennants, the effect completed by socks and peeping handkerchiefs in the same color motifs. On a clanking chain they led a large, angry tom-cat, painted to represent a tiger.

A good half of the station crowd was already staring at them, torn between horrified pity and riotous mirth, and as Phyllis, with her svelte jaw dropping, approached, the pair bent over and emitted a college cheer in loud, far-carrying voices, thoughtfully adding the name "Phyllis" to the end. She was vociferously greeted and escorted enthusiastically across the campus, followed by half a hundred village urchins—to the stifled laughter of hundreds of alumni and visitors, half of whom had no idea that this was a practical joke, but thought that Burne and Fred were two varsity sports showing their girl a collegiate time.

Phyllis's feelings as she was paraded by the Harvard and Princeton stands, where sat dozens of her former devotees, can be imagined. She tried to walk a little ahead, she tried to walk a little behind—but they stayed close, that there should be no doubt whom she was with, talking in loud voices of their friends on the football team, until she could almost hear her acquaintances whispering:

"Phyllis Styles must be *awfully hard up* to have to come with *those two.*"

That had been Burne, dynamically humorous, fundamentally serious. From that root had blossomed the energy that he was now trying to orient with progress. . . .

So the weeks passed and March came and the clay feet that Amory looked for failed to appear. About a hundred juniors and seniors resigned from their clubs in a final fury of righteousness, and the clubs in helplessness turned upon Burne their finest weapon: ridicule. Every one who knew him liked him—but what he stood for (and he began to stand for more all the time) came under the lash of many tongues, until a frailer man than he would have been snowed under.

"Don't you mind losing prestige?" asked Amory one night. They had taken to exchanging calls several times a week.

"Of course I don't. What's prestige, at best?"

"Some people say that you're just a rather original politician."

He roared with laughter.

"That's what Fred Sloane told me today. I suppose I have it coming."

One afternoon they dipped into a subject that had interested Amory for a long time—the matter of the bearing of physical attributes on a man's make-up. Burne had gone into the biology of this, and then:

"Of course health counts—a healthy man has twice the chance of being good," he said.

"I don't agree with you—I don't believe in 'muscular Christianity.' "

"I do—I believe Christ had great physical vigor."

"Oh, no," Amory protested. "He worked too hard for that. I imagine that when he died he was a broken-down man—and the great saints haven't been strong."

"Half of them have."

"Well, even granting that, I don't think health has anything to do with goodness; of course, it's valuable to a great saint to be able to stand enormous strains, but this fad of popular preachers rising on their toes in simulated virility, bellowing that calisthenics will save the world—no, Burne, I can't go that."

"Well, let's waive it—we won't get anywhere, and besides I haven't quite made up my mind about it myself. Now, here's something I *do* know—personal appearance has a lot to do with it."

"Coloring?" Amory asked eagerly.

"Yes."

"That's what Tom and I figured," Amory agreed. "We took the year-books for the last ten years and looked at the pictures of the senior council. I know you don't think much of that august body, but it does represent success here in a general way. Well, I suppose only about thirty-five per cent of every class here are blonds, are really light—yet *two-thirds* of every senior council are light. We looked at pictures of ten years of them, mind you; that means that out of every *fifteen* light-haired men in the senior class *one* is on the senior council, and of the dark-haired men it's only one in *fifty*."

"It's true," Burne agreed. "The light-haired man *is* a higher type, generally speaking. I worked the thing out with the Presidents of the United States once, and found that way over half of them were light-haired—yet think of the preponderant number of brunettes in the race."

"People unconsciously admit it," said Amory. "You'll notice a blond person is *expected* to talk. If a blond girl doesn't talk we call her a 'doll'; if a light-haired man is silent he's considered stupid. Yet the world is full of 'dark silent men' and 'languorous brunettes' who haven't a brain in their heads, but somehow are never accused of the dearth."

"And the large mouth and broad chin and rather big nose undoubtedly make the superior face."

"I'm not so sure." Amory was all for classical features.

"Oh, yes—I'll show you," and Burne pulled out of his desk a photographic collection of heavily bearded, shaggy celebrities—Tolstoi, Whitman, Carpenter, and others.

"Aren't they wonderful?"

Amory tried politely to appreciate them, and gave up laughingly.

"Burne, I think they're the ugliest-looking crowd I ever came across. They look like an old man's home."

"Oh, Amory, look at that forehead on Emerson; look at Tolstoi's eyes." His tone was reproachful.

Amory shook his head.

"No! Call them remarkable-looking or anything you want—but ugly they certainly are."

Unabashed, Burne ran his hand lovingly across the spacious foreheads, and piling up the pictures put them back in his desk.

Walking at night was one of his favorite pursuits, and one night he persuaded Amory to accompany him.

"I hate the dark," Amory objected. "I didn't use to—except when I was particularly imaginative, but now, I really do—I'm a regular fool about it."

"That's useless, you know."

"Quite possibly."

"We'll go east," Burne suggested, "and down that string of roads through the woods."

"Doesn't sound very appealing to me," admitted Amory reluctantly, "but let's go."

They set off at a good gait, and for an hour swung along in a brisk argument until the lights of Princeton were luminous white blots behind them.

"Any person with any imagination is bound to be afraid," said Burne earnestly. "And this very walking at night is one of the things I was afraid about. I'm going to tell you why I can walk anywhere now and not be afraid."

"Go on," Amory urged eagerly. They were striding toward the woods, Burne's nervous, enthusiastic voice warming to his subject.

"I used to come out here alone at night, oh, three months ago, and I always stopped at that cross-road we just passed. There were the woods looming up ahead, just as they do now, there were dogs howling and the shadows and no human sound. Of course, I peopled the woods with everything ghastly, just like you do; don't you?"

"I do," Amory admitted.

"Well, I began analyzing it—my imagination persisted in sticking horrors into the dark—so I stuck my imagination into the dark instead, and let it look out at me—I let it play stray dog or escaped convict or ghost, and then saw myself coming along the road. That made it all right—as it always makes everything all right to project yourself completely into another's place. I knew that if I were the dog or the convict or the ghost I wouldn't be a menace to Burne Holiday any more than he was a menace to me. Then I thought of my watch. I'd better go back and leave it and then essay the woods. No; I decided, it's better on the whole that I should lose a watch than that I should turn back—and I did go into them—not only followed the road through them, but walked into them until I wasn't frightened any more—did it until one night I sat down and dozed off in there; then I knew I was through being afraid of the dark."

"Lordy," Amory breathed. "I couldn't have done that. I'd have come out half-way, and the first time an automobile passed and made the dark thicker when its lamps disappeared, I'd have come in."

"Well," Burne said suddenly, after a few moments' silence, "we're half-way through, let's turn back."

On the return he launched into a discussion of will.

"It's the whole thing," he asserted. "It's the one dividing line between good and evil. I've never met a man who led a rotten life and didn't have a weak will."

"How about great criminals?"

"They're usually insane. If not, they're weak. There is no such thing as a strong, sane criminal."

"Burne, I disagree with you altogether; how about the superman?"

"Well?"

"He's evil, I think, yet he's strong and sane."

"I've never met him. I'll bet, though, that he's stupid or insane."

"I've met him over and over and he's neither. That's why I think you're wrong."

"I'm sure I'm not—and so I don't believe in imprisonment except for the insane."

On this point Amory could not agree. It seemed to him that life and history were rife with the strong criminal, keen, but often self-deluding; in politics and business one found him and among the old statesmen and kings and generals; but Burne never agreed and their courses began to split on that point.

Burne was drawing farther and farther away from the world about him. He resigned the vice-presidency of the senior class and took to reading and walking as almost his only pursuits. He voluntarily attended graduate lectures in philosophy and biology, and sat in all of them with a rather pathetically intent look in his eyes, as if waiting for something the lecturer would never quite come to. Sometimes Amory would see him squirm in his seat; and his face would light up; he was on fire to debate a point.

He grew more abstracted on the street and was even accused of becoming a snob, but Amory knew it was nothing of the sort, and once when Burne passed him four feet off, absolutely unseeingly, his mind a thousand miles away, Amory almost choked with the romantic joy of watching him. Burne seemed to be climbing heights where others would be forever unable to get a foothold.

"I tell you," Amory declared to Tom, "he's the first contemporary I've ever met whom I'll admit is my superior in mental capacity."

"It's a bad time to admit it—people are beginning to think he's odd."

"He's way over their heads—you know you think so yourself when you talk to him—Good Lord, Tom, you *used* to stand out against 'people.' Success has completely conventionalized you."

Tom grew rather annoyed.

"What's he trying to do—be excessively holy?"

"No! not like anybody you've ever seen. Never enters the Philadelphian Society. He has no faith in that rot. He doesn't believe that public swimming-pools and a kind word in time will right the wrongs of the world; moreover, he takes a drink whenever he feels like it."

"He certainly is getting in wrong."

"Have you talked to him lately?"

"No."

"Then you haven't any conception of him."

The argument ended nowhere, but Amory noticed more than ever how the sentiment toward Burne had changed on the campus.

"It's odd," Amory said to Tom one night when they had grown more amicable on the subject, "that the people who violently disapprove of Burne's radicalism are distinctly the Pharisee class—I mean they're the best-educated men in college—the editors of the papers, like yourself and Ferrenby, the younger professors. . . . The illiterate athletes like Langueduc think he's getting eccentric, but they just say, 'Good old Burne has got some queer ideas in his head,' and pass on— the Pharisee class—Gee! they ridicule him unmercifully."

The next morning he met Burne hurrying along McCosh walk after a recitation.

"Whither bound, Tsar?"

"Over to the *Prince* office to see Ferrenby," he waved a copy of the morning's *Princetonian* at Amory. "He wrote this editorial."

"Going to flay him alive?"

"No—but he's got me all balled up. Either I've misjudged him or he's suddenly become the world's worst radical."

Burne hurried on, and it was several days before Amory heard an account of the ensuing conversation. Burne had come into the editor's sanctum displaying the paper cheerfully.

"Hello, Jesse."

"Hello there, Savonarola."

"I just read your editorial."

"Good boy—didn't know you stooped that low."

"Jesse, you startled me."

"How so?"

"Aren't you afraid the faculty'll get after you if you pull this irreligious stuff?"

"What?"

"Like this morning."

"What the devil—that editorial was on the coaching system."

"Yes, but that quotation— —"

Jesse sat up.

"What quotation?"

"You know: 'He who is not with me is against me.'"

"Well—what about it?"

Jesse was puzzled but not alarmed.

"Well, you say here—let me see." Burne opened the paper and read: "*'He who is not with me is against me,'* as that gentleman said who was notoriously capable of only coarse distinctions and puerile generalities."

"What of it?" Ferrenby began to look alarmed. "Oliver Cromwell said it, didn't he? or was it Washington, or one of the saints? Good Lord, I've forgotten."

Burne roared with laughter.

"Oh, Jesse, oh, good, kind Jesse."

"Who said it, for Pete's sake?"

"Well," said Burne, recovering his voice, "St. Matthew attributes it to Christ."

"My God!" cried Jesse, and collapsed backward into the wastebasket.

AMORY WRITES A POEM

The weeks tore by. Amory wandered occasionally to New York on the chance of finding a new shining green autobus, that its stick-of-candy glamour might penetrate his disposition. One day he ventured into a stock-company revival of a play whose name was faintly familiar. The curtain rose—he watched casually as a girl entered. A few phrases rang in his ear and touched a faint chord of memory. Where—? When—?

Then he seemed to hear a voice whispering beside him, a very soft, vibrant voice: "Oh, I'm such a poor little fool; do tell me when I do wrong."

The solution came in a flash and he had a quick, glad memory of Isabelle.

He found a blank space on his programme, and began to scribble rapidly:

> *Here in the figured dark I watch once more,*
> *There, with the curtain, roll the years away;*
> *Two years of years—there was an idle day*
> *Of ours, when happy endings didn't bore*
> *Our unfermented souls; I could adore*
> *Your eager face beside me, wide-eyed, gay,*
> *Smiling a repertoire while the poor play*
> *Reached me as a faint ripple reaches shore.*
>
> *Yawning and wondering an evening through,*
> *I watch alone . . . and chatterings, of course,*
> *Spoil the one scene which, somehow, did have charms;*
> *You wept a bit, and I grew sad for you*
> *Right here! Where Mr. X defends divorce*
> *And what's-her-name falls fainting in his arms.*

STILL CALM

"Ghosts are such dumb things," said Alec, "they're slow-witted. I can always outguess a ghost."

"How?" asked Tom.

"Well, it depends where. Take a bedroom, for example. If you use *any* discretion a ghost can never get you in a bedroom."

"Go on, s'pose you think there's maybe a ghost in your bedroom— what measures do you take on getting home at night?" demanded Amory, interested.

"Take a stick," answered Alec, with ponderous reverence, "one about the length of a broom-handle. Now, the first thing to do is to get the room *cleared*—to do this you rush with your eyes closed into your study and turn on the lights—next, approaching the closet, carefully run the stick in the door three or four times. Then, if nothing happens, you can look in. *Always, always* run the stick in viciously first—*never* look first!"

"Of course, that's the ancient Celtic school," said Tom gravely.

"Yes—but they usually pray first. Anyway, you use this method to clear the closets and also for behind all doors— —"

"And the bed," Amory suggested.

"Oh, Amory, no!" cried Alec in horror. "That isn't the way—the bed requires different tactics—let the bed alone, as you value your reason—if there is a ghost in the room and that's only about a third of the time, it is *almost always* under the bed."

"Well—" Amory began.

Alec waved him into silence.

"Of *course* you never look. You stand in the middle of the floor and before he knows what you're going to do make a sudden leap for the bed—never walk near the bed; to a ghost your ankle is your most vulnerable part—once in bed, you're safe; he may lie around under the bed all night, but you're safe as daylight. If you still have doubts pull the blanket over your head."

"All that's very interesting," said Tom.

"Isn't it?" Alec beamed proudly. "All my own, too—the Sir Oliver Lodge of the new world."

Amory was enjoying college immensely again. The sense of going forward in a direct, determined line had come back; youth was stirring and shaking out a few new feathers. He had even stored enough surplus energy to sally into a new pose.

"What's the idea of all this 'distracted' stuff, Amory?" asked Alec one day, and then as Amory pretended to be cramped over his book in a daze: "Oh, don't try to act Burne, the mystic, to me."

Amory looked up innocently.

"What?"

"What?" mimicked Alec. "Are you trying to read yourself into a rhapsody with—let's see the book."

He snatched it; regarded it derisively.

"Well?" said Amory a little stiffly.

" 'The Life of St. Teresa,' " read Alec aloud. "Oh, my gosh!"

"Say, Alec."

"What?"

"Does it bother you?"

"Does what bother me?"

"My acting dazed and all that?"

"Why, no—of course it doesn't *bother* me."

"Well, then, don't spoil it. If I enjoy going around telling people guilelessly that I think I'm a genius, let me do it."

"You're getting a reputation for being eccentric," said Alec, laughing, "if that's what you mean."

Amory finally prevailed, and Alec agreed to accept his face value in the presence of others if he was allowed rest periods when they were alone; so Amory "ran it out" at a great rate, bringing the most eccentric characters to dinner, wild-eyed grad students, preceptors with strange theories of God and government, to the cynical amazement of the supercilious Cottage Club.

As February became slashed by sun and moved cheerfully into March, Amory went several times to spend weekends with Monsignor; once he took Burne, with great success, for he took equal pride and delight in displaying them to each other. Monsignor took him several times to see Thornton Hancock, and once or twice to the house of a Mrs. Lawrence, a type of Rome-haunting American whom Amory liked immediately.

Then one day came a letter from Monsignor, which appended an interesting P.S.:

Do you know, it ran, *that your third cousin, Clara Page, widowed six months and very poor, is living in Philadelphia? I don't think you've ever met her, but I wish, as a favor to me, you'd go to see her. To my mind, she's rather a remarkable woman, and just about your age.*

Amory sighed and decided to go, as a favor. . . .

CLARA

She was immemorial. . . . Amory wasn't good enough for Clara, Clara of ripply golden hair, but then no man was. Her goodness was above the prosy morals of the husband-seeker, apart from the dull literature of female virtue.

Sorrow lay lightly around her, and when Amory found her in Philadelphia he thought her steely blue eyes held only happiness; a latent strength, a realism, was brought to its fullest development by the facts that she was compelled to face. She was alone in the world, with two small children, little money, and, worst of all, a host of friends. He saw her that winter in Philadelphia entertaining a houseful of men for an evening, when he knew she had not a servant in the house except the little colored girl guarding the babies overhead. He saw one of the greatest libertines in that city, a man who was habitually drunk and notorious at home and abroad, sitting opposite her for an evening, discussing *girls' boarding-schools* with a sort of innocent excitement. What a twist Clara had to her mind! She could make fascinating and almost brilliant conversation out of the thinnest air that ever floated through a drawing-room.

The idea that the girl was poverty-stricken had appealed to Amory's sense of situation. He arrived in Philadelphia expecting to be told that 921 Ark Street was in a miserable lane of hovels. He was even disappointed when it proved to be nothing of the sort. It was an old house that had been in her husband's family for years. An elderly aunt, who objected to having it sold, had put ten years' taxes with a lawyer and pranced off to Honolulu, leaving Clara to struggle with the heating-problem as best she could. So no wild-haired woman with a hungry baby at her breast and a sad Amelia-like look greeted him. Instead, Amory would have thought from his reception that she had not a care in the world.

A calm virility and a dreamy humor, marked contrasts to her level-headedness—into these moods she slipped sometimes as a refuge. She could do the most prosy things (though she was wise enough never to stultify herself with such "household arts" as *knitting* and *embroidery*), yet immediately afterward pick up a book and let her imagination rove as a formless cloud with the wind. Deepest of all in her personality was the golden radiance that she diffused around her. As an open fire in a dark room throws romance and pathos into the quiet faces at its edge, so she cast her lights and shadows around the rooms that held her, until she made of her prosy old uncle a man of quaint and meditative

charm, metamorphosed the stray telegraph boy into a Puck-like creature of delightful originality. At first this quality of hers somehow irritated Amory. He considered his own uniqueness sufficient, and it
rather embarrassed him when she tried to read new interests into him
for the benefit of what other adorers were present. He felt as if a polite
but insistent stage-manager were attempting to make him give a new
interpretation of a part he had conned for years.

But Clara talking, Clara telling a slender tale of a hatpin and an
inebriated man and herself. . . . People tried afterward to repeat her
anecdotes but for the life of them they could make them sound like
nothing whatever. They gave her a sort of innocent attention and the
best smiles many of them had smiled for long; there were few tears in
Clara, but people smiled misty-eyed at her.

Very occasionally Amory stayed for little half-hours after the rest of
the court had gone, and they would have bread and jam and tea late in
the afternoon or "maple-sugar lunches," as she called them, at night.

"You *are* remarkable, aren't you!" Amory was becoming trite from
where he perched in the centre of the dining-room table one six
o'clock.

"Not a bit," she answered. She was searching out napkins in the
sideboard. "I'm really most humdrum and common-place. One of those
people who have no interest in anything but their children."

"Tell that to somebody else," scoffed Amory. "You know you're
perfectly effulgent." He asked her the one thing that he knew might
embarrass her. It was the remark that the first bore made to Adam.

"Tell me about yourself." And she gave the answer that Adam must
have given.

"There's nothing to tell."

But eventually Adam probably told the bore all the things he
thought about at night when the locusts sang in the sandy grass, and
he must have remarked patronizingly how *different* he was from Eve,
forgetting how different she was from him . . . at any rate, Clara told
Amory much about herself that evening. She had had a harried life
from sixteen on, and her education had stopped sharply with her leisure. Browsing in her library, Amory found a tattered gray book out of
which fell a yellow sheet that he impudently opened. It was a poem
that she had written at school about a gray convent wall on a gray day,
and a girl with her cloak blown by the wind sitting atop of it and
thinking about the many-colored world. As a rule such sentiment
bored him, but this was done with so much simplicity and atmosphere,
that it brought a picture of Clara to his mind, of Clara on such a cool,
gray day with her keen blue eyes staring out, trying to see her tragedies come marching over the gardens outside. He envied that poem.

How he would have loved to have come along and seen her on the wall and talked nonsense or romance to her, perched above him in the air. He began to be frightfully jealous of everything about Clara: of her past, of her babies, of the men and women who flocked to drink deep of her cool kindness and rest their tired minds as at an absorbing play.

"*Nobody* seems to bore you," he objected.

"About half the world do," she admitted, "but I think that's a pretty good average, don't you?" and she turned to find something in Browning that bore on the subject. She was the only person he ever met who could look up passages and quotations to show him in the middle of the conversation, and yet not be irritating to distraction. She did it constantly, with such a serious enthusiasm that he grew fond of watching her golden hair bent over a book, brow wrinkled ever so little at hunting her sentence.

Through early March he took to going to Philadelphia for weekends. Almost always there was someone else there and she seemed not anxious to see him alone, for many occasions presented themselves when a word from her would have given him another delicious half-hour of adoration. But he fell gradually in love and began to speculate wildly on marriage. Though this design flowed through his brain even to his lips, still he knew afterward that the desire had not been deeply rooted. Once he dreamt that it had come true and woke up in a cold panic, for in his dream she had been a silly, flaxen Clara, with the gold gone out of her hair and platitudes falling insipidly from her changeling tongue. But she was the first fine woman he ever knew and one of the few good people who ever interested him. She made her goodness such an asset. Amory had decided that most good people either dragged theirs after them as a liability, or else distorted it to artificial geniality, and of course there were the ever-present prig and Pharisee—(but Amory never included *them* as being among the saved).

ST. CECILIA

> *Over her gray and velvet dress,*
> *Under her molten, beaten hair,*
> *Color of rose in mock distress*
> *Flushes and fades and makes her fair;*
> *Fills the air from her to him*
> *With light and languor and little sighs,*
> *Just so subtly he scarcely knows . . .*
> *Laughing lightning, color of rose.*

"Do you like me?"

"Of course I do," said Clara seriously.

"Why?"

"Well, we have some qualities in common. Things that are spontaneous in each of us—or were originally."

"You're implying that I haven't used myself very well?"

Clara hesitated.

"Well, I can't judge. A man, of course, has to go through a lot more, and I've been sheltered."

"Oh, don't stall, please, Clara," Amory interrupted; "but do talk about me a little, won't you?"

"Surely, I'd adore to." She didn't smile.

"That's sweet of you. First answer some questions. Am I painfully conceited?"

"Well—no, you have tremendous vanity, but it'll amuse the people who notice its preponderance."

"I see."

"You're really humble at heart. You sink to the third hell of depression when you think you've been slighted. In fact, you haven't much self-respect."

"Centre of target twice, Clara. How do you do it? You never let me say a word."

"Of course not—I can never judge a man while he's talking. But I'm not through; the reason you have so little real self-confidence, even though you gravely announce to the occasional philistine that you think you're a genius, is that you've attributed all sorts of atrocious faults to yourself and are trying to live up to them. For instance, you're always saying that you are a slave to high-balls."

"But I am, potentially."

"And you say you're a weak character, that you've no will."

"Not a bit of will—I'm a slave to my emotions, to my likes, to my hatred of boredom, to most of my desires——"

"You are not!" She brought one little fist down onto the other. "You're a slave, a bound helpless slave to one thing in the world, your imagination."

"You certainly interest me. If this isn't boring you, go on."

"I notice that when you want to stay over an extra day from college you go about it in a sure way. You never decide at first while the merits of going or staying are fairly clear in your mind. You let your imagination shinny on the side of your desires for a few hours, and then you decide. Naturally your imagination, after a little freedom, thinks up a million reasons why you should stay, so your decision when it comes isn't true. It's biassed."

"Yes," objected Amory, "but isn't it lack of will-power to let my imagination shinny on the wrong side?"

"My dear boy, there's your big mistake. This has nothing to do with will-power; that's a crazy, useless word, anyway; you lack judgment—the judgment to decide at once when you know your imagination will play you false, given half a chance."

"Well, I'll be darned!" exclaimed Amory in surprise, "that's the last thing I expected."

Clara didn't gloat. She changed the subject immediately. But she had started him thinking and he believed she was partly right. He felt like a factory-owner who after accusing a clerk of dishonesty finds that his own son, in the office, is changing the books once a week. His poor, mistreated will that he had been holding up to the scorn of himself and his friends, stood before him innocent, and his judgment walked off to prison with the unconfinable imp, imagination, dancing in mocking glee beside him. Clara's was the only advice he ever asked without dictating the answer himself—except, perhaps, in his talks with Monsignor Darcy.

How he loved to do any sort of thing with Clara! Shopping with her was a rare, epicurean dream. In every store where she had ever traded she was whispered about as the beautiful Mrs. Page.

"I'll bet she won't stay single long."

"Well, don't scream it out. She ain't lookin' for no advice."

"*Ain't* she beautiful!"

(Enter a floor-walker—silence till he moves forward, smirking.)

"Society person, ain't she?"

"Yeah, but poor now, I guess; so they say."

"Gee! girls, *ain't* she some kid!"

And Clara beamed on all alike. Amory believed that trades-people gave her discounts, sometimes to her knowledge and sometimes without it. He knew she dressed very well, had always the best of everything in the house, and was inevitably waited upon by the head floor-walker at the very least.

Sometimes they would go to church together on Sunday and he would walk beside her and revel in her cheeks moist from the soft water in the new air. She was very devout, always had been, and God knows what heights she attained and what strength she drew down to herself when she knelt and bent her golden hair into the stained-glass light.

"St. Cecilia," he cried aloud one day, quite involuntarily, and the people turned and peered, and the priest paused in his sermon and Clara and Amory turned to fiery red.

That was the last Sunday they had, for he spoiled it all that night. He couldn't help it.

They were walking through the March twilight where it was as warm as June, and the joy of youth filled his soul so that he felt he must speak.

"I think," he said and his voice trembled, "that if I lost faith in you I'd lose faith in God."

She looked at him with such a startled face that he asked her the matter.

"Nothing," she said slowly, "only this: five men have said that to me before, and it frightens me."

"Oh, Clara, is that your fate!"

She did not answer.

"I suppose love to you is—" he began.

She turned like a flash.

"I have never been in love."

They walked along, and he realized slowly how much she had told him . . . never in love. . . . She seemed suddenly a daughter of light alone. His entity dropped out of her plane and he longed only to touch her dress with almost the realization that Joseph must have had of Mary's eternal significance. But quite mechanically he heard himself saying:

"And I love you—any latent greatness that I've got is . . . oh, I can't talk, but Clara, if I come back in two years in a position to marry you——"

She shook her head.

"No," she said; "I'd never marry again. I've got my two children and I want myself for them. I like you—I like all clever men, you more than any—but you know me well enough to know that I'd never marry a clever man—" She broke off suddenly.

"Amory."

"What?"

"You're not in love with me. You never wanted to marry me, did you?"

"It was the twilight," he said wonderingly. "I didn't feel as though I were speaking aloud. But I love you—or adore you—or worship you——"

"There you go—running through your catalogue of emotions in five seconds."

He smiled unwillingly.

"Don't make me out such a light-weight, Clara; you *are* depressing sometimes."

"You're not a light-weight, of all things," she said intently, taking his arm and opening wide her eyes—he could see their kindliness in the fading dusk. "A light-weight is an eternal nay."

"There's so much spring in the air—there's so much lazy sweetness in your heart."

She dropped his arm.

"You're all fine now, and I feel glorious. Give me a cigarette. You've never seen me smoke, have you? Well, I do, about once a month."

And then that wonderful girl and Amory raced to the corner like two mad children gone wild with pale-blue twilight.

"I'm going to the country for tomorrow," she announced, as she stood panting, safe beyond the flare of the corner lamppost. "These days are too magnificent to miss, though perhaps I feel them more in the city."

"Oh, Clara!" Amory said; "what a devil you could have been if the Lord had just bent your soul a little the other way!"

"Maybe," she answered; "but I think not. I'm never really wild and never have been. That little outburst was pure spring."

"And you are, too," said he.

They were walking along now.

"No—you're wrong again, how can a person of your own self-reputed brains be so constantly wrong about me? I'm the opposite of everything spring ever stood for. It's unfortunate, if I happen to look like what pleased some soppy old Greek sculptor, but I assure you that if it weren't for my face I'd be a quiet nun in the convent without"— then she broke into a run and her raised voice floated back to him as he followed—"my precious babies, which I must go back and see."

She was the only girl he ever knew with whom he could understand how another man might be preferred. Often Amory met wives whom he had known as debutantes, and looking intently at them imagined that he found something in their faces which said:

"Oh, if I could only have gotten *you!*" Oh, the enormous conceit of the man!

But that night seemed a night of stars and singing and Clara's bright soul still gleamed on the ways they had trod.

"Golden, golden is the air—" he chanted to the little pools of water. . . . "Golden is the air, golden notes from golden mandolins, golden frets of golden violins, fair, oh, wearily fair. . . . Skeins from braided basket, mortals may not hold; oh, what young extravagant God, who would know or ask it? . . . who could give such gold . . ."

AMORY IS RESENTFUL

Slowly and inevitably, yet with a sudden surge at the last, while Amory talked and dreamed, war rolled swiftly up the beach and washed the sands where Princeton played. Every night the gymnasium echoed as platoon after platoon swept over the floor and shuffled out the basket-ball markings. When Amory went to Washington the next week-end he caught some of the spirit of crisis which changed to repulsion in the Pullman car coming back, for the berths across from him were occupied by stinking aliens—Greeks, he guessed, or Russians. He thought how much easier patriotism had been to a homogeneous race, how much easier it would have been to fight as the Colonies fought, or as the Confederacy fought. And he did no sleeping that night, but listened to the aliens guffaw and snore while they filled the car with the heavy scent of latest America.

In Princeton every one bantered in public and told themselves privately that their deaths at least would be heroic. The literary students read Rupert Brooke passionately; the lounge-lizards worried over whether the government would permit the English-cut uniform for officers; a few of the hopelessly lazy wrote to the obscure branches of the War Department, seeking an easy commission and a soft berth.

Then, after a week, Amory saw Burne and knew at once that argument would be futile—Burne had come out as a pacifist. The socialist magazines, a great smattering of Tolstoi, and his own intense longing for a cause that would bring out whatever strength lay in him, had finally decided him to preach peace as a subjective ideal.

"When the German army entered Belgium," he began, "if the inhabitants had gone peaceably about their business, the German army would have been disorganized in——"

"I know," Amory interrupted, "I've heard it all. But I'm not going to talk propaganda with you. There's a chance that you're right—but even so we're hundreds of years before the time when non-resistance can touch us as a reality."

"But, Amory, listen——"

"Burne, we'd just argue——"

"Very well."

"Just one thing—I don't ask you to think of your family or friends, because I know they don't count a picayune with you beside your sense of duty—but, Burne, how do you know that the magazines you read and the societies you join and these idealists you meet aren't just plain *German?*"

"Some of them are, of course."

"How do you know they aren't *all* pro-German—just a lot of weak ones—with German-Jewish names."

"That's the chance, of course," he said slowly. "How much or how little I'm taking this stand because of propaganda I've heard, I don't know; naturally I think that it's my most innermost conviction—it seems a path spread before me just now."

Amory's heart sank.

"But think of the cheapness of it—no one's really going to martyr you for being a pacifist—it's just going to throw you in with the worst——"

"I doubt it," he interrupted.

"Well, it all smells of Bohemian New York to me."

"I know what you mean, and that's why I'm not sure I'll agitate."

"You're one man, Burne—going to talk to people who won't listen—with all God's given you."

"That's what Stephen must have thought many years ago. But he preached his sermon and they killed him. He probably thought as he was dying what a waste it all was. But you see, I've always felt that Stephen's death was the thing that occurred to Paul on the road to Damascus, and sent him to preach the word of Christ all over the world."

"Go on."

"That's all—this is my particular duty. Even if right now I'm just a pawn—just sacrificed. God! Amory—you don't think I like the Germans!"

"Well, I can't say anything else—I get to the end of all the logic about non-resistance, and there, like an excluded middle, stands the huge spectre of man as he is and always will be. And this spectre stands right beside the one logical necessity of Tolstoi's, and the other logical necessity of Nietzsche's—" Amory broke off suddenly. "When are you going?"

"I'm going next week."

"I'll see you, of course."

As he walked away it seemed to Amory that the look in his face bore a great resemblance to that in Kerry's when he had said good-by under Blair Arch two years before. Amory wondered unhappily why he could never go into anything with the primal honesty of those two.

"Burne's a fanatic," he said to Tom, "and he's dead wrong and, I'm inclined to think, just an unconscious pawn in the hands of anarchistic publishers and German-paid rag wavers—but he haunts me—just leaving everything worth while——"

Burne left in a quietly dramatic manner a week later. He sold all his possessions and came down to the room to say good-by, with a battered old bicycle, on which he intended to ride to his home in Pennsylvania.

"Peter the Hermit bidding farewell to Cardinal Richelieu," suggested Alec, who was lounging in the window-seat as Burne and Amory shook hands.

But Amory was not in the mood for that, and as he saw Burne's long legs propel his ridiculous bicycle out of sight beyond Alexander Hall, he knew he was going to have a bad week. Not that he doubted the war—Germany stood for everything repugnant to him; for materialism and the direction of tremendous licentious force; it was just that Burne's face stayed in his memory and he was sick of the hysteria he was beginning to hear.

"What on earth is the use of suddenly running down Goethe," he declared to Alec and Tom. "Why write books to prove he started the war—or that that stupid, overestimated Schiller is a demon in disguise?"

"Have you ever read anything of theirs?" asked Tom shrewdly.

"No," Amory admitted.

"Neither have I," he said laughing.

"People will shout," said Alec quietly, "but Goethe's on his same old shelf in the library—to bore any one that wants to read him!"

Amory subsided, and the subject dropped.

"What are you going to do, Amory?"

"Infantry or aviation, I can't make up my mind—I hate mechanics, but then of course aviation's the thing for me——"

"I feel as Amory does," said Tom. "Infantry or aviation—aviation sounds like the romantic side of the war, of course—like cavalry used to be, you know; but like Amory I don't know a horsepower from a piston-rod."

Somehow Amory's dissatisfaction with his lack of enthusiasm culminated in an attempt to put the blame for the whole war on the ancestors of his generation . . . all the people who cheered for Germany in 1870. . . . All the materialists rampant, all the idolizers of German science and efficiency. So he sat one day in an English lecture and heard "Locksley Hall" quoted and fell into a brown study with contempt for Tennyson and all he stood for—for he took him as a representative of the Victorians.

> *Victorians, Victorians, who never learned to weep*
> *Who sowed the bitter harvest that your children go to reap——*

scribbled Amory in his note-book. The lecture was saying something about Tennyson's solidity and fifty heads were bent to take notes. Amory turned over to a fresh page and began scrawling again.

They shuddered when they found what Mr. Darwin was about,
They shuddered when the waltz came in and Newman hurried out——

But the waltz came in much earlier; he crossed that out.

"And entitled *A Song in the Time of Order*," came the professor's voice, droning far away. "Time of Order"—Good Lord! Everything crammed in the box and the Victorians sitting on the lid smiling serenely. . . . With Browning in his Italian villa crying bravely: "All's for the best." Amory scribbled again.

You knelt up in the temple and he bent to hear you pray,
You thanked him for your "glorious gains"—reproached him for "Cathay."

Why could he never get more than a couplet at a time? Now he needed something to rhyme with:

You would keep Him straight with science, tho He had gone wrong
before . . .

Well, anyway. . . .

You met your children in your home—"I've fixed it up!" you cried,
Took your fifty years of Europe, and then virtuously—died.

"That was to a great extent Tennyson's idea," came the lecturer's voice. "Swinburne's *Song in the Time of Order* might well have been Tennyson's title. He idealized order against chaos, against waste."

At last Amory had it. He turned over another page and scrawled vigorously for the twenty minutes that was left of the hour. Then he walked up to the desk and deposited a page torn out of his note-book.

"Here's a poem to the Victorians, sir," he said coldly.

The professor picked it up curiously while Amory backed rapidly through the door.

Here is what he had written:

Songs in the time of order
You left for us to sing,
Proofs with excluded middles,
Answers to life in rhyme,
Keys of the prison warder
And ancient bells to ring,

Time was the end of riddles,
We were the end of time . . .

Here were domestic oceans
And a sky that we might reach,
Guns and a guarded border,
Gantlets—but not to fling,
Thousands of old emotions
And a platitude for each,
Songs in the time of order—
And tongues, that we might sing.

THE END OF MANY THINGS

Early April slipped by in a haze—a haze of long evenings on the club veranda with the graphophone playing "Poor Butterfly" inside . . . for "Poor Butterfly" had been the song of that last year. The war seemed scarcely to touch them and it might have been one of the senior springs of the past, except for the drilling every other afternoon, yet Amory realized poignantly that this was the last spring under the old régime.

"This is the great protest against the superman," said Amory.

"I suppose so," Alec agreed.

"He's absolutely irreconcilable with any Utopia. As long as he occurs, there's trouble and all the latent evil that makes a crowd list and sway when he talks."

"And of course all that he is is a gifted man without a moral sense."

"That's all. I think the worst thing to contemplate is this—it's all happened before, how soon will it happen again? Fifty years after Waterloo Napoleon was as much a hero to English school children as Wellington. How do we know our grandchildren won't idolize Von Hindenburg the same way?"

"What brings it about?"

"Time, damn it, and the historian. If we could only learn to look on evil *as* evil, whether it's clothed in filth or monotony or magnificence."

"God! Haven't we raked the universe over the coals for four years?"

Then the night came that was to be the last. Tom and Amory, bound in the morning for different training-camps, paced the shadowy walks as usual and seemed still to see around them the faces of the men they knew.

"The grass is full of ghosts tonight."

"The whole campus is alive with them."

They paused by Little and watched the moon rise, to make silver of the slate roof of Dodd and blue the rustling trees.

"You know," whispered Tom, "what we feel now is the sense of all the gorgeous youth that has rioted through here in two hundred years."

A last burst of singing flooded up from Blair Arch—broken voices for some long parting.

"And what we leave here is more than this class; it's the whole heritage of youth. We're just one generation—we're breaking all the links that seemed to bind us here to top-booted and high-stocked generations. We've walked arm and arm with Burr and Light-Horse Harry Lee through half these deep-blue nights."

"That's what they are," Tom tangented off, "deep blue—a bit of color would spoil them, make them exotic. Spires, against a sky that's a promise of dawn, and blue light on the slate roofs—it hurts . . . rather——"

"Good-by, Aaron Burr," Amory called toward deserted Nassau Hall, "you and I knew strange corners of life."

His voice echoed in the stillness.

"The torches are out," whispered Tom. "Ah, Messalina, the long shadows are building minarets on the stadium——"

For an instant the voices of freshman year surged around them and then they looked at each other with faint tears in their eyes.

"Damn!"

"Damn!"

The last light fades and drifts across the land—the low, long land, the sunny land of spires; the ghosts of evening tune again their lyres and wander singing in a plaintive band down the long corridors of trees; pale fires echo the night from tower top to tower: Oh, sleep that dreams, and dream that never tires, press from the petals of the lotus flower something of this to keep, the essence of an hour.

No more to wait the twilight of the moon in this sequestered vale of star and spire, for one eternal morning of desire passes to time and earthly afternoon. Here, Heraclitus, did you find in fire and shifting things the prophecy you hurled down the dead years; this midnight my desire will see, shadowed among the embers, furled in flame, the splendor and the sadness of the world.

Interlude

May, 1917–February, 1919

A LETTER DATED JANUARY, 1918, WRITTEN BY Monsignor Darcy to Amory, who is a second lieutenant in the 171st Infantry, Port of Embarkation, Camp Mills, Long Island.

My dear Boy:—
All you need tell me of yourself is that you still are; for the rest I merely search back in a restive memory, a thermometer that records only fevers, and match you with what I was at your age. But men will chatter and you and I will still shout our futilities to each other across the stage until the last silly curtain falls plump! *upon our bobbing heads. But you are starting the spluttering magic-lantern show of life with much the same array of slides as I had, so I need to write you if only to shriek the colossal stupidity of people. . . .*

This is the end of one thing: for better or worse you will never again be quite the Amory Blaine that I knew, never again will we meet as we have met, because your generation is growing hard, much harder than mine ever grew, nourished as they were on the stuff of the nineties.

Amory, lately I reread Æschylus and there in the divine irony of the "Agamemnon" I find the only answer to this bitter age—all the world tumbled about our ears, and the closest parallel ages back in that hopeless resignation. There are times when I think of the men out there as Roman legionaries, miles from their corrupt city, stemming back the hordes . . . hordes a little more menacing, after all, than the corrupt city . . . another blind blow at the race, furies that we passed with ovations years ago, over whose corpses we bleated triumphantly all through the Victorian era. . . .

And afterward an out-and-out materialistic world—and the Catholic Church. I wonder where you'll fit in. Of one thing I'm sure—Celtic you'll live and Celtic you'll die; so if you don't use heaven as a continual referendum for your ideas you'll find earth a continual recall to your ambitions.

Amory, I've discovered suddenly that I'm an old man. Like all old men, I've had dreams sometimes and I'm going to tell you of them. I've enjoyed imagining that you were my son, that perhaps when I was young I went into a state of coma and begat you, and when I came to, had no recollection of it . . . it's the paternal instinct, Amory—celibacy goes deeper than the flesh. . . .

Sometimes I think that the explanation of our deep resemblance is some common ancestor, and I find that the only blood that the Darcys and the O'Haras have in common is that of the O'Donahues . . . Stephen was his name, I think. . . .

When the lightning strikes one of us it strikes both: you had hardly arrived at the port of embarkation when I got my papers to start for Rome, and I am waiting every moment to be told where to take ship. Even before you get this letter I shall be on the ocean; then will come your turn. You went to war as a gentleman should, just as you went to school and college, because it was the thing to do. It's better to leave the blustering and tremulo-heroism to the middle classes; they do it so much better.

Do you remember that week-end last March when you brought Burne Holiday from Princeton to see me? What a magnificent boy he is! It gave me a frightful shock afterward when you wrote that he thought me splendid; how could he be so deceived? Splendid is the one thing that neither you nor I are. We are many other things—we're extraordinary, we're clever, we could be said, I suppose, to be brilliant. We can attract people, we can make atmosphere, we can almost lose our Celtic souls in Celtic subtleties, we can almost always have our own way; but splendid—rather not!

I am going to Rome with a wonderful dossier and letters of introduction that cover every capital in Europe, and there will be "no small stir" when I get there. How I wish you were with me! This sounds like a rather cynical paragraph, not at all the sort of thing that a middle-aged clergyman should write to a youth about to depart for the war; the only excuse is that the middle-aged clergyman is talking to himself. There are deep things in us and you know what they are as well as I do. We have great faith, though yours at present is uncrystallized; we have a terrible honesty that all our sophistry cannot destroy and, above all, a childlike simplicity that keeps us from ever being really malicious.

I have written a keen for you which follows. I am sorry your cheeks are not up to the description I have written of them, but you will smoke and read all night— —

At any rate here it is:

A Lament for a Foster Son, and He Going to the War Against the King of Foreign.

Ochone
He is gone from me the son of my mind
And he in his golden youth like Angus Oge
Angus of the bright birds
And his mind strong and subtle like the mind of Cuchulin
on Muirtheme.

Awirra sthrue
His brow is as white as the milk of the cows of Maeve
And his cheeks like the cherries of the tree
And it bending down to Mary and she feeding the Son of God.

Aveelia Vrone
His hair is like the golden collar of the Kings at Tara
And his eyes like the four gray seas of Erin.
And they swept with the mists of rain.

Mavrone go Gudyo
He to be in the joyful and red battle
Amongst the chieftains and they doing great deeds of valor
His life to go from him
It is the chords of my own soul would be loosed.

A Vich Deelish
My heart is in the heart of my son
And my life is in his life surely

A man can be twice young
  In the life of his sons only.

Jia du Vaha Alanav
May the Son of God be above him and beneath him,
    before him and behind him
May the King of the elements cast a mist over the eyes of
    the King of Foreign,
May the Queen of the Graces lead him by the hand
    the way he can go through the midst of his enemies
    and they not seeing him

  May Patrick of the Gael and Collumb of the Churches and
      the five thousand Saints of Erin be better than a shield to him
And he got into the fight.
Och Ochone.

Amory—Amory—I feel, somehow, that this is all; one or both of us is not going to last out this war. . . . I've been trying to tell you how much this reincarnation of myself in you has meant in the last few years . . . curiously alike we are . . . curiously unlike.

  Good-by, dear boy, and God be with you.
                    Thayer Darcy.

EMBARKING AT NIGHT

Amory moved forward on the deck until he found a stool under an electric light. He searched in his pocket for notebook and pencil and then began to write, slowly, laboriously:

We leave tonight . . .
    Silent, we filled the still, deserted street,
        A column of dim gray,
    And ghosts rose startled at the muffled beat
        Along the moonless way;
    The shadowy shipyards echoed to the feet
        That turned from night and day.

  And so we linger on the windless decks,
      See on the spectre shore

Shades of a thousand days, poor gray-ribbed wrecks . . .
   Oh, shall we then deplore
Those futile years!
         See how the sea is white!
The clouds have broken and the heavens burn
   To hollow highways, paved with gravelled light
The churning of the waves about the stern
   Rises to one voluminous nocturne,
            . . . We leave tonight.

A letter from Amory, headed "Brest, January 11th, 1919," to Lieutenant T. P. D'Invilliers, Camp Gordon, Ga.

Dear Baudelaire:—
We meet in Manhattan on the 30th of this very mo.; we then proceed to take a very sporty apartment, you and I and Alec, who is at me elbow as I write. I don't know what I'm going to do but I have a vague dream of going into politics. Why is it that the pick of the young Englishmen from Oxford and Cambridge go into politics and in the U. S. A. we leave it to the muckers?— raised in the ward, educated in the assembly and sent to Congress, fat-paunched bundles of corruption, devoid of "both ideas and ideals" as the debaters used to say. Even forty years ago we had good men in politics, but we, we are brought up to pile up a million and "show what we are made of." Sometimes I wish I'd been an Englishman; American life is so damned dumb and stupid and healthy.

Since poor Beatrice died I'll probably have a little money, but very darn little. I can forgive mother almost everything except the fact that in a sudden burst of religiosity toward the end, she left half of what remained to be spent in stained-glass windows and seminary endowments. Mr. Barton, my lawyer, writes me that my thousands are mostly in street railways and that the said Street R.R.s are losing money because of the five-cent fares. Imagine a salary list that gives $350 a month to a man that can't read and write!— yet I believe in it, even though I've seen what was once a sizable fortune melt away between speculation, extravagance, the democratic administration, and the income tax—modern, that's me all over, Mabel.

At any rate we'll have really knock-out rooms—you can get a job on some fashion magazine, and Alec can go into the Zinc Company or whatever it is that his people own—he's looking over my shoulder and he says it's a brass company, but I don't think it matters much, do you? There's probably as much corruption in zinc-made money as brass-made money. As for the well-known Amory, he would write immortal literature if he were sure enough about anything to risk telling any one else about it. There is no more dangerous gift to posterity than a few cleverly turned platitudes.

Tom, why don't you become a Catholic? Of course to be a good one you'd have to give up those violent intrigues you used to tell me about, but you'd write better poetry if you were linked up to tall golden candlesticks and long, even chants, and even if the American priests are rather bourgeois, as Beatrice used to say, still you need only go to the sporty churches, and I'll introduce you to Monsignor Darcy who really is a wonder.

Kerry's death was a blow, so was Jesse's to a certain extent. And I have a great curiosity to know what queer corner of the world has swallowed Burne. Do you suppose he's in prison under some false name? I confess that the war instead of making me orthodox, which is the correct reaction, has made me a passionate agnostic. The Catholic Church has had its wings clipped so often lately that its part was timidly negligible, and they haven't any good writers any more. I'm sick of Chesterton.

I've only discovered one soldier who passed through the much-advertised spiritual crisis, like this fellow, Donald Hankey, and the one I knew was already studying for the ministry, so he was ripe for it. I honestly think that's all pretty much rot, though it seemed to give sentimental comfort to those at home; and may make fathers and mothers appreciate their children. This crisis-inspired religion is rather valueless and fleeting at best. I think four men have discovered Paris to one that discovered God.

But us—you and me and Alec—oh, we'll get a Jap butler and dress for dinner and have wine on the table and lead a contemplative, emotionless life until we decide to use machine-guns with the property owners—or throw bombs with the Bolshevik. God! Tom, I hope something happens. I'm restless as the devil and have a horror of getting fat or falling in love and growing domestic.

The place at Lake Geneva is now for rent but when I land I'm going West to see Mr. Barton and get some details. Write me care of the Blackstone, Chicago.

S'ever, dear Boswell,
Samuel Johnson.

BOOK TWO

The Education

of a

Personage

One

The Débutante

*T*he time is February. The place is a large, dainty bedroom in the Connage
house on Sixty-eighth Street, New York. A girl's room: pink walls and
curtains and a pink bedspread on a cream-colored bed. Pink and cream are
the motifs of the room, but the only article of furniture in full view is a
luxurious dressing-table with a glass top and a three-sided mirror. On the
walls there is an expensive print of "Cherry Ripe," a few polite dogs by
Landseer, and the "King of the Black Isles," by Maxfield Parrish.

Great disorder consisting of the following items: (1) seven or eight empty
cardboard boxes, with tissue-paper tongues hanging panting from their
mouths; (2) an assortment of street dresses mingled with their sisters of the
evening, all upon the table, all evidently new; (3) a roll of tulle, which has
lost its dignity and wound itself tortuously around everything in sight, and
(4) upon the two small chairs, a collection of lingerie that beggars description. One would enjoy seeing the bill called forth by the finery displayed and

*one is possessed by a desire to see the princess for whose benefit — Look!
There's some one! Disappointment! This is only a maid hunting for something — she lifts a heap from a chair — Not there; another heap, the dressing-
table, the chiffonier drawers. She brings to light several beautiful chemises
and an amazing pajama but this does not satisfy her — she goes out.*

An indistinguishable mumble from the next room.

*Now, we are getting warm. This is Alec's mother, Mrs. Connage, ample,
dignified, rouged to the dowager point and quite worn out. Her lips move
significantly as she looks for IT. Her search is less thorough than the
maid's but there is a touch of fury in it, that quite makes up for its
sketchiness. She stumbles on the tulle and her "damn" is quite audible. She
retires, empty-handed.*

*More chatter outside and a girl's voice, a very spoiled voice, says: "Of all
the stupid people — —"*

*After a pause a third seeker enters, not she of the spoiled voice, but a
younger edition. This is Cecelia Connage, sixteen, pretty, shrewd, and constitutionally good-humored. She is dressed for the evening in a gown the
obvious simplicity of which probably bores her. She goes to the nearest pile,
selects a small pink garment and holds it up appraisingly.*

CECELIA: Pink?

ROSALIND: *(Outside)* Yes!

CECELIA: *Very* snappy?

ROSALIND: Yes!

CECELIA: I've got it!

*(She sees herself in the mirror of the dressing-table and commences to
shimmy enthusiastically.)*

ROSALIND: *(Outside)* What are you doing — trying it on?

*(CECELIA ceases and goes out carrying the garment at the right shoulder.
From the other door, enters ALEC CONNAGE. He looks around quickly and
in a huge voice shouts: Mama! There is a chorus of protest from next door
and encouraged he starts toward it, but is repelled by another chorus.)*

ALEC: So *that's* where you all are! Amory Blaine is here.

CECELIA: *(Quickly)* Take him down-stairs.

ALEC: Oh, he *is* down-stairs.

MRS. CONNAGE: Well, you can show him where his room is. Tell
him I'm sorry that I can't meet him now.

ALEC: He's heard a lot about you all. I wish you'd hurry. Father's
telling him all about the war and he's restless. He's sort of temperamental.

(This last suffices to draw CECELIA into the room.)

CECELIA: *(Seating herself high upon lingerie)* How do you mean —
temperamental? You used to say that about him in letters.

ALEC: Oh, he writes stuff.

CECELIA: Does he play the piano?

ALEC: Don't think so.

CECELIA: *(Speculatively)* Drink?

ALEC: Yes—nothing queer about him.

CECELIA: Money?

ALEC: Good Lord—ask him, he used to have a lot, and he's got some income now.

(MRS. CONNAGE appears.)

MRS. CONNAGE: Alec, of course we're glad to have any friend of yours— —

ALEC: You certainly ought to meet Amory.

MRS. CONNAGE: Of course, I want to. But I think it's so childish of you to leave a perfectly good home to go and live with two other boys in some impossible apartment. I hope it isn't in order that you can all drink as much as you want. *(She pauses.)* He'll be a little neglected tonight. This is Rosalind's week, you see. When a girl comes out, she needs *all* the attention.

ROSALIND: *(Outside)* Well, then, prove it by coming here and hooking me.

(MRS. CONNAGE goes.)

ALEC: Rosalind hasn't changed a bit.

CECELIA: *(In a lower tone)* She's awfully spoiled.

ALEC: She'll meet her match tonight.

CECELIA: Who—Mr. Amory Blaine?

(ALEC nods.)

CECELIA: Well, Rosalind has still to meet the man she can't outdistance. Honestly, Alec, she treats men terribly. She abuses them and cuts them and breaks dates with them and yawns in their faces—and they come back for more.

ALEC: They love it.

CECELIA: They hate it. She's a—she's a sort of vampire, I think—and she can make girls do what she wants usually—only she hates girls.

ALEC: Personality runs in our family.

CECELIA: *(Resignedly)* I guess it ran out before it got to me.

ALEC: Does Rosalind behave herself?

CECELIA: Not particularly well. Oh, she's average—smokes sometimes, drinks punch, frequently kissed—Oh, yes—common knowledge—one of the effects of the war, you know.

(Emerges MRS. CONNAGE.)

MRS. CONNAGE: Rosalind's almost finished so I can go down and meet your friend.

(ALEC and his mother go out.)

ROSALIND: *(Outside)* Oh, mother— —

CECELIA: Mother's gone down.

(And now ROSALIND *enters.* ROSALIND *is—utterly* ROSALIND. *She is one of those girls who need never make the slightest effort to have men fall in love with them. Two types of men seldom do: dull men are usually afraid of her cleverness and intellectual men are usually afraid of her beauty. All others are hers by natural prerogative.*

If ROSALIND *could be spoiled the process would have been complete by this time, and as a matter of fact, her disposition is not all it should be; she wants what she wants when she wants it and she is prone to make every one around her pretty miserable when she doesn't get it—but in the true sense she is not spoiled. Her fresh enthusiasm, her will to grow and learn, her endless faith in the inexhaustibility of romance, her courage and fundamental honesty—these things are not spoiled.*

There are long periods when she cordially loathes her whole family. She is quite unprincipled; her philosophy is carpe diem *for herself and* laissez-faire *for others. She loves shocking stories: she has that coarse streak that usually goes with natures that are both fine and big. She wants people to like her, but if they do not it never worries her or changes her.*

She is by no means a model character.

The education of all beautiful women is the knowledge of men. ROSALIND *had been disappointed in man after man as individuals, but she had great faith in man as a sex. Women she detested. They represented qualities that she felt and despised in herself—incipient meanness, conceit, cowardice, and petty dishonesty. She once told a roomful of her mother's friends that the only excuse for women was the necessity for a disturbing element among men. She danced exceptionally well, drew cleverly but hastily, and had a startling facility with words, which she used only in love-letters.*

But all criticism of ROSALIND *ends in her beauty. There was that shade of glorious yellow hair, the desire to imitate which supports the dye industry. There was the eternal kissable mouth, small, slightly sensual, and utterly disturbing. There were gray eyes and an unimpeachable skin with two spots of vanishing color. She was slender and athletic, without underdevelopment, and it was a delight to watch her move about a room, walk along a street, swing a golf club, or turn a "cartwheel."*

A last qualification—her vivid, instant personality escaped that conscious, theatrical quality that AMORY *had found in* ISABELLE. MONSIGNOR DARCY *would have been quite up a tree whether to call her a personality or a personage. She was perhaps the delicious, inexpressible, once-in-a-century blend.*

On the night of her début she is, for all her strange, stray wisdom, quite like a happy little girl. Her mother's maid has just done her hair, but she has decided impatiently that she can do a better job herself. She is too nervous just now to stay in one place. To that we owe her presence in this littered room. She is going to speak. ISABELLE's *alto tones had been like a violin, but if you could hear* ROSALIND, *you would say her voice was musical as a waterfall.*

ROSALIND: Honestly, there are only two costumes in the world that I really enjoy being in— *(Combing her hair at the dressing-table.)* One's a hoop skirt with pantaloons; the other's a one-piece bathing-suit. I'm quite charming in both of them.

CECELIA: Glad you're coming out?

ROSALIND: Yes; aren't you?

CECELIA: *(Cynically)* You're glad so you can get married and live on Long Island with the *fast younger married set.* You want life to be a chain of flirtation with a man for every link.

ROSALIND: *Want* it to be one! You mean I've *found* it one.

CECELIA: Ha!

ROSALIND: Cecelia, darling, you don't know what a trial it is to be—like me. I've got to keep my face like steel in the street to keep men from winking at me. If I laugh hard from a front row in the theatre, the comedian plays to me for the rest of the evening. If I drop my voice, my eyes, my handkerchief at a dance, my partner calls me up on the 'phone every day for a week.

CECELIA: It must be an awful strain.

ROSALIND: The unfortunate part is that the only men who interest me at all are the totally ineligible ones. Now—if I were poor I'd go on the stage.

CECELIA: Yes, you might as well get paid for the amount of acting you do.

ROSALIND: Sometimes when I've felt particularly radiant I've thought, why should this be wasted on one man?

CECELIA: Often when you're particularly sulky, I've wondered why it should all be wasted on just one family. *(Getting up.)* I think I'll go down and meet Mr. Amory Blaine. I like temperamental men.

ROSALIND: There aren't any. Men don't know how to be really angry or really happy—and the ones that do, go to pieces.

CECELIA: Well, I'm glad I don't have all your worries. I'm engaged.

ROSALIND: *(With a scornful smile)* Engaged? Why, you little lunatic! If mother heard you talking like that she'd send you off to boarding-school, where you belong.

CECELIA: You won't tell her, though, because I know things I could tell—and you're too selfish!

ROSALIND: *(A little annoyed)* Run along, little girl! Who are you engaged to, the iceman? the man that keeps the candy-store?

CECELIA: Cheap wit—good-by, darling, I'll see you later.

ROSALIND: Oh, be *sure* and do that—you're *such* a help.

(*Exit* CECELIA. ROSALIND *finishes her hair and rises, humming. She goes up to the mirror and starts to dance in front of it on the soft carpet. She watches not her feet, but her eyes—never casually but always intently, even when she smiles. The door suddenly opens and then slams behind* AMORY, *very cool and handsome as usual. He melts into instant confusion.*)

HE: Oh, I'm sorry. I thought— —

SHE: (*Smiling radiantly*) Oh, you're Amory Blaine, aren't you?

HE: (*Regarding her closely*) And you're Rosalind?

SHE: I'm going to call you Amory—oh, come in—it's all right—mother'll be right in—(*under her breath*) unfortunately.

HE: (*Gazing around*) This is sort of a new wrinkle for me.

SHE: This is No Man's Land.

HE: This is where you—you—(*pause*)

SHE: Yes—all those things. (*She crosses to the bureau.*) See, here's my rouge—eye pencils.

HE: I didn't know you were that way.

SHE: What did you expect?

HE: I thought you'd be sort of—sort of—sexless, you know, swim and play golf.

SHE: Oh, I do—but not in business hours.

HE: Business?

SHE: Six to two—strictly.

HE: I'd like to have some stock in the corporation.

SHE: Oh, it's not a corporation—it's just "Rosalind, Unlimited." Fifty-one shares, name, good-will, and everything goes at $25,000 a year.

HE: (*Disapprovingly*) Sort of a chilly proposition.

SHE: Well, Amory, you don't mind—do you? When I meet a man that doesn't bore me to death after two weeks, perhaps it'll be different.

HE: Odd, you have the same point of view on men that I have on women.

SHE: I'm not really feminine, you know—in my mind.

HE: (*Interested*) Go on.

SHE: No, you—you go on—you've made me talk about myself. That's against the rules.

HE: Rules?

SHE: My own rules—but you— Oh, Amory, I hear you're brilliant. The family expects *so* much of you.

HE: How encouraging!

SHE: Alec said you'd taught him to think. Did you? I didn't believe any one could.

HE: No. I'm really quite dull.

(He evidently doesn't intend this to be taken seriously.)

SHE: Liar.

HE: I'm—I'm religious—I'm literary. I've—I've even written poems.

SHE: Vers libre—splendid! *(She declaims.)*

> The trees are green,
> The birds are singing in the trees,
> The girl sips her poison
> The bird flies away the girl dies.

HE: *(Laughing)* No, not that kind.

SHE: *(Suddenly)* I like you.

HE: Don't.

SHE: Modest too— —

HE: I'm afraid of you. I'm always afraid of a girl—until I've kissed her.

SHE: *(Emphatically)* My dear boy, the war is over.

HE: So I'll always be afraid of you.

SHE: *(Rather sadly)* I suppose you will.

(A slight hesitation on both their parts.)

HE: *(After due consideration)* Listen. This is a frightful thing to ask.

SHE: *(Knowing what's coming)* After five minutes.

HE: But will you—kiss me? Or are you afraid?

SHE: I'm never afraid—but your reasons are so poor.

HE: Rosalind, I really *want* to kiss you.

SHE: So do I.

(They kiss— definitely and thoroughly.)

HE: *(After a breathless second)* Well, is your curiosity satisfied?

SHE: Is yours?

HE: No, it's only aroused.

(He looks it.)

SHE: *(Dreamily)* I've kissed dozens of men. I suppose I'll kiss dozens more.

HE: *(Abstractedly)* Yes, I suppose you could—like that.

SHE: Most people like the way I kiss.

HE: *(Remembering himself)* Good Lord, yes. Kiss me once more, Rosalind.

SHE: No—my curiosity is generally satisfied at one.

HE: *(Discouraged)* Is that a rule?

SHE: I make rules to fit the cases.

HE: You and I are somewhat alike—except that I'm years older in experience.

SHE: How old are you?

HE: Almost twenty-three. You?

SHE: Nineteen—just.

HE: I suppose you're the product of a fashionable school.

SHE: No—I'm fairly raw material. I was expelled from Spence—I've forgotten why.

HE: What's your general trend?

SHE: Oh, I'm bright, quite selfish, emotional when aroused, fond of admiration——

HE: *(Suddenly)* I don't want to fall in love with you——

SHE: *(Raising her eyebrows)* Nobody asked you to.

HE: *(Continuing coldly)* But I probably will. I love your mouth.

SHE: Hush! Please don't fall in love with my mouth—hair, eyes, shoulders, slippers—but *not* my mouth. Everybody falls in love with my mouth.

HE: It's quite beautiful.

SHE: It's too small.

HE: No it isn't—let's see.

(He kisses her again with the same thoroughness.)

SHE: *(Rather moved)* Say something sweet.

HE: *(Frightened)* Lord help me.

SHE: *(Drawing away)* Well, don't—if it's so hard.

HE: Shall we pretend? So soon?

SHE: We haven't the same standards of time as other people.

HE: Already it's—other people.

SHE: Let's pretend.

HE: No—I can't—it's sentiment.

SHE: You're not sentimental?

HE: No, I'm romantic—a sentimental person thinks things will last—a romantic person hopes against hope that they won't. Sentiment is emotional.

SHE: And you're not? *(With her eyes half-closed.)* You probably flatter yourself that that's a superior attitude.

HE: Well—Rosalind, Rosalind, don't argue—kiss me again.

SHE: *(Quite chilly now)* No—I have no desire to kiss you.

HE: *(Openly taken aback)* You wanted to kiss me a minute ago.

SHE: This is now.

HE: I'd better go.

SHE: I suppose so.

(He goes toward the door.)

SHE: Oh!

(He turns.)

SHE: *(Laughing)* Score—Home Team: One hundred—Opponents: Zero.

(He starts back.)

SHE: *(Quickly)* Rain—no game.

(He goes out.)

    (She goes quietly to the chiffonier, takes out a cigarette-case and hides it in the side drawer of a desk. Her mother enters, note-book in hand.)

MRS. CONNAGE: Good—I've been wanting to speak to you alone before we go down-stairs.

ROSALIND: Heavens! you frighten me!

MRS. CONNAGE: Rosalind, you've been a very expensive proposition.

ROSALIND: *(Resignedly)* Yes.

MRS. CONNAGE: And you know your father hasn't what he once had.

ROSALIND: *(Making a wry face)* Oh, please don't talk about money.

MRS. CONNAGE: You can't do anything without it. This is our last year in this house—and unless things change Cecelia won't have the advantages you've had.

ROSALIND: *(Impatiently)* Well—what is it?

MRS. CONNAGE: So I ask you to please mind me in several things I've put down in my note-book. The first one is: don't disappear with young men. There may be a time when it's valuable, but at present I want you on the dance-floor where I can find you. There are certain men I want to have you meet and I don't like finding you in some corner of the conservatory exchanging silliness with any one—or listening to it.

ROSALIND: *(Sarcastically)* Yes, listening to it *is* better.

MRS. CONNAGE: And don't waste a lot of time with the college set—little boys nineteen and twenty years old. I don't mind a prom or a football game, but staying away from advantageous parties to eat in little cafés down-town with Tom, Dick, and Harry——

ROSALIND: *(Offering her code, which is, in its way, quite as high as her mother's)* Mother, it's done—you can't run everything now the way you did in the early nineties.

MRS. CONNAGE: *(Paying no attention)* There are several bachelor friends of your father's that I want you to meet tonight—youngish men.

ROSALIND: *(Nodding wisely)* About forty-five?

MRS. CONNAGE: *(Sharply)* Why not?

ROSALIND: Oh, *quite* all right—they know life and are so adorably tired looking *(shakes her head)*—but they *will* dance.

MRS. CONNAGE: I haven't met Mr. Blaine—but I don't think you'll care for him. He doesn't sound like a money-maker.

ROSALIND: Mother, I never *think* about money.

MRS. CONNAGE: You never keep it long enough to think about it.

ROSALIND: (*Sighs*) Yes, I suppose some day I'll marry a ton of it— out of sheer boredom.

MRS. CONNAGE: (*Referring to note-book*) I had a wire from Hartford. Dawson Ryder is coming up. Now there's a young man I like, and he's floating in money. It seems to me that since you seem tired of Howard Gillespie you might give Mr. Ryder some encouragement. This is the third time he's been up in a month.

ROSALIND: How did you know I was tired of Howard Gillespie?

MRS. CONNAGE: The poor boy looks so miserable every time he comes.

ROSALIND: That was one of those romantic, pre-battle affairs. They're all wrong.

MRS. CONNAGE: (*Her say said*) At any rate, make us proud of you tonight.

ROSALIND: Don't you think I'm beautiful?

MRS. CONNAGE: You know you are.

(*From down-stairs is heard the moan of a violin being tuned, the roll of a drum. MRS. CONNAGE turns quickly to her daughter.*)

MRS. CONNAGE: Come!

ROSALIND: One minute!

(*Her mother leaves. ROSALIND goes to the glass where she gazes at herself with great satisfaction. She kisses her hand and touches her mirrored mouth with it. Then she turns out the lights and leaves the room. Silence for a moment. A few chords from the piano, the discreet patter of faint drums, the rustle of new silk, all blend on the staircase outside and drift in through the partly opened door. Bundled figures pass in the lighted hall. The laughter heard below becomes doubled and multiplied. Then some one comes in, closes the door, and switches on the lights. It is CECELIA. She goes to the chiffonier, looks in the drawers, hesitates— then to the desk whence she takes the cigarette-case and extracts one. She lights it and then, puffing and blowing, walks toward the mirror.*)

CECELIA: (*In tremendously sophisticated accents*) Oh, yes, coming out is *such* a farce nowadays, you know. One really plays around so much before one is seventeen, that it's positively anticlimax. (*Shaking hands with a visionary middle-aged nobleman.*) Yes, your grace—I b'lieve I've heard my sister speak of you. Have a puff—they're very good. They're—they're Coronas. You don't smoke? What a pity! The king doesn't allow it, I suppose. Yes, I'll dance.

(So she dances around the room to a tune from down-stairs, her arms outstretched to an imaginary partner, the cigarette waving in her hand.)

SEVERAL HOURS LATER

The corner of a den down-stairs, filled by a very comfortable leather lounge. A small light is on each side above, and in the middle, over the couch hangs a painting of a very old, very dignified gentleman, period 1860. Outside the music is heard in a fox-trot.

ROSALIND *is seated on the lounge and on her left is* HOWARD GILLESPIE, *a vapid youth of about twenty-four. He is obviously very unhappy, and she is quite bored.*

GILLESPIE: *(Feebly)* What do you mean I've changed. I feel the same toward you.

ROSALIND: But you don't look the same to me.

GILLESPIE: Three weeks ago you used to say that you liked me because I was so blasé, so indifferent—I still am.

ROSALIND: But not about me. I used to like you because you had brown eyes and thin legs.

GILLESPIE: *(Helplessly)* They're still thin and brown. You're a vampire, that's all.

ROSALIND: The only thing I know about vamping is what's on the piano score. What confuses men is that I'm perfectly natural. I used to think you were never jealous. Now you follow me with your eyes wherever I go.

GILLESPIE: I love you.

ROSALIND: *(Coldly)* I know it.

GILLESPIE: And you haven't kissed me for two weeks. I had an idea that after a girl was kissed she was—was—won.

ROSALIND: Those days are over. I have to be won all over again every time you see me.

GILLESPIE: Are you serious?

ROSALIND: About as usual. There used to be two kinds of kisses: First when girls were kissed and deserted; second, when they were engaged. Now there's a third kind, where the man is kissed and deserted. If Mr. Jones of the nineties bragged he'd kissed a girl, every one knew he was through with her. If Mr. Jones of 1919 brags the same every one knows it's because he can't kiss her any more. Given a decent start any girl can beat a man nowadays.

GILLESPIE: Then why do you play with men?

ROSALIND: *(Leaning forward confidentially)* For that first moment, when he's interested. There is a moment—Oh, just before the first kiss, a whispered word—something that makes it worth while.

GILLESPIE: And then?

ROSALIND: Then after that you make him talk about himself. Pretty soon he thinks of nothing but being alone with you—he sulks, he won't fight, he doesn't want to play— Victory!

(Enter DAWSON RYDER, twenty-six, handsome, wealthy, faithful to his own, a bore perhaps, but steady and sure of success.)

RYDER: I believe this is my dance, Rosalind.

ROSALIND: Well, Dawson, so you recognize me. Now I know I haven't got too much paint on. Mr. Ryder, this is Mr. Gillespie.

(They shake hands and GILLESPIE leaves, tremendously downcast.)

RYDER: Your party is certainly a success.

ROSALIND: Is it— I haven't seen it lately. I'm weary— Do you mind sitting out a minute?

RYDER: Mind—I'm delighted. You know I loathe this "rushing" idea. See a girl yesterday, today, tomorrow.

ROSALIND: Dawson!

RYDER: What?

ROSALIND: I wonder if you know you love me.

RYDER: *(Startled)* What— Oh—you know you're remarkable!

ROSALIND: Because you know I'm an awful proposition. Any one who marries me will have his hands full. I'm mean—mighty mean.

RYDER: Oh, I wouldn't say that.

ROSALIND: Oh, yes, I am—especially to the people nearest to me. *(She rises.)* Come, let's go. I've changed my mind and I want to dance. Mother is probably having a fit.

(Exeunt. Enter ALEC and CECELIA.)

CECELIA: Just my luck to get my own brother for an intermission.

ALEC: *(Gloomily)* I'll go if you want me to.

CECELIA: Good heavens, no—with whom would I begin the next dance? *(Sighs.)* There's no color in a dance since the French officers went back.

ALEC: *(Thoughtfully)* I don't want Amory to fall in love with Rosalind.

CECELIA: Why, I had an idea that that was just what you did want.

ALEC: I did, but since seeing these girls—I don't know. I'm awfully attached to Amory. He's sensitive and I don't want him to break his heart over somebody who doesn't care about him.

CECELIA: He's very good looking.

ALEC: *(Still thoughtfully)* She won't marry him, but a girl doesn't have to marry a man to break his heart.

CECELIA: What does it? I wish I knew the secret.

ALEC: Why, you cold-blooded little kitty. It's lucky for some that the Lord gave you a pug nose.

(Enter MRS. CONNAGE.)

MRS. CONNAGE: Where on earth is Rosalind?

ALEC: *(Brilliantly)* Of course you've come to the best people to find out. She'd naturally be with us.

MRS. CONNAGE: Her father has marshalled eight bachelor millionaires to meet her.

ALEC: You might form a squad and march through the halls.

MRS. CONNAGE: I'm perfectly serious—for all I know she may be at the Cocoanut Grove with some football player on the night of her début. You look left and I'll——

ALEC: *(Flippantly)* Hadn't you better send the butler through the cellar?

MRS. CONNAGE: *(Perfectly serious)* Oh, you don't think she'd be there?

CECELIA: He's only joking, mother.

ALEC: Mother had a picture of her tapping a keg of beer with some high hurdler.

MRS. CONNAGE: Let's look right away.

(They go out. ROSALIND comes in with GILLESPIE.)

GILLESPIE: Rosalind— Once more I ask you. Don't you care a blessed thing about me?

(AMORY walks in briskly.)

AMORY: My dance.

ROSALIND: Mr. Gillespie, this is Mr. Blaine.

GILLESPIE: I've met Mr. Blaine. From Lake Geneva, aren't you?

AMORY: Yes.

GILLESPIE: *(Desperately)* I've been there. It's in the—the Middle West, isn't it?

AMORY: *(Spicily)* Approximately. But I always felt that I'd rather be provincial hot-tamale than soup without seasoning.

GILLESPIE: What!

AMORY: Oh, no offense.

(GILLESPIE bows and leaves.)

ROSALIND: He's too much *people.*

AMORY: I was in love with a *people* once.

ROSALIND: So?

AMORY: Oh, yes—her name was Isabelle—nothing at all to her except what I read into her.

ROSALIND: What happened?

AMORY: Finally I convinced her that she was smarter than I was—then she threw me over. Said I was critical and impractical, you know.

ROSALIND: What do you mean impractical?

AMORY: Oh—drive a car, but can't change a tire.

ROSALIND: What are you going to do?

AMORY: Can't say—run for President, write——

ROSALIND: Greenwich Village?

AMORY: Good heavens, no—I said write—not drink.

ROSALIND: I like business men. Clever men are usually so homely.

AMORY: I feel as if I'd known you for ages.

ROSALIND: Oh, are you going to commence the "pyramid" story?

AMORY: No—I was going to make it French. I was Louis XIV and you were one of my—my— *(Changing his tone.)* Suppose—we fell in love.

ROSALIND: I've suggested pretending.

AMORY: If we did it would be very big.

ROSALIND: Why?

AMORY: Because selfish people are in a way terribly capable of great loves.

ROSALIND: *(Turning her lips up)* Pretend.

(Very deliberately they kiss.)

AMORY: I can't say sweet things. But you *are* beautiful.

ROSALIND: Not that.

AMORY: What then?

ROSALIND: *(Sadly)* Oh, nothing—only I want sentiment, real sentiment—and I never find it.

AMORY: I never find anything else in the world—and I loathe it.

ROSALIND: It's so hard to find a male to gratify one's artistic taste.

(Some one has opened a door and the music of a waltz surges into the room. ROSALIND rises.)

ROSALIND: Listen! they're playing "Kiss Me Again."

(He looks at her.)

AMORY: Well?

ROSALIND: Well?

AMORY: *(Softly—the battle lost)* I love you.

ROSALIND: I love you—now.

(They kiss.)

AMORY: Oh, God, what have I done?

ROSALIND: Nothing. Oh, don't talk. Kiss me again.

AMORY: I don't know why or how, but I love you—from the moment I saw you.

ROSALIND: Me too—I—I—oh, tonight's tonight.

(Her brother strolls in, starts and then in a loud voice says: "Oh, excuse me," and goes.)

ROSALIND: *(Her lips scarcely stirring)* Don't let me go—I don't care who knows what I do.

AMORY: Say it!

ROSALIND: I love you—now. *(They part.)* Oh—I am very youthful, thank God—and rather beautiful, thank God—and happy, thank God, thank God—*(She pauses and then, in an odd burst of prophecy, adds)* Poor Amory!

(He kisses her again.)

KISMET

Within two weeks Amory and Rosalind were deeply and passionately in love. The critical qualities which had spoiled for each of them a dozen romances were dulled by the great wave of emotion that washed over them.

"It may be an insane love-affair," she told her anxious mother, "but it's not inane."

The wave swept Amory into an advertising agency early in March, where he alternated between astonishing bursts of rather exceptional work and wild dreams of becoming suddenly rich and touring Italy with Rosalind.

They were together constantly, for lunch, for dinner, and nearly every evening—always in a sort of breathless hush, as if they feared that any minute the spell would break and drop them out of this paradise of rose and flame. But the spell became a trance, seemed to increase from day to day; they began to talk of marrying in July—in June. All life was transmitted into terms of their love, all experience, all desires, all ambitions, were nullified—their senses of humor crawled into corners to sleep; their former love-affairs seemed faintly laughable and scarcely regretted juvenilia.

For the second time in his life Amory had had a complete bouleversement and was hurrying into line with his generation.

A LITTLE INTERLUDE

Amory wandered slowly up the avenue and thought of the night as inevitably his—the pageantry and carnival of rich dusk and dim streets . . . it seemed that he had closed the book of fading harmonies at last and stepped into the sensuous vibrant walks of life. Everywhere these countless lights, this promise of a night of streets and singing—he moved in a half-dream through the crowd as if expecting to meet Rosalind hurrying toward him with eager feet from every corner. . . . How the unforgettable faces of dusk would blend to hers, the myriad footsteps, a thousand overtures, would blend to her footsteps; and there would be more drunkenness than wine in the softness of her eyes on his. Even his dreams now were faint violins drifting like summer sounds upon the summer air.

The room was in darkness except for the faint glow of Tom's cigarette where he lounged by the open window. As the door shut behind him, Amory stood a moment with his back against it.

"Hello, Benvenuto Blaine. How went the advertising business to-day?"

Amory sprawled on a couch.

"I loathed it as usual!" The momentary vision of the bustling agency was displaced quickly by another picture.

"My God! She's wonderful!"

Tom sighed.

"I can't tell you," repeated Amory, "just how wonderful she is. I don't want you to know. I don't want any one to know."

Another sigh came from the window—quite a resigned sigh.

"She's life and hope and happiness, my whole world now."

He felt the quiver of a tear on his eyelid.

"Oh, *golly*, Tom!"

BITTER SWEET

"Sit like we do," she whispered.

He sat in the big chair and held out his arms so that she could nestle inside them.

"I knew you'd come tonight," she said softly, "like summer, just when I needed you most . . . darling . . . darling . . ."

His lips moved lazily over her face.

"You *taste* so good," he sighed.

"How do you mean, lover?"

"Oh, just sweet, just sweet . . ." he held her closer.

"Amory," she whispered, "when you're ready for me I'll marry you."

"We won't have much at first."

"Don't!" she cried. "It hurts when you reproach yourself for what you can't give me. I've got your precious self—and that's enough for me."

"Tell me . . ."

"You know, don't you? Oh, you know."

"Yes, but I want to hear you say it."

"I love you, Amory, with all my heart."

"Always, will you?"

"All my life— Oh, Amory——"

"What?"

"I want to belong to you. I want your people to be my people. I want to have your babies."

"But I haven't any people."

"Don't laugh at me, Amory. Just kiss me."

"I'll do what you want," he said.

"No, I'll do what *you* want. We're *you*—not me. Oh, you're so much a part, so much all of me . . ."

He closed his eyes.

"I'm so happy that I'm frightened. Wouldn't it be awful if this was—was the high point? . . ."

She looked at him dreamily.

"Beauty and love pass, I know. . . . Oh, there's sadness, too. I suppose all great happiness is a little sad. Beauty means the scent of roses and then the death of roses——"

"Beauty means the agony of sacrifice and the end of agony. . . ."

"And, Amory, we're beautiful, I know. I'm sure God loves us——"

"He loves you. You're his most precious possession."

"I'm not his, I'm yours. Amory, I belong to you. For the first time I regret all the other kisses; now I know how much a kiss can mean."

Then they would smoke and he would tell her about his day at the office—and where they might live. Sometimes, when he was particularly loquacious, she went to sleep in his arms, but he loved that Rosalind—all Rosalinds—as he had never in the world loved any one else. Intangibly fleeting, unrememberable hours.

AQUATIC INCIDENT

One day Amory and Howard Gillespie meeting by accident downtown took lunch together, and Amory heard a story that delighted him. Gillespie after several cocktails was in a talkative mood; he began by telling Amory that he was sure Rosalind was slightly eccentric.

He had gone with her on a swimming party up in Westchester County, and some one mentioned that Annette Kellerman had been there one day on a visit and had dived from the top of a rickety, thirty-foot summer-house. Immediately Rosalind insisted that Howard should climb up with her to see what it looked like.

A minute later, as he sat and dangled his feet on the edge, a form shot by him; Rosalind, her arms spread in a beautiful swan dive, had sailed through the air into the clear water.

"Of course *I* had to go, after that—and I nearly killed myself. I thought I was pretty good to even try it. Nobody else in the party tried it. Well, afterward Rosalind had the nerve to ask me why I stooped over when I dove. 'It didn't make it any easier,' she said, 'it just took all the courage out of it.' I ask you, what can a man do with a girl like that? Unnecessary, I call it."

Gillespie failed to understand why Amory was smiling delightedly all through lunch. He thought perhaps he was one of these hollow optimists.

FIVE WEEKS LATER

Again the library of the Connage house. ROSALIND *is alone, sitting on the lounge staring very moodily and unhappily at nothing. She has changed perceptibly—she is a trifle thinner for one thing; the light in her eyes is not so bright; she looks easily a year older.*

Her mother comes in, muffled in an opera-cloak. She takes in ROSALIND *with a nervous glance.*

MRS. CONNAGE: Who is coming tonight?

(ROSALIND *fails to hear her, at least takes no notice.*)

MRS. CONNAGE: Alec is coming up to take me to this Barrie play, "Et tu, Brutus." (*She perceives that she is talking to herself.*) Rosalind! I asked you who is coming tonight?

ROSALIND: (*Starting*) Oh—what—oh—Amory——

MRS. CONNAGE: (*Sarcastically*) You have so *many* admirers lately that I couldn't imagine *which* one. (ROSALIND *doesn't answer.*) Dawson Ryder is more patient than I thought he'd be. You haven't given him an evening this week.

ROSALIND: (*With a very weary expression that is quite new to her face.*) Mother—please——

MRS. CONNAGE: Oh, *I* won't interfere. You've already wasted over two months on a theoretical genius who hasn't a penny to his name, but *go* ahead, waste your life on him. *I* won't interfere.

ROSALIND: (*As if repeating a tiresome lesson*) You know he has a little income—and you know he's earning thirty-five dollars a week in advertising——

MRS. CONNAGE: And it wouldn't buy your clothes. (*She pauses but* ROSALIND *makes no reply.*) I have your best interests at heart when I tell you not to take a step you'll spend your days regretting. It's not as if your father could help you. Things have been hard for him lately and he's an old man. You'd be dependent absolutely on a dreamer, a nice, well-born boy, but a dreamer—merely *clever. (She implies that this quality in itself is rather vicious.)*

ROSALIND: For heaven's sake, mother— —

(A maid appears, announces Mr. Blaine who follows immediately. AMORY's friends have been telling him for ten days that he "looks like the wrath of God," and he does. As a matter of fact he has not been able to eat a mouthful in the last thirty-six hours.)

AMORY: Good evening, Mrs. Connage.

MRS. CONNAGE: *(Not unkindly)* Good evening, Amory.

(AMORY and ROSALIND exchange glances—and ALEC comes in. ALEC's attitude throughout has been neutral. He believes in his heart that the marriage would make AMORY mediocre and ROSALIND miserable, but he feels a great sympathy for both of them.)

ALEC: Hi, Amory!

AMORY: Hi, Alec! Tom said he'd meet you at the theatre.

ALEC: Yeah, just saw him. How's the advertising to-day? Write some brilliant copy?

AMORY: Oh, it's about the same. I got a raise—*(Every one looks at him rather eagerly)*—of two dollars a week. *(General collapse.)*

MRS. CONNAGE: Come, Alec, I hear the car.

(A good night, rather chilly in sections. After MRS. CONNAGE and ALEC go out there is a pause. ROSALIND still stares moodily at the fireplace. AMORY goes to her and puts his arm around her.)

AMORY: Darling girl.

(They kiss. Another pause and then she seizes his hand, covers it with kisses and holds it to her breast.)

ROSALIND: *(Sadly)* I love your hands, more than anything. I see them often when you're away from me—so tired; I know every line of them. Dear hands!

(Their eyes meet for a second and then she begins to cry—a tearless sobbing.)

AMORY: Rosalind!

ROSALIND: Oh, we're so darned pitiful!

AMORY: Rosalind!

ROSALIND: Oh, I want to die!

AMORY: Rosalind, another night of this and I'll go to pieces. You've been this way four days now. You've got to be more encouraging or I can't work or eat or sleep. *(He looks around helplessly as if searching for new words to clothe an old, shopworn phrase.)* We'll have to make a start. I *like* having to make a start together. *(His forced hopefulness fades as he sees her unresponsive.)* What's the matter? *(He gets up suddenly and starts to pace the floor.)* It's Dawson Ryder, that's what it is. He's been working on your nerves. You've been with him every afternoon for a week. People come and tell me they've seen you together, and I have to smile and nod and pretend it hasn't the slightest significance for me. And you won't tell me anything as it develops.

ROSALIND: Amory, if you don't sit down I'll scream.

AMORY: *(Sitting down suddenly beside her)* Oh, Lord.

ROSALIND: *(Taking his hand gently)* You know I love you, don't you?

AMORY: Yes.

ROSALIND: You know I'll always love you — —

AMORY: Don't talk that way; you frighten me. It sounds as if we weren't going to have each other. *(She cries a little and rising from the couch goes to the armchair.)* I've felt all afternoon that things were worse. I nearly went wild down at the office — couldn't write a line. Tell me everything.

ROSALIND: There's nothing to tell, I say. I'm just nervous.

AMORY: Rosalind, you're playing with the idea of marrying Dawson Ryder.

ROSALIND: *(After a pause)* He's been asking me to all day.

AMORY: Well, he's got his nerve!

ROSALIND: *(After another pause)* I like him.

AMORY: Don't say that. It hurts me.

ROSALIND: Don't be a silly idiot. You know you're the only man I've ever loved, ever will love.

AMORY: *(Quickly)* Rosalind, let's get married — next week.

ROSALIND: We can't.

AMORY: Why not?

ROSALIND: Oh, we can't. I'd be your squaw — in some horrible place.

AMORY: We'll have two hundred and seventy-five dollars a month all told.

ROSALIND: Darling, I don't even do my own hair, usually.

AMORY: I'll do it for you.

ROSALIND: *(Between a laugh and a sob)* Thanks.

AMORY: Rosalind, you *can't* be thinking of marrying some one else. Tell me! You leave me in the dark. I can help you fight it out if you'll only tell me.

ROSALIND: It's just — us. We're pitiful, that's all. The very qualities I love you for are the ones that will always make you a failure.

AMORY: *(Grimly)* Go on.

ROSALIND: Oh — it *is* Dawson Ryder. He's so reliable, I almost feel that he'd be a — a background.

AMORY: You don't love him.

ROSALIND: I know, but I respect him, and he's a good man and a strong one.

AMORY: *(Grudgingly)* Yes—he's that.

ROSALIND: Well—here's one little thing. There was a little poor boy we met in Rye Tuesday afternoon—and, oh, Dawson took him on his lap and talked to him and promised him an Indian suit—and next day he remembered and bought it—and, oh, it was so sweet and I couldn't help thinking he'd be so nice to—to our children—take care of them—and I wouldn't have to worry.

AMORY: *(In despair)* Rosalind! Rosalind!

ROSALIND: *(With a faint roguishness)* Don't look so consciously suffering.

AMORY: What power we have of hurting each other!

ROSALIND: *(Commencing to sob again)* It's been so perfect—you and I. So like a dream that I'd longed for and never thought I'd find. The first real unselfishness I've ever felt in my life. And I can't see it fade out in a colorless atmosphere!

AMORY: It won't—it won't!

ROSALIND: I'd rather keep it as a beautiful memory—tucked away in my heart.

AMORY: Yes, women can do that—but not men. I'd remember always, not the beauty of it while it lasted, but just the bitterness, the long bitterness.

ROSALIND: Don't!

AMORY: All the years never to see you, never to kiss you, just a gate shut and barred—you don't dare be my wife.

ROSALIND: No—no—I'm taking the hardest course, the strongest course. Marrying you would be a failure and I never fail—if you don't stop walking up and down I'll scream!

(Again he sinks despairingly onto the lounge.)

AMORY: Come over here and kiss me.

ROSALIND: No.

AMORY: Don't you *want* to kiss me?

ROSALIND: Tonight I want you to love me calmly and coolly.

AMORY: The beginning of the end.

ROSALIND: *(With a burst of insight)* Amory, you're young. I'm young. People excuse us now for our poses and vanities, for treating people like Sancho and yet getting away with it. They excuse us now. But you've got a lot of knocks coming to you——

AMORY: And you're afraid to take them with me.

ROSALIND: No, not that. There was a poem I read somewhere—you'll say Ella Wheeler Wilcox and laugh—but listen:

For this is wisdom—to love and live,
To take what fate or the gods may give,
To ask no question, to make no prayer,
To kiss the lips and caress the hair,
Speed passion's ebb as we greet its flow,
To have and to hold, and, in time—let go.

AMORY: But we haven't had.

ROSALIND: Amory, I'm yours—you know it. There have been times in the last month I'd have been completely yours if you'd said so. But I can't marry you and ruin both our lives.

AMORY: We've got to take our chance for happiness.

ROSALIND: Dawson says I'd learn to love him.

(AMORY *with his head sunk in his hands does not move. The life seems suddenly gone out of him.*)

ROSALIND: Lover! Lover! I can't do with you, and I can't imagine life without you.

AMORY: Rosalind, we're on each other's nerves. It's just that we're both high-strung, and this week——

(*His voice is curiously old. She crosses to him and taking his face in her hands, kisses him.*)

ROSALIND: I can't, Amory. I can't be shut away from the trees and flowers, cooped up in a little flat, waiting for you. You'd hate me in a narrow atmosphere. I'd make you hate me.

(*Again she is blinded by sudden uncontrolled tears.*)

AMORY: Rosalind——

ROSALIND: Oh, darling, go— Don't make it harder! I can't stand it——

AMORY: (*His face drawn, his voice strained*) Do you know what you're saying? Do you mean forever?

(*There is a difference somehow in the quality of their suffering.*)

ROSALIND: Can't you see——

AMORY: I'm afraid I can't if you love me. You're afraid of taking two years' knocks with me.

ROSALIND: I wouldn't be the Rosalind you love.

AMORY: (*A little hysterically*) I can't give you up! I can't, that's all! I've got to have you!

ROSALIND: (*A hard note in her voice*) You're being a baby now.

AMORY: (*Wildly*) I don't care! You're spoiling our lives!

ROSALIND: I'm doing the wise thing, the only thing.

AMORY: Are you going to marry Dawson Ryder?

ROSALIND: Oh, don't ask me. You know I'm old in some ways—in others—well, I'm just a little girl. I like sunshine and pretty things and cheerfulness—and I dread responsibility. I don't want to think about pots and kitchens and brooms. I want to worry whether my legs will get slick and brown when I swim in the summer.

AMORY: And you love me.

ROSALIND: That's just why it has to end. Drifting hurts too much. We can't have any more scenes like this.

(She draws his ring from her finger and hands it to him. Their eyes blind again with tears.)

AMORY: *(His lips against her wet cheek)* Don't! Keep it, please—oh, don't break my heart!

(She presses the ring softly into his hand.)

ROSALIND: *(Brokenly)* You'd better go.

AMORY: Good-by— —

(She looks at him once more, with infinite longing, infinite sadness.)

ROSALIND: Don't ever forget me, Amory— —

AMORY: Good-by— —

(He goes to the door, fumbles for the knob, finds it—she sees him throw back his head—and he is gone. Gone—she half starts from the lounge and then sinks forward on her face into the pillows.)

ROSALIND: Oh, God, I want to die! *(After a moment she rises and with her eyes closed feels her way to the door. Then she turns and looks once more at the room. Here they had sat and dreamed: that tray she had so often filled with matches for him; that shade that they had discreetly lowered one long Sunday afternoon. Misty-eyed she stands and remembers; she speaks aloud.)* Oh, Amory, what have I done to you?

(And deep under the aching sadness that will pass in time, Rosalind feels that she has lost something, she knows not what, she knows not why.)

Two

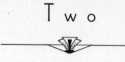

Experiments

in Convalescence

THE KNICKERBOCKER BAR, BEAMED UPON BY
Maxfield Parrish's jovial, colorful "Old King Cole," was well
crowded. Amory stopped in the entrance and looked at his wrist-
watch; he wanted particularly to know the time, for something in his
mind that catalogued and classified liked to chip things off cleanly.
Later it would satisfy him in a vague way to be able to think "that
thing ended at exactly twenty minutes after eight on Thursday, June
10, 1919." This was allowing for the walk from her house—a walk
concerning which he had afterward not the faintest recollection.

He was in rather grotesque condition: two days of worry and nervousness, of sleepless nights, of untouched meals, culminating in the
emotional crisis and Rosalind's abrupt decision—the strain of it had
drugged the foreground of his mind into a merciful coma. As he fum-

bled clumsily with the olives at the free-lunch table, a man approached and spoke to him, and the olives dropped from his nervous hands.

"Well, Amory . . ."

It was some one he had known at Princeton; he had no idea of the name.

"Hello, old boy—" he heard himself saying.

"Name's Jim Wilson—you've forgotten."

"Sure, you bet, Jim. I remember."

"Going to reunion?"

"You know!" Simultaneously he realized that he was not going to reunion.

"Get overseas?"

Amory nodded, his eyes staring oddly. Stepping back to let some one pass, he knocked the dish of olives to a crash on the floor.

"Too bad," he muttered. "Have a drink?"

Wilson, ponderously diplomatic, reached over and slapped him on the back.

"You've had plenty, old boy."

Amory eyed him dumbly until Wilson grew embarrassed under the scrutiny.

"Plenty, hell!" said Amory finally. "I haven't had a drink to-day."

Wilson looked incredulous.

"Have a drink or not?" cried Amory rudely.

Together they sought the bar.

"Rye high."

"I'll just take a Bronx."

Wilson had another; Amory had several more. They decided to sit down. At ten o'clock Wilson was displaced by Carling, class of '15. Amory, his head spinning gorgeously, layer upon layer of soft satisfaction setting over the bruised spots of his spirit, was discoursing volubly on the war.

"'S a mental was'e," he insisted with owl-like wisdom. "Two years my life spent inalleshual vacuity. Los' idealism, got be physcal anmal," he shook his fist expressively at Old King Cole, "got be Prussian 'bout ev'thing, women 'specially. Use' be straight 'bout women college. Now don' givadam." He expressed his lack of principle by sweeping a seltzer bottle with a broad gesture to noisy extinction on the floor, but this did not interrupt his speech. "Seek pleasure where find it for tomorrow die. 'At's philos'phy for me now on."

Carling yawned, but Amory, waxing brilliant, continued:

"Use' wonder 'bout things—people satisfied compromise, fif'y-fif'y att'tude on life. Now don' wonder, don' wonder—" He became so emphatic in impressing on Carling the fact that he didn't wonder that he lost the thread of his discourse and concluded by announcing to the bar at large that he was a "physcal anmal."

"What are you celebrating, Amory?"

Amory leaned forward confidentially.

"Cel'brating blowmylife. Great moment blow my life. Can't tell you 'bout it— —"

He heard Carling addressing a remark to the bartender:

"Give him a bromo-seltzer."

Amory shook his head indignantly.

"None that stuff!"

"But listen, Amory, you're making yourself sick. You're white as a ghost."

Amory considered the question. He tried to look at himself in the mirror but even by squinting up one eye could only see as far as the row of bottles behind the bar.

"Like som'n solid. We go get some—some salad."

He settled his coat with an attempt at nonchalance, but letting go of the bar was too much for him, and he slumped against a chair.

"We'll go over to Shanley's," suggested Carling, offering an elbow.

With this assistance Amory managed to get his legs in motion enough to propel him across Forty-second Street.

Shanley's was very dim. He was conscious that he was talking in a loud voice, very succinctly and convincingly, he thought, about a desire to crush people under his heel. He consumed three club sandwiches, devouring each as though it were no larger than a chocolate-drop. Then Rosalind began popping into his mind again, and he found his lips forming her name over and over. Next he was sleepy, and he had a hazy, listless sense of people in dress suits, probably waiters, gathering around the table. . . .

. . . He was in a room and Carling was saying something about a knot in his shoe-lace.

"Nemmine," he managed to articulate drowsily. "Sleep in 'em. . . ."

STILL ALCOHOLIC

He awoke laughing and his eyes lazily roamed his surroundings, evidently a bedroom and bath in a good hotel. His head was whirring and picture after picture was forming and blurring and melting before his eyes, but beyond the desire to laugh he had no entirely conscious reaction. He reached for the 'phone beside his bed.

"Hello—what hotel is this—?

"Knickerbocker? All right, send up two rye high-balls——"

He lay for a moment and wondered idly whether they'd send up a bottle or just two of those little glass containers. Then, with an effort, he struggled out of bed and ambled into the bathroom.

When he emerged, rubbing himself lazily with a towel, he found the bar boy with the drinks and had a sudden desire to kid him. On reflection he decided that this would be undignified, so he waved him away.

As the new alcohol tumbled into his stomach and warmed him, the isolated pictures began slowly to form a cinema reel of the day before. Again he saw Rosalind curled weeping among the pillows, again he felt her tears against his cheek. Her words began ringing in his ears: "Don't ever forget me, Amory—don't ever forget me——"

"Hell!" he faltered aloud, and then he choked and collapsed on the bed in a shaken spasm of grief. After a minute he opened his eyes and regarded the ceiling.

"Damned fool!" he exclaimed in disgust, and with a voluminous sigh rose and approached the bottle. After another glass he gave way loosely to the luxury of tears. Purposely he called up into his mind little incidents of the vanished spring, phrased to himself emotions that would make him react even more strongly to sorrow.

"We were so happy," he intoned dramatically, "so very happy." Then he gave way again and knelt beside the bed, his head half-buried in the pillow.

"My own girl—my own—Oh——"

He clenched his teeth so that the tears streamed in a flood from his eyes.

"Oh . . . my baby girl, all I had, all I wanted! . . . Oh, my girl, come back, come back! I need you . . . need you . . . we're so pitiful . . . just misery we brought each other. . . . She'll be shut away from me. . . . I can't see her; I can't be her friend. It's got to be that way—it's got to be——"

And then again:

"We've been so happy, so very happy. . . ."

He rose to his feet and threw himself on the bed in an ecstasy of sentiment, and then lay exhausted while he realized slowly that he had been very drunk the night before, and that his head was spinning again wildly. He laughed, rose, and crossed again to Lethe. . . .

At noon he ran into a crowd in the Biltmore bar, and the riot began again. He had a vague recollection afterward of discussing French poetry with a British officer who was introduced to him as "Captain Corn, of his Majesty's Foot," and he remembered attempting to recite "Clair de Lune" at luncheon; then he slept in a big, soft chair until almost five o'clock when another crowd found and woke him; there followed an alcoholic dressing of several temperaments for the ordeal of dinner. They selected theatre tickets at Tyson's for a play that had a four-drink programme—a play with two monotonous voices, with turbid, gloomy scenes, and lighting effects that were hard to follow when his eyes behaved so amazingly. He imagined afterward that it must have been "The Jest.". . .

. . . Then the Cocoanut Grove, where Amory slept again on a little balcony outside. Out in Shanley's, Yonkers, he became almost logical, and by a careful control of the number of high-balls he drank, grew quite lucid and garrulous. He found that the party consisted of five men, two of whom he knew slightly; he became righteous about paying his share of the expense and insisted in a loud voice on arranging everything then and there to the amusement of the tables around him. . . .

Some one mentioned that a famous cabaret star was at the next table, so Amory rose and, approaching gallantly, introduced himself . . . this involved him in an argument, first with her escort and then with the head-waiter—Amory's attitude being a lofty and exaggerated courtesy . . . he consented, after being confronted with irrefutable logic, to being led back to his own table.

"Decided to commit suicide," he announced suddenly.

"When? Next year?"

"Now. Tomorrow morning. Going to take a room at the Commodore, get into a hot bath and open a vein."

"He's getting morbid!"

"You need another rye, old boy!"

"We'll all talk it over tomorrow."

But Amory was not to be dissuaded, from argument at least.

"Did you ever get that way?" he demanded confidentially fortaccio.

"Sure!"

"Often?"

"My chronic state."

This provoked discussion. One man said that he got so depressed sometimes that he seriously considered it. Another agreed that there was nothing to live for. "Captain Corn," who had somehow rejoined the party, said that in his opinion it was when one's health was bad that one felt that way most. Amory's suggestion was that they should each order a Bronx, mix broken glass in it, and drink it off. To his relief no one applauded the idea, so having finished his high-ball, he balanced his chin in his hand and his elbow on the table—a most delicate, scarcely noticeable sleeping position, he assured himself—and went into a deep stupor. . . .

He was awakened by a woman clinging to him, a pretty woman, with brown, disarranged hair and dark blue eyes.

"Take me home!" she cried.

"Hello!" said Amory, blinking.

"I like you," she announced tenderly.

"I like you too."

He noticed that there was a noisy man in the background and that one of his party was arguing with him.

"Fella I was with's a damn fool," confided the blue-eyed woman. "I hate him. I want to go home with you."

"You drunk?" queried Amory with intense wisdom.

She nodded coyly.

"Go home with him," he advised gravely. "He brought you."

At this point the noisy man in the background broke away from his detainers and approached.

"Say!" he said fiercely. "I brought this girl out here and you're butting in!"

Amory regarded him coldly, while the girl clung to him closer.

"You let go that girl!" cried the noisy man.

Amory tried to make his eyes threatening.

"You go to hell!" he directed finally, and turned his attention to the girl.

"Love first sight," he suggested.

"I love you," she breathed and nestled close to him. She *did* have beautiful eyes.

Some one leaned over and spoke in Amory's ear.

"That's just Margaret Diamond. She's drunk and this fellow here brought her. Better let her go."

"Let him take care of her, then!" shouted Amory furiously. "I'm no W. Y. C. A. worker, am I? —am I?"

"Let her go!"

"It's *her* hanging on, damn it! Let her hang!"

The crowd around the table thickened. For an instant a brawl threatened, but a sleek waiter bent back Margaret Diamond's fingers until she released her hold on Amory, whereupon she slapped the waiter furiously in the face and flung her arms about her raging original escort.

"Oh, Lord!" cried Amory.

"Let's go!"

"Come on, the taxis are getting scarce!"

"Check, waiter."

"C'mon, Amory. Your romance is over."

Amory laughed.

"You don't know how true you spoke. No idea. 'At's the whole trouble."

AMORY ON THE LABOR QUESTION

Two mornings later he knocked at the president's door at Bascome and Barlow's advertising agency.

"Come in!"

Amory entered unsteadily.

"'Morning, Mr. Barlow."

Mr. Barlow brought his glasses to the inspection and set his mouth slightly ajar that he might better listen.

"Well, Mr. Blaine. We haven't seen you for several days."

"No," said Amory. "I'm quitting."

"Well—well—this is——"

"I don't like it here."

"I'm sorry. I thought our relations had been quite—ah—pleasant. You seemed to be a hard worker—a little inclined perhaps to write fancy copy——"

"I just got tired of it," interrupted Amory rudely. "It didn't matter a damn to me whether Harebell's flour was any better than any one else's. In fact, I never ate any of it. So I got tired of telling people about it—oh, I know I've been drinking——"

Mr. Barlow's face steeled by several ingots of expression.

"You asked for a position——"

Amory waved him to silence.

"And I think I was rottenly underpaid. Thirty-five dollars a week— less than a good carpenter."

"You had just started. You'd never worked before," said Mr. Barlow coolly.

"But it took about ten thousand dollars to educate me where I could write your darned stuff for you. Anyway, as far as length of service goes, you've got stenographers here you've paid fifteen a week for five years."

"I'm not going to argue with you, sir," said Mr. Barlow rising.

"Neither am I. I just wanted to tell you I'm quitting."

They stood for a moment looking at each other impassively and then Amory turned and left the office.

A LITTLE LULL

Four days after that he returned at last to the apartment. Tom was engaged on a book review for *The New Democracy* on the staff of which he was employed. They regarded each other for a moment in silence.

"Well?"

"Well?"

"Good Lord, Amory, where'd you get the black eye—and the jaw?"

Amory laughed.

"That's a mere nothing."

He peeled off his coat and bared his shoulders.

"Look here!"

Tom emitted a low whistle.

"What hit you?"

Amory laughed again.

"Oh, a lot of people. I got beaten up. Fact." He slowly replaced his shirt. "It was bound to come sooner or later and I wouldn't have missed it for anything."

"Who was it?"

"Well, there were some waiters and a couple of sailors and a few stray pedestrians, I guess. It's the strangest feeling. You ought to get beaten up just for the experience of it. You fall down after a while and everybody sort of slashes in at you before you hit the ground—then they kick you."

Tom lighted a cigarette.

"I spent a day chasing you all over town, Amory. But you always kept a little ahead of me. I'd say you've been on some party."

Amory tumbled into a chair and asked for a cigarette.

"You sober now?" asked Tom quizzically.

"Pretty sober. Why?"

"Well, Alec has left. His family had been after him to go home and live, so he——"

A spasm of pain shook Amory.

"Too bad."

"Yes, it is too bad. We'll have to get some one else if we're going to stay here. The rent's going up."

"Sure. Get anybody. I'll leave it to you, Tom."

Amory walked into his bedroom. The first thing that met his glance was a photograph of Rosalind that he had intended to have framed, propped up against a mirror on his dresser. He looked at it unmoved. After the vivid mental pictures of her that were his portion at present, the portrait was curiously unreal. He went back into the study.

"Got a cardboard box?"

"No," answered Tom, puzzled. "Why should I have? Oh, yes— there may be one in Alec's room."

Eventually Amory found what he was looking for and, returning to his dresser, opened a drawer full of letters, notes, part of a chain, two little handkerchiefs, and some snap-shots. As he transferred them carefully to the box his mind wandered to some place in a book where the hero, after preserving for a year a cake of his lost love's soap, finally washed his hands with it. He laughed and began to hum "After you've gone" . . . ceased abruptly . . .

The string broke twice, and then he managed to secure it, dropped the package into the bottom of his trunk, and having slammed the lid returned to the study.

"Going out?" Tom's voice held an undertone of anxiety.

"Uh-huh."

"Where?"

"Couldn't say, old keed."

"Let's have dinner together."

"Sorry. I told Sukey Brett I'd eat with him."

"Oh."

"By-by."

Amory crossed the street and had a high-ball; then he walked to Washington Square and found a top seat on a bus. He disembarked at Forty-third Street and strolled to the Biltmore bar.

"Hi, Amory!"

"What'll you have?"

"Yoho! Waiter!"

TEMPERATURE NORMAL

The advent of prohibition with the "thirsty-first" put a sudden stop to the submerging of Amory's sorrows, and when he awoke one morning to find that the old bar-to-bar days were over, he had neither remorse for the past three weeks nor regret that their repetition was impossible. He had taken the most violent, if the weakest, method to shield himself from the stabs of memory, and while it was not a course he would have prescribed for others, he found in the end that it had done its business: he was over the first flush of pain.

Don't misunderstand! Amory had loved Rosalind as he would

never love another living person. She had taken the first flush of his youth and brought from his unplumbed depths tenderness that had surprised him, gentleness and unselfishness that he had never given to another creature. He had later love-affairs, but of a different sort: in those he went back to that, perhaps, more typical frame of mind, in which the girl became the mirror of a mood in him. Rosalind had drawn out what was more than passionate admiration; he had a deep, undying affection for Rosalind.

But there had been, near the end, so much dramatic tragedy, culminating in the arabesque nightmare of his three weeks' spree, that he was emotionally worn out. The people and surroundings that he remembered as being cool or delicately artificial seemed to promise him a refuge. He wrote a cynical story which featured his father's funeral and despatched it to a magazine, receiving in return a check for sixty dollars and a request for more of the same tone. This tickled his vanity, but inspired him to no further effort.

He read enormously. He was puzzled and depressed by "A Portrait of the Artist as a Young Man"; intensely interested by "Joan and Peter" and "The Undying Fire," and rather surprised by his discovery through a critic named Mencken of several excellent American novels: "Vandover and the Brute," "The Damnation of Theron Ware," and "Jennie Gerhardt." Mackenzie, Chesterton, Galsworthy, Bennett had sunk in his appreciation from sagacious, life-saturated geniuses to merely diverting contemporaries. Shaw's aloof clarity and brilliant consistency and the gloriously intoxicated efforts of H. G. Wells to fit the key of romantic symmetry into the elusive lock of truth alone won his rapt attention.

He wanted to see Monsignor Darcy, to whom he had written when he landed, but he had not heard from him; besides he knew that a visit to Monsignor would entail the story of Rosalind, and the thought of repeating it turned him cold with horror.

In his search for cool people he remembered Mrs. Lawrence, a very intelligent, very dignified lady, a convert to the church, and a great devotee of Monsignor's.

He called her on the 'phone one day. Yes, she remembered him perfectly; no, Monsignor wasn't in town, was in Boston she thought; he'd promised to come to dinner when he returned. Couldn't Amory take luncheon with her?

"I thought I'd better catch up, Mrs. Lawrence," he said rather ambiguously when he arrived.

"Monsignor was here just last week," said Mrs. Lawrence regretfully. "He was very anxious to see you, but he'd left your address at home."

"Did he think I'd plunged into Bolshevism?" asked Amory, interested.

"Oh, he's having a frightful time."

"Why?"

"About the Irish Republic. He thinks it lacks dignity."

"So?"

"He went to Boston when the Irish President arrived and he was greatly distressed because the receiving committee, when they rode in an automobile, *would* put their arms around the President."

"I don't blame him."

"Well, what impressed you more than anything while you were in the army? You look a great deal older."

"That's from another, more disastrous battle," he answered, smiling in spite of himself. "But the army—let me see—well, I discovered that physical courage depends to a great extent on the physical shape a man is in. I found that I was as brave as the next man—it used to worry me before."

"What else?"

"Well, the idea that men can stand anything if they get used to it, and the fact that I got a high mark in the psychological examination."

Mrs. Lawrence laughed. Amory was finding it a great relief to be in this cool house on Riverside Drive, away from more condensed New York and the sense of people expelling great quantities of breath into a little space. Mrs. Lawrence reminded him vaguely of Beatrice, not in temperament, but in her perfect grace and dignity. The house, its furnishings, the manner in which dinner was served, were in immense contrast to what he had met in the great places on Long Island, where the servants were so obtrusive that they had positively to be bumped out of the way, or even in the houses of more conservative "Union Club" families. He wondered if this air of symmetrical restraint, this grace, which he felt was continental, was distilled through Mrs. Lawrence's New England ancestry or acquired in long residence in Italy and Spain.

Two glasses of sauterne at luncheon loosened his tongue, and he talked, with what he felt was something of his old charm, of religion and literature and the menacing phenomena of the social order. Mrs. Lawrence was ostensibly pleased with him, and her interest was especially in his mind; he wanted people to like his mind again—after a while it might be such a nice place in which to live.

"Monsignor Darcy still thinks that you're his reincarnation, that your faith will eventually clarify."

"Perhaps," he assented. "I'm rather pagan at present. It's just that religion doesn't seem to have the slightest bearing on life at my age."

When he left her house he walked down Riverside Drive with a feeling of satisfaction. It was amusing to discuss again such subjects as this young poet, Stephen Vincent Benét, or the Irish Republic. Between the rancid accusations of Edward Carson and Justice Cohalan he had completely tired of the Irish question; yet there had been a time when his own Celtic traits were pillars of his personal philosophy.

There seemed suddenly to be much left in life, if only this revival of old interests did not mean that he was backing away from it again — backing away from life itself.

RESTLESSNESS

"I'm très old and très bored, Tom," said Amory one day, stretching himself at ease in the comfortable window-seat. He always felt most natural in a recumbent position.

"You used to be entertaining before you started to write," he continued. "Now you save any idea that you think would do to print."

Existence had settled back to an ambitionless normality. They had decided that with economy they could still afford the apartment, which Tom, with the domesticity of an elderly cat, had grown fond of. The old English hunting prints on the wall were Tom's, and the large tapestry by courtesy, a relic of decadent days in college, and the great profusion of orphaned candlesticks and the carved Louis XV chair in which no one could sit more than a minute without acute spinal disorders — Tom claimed that this was because one was sitting in the lap of Montespan's wraith — at any rate, it was Tom's furniture that decided them to stay.

They went out very little: to an occasional play, or to dinner at the Ritz or the Princeton Club. With prohibition the great rendezvous had received their death wounds; no longer could one wander to the Biltmore bar at twelve or five and find congenial spirits, and both Tom and Amory had outgrown the passion for dancing with mid-Western or New Jersey debbies at the Club-de-Vingt (nick-named the "Club de Gink") or the Plaza Rose Room — besides even that required several cocktails "to come down to the intellectual level of the women present," as Amory had once put it to a horrified matron.

Amory had lately received several alarming letters from Mr. Barton — the Lake Geneva house was too large to be easily rented; the best rent obtainable at present would serve this year to little more than pay for the taxes and necessary improvements; in fact, the lawyer suggested that the whole property was simply a white elephant on Amory's hands. Nevertheless, even though it might not yield a cent for the next three years, Amory decided with a vague sentimentality that for the present, at any rate, he would not sell the house.

This particular day on which he announced his ennui to Tom had been quite typical. He had risen at noon, lunched with Mrs. Lawrence, and then ridden abstractedly homeward atop one of his beloved buses.

"Why shouldn't you be bored," yawned Tom. "Isn't that the conventional frame of mind for the young man of your age and condition?"

"Yes," said Amory speculatively, "but I'm more than bored; I'm restless."

"Love and war did for you."

"Well," Amory considered, "I'm not sure that the war itself had any great effect on either you or me—but it certainly ruined the old backgrounds, sort of killed individualism out of our generation."

Tom looked up in surprise.

"Yes it did," insisted Amory. "I'm not sure it didn't kill it out of the whole world. Oh, Lord, what a pleasure it used to be to dream I might be a really great dictator or writer or religious or political leader—and now even a Leonardo da Vinci or Lorenzo de Medici couldn't be a real old-fashioned bolt in the world. Life is too huge and complex. The world is so overgrown that it can't lift its own fingers, and I was planning to be such an important finger——"

"I don't agree with you," Tom interrupted. "There never were men placed in such egotistic positions since—oh, since the French Revolution."

Amory disagreed violently.

"You're mistaking this period when every nut is an individualist for a period of individualism. Wilson has only been powerful when he has represented; he's had to compromise over and over again. Just as soon as Trotsky and Lenin take a definite, consistent stand they'll become two-minute figures like Kerensky. Even Foch hasn't half the significance of Stonewall Jackson. War used to be the most individualistic pursuit of man, and yet the popular heroes of the war had neither authority nor responsibility: Guynemer and Sergeant York. How could a schoolboy make a hero of Pershing? A big man has no time really to do anything but just sit and be big."

"Then you don't think there will be any more permanent world heroes?"

"Yes—in history—not in life. Carlyle would have difficulty getting material for a new chapter on 'The Hero as a Big Man.'"

"Go on. I'm a good listener to-day."

"People try so hard to believe in leaders now, pitifully hard. But we no sooner get a popular reformer or politican or soldier or writer or philosopher—a Roosevelt, a Tolstoi, a Wood, a Shaw, a Nietzsche, than the cross-currents of criticism wash him away. My Lord, no man can stand prominence these days. It's the surest path to obscurity. People get sick of hearing the same name over and over."

"Then you blame it on the press?"

"Absolutely. Look at you; you're on *The New Democracy*, considered the most brilliant weekly in the country, read by the men who do things and all that. What's your business? Why, to be as clever, as interesting, and as brilliantly cynical as possible about every man, doctrine, book, or policy that is assigned you to deal with. The more strong lights, the more spiritual scandal you can throw on the matter, the more money they pay you, the more the people buy the issue. You, Tom d'Invilliers, a blighted Shelley, changing, shifting, clever, unscrupulous, represent the critical consciousness of the race—Oh, don't protest, I know the stuff. I used to write book reviews in college; I considered it rare sport to refer to the latest honest, conscientious effort to propound a theory or a remedy as a 'welcome addition to our light summer reading.' Come on now, admit it."

Tom laughed, and Amory continued triumphantly.

"We *want* to believe. Young students try to believe in older authors, constituents try to believe in their Congressmen, countries try to believe in their statesmen, but they *can't*. Too many voices, too much scattered, illogical, ill-considered criticism. It's worse in the case of newspapers. Any rich, unprogressive old party with that particularly grasping, acquisitive form of mentality known as financial genius can own a paper that is the intellectual meat and drink of thousands of tired, hurried men, men too involved in the business of modern living to swallow anything but predigested food. For two cents the voter buys his politics, prejudices, and philosophy. A year later there is a new political ring or a change in the paper's ownership, consequence: more confusion, more contradiction, a sudden inrush of new ideas, their tempering, their distillation, the reaction against them— —"

He paused only to get his breath.

"And that is why I have sworn not to put pen to paper until my ideas either clarify or depart entirely; I have quite enough sins on my soul without putting dangerous, shallow epigrams into people's heads; I might cause a poor, inoffensive capitalist to have a vulgar liaison with a bomb, or get some innocent little Bolshevik tangled up with a machine-gun bullet— —"

Tom was growing restless under this lampooning of his connection with *The New Democracy*.

"What's all this got to do with your being bored?"

Amory considered that it had much to do with it.

"How'll I fit in?" he demanded. "What am I for? To propagate the race? According to the American novels we are led to believe that the 'healthy American boy' from nineteen to twenty-five is an entirely sexless animal. As a matter of fact, the healthier he is the less that's true. The only alternative to letting it get you is some violent interest. Well, the war is over; I believe too much in the responsibilities of authorship to write just now; and business, well, business speaks for itself. It has no connection with anything in the world that I've ever been interested in, except a slim, utilitarian connection with economics. What I'd see of it, lost in a clerkship, for the next and best ten years of my life would have the intellectual content of an industrial movie."

"Try fiction," suggested Tom.

"Trouble is I get distracted when I start to write stories—get afraid I'm doing it instead of living—get thinking maybe life is waiting for me in the Japanese gardens at the Ritz or at Atlantic City or on the lower East Side.

"Anyway," he continued, "I haven't the vital urge. I wanted to be a regular human being but the girl couldn't see it that way."

"You'll find another."

"God! Banish the thought. Why don't you tell me that 'if the girl had been worth having she'd have waited for you'? No, sir, the girl really worth having won't wait for anybody. If I thought there'd be another I'd lose my remaining faith in human nature. Maybe I'll play— but Rosalind was the only girl in the wide world that could have held me."

"Well," yawned Tom, "I've played confidant a good hour by the clock. Still, I'm glad to see you're beginning to have violent views again on something."

"I am," agreed Amory reluctantly. "Yet when I see a happy family it makes me sick at my stomach— —"

"Happy families try to make people feel that way," said Tom cynically.

TOM THE CENSOR

There were days when Amory listened. These were when Tom, wreathed in smoke, indulged in the slaughter of American literature. Words failed him.

"Fifty thousand dollars a year," he would cry. "My God! Look at them, look at them—Edna Ferber, Gouverneur Morris, Fannie Hurst, Mary Roberts Rinehart—not producing among 'em one story or novel that will last ten years. This man Cobb—I don't think he's either clever or amusing—and what's more, I don't think very many people do, except the editors. He's just groggy with advertising. And—oh Harold Bell Wright oh Zane Grey——"

"They try."

"No, they don't even try. Some of them *can* write, but they won't sit down and do one honest novel. Most of them *can't* write, I'll admit. I believe Rupert Hughes tries to give a real, comprehensive picture of American life, but his style and perspective are barbarous. Ernest Poole and Dorothy Canfield try but they're hindered by their absolute lack of any sense of humor; but at least they crowd their work instead of spreading it thin. Every author ought to write every book as if he were going to be beheaded the day he finished it."

"Is that *double entente?*"

"Don't slow me up! Now there's a few of 'em that seem to have some cultural background, some intelligence and a good deal of literary felicity but they just simply won't write honestly; they'd all claim there was no public for good stuff. Then why the devil is it that Wells, Conrad, Galsworthy, Shaw, Bennett, and the rest depend on America for over half their sales?"

"How does little Tommy like the poets?"

Tom was overcome. He dropped his arms until they swung loosely beside the chair and emitted faint grunts.

"I'm writing a satire on 'em now, calling it 'Boston Bards and Hearst Reviewers.' "

"Let's hear it," said Amory eagerly.

"I've only got the last few lines done."

"That's very modern. Let's hear 'em, if they're funny."

Tom produced a folded paper from his pocket and read aloud, pausing at intervals so that Amory could see that it was free verse:

> *So*
> *Walter Arensberg,*
> *Alfred Kreymborg,*
> *Carl Sandburg,*
> *Louis Untermeyer,*
> *Eunice Tietjens,*
> *Clara Shanafelt,*
> *James Oppenheim,*
> *Maxwell Bodenheim,*
> *Richard Glaenzer,*
> *Scharmel Iris,*
> *Conrad Aiken,*
> *I place your names here*

So that you may live
If only as names,
Sinuous, mauve-colored names,
In the juvenilia
Of my collected editions.

Amory roared.

"You win the iron pansy. I'll buy you a meal on the arrogance of the last two lines."

Amory did not entirely agree with Tom's sweeping damnation of American novelists and poets. He enjoyed both Vachel Lindsay and Booth Tarkington, and admired the conscientious, if slender, artistry of Edgar Lee Masters.

"What I hate is this idiotic drivel about 'I am God—I am man—I ride the winds—I look through the smoke—I am the life sense.' "

"It's ghastly!"

"And I wish American novelists would give up trying to make business romantically interesting. Nobody wants to read about it, unless it's crooked business. If it was an entertaining subject they'd buy the life of James J. Hill and not one of these long office tragedies that harp along on the significance of smoke——"

"And gloom," said Tom. "That's another favorite, though I'll admit the Russians have the monopoly. Our specialty is stories about little girls who break their spines and get adopted by grouchy old men because they smile so much. You'd think we were a race of cheerful cripples and that the common end of the Russian peasant was suicide——"

"Six o'clock," said Amory, glancing at his wrist-watch. "I'll buy you a grea' big dinner on the strength of the juvenilia of your collected editions."

LOOKING BACKWARD

July sweltered out with a last hot week, and Amory in another surge of unrest realized that it was just five months since he and Rosalind had met. Yet it was already hard for him to visualize the heart-whole boy who had stepped off the transport, passionately desiring the adventure of life. One night while the heat, overpowering and enervating, poured into the windows of his room he struggled for several hours in a vague effort to immortalize the poignancy of that time.

The February streets, wind-washed by night, blow full of strange half-intermittent damps, bearing on wasted walks in shining sight wet snow plashed into gleams under the lamps, like golden oil from some divine machine, in an hour of thaw and stars.

Strange damps—full of the eyes of many men, crowded with life borne in upon a lull. . . . Oh, I was young, for I could turn again to you, most finite and most beautiful, and taste the stuff of half-remembered dreams, sweet and new on your mouth.

. . . There was a tanging in the midnight air—silence was dead and sound not yet awoken—Life cracked like ice!—one brilliant note and there, radiant and pale, you stood . . . and spring had broken. (The icicles were short upon the roofs and the changeling city swooned.)

Our thoughts were frosty mist along the eaves; our two ghosts kissed, high on the long, mazed wires—eerie half-laughter echoes here and leaves only a fatuous sigh for young desires; regret has followed after things she loved, leaving the great husk.

ANOTHER ENDING

In mid-August came a letter from Monsignor Darcy, who had evidently just stumbled on his address:

My dear Boy:—
Your last letter was quite enough to make me worry about you. It was not a bit like yourself. Reading between the lines I should imagine that your engagement to this girl is making you rather unhappy, and I see you have lost all the feeling of romance that you had before the war. You make a great mistake if you think you can be romantic without religion. Sometimes I think that with both of us the secret of success, when we find it, is the mystical element in us: something flows into us that enlarges our personalities, and when it ebbs out our personalities shrink; I should call your last two letters rather shrivelled. Beware of losing yourself in the personality of another being, man or woman.

His Eminence Cardinal O'Neill and the Bishop of Boston are staying with me at present, so it is hard for me to get a moment to write, but I wish you would come up here later if only for a weekend. I go to Washington this week.

What I shall do in the future is hanging in the balance. Absolutely between ourselves I should not be surprised to see the red hat of a cardinal descend upon my unworthy head within the next eight months. In any event, I should like to have a house in New York or Washington where you could drop in for week-ends.

Amory, I'm very glad we're both alive; this war could easily have been the end of a brilliant family. But in regard to matrimony, you are now at the most dangerous period of your life. You might marry in haste and repent at leisure, but I think you won't. From what you write me about the present calamitous state of your finances, what you want is naturally impossible. However, if I judge you by the means I usually choose, I should say that there will be something of an emotional crisis within the next year.

Do write me. I feel annoyingly out of date on you.

With greatest affection,
Thayer Darcy.

Within a week after the receipt of this letter their little household fell precipitously to pieces. The immediate cause was the serious and probably chronic illness of Tom's mother. So they stored the furniture, gave instructions to sublet and shook hands gloomily in the Pennsylvania Station. Amory and Tom seemed always to be saying good-by.

Feeling very much alone, Amory yielded to an impulse and set off southward, intending to join Monsignor in Washington. They missed connections by two hours, and, deciding to spend a few days with an ancient, remembered uncle, Amory journeyed up through the luxuriant fields of Maryland into Ramilly County. But instead of two days his stay lasted from mid-August nearly through September, for in Maryland he met Eleanor.

Three

Young Irony

FOR YEARS AFTERWARD WHEN AMORY THOUGHT of Eleanor he seemed still to hear the wind sobbing around him and sending little chills into the places beside his heart. The night when they rode up the slope and watched the cold moon float through the clouds, he lost a further part of him that nothing could restore; and when he lost it he lost also the power of regretting it. Eleanor was, say, the last time that evil crept close to Amory under the mask of beauty, the last weird mystery that held him with wild fascination and pounded his soul to flakes.

With her his imagination ran riot and that is why they rode to the highest hill and watched an evil moon ride high, for they knew then that they could see the devil in each other. But Eleanor—did Amory dream her? Afterward their ghosts played, yet both of them hoped from their souls never to meet. Was it the infinite sadness of her eyes that drew him or the mirror of himself that he found in the gorgeous clarity of her mind? She will have no other adventure like Amory, and if she reads this she will say:

"And Amory will have no other adventure like me."

Nor will she sigh, any more than he would sigh.

Eleanor tried to put it on paper once:

> *The fading things we only know*
> *We'll have forgotten . . .*
> *Put away . . .*
> *Desires that melted with the snow,*
> *And dreams begotten*
> *This today:*
> *The sudden dawns we laughed to greet,*
> *That all could see, that none could share,*
> *Will be but dawns . . . and if we meet*
> *We shall not care.*

> *Dear . . . not one tear will rise for this . . .*
> *A little while hence*
> *No regret*
> *Will stir for a remembered kiss —*
> *Not even silence,*
> *When we've met,*
> *Will give old ghosts a waste to roam,*
> *Or stir the surface of the sea . . .*
> *If gray shapes drift beneath the foam*
> *We shall not see.*

They quarrelled dangerously because Amory maintained that *sea* and *see* couldn't possibly be used as a rhyme. And then Eleanor had part of another verse that she couldn't find a beginning for:

> *. . . But wisdom passes . . . still the years*
> *Will feed us wisdom. . . . Age will go*
> *Back to the old — For all our tears*
> *We shall not know.*

Eleanor hated Maryland passionately. She belonged to the oldest of the old families of Ramilly County and lived in a big, gloomy house with her grandfather. She had been born and brought up in France. . . . I see I am starting wrong. Let me begin again.

Amory was bored, as he usually was in the country. He used to go for far walks by himself—and wander along reciting "Ulalume" to the corn-fields, and congratulating Poe for drinking himself to death in that atmosphere of smiling complacency. One afternoon he had strolled for several miles along a road that was new to him, and then through a wood on bad advice from a colored woman . . . losing himself entirely. A passing storm decided to break out, and to his great impatience the sky grew black as pitch and the rain began to splatter down through the trees, become suddenly furtive and ghostly. Thunder rolled with menacing crashes up the valley and scattered through the woods in intermittent batteries. He stumbled blindly on, hunting for a way out, and finally, through webs of twisted branches, caught sight of a rift in the trees where the unbroken lightning showed open country. He rushed to the edge of the woods and then hesitated whether or not to cross the fields and try to reach the shelter of the little house marked by a light far down the valley. It was only half past five, but he could see scarcely ten steps before him, except when the lightning made everything vivid and grotesque for great sweeps around.

Suddenly a strange sound fell on his ears. It was a song, in a low, husky voice, a girl's voice, and whoever was singing was very close to him. A year before he might have laughed, or trembled; but in his restless mood he only stood and listened while the words sank into his consciousness:

> *Les sanglots longs*
> *Des violins*
> > *De l'automne*
> *Blessent mon coeur*
> *D'une langueur*
> > *Monotone.*

The lightning split the sky, but the song went on without a quaver. The girl was evidently in the field and the voice seemed to come vaguely from a haystack about twenty feet in front of him.

Then it ceased; ceased and began again in a weird chant that soared and hung and fell and blended with the rain:

> *Tout suffocant*
> *Et blême quand*
> > *Sonne l'heure*
> *Je me souviens*
> *Des jours anciens*
> > *Et je pleure. . . .*

"Who the devil is there in Ramilly County," muttered Amory aloud, "who would deliver Verlaine in an extemporaneous tune to a soaking haystack?"

"Somebody's there!" cried the voice unalarmed. "Who are you? — Manfred, St. Christopher, or Queen Victoria?"

"I'm Don Juan!" Amory shouted on impulse, raising his voice above the noise of the rain and the wind.

A delighted shriek came from the haystack.

"I know who you are — you're the blond boy that likes 'Ulalume' — I recognize your voice."

"How do I get up?" he cried from the foot of the haystack, whither he had arrived, dripping wet. A head appeared over the edge — it was so dark that Amory could just make out a patch of damp hair and two eyes that gleamed like a cat's.

"Run back!" came the voice, "and jump and I'll catch your hand — no, not there — on the other side."

He followed directions and as he sprawled up the side, knee-deep in hay, a small, white hand reached out, gripped his, and helped him onto the top.

"Here you are, Juan," cried she of the damp hair. "Do you mind if I drop the Don?"

"You've got a thumb like mine!" he exclaimed.

"And you're holding my hand, which is dangerous without seeing my face." He dropped it quickly.

As if in answer to his prayers came a flash of lightning and he looked eagerly at her who stood beside him on the soggy haystack, ten feet above the ground. But she had covered her face and he saw nothing but a slender figure, dark, damp, bobbed hair, and the small white hands with the thumbs that bent back like his.

"Sit down," she suggested politely, as the dark closed in on them. "If you'll sit opposite me in this hollow you can have half of the raincoat, which I was using as a water-proof tent until you so rudely interrupted me."

"I was asked," Amory said joyfully; "you asked me — you know you did."

"Don Juan always manages that," she said, laughing, "but I shan't call you that any more, because you've got reddish hair. Instead you can recite 'Ulalume' and I'll be Psyche, your soul."

Amory flushed, happily invisible under the curtain of wind and rain. They were sitting opposite each other in a slight hollow in the hay with the raincoat spread over most of them, and the rain doing for the rest. Amory was trying desperately to see Psyche, but the lightning refused to flash again, and he waited impatiently. Good Lord! suppos-

ing she wasn't beautiful—supposing she was forty and pedantic—
heavens! Suppose, only suppose, she was mad. But he knew the last
was unworthy. Here had Providence sent a girl to amuse him just as it
sent Benvenuto Cellini men to murder, and he was wondering if she
was mad, just because she exactly filled his mood.

"I'm not," she said.

"Not what?"

"Not mad. I didn't think you were mad when I first saw you, so it
isn't fair that you should think so of me."

"How on earth——"

As long as they knew each other Eleanor and Amory could be "on
a subject" and stop talking with the definite thought of it in their
heads, yet ten minutes later speak aloud and find that their minds had
followed the same channels and led them each to a parallel idea, an
idea that others would have found absolutely unconnected with the
first.

"Tell me," he demanded, leaning forward eagerly, "how do you
know about 'Ulalume'—how did you know the color of my hair?
What's your name? What were you doing here? Tell me all at once!"

Suddenly the lightning flashed in with a leap of over-reaching light
and he saw Eleanor, and looked for the first time into those eyes of
hers. Oh, she was magnificent—pale skin, the color of marble in starlight, slender brows, and eyes that glittered green as emeralds in the
blinding glare. She was a witch, of perhaps nineteen, he judged, alert
and dreamy and with the tell-tale white line over her upper lip that was
a weakness and a delight. He sank back with a gasp against the wall of
hay.

"Now you've seen me," she said calmly, "and I suppose you're
about to say that my green eyes are burning into your brain."

"What color is your hair?" he asked intently. "It's bobbed, isn't it?"

"Yes, it's bobbed. I don't know what color it is," she answered,
musing, "so many men have asked me. It's medium, I suppose— No
one ever looks long at my hair. I've got beautiful eyes, though, haven't
I. I don't care what you say, I have beautiful eyes."

"Answer my question, Madeline."

"Don't remember them all—besides my name isn't Madeline, it's
Eleanor."

"I might have guessed it. You *look* like Eleanor—you have that
Eleanor look. You know what I mean."

There was a silence as they listened to the rain.

"It's going down my neck, fellow lunatic," she offered finally.

"Answer my questions."

"Well—name of Savage, Eleanor; live in big old house mile down road; nearest living relation to be notified, grandfather—Ramilly Savage; height, five feet four inches; number on watch-case, 3077 W; nose, delicate aquiline, temperament, uncanny——"

"And me," Amory interrupted, "where did you see me?"

"Oh, you're one of *those* men," she answered haughtily, "must lug old self into conversation. Well, my boy, I was behind a hedge sunning myself one day last week, and along comes a man saying in a pleasant, conceited way of talking:

> *"And now when the night was senescent"*
> *(says he)*
> *"And the star dials pointed to morn*
> *At the end of the path a liquescent"*
> *(says he)*
> *"And nebulous lustre was born."*

So I poked my eyes up over the hedge, but you had started to run, for some unknown reason, and so I saw but the back of your beautiful head. 'Oh!' says I, 'there's a man for whom many of us might sigh,' and I continued in my best Irish——"

"All right," Amory interrupted. "Now go back to yourself."

"Well, I will. I'm one of those people who go through the world giving other people thrills, but getting few myself except those I read into men on such nights as these. I have the social courage to go on the stage, but not the energy; I haven't the patience to write books; and I never met a man I'd marry. However, I'm only eighteen."

The storm was dying down softly and only the wind kept up its ghostly surge and made the stack lean and gravely settle from side to side. Amory was in a trance. He felt that every moment was precious. He had never met a girl like this before—she would never seem quite the same again. He didn't at all feel like a character in a play, the appropriate feeling in an unconventional situation—instead, he had a sense of coming home.

"I have just made a great decision," said Eleanor after another pause, "and that is why I'm here, to answer another of your questions. I have just decided that I don't believe in immortality."

"Really! how banal!"

"Frightfully so," she answered, "but depressing with a stale, sickly depression, nevertheless. I came out here to get wet—like a wet hen; wet hens always have great clarity of mind," she concluded.

"Go on," Amory said politely.

"Well—I'm not afraid of the dark, so I put on my slicker and rubber boots and came out. You see I was always afraid, before, to say

I didn't believe in God—because the lightning might strike me—but here I am and it hasn't, of course, but the main point is that this time I wasn't any more afraid of it than I had been when I was a Christian Scientist, like I was last year. So now I know I'm a materialist and I was fraternizing with the hay when you came out and stood by the woods, scared to death."

"Why, you little wretch—" cried Amory indignantly. "Scared of what?"

"*Yourself!*" she shouted, and he jumped. She clapped her hands and laughed. "See—see! Conscience—kill it like me! Eleanor Savage, materiologist—no jumping, no starting, come early——"

"But I *have* to have a soul," he objected. "I can't be rational—and I won't be molecular."

She leaned toward him, her burning eyes never leaving his own and whispered with a sort of romantic finality:

"I thought so, Juan, I feared so—you're sentimental. You're not like me. I'm a romantic little materialist."

"I'm not sentimental—I'm as romantic as you are. The idea, you know, is that the sentimental person thinks things will last—the romantic person has a desperate confidence that they won't." (This was an ancient distinction of Amory's.)

"Epigrams. I'm going home," she said sadly. "Let's get off the haystack and walk to the cross-roads."

They slowly descended from their perch. She would not let him help her down and motioning him away arrived in a graceful lump in the soft mud where she sat for an instant, laughing at herself. Then she jumped to her feet and slipped her hand into his, and they tip-toed across the fields, jumping and swinging from dry spot to dry spot. A transcendent delight seemed to sparkle in every pool of water, for the moon had risen and the storm had scurried away into western Maryland: When Eleanor's arm touched his he felt his hands grow cold with deadly fear lest he should lose the shadow brush with which his imagination was painting wonders of her. He watched her from the corners of his eyes as ever he did when he walked with her—she was a feast and a folly and he wished it had been his destiny to sit forever on a haystack and see life through her green eyes. His paganism soared that night and when she faded out like a gray ghost down the road, a deep singing came out of the fields and filled his way homeward. All night the summer moths flitted in and out of Amory's window; all night large looming sounds swayed in mystic revery through the silver grain—and he lay awake in the clear darkness.

SEPTEMBER

Amory selected a blade of grass and nibbled at it scientifically.

"I never fall in love in August or September," he proffered.

"When then?"

"Christmas or Easter. I'm a liturgist."

"Easter!" She turned up her nose. "Huh! Spring in corsets!"

"Easter *would* bore spring, wouldn't she? Easter has her hair braided, wears a tailored suit."

> *Bind on thy sandals, oh, thou most fleet.*
> *Over the splendor and speed of thy feet— —*

quoted Eleanor softly, and then added: "I suppose Hallowe'en is a better day for autumn than Thanksgiving."

"Much better—and Christmas Eve does very well for winter, but summer . . ."

"Summer has no day," she said. "We can't possibly have a summer love. So many people have tried that the name's become proverbial. Summer is only the unfulfilled promise of spring, a charlatan in place of the warm balmy nights I dream of in April. It's a sad season of life without growth. . . . It has no day."

"Fourth of July," Amory suggested facetiously.

"Don't be funny!" she said, raking him with her eyes.

"Well, what could fulfill the promise of spring?"

She thought a moment.

"Oh, I suppose heaven would, if there was one," she said finally, "a sort of pagan heaven—you ought to be a materialist," she continued irrelevantly.

"Why?"

"Because you look a good deal like the pictures of Rupert Brooke."

To some extent Amory tried to play Rupert Brooke as long as he knew Eleanor. What he said, his attitude toward life, toward her, toward himself, were all reflexes of the dead Englishman's literary moods. Often she sat in the grass, a lazy wind playing with her short hair, her voice husky as she ran up and down the scale from Grant-chester to Waikiki. There was something most passionate in Eleanor's reading aloud. They seemed nearer, not only mentally, but physically, when they read, than when she was in his arms, and this was often, for they fell half into love almost from the first. Yet was Amory capable of love now? He could, as always, run through the emotions in a half

hour, but even while they revelled in their imaginations, he knew that
neither of them could care as he had cared once before — I suppose that
was why they turned to Brooke, and Swinburne, and Shelley. Their
chance was to make everything fine and finished and rich and imagini-
tive; they must bend tiny golden tenacles from his imagination to hers,
that would take the place of the great, deep love that was never so
near, yet never so much of a dream.

One poem they read over and over; Swinburne's "Triumph of
Time," and four lines of it rang in his memory afterward on warm
nights when he saw the fireflies among dusky tree trunks and heard
the low drone of many frogs. Then Eleanor seemed to come out of the
night and stand by him, and he heard her throaty voice, with its tone of
a fleecy-headed drum, repeating:

> *Is it worth a tear, is it worth an hour,*
> *To think of things that are well outworn;*
> *Of fruitless husks and fugitive flower,*
> *The dream foregone and the deed foreborne?*

They were formally introduced two days later, and his aunt told
him her history. The Ramillys were two: old Mr. Ramilly and his
granddaughter, Eleanor. She had lived in France with a restless
mother whom Amory imagined to have been very like his own, on
whose death she had come to America, to live in Maryland. She had
gone to Baltimore first to stay with a bachelor uncle, and there she
insisted on being a débutante at the age of seventeen. She had a wild
winter and arrived in the country in March, having quarrelled frantically with all her Baltimore relatives, and shocked them into fiery protest. A rather fast crowd had come out, who drank cocktails in
limousines and were promiscuously condescending and patronizing
toward older people, and Eleanor with an esprit that hinted strongly of
the boulevards, led many innocents still redolent of St. Timothy's and
Farmington, into paths of Bohemian naughtiness. When the story
came to her uncle, a forgetful cavalier of a more hypocritical era, there
was a scene, from which Eleanor emerged, subdued but rebellious and
indignant, to seek haven with her grandfather who hovered in the
country on the near side of senility. That's as far as her story went; she
told him the rest herself, but that was later.

Often they swam and as Amory floated lazily in the water he shut
his mind to all thoughts except those of hazy soap-bubble lands where
the sun splattered through wind-drunk trees. How could any one possibly think or worry, or do anything except splash and dive and loll
there on the edge of time while the flower months failed. Let the days

move over—sadness and memory and pain recurred outside, and here, once more, before he went on to meet them he wanted to drift and be young.

There were days when Amory resented that life had changed from an even progress along a road stretching ever in sight, with the scenery merging and blending, into a succession of quick, unrelated scenes—two years of sweat and blood, that sudden absurd instinct for paternity that Rosalind had stirred; the half-sensual, half-neurotic quality of this autumn with Eleanor. He felt that it would take all time, more than he could ever spare, to glue these strange cumbersome pictures into the scrap-book of his life. It was all like a banquet where he sat for this half-hour of his youth and tried to enjoy brilliant epicurean courses.

Dimly he promised himself a time where all should be welded together. For months it seemed that he had alternated between being borne along a stream of love or fascination, or left in an eddy, and in the eddies he had not desired to think, rather to be picked up on a wave's top and swept along again.

"The despairing, dying autumn and our love—how well they harmonize!" said Eleanor sadly one day as they lay dripping by the water.

"The Indian summer of our hearts—" he ceased.

"Tell me," she said finally, "was she light or dark?"

"Light."

"Was she more beautiful than I am?"

"I don't know," said Amory shortly.

One night they walked while the moon rose and poured a great burden of glory over the garden until it seemed fairyland with Amory and Eleanor, dim phantasmal shapes, expressing eternal beauty and curious elfin love moods. Then they turned out of the moonlight into the trellised darkness of a vine-hung pagoda, where there were scents so plaintive as to be nearly musical.

"Light a match," she whispered. "I want to see you."

Scratch! Flare!

The night and the scarred trees were like scenery in a play, and to be there with Eleanor, shadowy and unreal, seemed somehow oddly familiar. Amory thought how it was only the past that ever seemed strange and unbelievable. The match went out.

"It's black as pitch."

"We're just voices now," murmured Eleanor, "little lonesome voices. Light another."

"That was my last match."

Suddenly he caught her in his arms.

"You *are* mine—you know you're mine!" he cried wildly . . . the moonlight twisted in through the vines and listened . . . the fireflies hung upon their whispers as if to win his glance from the glory of their eyes.

THE END OF SUMMER

"No wind is stirring in the grass; not one wind stirs . . . the water in the hidden pools, as glass, fronts the full moon and so inters the golden token in its icy mass," chanted Eleanor to the trees that skeletoned the body of the night. "Isn't it ghostly here? If you can hold your horse's feet up, let's cut through the woods and find the hidden pools."

"It's after one, and you'll get the devil," he objected, "and I don't know enough about horses to put one away in the pitch dark."

"Shut up, you old fool," she whispered irrelevantly, and, leaning over, she patted him lazily with her riding-crop. "You can leave your old plug in our stable and I'll send him over tomorrow."

"But my uncle has got to drive me to the station with this old plug at seven o'clock."

"Don't be a spoilsport—remember, you have a tendency toward wavering that prevents you from being the entire light of my life."

Amory drew his horse up close beside, and, leaning toward her, grasped her hand.

"Say I am—*quick*, or I'll pull you over and make you ride behind me."

She looked up and smiled and shook her head excitedly.

"Oh, do!—or rather, don't! Why are all the exciting things so uncomfortable, like fighting and exploring and skiing in Canada? By the way, we're going to ride up Harper's Hill. I think that comes in our programme about five o'clock.

"You little devil," Amory growled. "You're going to make me stay up all night and sleep in the train like an immigrant all day tomorrow, going back to New York."

"Hush! some one's coming along the road—let's go! *Whoo-ee-oop!*" And with a shout that probably gave the belated traveller a series of shivers, she turned her horse into the woods and Amory followed slowly, as he had followed her all day for three weeks.

The summer was over, but he had spent the days in watching Eleanor, a graceful, facile Manfred, build herself intellectual and imaginative pyramids while she revelled in the artificialities of the temperamental teens and they wrote poetry at the dinner-table.

❊　❊　❊

When Vanity kissed Vanity, a hundred happy Junes ago, he pondered o'er her breathlessly, and, that all men might ever know, he
rhymed her eyes with life and death:

"Thru Time I'll save my love!" he said . . . yet Beauty vanished
with his breath, and, with her lovers, she was dead . . .

—Ever his wit and not her eyes, ever his art and not her hair:

"Who'd learn a trick in rhyme, be wise and pause before his sonnet
there" . . . So all my words, however true, might sing you to a thou-
sandth June, and no one ever know that you were Beauty for an
afternoon.

So he wrote one day, when he pondered how coldly we thought of
the "Dark Lady of the Sonnets," and how little we remembered her as
the great man wanted her remembered. For what Shakespeare *must*
have desired, to have been able to write with such divine despair, was
that the lady should live . . . and now we have no real interest in her.
. . . The irony of it is that if he had cared *more* for the poem than for
the lady the sonnet would be only obvious, imitative rhetoric and no
one would ever have read it after twenty years. . . .

This was the last night Amory ever saw Eleanor. He was leaving in
the morning and they had agreed to take a long farewell trot by the
cold moonlight. She wanted to talk, she said—perhaps the last time in
her life that she could be rational (she meant pose with comfort). So
they had turned into the woods and rode for half an hour with scarcely
a word, except when she whispered "Damn!" at a bothersome
branch—whispered it as no other girl was ever able to whisper it. Then
they started up Harper's Hill, walking their tired horses.

"Good Lord! It's quiet here!" whispered Eleanor; "much more
lonesome than the woods."

"I hate woods," Amory said, shuddering. "Any kind of foliage or
underbrush at night. Out here it's so broad and easy on the spirit."

"The long slope of a long hill."

"And the cold moon rolling moonlight down it."

"And thee and me, last and most important."

It was quiet that night—the straight road they followed up to the
edge of the cliff knew few footsteps at any time. Only an occasional
Negro cabin, silver-gray in the rock-ribbed moonlight, broke the long
line of bare ground; behind lay the black edge of the woods like a dark
frosting on white cake, and ahead the sharp, high horizon. It was much
colder—so cold that it settled on them and drove all the warm nights
from their minds.

"The end of summer," said Eleanor softly. "Listen to the beat of
our horses' hoofs—'tump-tump-tump-a-tump.' Have you ever been fe-

verish and had all noises divide into 'tump-tump-tump' until you could swear eternity was divisible into so many tumps? That's the way I feel—old horses go tump-tump. . . . I guess that's the only thing that separates horses and clocks from us. Human beings can't go 'tump-tump-tump' without going crazy."

The breeze freshened and Eleanor pulled her cape around her and shivered.

"Are you very cold?" asked Amory.

"No, I'm thinking about myself—my black old inside self, the real one, with the fundamental honesty that keeps me from being absolutely wicked by making me realize my own sins."

They were riding up close by the cliff and Amory gazed over. Where the fall met the ground a hundred feet below, a black stream made a sharp line, broken by tiny glints in the swift water.

"Rotten, rotten old world," broke out Eleanor suddenly, "and the wretchedest thing of all is me—oh, *why* am I a girl? Why am I not a stupid—? Look at you; you're stupider than I am, not much, but some, and you can lope about and get bored and then lope somewhere else, and you can play around with girls without being involved in meshes of sentiment, and you can do anything and be justified—and here am I with the brains to do everything, yet tied to the sinking ship of future matrimony. If I were born a hundred years from now, well and good, but now what's in store for me—I have to marry, that goes without saying. Who? I'm too bright for most men, and yet I have to descend to their level and let them patronize my intellect in order to get their attention. Every year that I don't marry I've got less chance for a first-class man. At the best I can have my choice from one or two cities and, of course, I have to marry into a dinner-coat.

"Listen," she leaned close again, "I like clever men and good-looking men, and, of course, no one cares more for personality than I do. Oh, just one person in fifty has any glimmer of what sex is. I'm hipped on Freud and all that, but it's rotten that every bit of *real* love in the world is ninety-nine per cent passion and one little soupçon of jealousy." She finished as suddenly as she began.

"Of course, you're right," Amory agreed. "It's a rather unpleasant overpowering force that's part of the machinery under everything. It's like an actor that lets you see his mechanics! Wait a minute till I think this out. . . ."

He paused and tried to get a metaphor. They had turned the cliff and were riding along the road about fifty feet to the left.

"You see every one's got to have some cloak to throw around it. The mediocre intellects, Plato's second class, use the remnants of romantic chivalry diluted with Victorian sentiment—and we who consider ourselves the intellectuals cover it up by pretending that it's another side of us, has nothing to do with our shining brains; we pretend that the fact that we realize it is really absolving us from being a prey to it. But the truth is that sex is right in the middle of our purest abstractions, so close that it obscures vision. . . . I can kiss you now and will. . . ." He leaned toward her in his saddle, but she drew away.

"I can't—I can't kiss you now—I'm more sensitive."

"You're more stupid then," he declared rather impatiently. "Intellect is no protection from sex any more than convention is . . ."

"What is?" she fired up. "The Catholic Church or the maxims of Confucius?"

Amory looked up, rather taken aback.

"That's your panacea, isn't it?" she cried. "Oh, you're just an old hypocrite, too. Thousands of scowling priests keeping the degenerate Italians and illiterate Irish repentant with gabble-gabble about the sixth and ninth commandments. It's just all cloaks, sentiment and spiritual rouge and panaceas. I'll tell you there *is* no God, not even a definite abstract goodness; so it's all got to be worked out for the individual by the individual here in high white foreheads like mine, and you're too much the prig to admit it." She let go her reins and shook her little fists at the stars.

"If there's a God let him strike me—strike me!"

"Talking about God again after the manner of atheists," Amory said sharply. His materialism, always a thin cloak, was torn to shreds by Eleanor's blasphemy. . . . She knew it and it angered him that she knew it.

"And like most intellectuals who don't find faith convenient," he continued coldly, "like Napoleon and Oscar Wilde and the rest of your type, you'll yell loudly for a priest on your death-bed."

Eleanor drew her horse up sharply and he reined in beside her.

"Will I?" she said in a queer voice that scared him. "Will I? Watch! *I'm going over the cliff!*" And before he could interfere she had turned and was riding breakneck for the end of the plateau.

He wheeled and started after her, his body like ice, his nerves in a vast clangor. There was no chance of stopping her. The moon was under a cloud and her horse would step blindly over. Then some ten feet from the edge of the cliff she gave a sudden shriek and flung herself sideways—plunged from her horse and, rolling over twice, landed in a pile of brush five feet from the edge. The horse went over with a frantic whinny. In a minute he was by Eleanor's side and saw that her eyes were open.

"Eleanor!" he cried.

She did not answr, but her lips moved and her eyes filled with sudden tears.

"Eleanor, are you hurt?"

"No; I don't think so," she said faintly, and then began weeping.

"My horse dead?"

"Good God—Yes!"

"Oh!" she wailed. "I thought I was going over. I didn't know——"

He helped her gently to her feet and boosted her onto his saddle. So they started homeward; Amory walking and she bent forward on the pommel, sobbing bitterly.

"I've got a crazy streak," she faltered, "twice before I've done things like that. When I was eleven mother went—went mad—stark raving crazy. We were in Vienna——"

All the way back she talked haltingly about herself, and Amory's love waned slowly with the moon. At her door they started from habit to kiss good night, but she could not run into his arms, nor were they stretched to meet her as in the week before. For a minute they stood there, hating each other with a bitter sadness. But as Amory had loved himself in Eleanor, so now what he hated was only a mirror. Their poses were strewn about the pale dawn like broken glass. The stars were long gone and there were left only the little sighing gusts of wind and the silences between . . . but naked souls are poor things ever, and soon he turned homeward and let new lights come in with the sun.

A POEM THAT ELEANOR SENT AMORY
SEVERAL YEARS LATER

Here, Earth-born, over the lilt of the water,
Lisping its music and bearing a burden of light,
Bosoming day as a laughing and radiant daughter . . .
Here we may whisper unheard, unafraid of the night.
Walking alone . . . was it splendor, or what, we were bound with,
Deep in the time when summer lets down her hair?
Shadows we loved and the patterns they covered the ground with
Tapestries, mystical, faint in the breathless air.

That was the day . . . and the night for another story,
Pale as a dream and shadowed with pencilled trees—
Ghosts of the stars came by who had sought for glory,
Whispered to us of peace in the plaintive breeze,
Whispered of old dead faiths that the day had shattered,

Youth the penny that bought delight of the moon;
That was the urge that we knew and the language that mattered
That was the debt that we paid to the usurer June.

Here, deepest of dreams, by the waters that bring not
Anything back of the past that we need not know,
What if the light is but sun and the little streams sing not,
We are together, it seems . . . I have loved you so . . .
What did the last night hold, with the summer over,
Drawing us back to the home in the changing glade?
What leered out of the dark in the ghostly clover?
God! . . . till you stirred in your sleep . . . and were wild afraid . . .

Well . . . we have passed . . . we are chronicle now to the eerie.
Curious metal from meteors that failed in the sky;
Earth-born the tireless is stretched by the water, quite weary,
Close to this ununderstandable changeling that's I . . .
Fear is an echo we traced to Security's daughter;
Now we are faces and voices . . . and less, too soon,
Whispering half-love over the lilt of the water . . .
Youth the penny that bought delight of the moon.

A POEM AMORY SENT TO ELEANOR AND WHICH HE CALLED "SUMMER STORM"

Faint winds, and a song fading and leaves falling,
Faint winds, and far away a fading laughter . . .
And the rain and over the fields a voice calling . . .
Our gray blown cloud scurries and lifts above,
Slides on the sun and flutters there to waft her
Sisters on. The shadow of a dove
Falls on the cote, the trees are filled with wings;
And down the valley through the crying trees
The body of the darker storm flies; brings
With its new air the breath of sunken seas
And slender tenuous thunder . . .

> *But I wait . . .*
Wait for the mists and for the blacker rain —
Heavier winds that stir the veil of fate,
Happier winds that pile her hair;

> *Again*

They tear me, teach me, strew the heavy air
Upon me, winds that I know, and storm.

There was a summer every rain was rare;
There was a season every wind was warm. . . .
And now you pass me in the mist . . . your hair
Rain-blown about you, damp lips curved once more
In that wild irony, that gay despair
That made you old when we have met before;
Wraith-like you drift on out before the rain,
Across the fields, blown with the stemless flowers,
With your old hopes, dead leaves and loves again—
Dim as a dream and wan with all old hours
(Whispers will creep into the growing dark . . .
Tumult will die over the trees)
                                        Now night
Tears from her wetted breast the splattered blouse
Of day, glides down the dreaming hills, tear-bright,
To cover with her hair the eerie green . . .
Love for the dusk . . . Love for the glistening after;
Quiet the trees to their last tops . . . serene . . .

Faint winds, and far away a fading laughter . . .

Four

The Supercilious

Sacrifice

ATLANTIC CITY. AMORY PACED THE BOARD
walk at day's end, lulled by the everlasting surge of changing
waves, smelling the half-mournful odor of the salt breeze. The sea, he
thought, had treasured its memories deeper than the faithless land. It
seemed still to whisper of Norse galleys ploughing the water world
under raven-figured flags, of the British dreadnoughts, gray bulwarks
of civilization steaming up through the fog of one dark July into the
North Sea.

"Well—Amory Blaine!"

Amory looked down into the street below. A low racing car had
drawn to a stop and a familiar cheerful face protruded from the
driver's seat.

"Come on down, goopher!" cried Alec.

Amory called a greeting and descending a flight of wooden steps approached the car. He and Alec had been meeting intermittently, but the barrier of Rosalind lay always between them. He was sorry for this; he hated to lose Alec.

"Mr. Blaine, this is Miss Waterson, Miss Wayne, and Mr. Tully."

"How d'y do?"

"Amory," said Alec exuberantly, "if you'll jump in we'll take you to some secluded nook and give you a wee jolt of Bourbon."

Amory considered.

"That's an idea."

"Step in—move over, Jill, and Amory will smile very handsomely at you."

Amory squeezed into the back seat beside a gaudy, vermilion-lipped blonde.

"Hello, Doug Fairbanks," she said flippantly. "Walking for exercise or hunting for company?"

"I was counting the waves," replied Amory gravely. "I'm going in for statistics."

"Don't kid me, Doug."

When they reached an unfrequented side street Alec stopped the car among deep shadows.

"What you doing down here these cold days, Amory?" he demanded, as he produced a quart of Bourbon from under the fur rug.

Amory avoided the question. Indeed, he had had no definite reason for coming to the coast.

"Do you remember that party of ours, sophomore year?" he asked instead.

"Do I? When we slept in the pavilions up in Asbury Park——"

"Lord, Alec! It's hard to think that Jesse and Dick and Kerry are all three dead."

Alec shivered.

"Don't talk about it. These dreary fall days depress me enough."

Jill seemed to agree.

"Doug here is sorta gloomy anyways," she commented. "Tell him to drink deep—it's good and scarce these days."

"What I really want to ask you, Amory, is where you are——"

"Why, New York, I suppose——"

"I mean tonight, because if you haven't got a room yet you'd better help me out."

"Glad to."

"You see, Tully and I have two rooms with bath between at the Ranier, and he's got to go back to New York. I don't want to have to move. Question is, will you occupy one of the rooms?"

Amory was willing, if he could get in right away.

"You'll find the key in the office; the rooms are in my name."

Declining further locomotion or further stimulation, Amory left the car and sauntered back along the board walk to the hotel.

He was in an eddy again, a deep, lethargic gulf, without desire to work or write, love or dissipate. For the first time in his life he rather longed for death to roll over his generation, obliterating their petty fevers and struggles and exultations. His youth seemed never so vanished as now in the contrast between the utter loneliness of this visit and that riotous, joyful party of four years before. Things that had been the merest commonplaces of his life then, deep sleep, the sense of beauty around him, all desire, had flown away and the gaps they left were filled only with the great listlessness of his disillusion.

"To hold a man a woman has to appeal to the worst in him." This sentence was the thesis of most of his bad nights, of which he felt this was to be one. His mind had already started to play variations on the subject. Tireless passion, fierce jealousy, longing to possess and crush—these alone were left of all his love for Rosalind; these remained to him as payment for the loss of his youth—bitter calomel under the thin sugar of love's exaltation.

In his room he undressed and wrapping himself in blankets to keep out the chill October air drowsed in an armchair by the open window. He remembered a poem he had read months before:

> *Oh staunch old heart who toiled so long for me,*
> *I waste my years sailing along the sea— —*

Yet he had no sense of waste, no sense of the present hope that waste implied. He felt that life had rejected him.

"Rosalind! Rosalind!" He poured the words softly into the half-darkness until she seemed to permeate the room; the wet salt breeze filled his hair with moisture; the rim of a moon seared the sky and made the curtains dim and ghostly. He fell asleep.

When he awoke it was very late and quiet. The blanket had slipped partly off his shoulders and he touched his skin to find it damp and cold.

Then he became aware of a tense whispering not ten feet away.

He became rigid.

"Don't make a sound!" It was Alec's voice. *"Jill—do you hear me?"*

"Yes— " breathed very low, very frightened. They were in the bathroom.

Then his ears caught a louder sound from somewhere along the corridor outside. It was a mumbling of men's voices and a repeated muffled rapping. Amory threw off the blankets and moved close to the bathroom door.

"My God!" came the girl's voice again. "You'll have to let them in."

"*Sh!*"

Suddenly a steady, insistent knocking began at Amory's hall door and simultaneously out of the bathroom came Alec, followed by the vermilion-lipped girl. They were both clad in pajamas.

"Amory!" an anxious whisper.

"What's the trouble?"

"It's house detectives. My God, Amory—they're just looking for a test-case— —"

"Well, better let them in."

"You don't understand. They can get me under the Mann Act."

The girl followed him slowly, a rather miserable, pathetic figure in the darkness.

Amory tried to plan quickly.

"You make a racket and let them in your room," he suggested anxiously, "and I'll get her out by this door."

"They're here too, though. They'll watch this door."

"Can't you give a wrong name?"

"No chance. I registered under my own name; besides, they'd trail the auto license number."

"Say you're married."

"Jill says one of the house detectives knows her."

The girl had stolen to the bed and tumbled upon it; lay there listening wretchedly to the knocking which had grown gradually to a pounding. Then came a man's voice, angry and imperative:

"Open up or we'll break the door in!"

In the silence when this voice ceased Amory realized that there were other things in the room besides people . . . over and around the figure crouched on the bed there hung an aura, gossamer as a moonbeam, tainted as stale, weak wine, yet a horror, diffusively brooding already over the three of them . . . and over by the window among the stirring curtains stood something else, featureless and indistinguishable, yet strangely familiar. . . . Simultaneously two great cases presented themselves side by side to Amory; all that took place in his mind, then, occupied in actual time less than ten seconds.

The first fact that flashed radiantly on his comprehension was the great impersonality of sacrifice—he perceived that what we call love and hate, reward and punishment, had no more to do with it than the date of the month. He quickly recapitulated the story of a sacrifice he had heard of in college: a man had cheated in an examination; his roommate in a gust of sentiment had taken the entire blame—due to the shame of it the innocent one's entire future seemed shrouded in regret and failure, capped by the ingratitude of the real culprit. He had finally taken his own life—years afterward the facts had come out. At the time the story had both puzzled and worried Amory. Now he realized the truth; that sacrifice was no purchase of freedom. It was like a great elective office, it was like an inheritance of power—to certain people at certain times an essential luxury, carrying with it not a guarantee but a responsibility, not a security but an infinite risk. Its very momentum might drag him down to ruin—the passing of the emotional wave that made it possible might leave the one who made it high and dry forever on an island of despair.

. . . Amory knew that afterward Alec would secretly hate him for having done so much for him. . . .

. . . All this was flung before Amory like an opened scroll, while ulterior to him and speculating upon him were those two breathless, listening forces: the gossamer aura that hung over and about the girl and that familiar thing by the window.

Sacrifice by its very nature was arrogant and impersonal; sacrifice should be eternally supercilious.

Weep not for me but for thy children.

That—thought Amory—would be somehow the way God would talk to me.

Amory felt a sudden surge of joy and then like a face in a motion-picture the aura over the bed faded out; the dynamic shadow by the window, that was as near as he could name it, remained for the fraction of a moment and then the breeze seemed to lift it swiftly out of the room. He clinched his hands in quick ecstatic excitement . . . the ten seconds were up. . . .

"Do what I say, Alec—do what I say. Do you understand?"

Alec looked at him dumbly—his face a tableau of anguish.

"You have a family," continued Amory slowly. "You have a family and its important that you should get out of this. Do you hear me?" He repeated clearly what he had said. "Do you hear me?"

"I hear you." The voice was curiously strained, the eyes never for a second left Amory's.

"Alec, you're going to lie down here. If any one comes in you act drunk. You do what I say—if you don't I'll probably take a paste at you."

There was another moment while they stared at each other. Then Amory went briskly to the bureau and, taking his pocketbook, beckoned peremptorily to the girl. He heard one word from Alec that sounded like "penitentiary," then he and Jill were in the bathroom with the door bolted behind them.

"You're here with me," he said sternly. "You've been with me all evening."

She nodded, gave a little half cry.

In a second he had the door of the other room open and three men entered. There was an immediate flood of electric light and he stood there blinking.

"You've been playing a little too dangerous a game, young man!"

Amory laughed.

"Well?"

The leader of the trio nodded authoritatively at a burly man in a check suit.

"All right, Olson."

"I got you, Mr. O'May," said Olson, nodding. The other two took a curious glance at their quarry and then withdrew, closing the door angrily behind them.

The burly man regarded Amory contemptuously.

"Didn't you ever hear of the Mann Act? Coming down here with her," he indicated the girl with his thumb, "with a New York license on your car—to a hotel like *this.*" He shook his head implying that he had struggled over Amory but now gave him up.

"Well," said Amory rather impatiently, "what do you want us to do?"

"Get dressed, quick—and tell your friend not to make such a racket." Jill was sobbing noisily on the bed, but at these words she subsided sulkily and, gathering up her clothes, retired to the bathroom. As Amory slipped into Alec's B.V.D.'s he found that his attitude toward the situation was agreeably humorous. The aggrieved virtue of the burly man made him want to laugh.

"Anybody else here?" demanded Olson, trying to look keen and ferret-like.

"Fellow who had the rooms," said Amory carelessly. "He's drunk as an owl, though. Been in there asleep since six o'clock."

"I'll take a look at him presently."

"How did you find out?" asked Amory curiously.

"Night clerk saw you go upstairs with this woman."

Amory nodded; Jill reappeared from the bathroom, completely if rather untidily arrayed.

"Now then," began Olson, producing a note-book, "I want your real names—no damn John Smith or Mary Brown."

"Wait a minute," said Amory quietly. "Just drop that big-bully stuff. We merely got caught, that's all."

Olson glared at him.

"Name?" he snapped.

Amory gave his name and New York address.

"And the lady?"

"Miss Jill——"

"Say," cried Olson indignantly, "just ease up on the nursery rhymes. What's your name? Sarah Murphy? Minnie Jackson?"

"Oh, my God!" cried the girl cupping her tear-stained face in her hands. "I don't want my mother to know. I don't want my mother to know."

"Come on now!"

"Shut up!" cried Amory at Olson.

An instant's pause.

"Stella Robbins," she faltered finally. "General Delivery, Rugway, New Hampshire."

Olson snapped his note-book shut and looked at them very ponderously.

"By rights the hotel could turn the evidence over to the police and you'd go to penitentiary, you would, for bringin' a girl from one State to 'nother f'r immoral purp'ses—" He paused to let the majesty of his words sink in. "But—the hotel is going to let you off."

"It doesn't want to get in the papers," cried Jill fiercely. "Let us off! Huh!"

A great lightness surrounded Amory. He realized that he was safe and only then did he appreciate the full enormity of what he might have incurred.

"However," continued Olson, "there's a protective association among the hotels. There's been too much of this stuff, and we got a 'rangement with the newspapers so that you get a little free publicity. Not the name of the hotel, but just a line sayin' that you had a little trouble in 'lantic City. See?"

"I see."

"You're gettin' off light—damn light—but——"

"Come on," said Amory briskly. "Let's get out of here. We don't need a valedictory."

Olson walked through the bathroom and took a cursory glance at Alec's still form. Then he extinguished the lights and motioned them to follow him. As they walked into the elevator Amory considered a piece of bravado—yielded finally. He reached out and tapped Olson on the arm.

"Would you mind taking off your hat? There's a lady in the elevator."

Olson's hat came off slowly. There was a rather embarrassing two minutes under the lights of the lobby while the night clerk and a few belated guests stared at them curiously; the loudly dressed girl with bent head, the handsome young man with his chin several points aloft; the inference was quite obvious. Then the chill outdoors—where the salt air was fresher and keener still with the first hints of morning.

"You can get one of those taxis and beat it," said Olson, pointing to the blurred outline of two machines whose drivers were presumably asleep inside.

"Good-by," said Olson. He reached in his pocket suggestively, but Amory snorted, and, taking the girl's arm, turned away.

"Where did you tell the driver to go?" she asked as they whirled along the dim street.

"The station."

"If that guy writes my mother——"

"He won't. Nobody'll ever know about this—except our friends and enemies."

Dawn was breaking over the sea.

"It's getting blue," she said.

"It does very well," agreed Amory critically, and then as an afterthought: "It's almost breakfast-time—do you want something to eat?"

"Food—" she said with a cheerful laugh. "Food is what queered the party. We ordered a big supper to be sent up to the room about two o'clock. Alec didn't give the waiter a tip, so I guess the little bastard snitched."

Jill's low spirits seemed to have gone faster than the scattering night. "Let me tell you," she said emphatically, "when you want to stage that sorta party stay away from liquor, and when you want to get tight stay away from bedrooms."

"I'll remember."

He tapped suddenly at the glass and they drew up at the door of an all-night restaurant.

"Is Alec a great friend of yours?" asked Jill as they perched themselves on high stools inside, and set their elbows on the dingy counter.

"He used to be. He probably won't want to be any more—and never understand why."

"It was sorta crazy you takin' all that blame. Is he pretty important? Kinda more important than you are?"

Amory laughed.

"That remains to be seen," he answered. "That's the question."

THE COLLAPSE OF SEVERAL PILLARS

Two days later back in New York Amory found in a newspaper what he had been searching for—a dozen lines which announced to whom it might concern that Mr. Amory Blaine, who "gave his address" as, etc., had been requested to leave his hotel in Atlantic City because of entertaining in his room a lady *not* his wife.

Then he started, and his fingers trembled, for directly above was a longer paragraph of which the first words were:

"Mr. and Mrs. Leland R. Connage are announcing the engagement of their daughter, Rosalind, to Mr. J. Dawson Ryder, of Hartford, Connecticut — —"

He dropped the paper and lay down on his bed with a frightened, sinking sensation in the pit of his stomach. She was gone, definitely, finally gone. Until now he had half unconsciously cherished the hope deep in his heart that some day she would need him and send for him, cry that it had been a mistake, that her heart ached only for the pain she had caused him. Never again could he find even the sombre luxury of wanting her—not this Rosalind, harder, older—nor any beaten, broken woman that his imagination brought to the door of his forties— Amory had wanted her youth, the fresh radiance of her mind and body, the stuff that she was selling now once and for all. So far as he was concerned, young Rosalind was dead.

A day later came a crisp, terse letter from Mr. Barton in Chicago, which informed him that as three more street-car companies had gone into the hands of receivers he could expect for the present no further remittances. Last of all, on a dazed Sunday night, a telegram told him of Monsignor Darcy's sudden death in Philadelphia five days before.

He knew then what it was that he had perceived among the curtains of the room in Atlantic City.

The Egotist Becomes

a Personage

A fathom deep in sleep I lie
*   With old desires, restrained before,*
To clamor lifeward with a cry,
*   As dark flies out the greying door;*
And so in quest of creeds to share
*   I seek assertive day again . . .*
But old monotony is there:
*   Endless avenues of rain.*

Oh, might I rise again! Might I
*   Throw off the heat of that old wine,*
See the new morning mass the sky
*   With fairy towers, line on line;*
Find each mirage in the high air
*   A symbol, not a dream again . . .*
But old monotony is there:
*   Endless avenues of rain.*

UNDER THE GLASS PORTE-COCHERE OF A THE-
atre Amory stood, watching the first great drops of rain splatter
down and flatten to dark stains on the sidewalk. The air became gray
and opalescent; a solitary light suddenly outlined a window over the
way; then another light; then a hundred more danced and glimmered
into vision. Under his feet a thick, iron-studded skylight turned yellow;
in the street the lamps of the taxicabs sent out glistening sheens along

the already black pavement. The unwelcome November rain had per-
versely stolen the day's last hour and pawned it with that ancient fence,
the night.

The silence of the theatre behind him ended with a curious snapping sound, followed by the heavy roaring of a rising crowd and the
interlaced clatter of many voices. The matinée was over.

He stood aside, edged a little into the rain to let the throng pass. A
small boy rushed out, sniffed in the damp, fresh air and turned up the
collar of his coat; came three or four couples in a great hurry; came a
further scattering of people whose eyes as they emerged glanced invariably, first at the wet street, then at the rain-filled air, finally at the
dismal sky; last a dense, strolling mass that depressed him with its
heavy odor compounded of the tobacco smell of the men and the fetid
sensuousness of stale powder on women. After the thick crowd came
another scattering; a stray half-dozen; a man on crutches; finally the
rattling bang of folding seats inside announced that the ushers were at
work.

New York seemed not so much awakening as turning over in its bed.
Pallid men rushed by, pinching together their coat-collars; a great
swarm of tired, magpie girls from a department-store crowded along
with shrieks of strident laughter, three to an umbrella; a squad of marching policemen passed, already miraculously protected by oilskin capes.

The rain gave Amory a feeling of detachment, and the numerous
unpleasant aspects of city life without money occurred to him in threatening procession. There was the ghastly, stinking crush of the subway—the car cards thrusting themselves at one, leering out like dull
bores who grab your arm with another story; the querulous worry as
to whether some one isn't leaning on you; a man deciding not to give
his seat to a woman, hating her for it; the woman hating him for not
doing it; at worst a squalid phantasmagoria of breath, and old cloth on
human bodies and the smells of the food men ate—at best just people—too hot or too cold, tired, worried.

He pictured the rooms where these people lived—where the patterns of the blistered wall-papers were heavy reiterated sunflowers on
green and yellow backgrounds, where there were tin bathtubs and
gloomy hallways and verdureless, unnamable spaces in back of the
buildings; where even love dressed as seduction—a sordid murder
around the corner, illicit motherhood in the flat above. And always
there was the economical stuffiness of indoor winter, and the long
summers, nightmares of perspiration between sticky enveloping walls
. . . dirty restaurants where careless, tired people helped themselves
to sugar with their own used coffee-spoons, leaving hard brown depos-
its in the bowl.

It was not so bad where there were only men or else only women; it was when they were vilely herded that it all seemed so rotten. It was some shame that women gave off at having men see them tired and poor—it was some disgust that men had for women who were tired and poor. It was dirtier than any battle-field he had seen, harder to contemplate than any actual hardship moulded of mire and sweat and danger, it was an atmosphere wherein birth and marriage and death were loathsome, secret things.

He remembered one day in the subway when a delivery boy had brought in a great funeral wreath of fresh flowers, how the smell of it had suddenly cleared the air and given every one in the car a momentary glow.

"I detest poor people," thought Amory suddenly. "I hate them for being poor. Poverty may have been beautiful once, but it's rotten now. It's the ugliest thing in the world. It's essentially cleaner to be corrupt and rich than it is to be innocent and poor." He seemed to see again a figure whose significance had once impressed him—a well-dressed young man gazing from a club window on Fifth Avenue and saying something to his companion with a look of utter disgust. Probably, thought Amory, what he said was: "My God! Aren't people horrible!"

Never before in his life had Amory considered poor people. He thought cynically how completely he was lacking in all human sympathy. O. Henry had found in these people romance, pathos, love, hate— Amory saw only coarseness, physical filth, and stupidity. He made no self-accusations: never any more did he reproach himself for feelings that were natural and sincere. He accepted all his reactions as a part of him, unchangeable, unmoral. This problem of poverty transformed, magnified, attached to some grander, more dignified attitude might some day even be his problem; at present it roused only his profound distaste.

He walked over to Fifth Avenue, dodging the blind, black menace of umbrellas, and standing in front of Delmonico's hailed an autobus. Buttoning his coat closely around him he climbed to the roof, where he rode in solitary state through the thin, persistent rain, stung into alertness by the cool moisture perpetually reborn on his check. Somewhere in his mind a conversation began, rather resumed its place in his attention. It was composed not of two voices, but of one, which acted alike as questioner and answerer:

Question.—Well—what's the situation?

Answer.—That I have about twenty-four dollars to my name.

Q.—You have the Lake Geneva estate.

A.—But I intend to keep it.

Q.—Can you live?

A. —I can't imagine not being able to. People make money in books and I've found that I can always do the things that people do in books. Really they are the only things I can do.

Q. —Be definite.

A. —I don't know what I'll do—nor have I much curiosity. Tomorrow I'm going to leave New York for good. It's a bad town unless you're on top of it.

Q. —Do you want a lot of money?

A. —No. I am merely afraid of being poor.

Q. —Very afraid?

A. —Just passively afraid.

Q. —Where are you drifting?

A. —Don't ask *me!*

Q. —Don't you care?

A. —Rather. I don't want to commit moral suicide.

Q. —Have you no interests left?

A. —None. I've no more virtue to lose. Just as a cooling pot gives off heat, so all through youth and adolescence we give off calories of virtue. That's what's called ingenuousness.

Q. —An interesting idea.

A. —That's why a "good man going wrong" attracts people. They stand around and literally *warm themselves* at the calories of virtue he gives off. Sarah makes an unsophisticated remark and the faces simper in delight—"How *innocent* the poor child is!" They're warming themselves at her virtue. But Sarah sees the simper and never makes that remark again. Only she feels a little colder after that.

Q. —All your calories gone?

A. —All of them. I'm beginning to warm myself at other people's virtue.

Q. —Are you corrupt?

A. —I think so. I'm not sure. I'm not sure about good and evil at all any more.

Q. —Is that a bad sign in itself?

A. —Not necessarily.

Q. —What would be the test of corruption?

A. —Becoming really insincere—calling myself "not such a bad fellow," thinking I regretted my lost youth when I only envy the delights of losing it. Youth is like having a big plate of candy. Sentimentalists think they want to be in the pure, simple state they were in before they ate the candy. They don't. They just want the fun of eating it all over again. The matron doesn't want to repeat her girlhood—she wants to repeat her honeymoon. I don't want to repeat my innocence. I want the pleasure of losing it again.

Q.—Where are you drifting?

This dialogue merged grotesquely into his mind's most familiar state—a grotesque blending of desires, worries, exterior impressions and physical reactions.

One Hundred and Twenty-seventh Street—or One Hundred and Thirty-seventh Street. . . . Two and three look alike—no, not much. Seat damp . . . are clothes absorbing wetness from seat, or seat absorbing dryness from clothes? . . . Sitting on wet substance gave appendicitis, so Froggy Parker's mother said. Well, he'd had it—I'll sue the steamboat company, Beatrice said, and my uncle has a quarter interest—did Beatrice go to heaven? . . . probably not— He represented Beatrice's immortality, also love-affairs of numerous dead men who surely had never thought of him . . . if it wasn't appendicitis, influenza maybe. What? One Hundred and Twentieth Street? That must have been One Hundred and Twelfth back there. One O Two instead of One Two Seven. Rosalind not like Beatrice, Eleanor like Beatrice, only wilder and brainier. Apartments along here expensive— probably hundred and fifty a month—maybe two hundred. Uncle had only paid hundred a month for whole great big house in Minneapolis. Question—were the stairs on the left or right as you came in? Anyway, in 12 Univee they were straight back and to the left. What a dirty river—want to go down there and see if it's dirty—French rivers all brown or black, so were Southern rivers. Twenty-four dollars meant four hundred and eighty doughnuts. He could live on it three months and sleep in the park. Wonder where Jill was—Jill Bayne, Fayne, Sayne—what the devil—neck hurts, darned uncomfortable seat. No desire to sleep with Jill, what could Alec see in her? Alec had a coarse taste in women. Own taste the best; Isabelle, Clara, Rosalind, Eleanor, were all-American. Eleanor would pitch, probably southpaw. Rosalind was outfield, wonderful hitter; Clara first base, maybe. Wonder what Humbird's body looked like now. If he himself hadn't been bayonet instructor he'd have gone up to line three months sooner, probably been killed. Where's the darned bell——

The street numbers of Riverside Drive were obscured by the mist and dripping trees from anything but the swiftest scrutiny, but Amory had finally caught sight of one—One Hundred and Twenty-seventh Street. He got off and with no distinct destination followed a winding, descending sidewalk and came out facing the river, in particular a long pier and a partioned litter of shipyards for miniature craft: small launches, canoes, rowboats, and catboats. He turned northward and followed the shore, jumped a small wire fence and found himself in a great disorderly yard adjoining a dock. The hulls of many boats in various stages of repair were around him; he smelled sawdust and paint and the scarcely distinguishable flat odor of the Hudson. A man approached through the heavy gloom.

"Hello," said Amory.

"Got a pass?"

"No. Is this private?"

"This is the Hudson River Sporting and Yacht Club."

"Oh! I didn't know. I'm just resting."

"Well—" began the man dubiously.

"I'll go if you want me to."

The man made non-committal noises in his throat and passed on. Amory seated himself on an overturned boat and leaned forward thoughtfully until his chin rested in his hand.

"Misfortune is liable to make me a damn bad man," he said slowly.

IN THE DROOPING HOURS

While the rain drizzled on Amory looked futilely back at the stream of his life, all its glitterings and dirty shallows. To begin with, he was still afraid—not physically afraid any more, but afraid of people and prejudice and misery and monotony. Yet, deep in his bitter heart, he wondered if he was after all worse than this man or the next. He knew that he could sophisticate himself finally into saying that his own weakness was just the result of circumstances and environment; that often when he raged at himself as an egotist something would whisper ingratiatingly: "No. Genius!" That was one manifestation of fear, that voice which whispered that he could not be both great and good, that genius was the exact combination of those inexplicable grooves and twists in his mind, that any discipline would curb it to mediocrity. Probably more than any concrete vice or failing Amory despised his own personality—he loathed knowing that tomorrow and the thousand days after he would swell pompously at a compliment and sulk at an ill word like a third-rate musician or a first-class actor. He was ashamed of the fact that very simple and honest people usually distrusted him; that he had been cruel, often, to those who had sunk their personalities in him— several girls, and a man here and there through college, that he had been an evil influence on; people who had followed him here and there into mental adventures from which he alone rebounded unscathed.

Usually, on nights like this, for there had been many lately, he could escape from this consuming introspection by thinking of children and the infinite possibilities of children—he leaned and listened and he heard a startled baby awake in a house across the street and lend a tiny whimper to the still night. Quick as a flash he turned away, wondering with a touch of panic whether something in the brooding despair of his mood had made a darkness in its tiny soul. He shivered. What if some day the balance was overturned, and he became a thing that frightened children and crept into rooms in the dark, approached dim communion with those phantoms who whispered shadowy secrets to the mad of that dark continent upon the moon. . . .

Amory smiled a bit.

"You're too much wrapped up in yourself," he heard some one say. And again — —

"Get out and do some real work — —"

"Stop worrying — —"

He fancied a possible future comment of his own.

"Yes — I was perhaps an egotist in youth, but I soon found it made me morbid to think too much about myself."

Suddenly he felt an overwhelming desire to let himself go to the devil — not to go violently as a gentleman should, but to sink safely and sensuously out of sight. He pictured himself in an adobe house in Mexico, half-reclining on a rug-covered couch, his slender, artistic fingers closed on a cigarette while he listened to guitars strumming melancholy undertones to an age-old dirge of Castile and an olive-skinned, carmine-lipped girl caressed his hair. Here he might live a strange litany, delivered from right and wrong and from the hound of heaven and from every God (except the exotic Mexican one who was pretty slack himself and rather addicted to Oriental scents)—delivered from success and hope and poverty into that long chute of indulgence which led, after all, only to the artificial lake of death.

There were so many places where one might deteriorate pleasantly: Port Said, Shanghai, parts of Turkestan, Constantinople, the South Seas—all lands of sad, haunting music and many odors, where lust could be a mode and expression of life, where the shades of night skies and sunsets would seem to reflect only moods of passion: the colors of lips and poppies.

STILL WEEDING

Once he had been miraculously able to scent evil as a horse detects a broken bridge at night, but the man with the queer feet in Phoebe's room had diminished to the aura over Jill. His instinct perceived the fetidness of poverty, but no longer ferreted out the deeper evils in pride and sensuality.

There were no more wise men; there were no more heroes; Burne

Holiday was sunk from sight as though he had never lived; Monsignor was dead. Amory had grown up to a thousand books, a thousand lies; he had listened eagerly to people who pretended to know, who knew nothing. The mystical reveries of saints that had once filled him with awe in the still hours of night, now vaguely repelled him. The Byrons and Brookes who had defied life from mountain tops were in the end but flaneurs and poseurs, at best mistaking the shadow of courage for the substance of wisdom. The pageantry of his disillusion took shape in a world-old procession of Prophets, Athenians, Martyrs, Saints, Scientists, Don Juans, Jesuits, Puritans, Fausts, Poets, Pacifists; like costumed alumni at a college reunion they streamed before him as their dreams, personalities, and creeds had in turn thrown colored lights on his soul; each had tried to express the glory of life and the tremendous significance of man; each had boasted of synchronizing what had gone before into his own rickety generalities; each had depended after all on the set stage and the convention of the theatre, which is that man in his hunger for faith will feed his mind with the nearest and most convenient food.

Women—of whom he had expected so much; whose beauty he had hoped to transmute into modes of art; whose unfathomable instincts, marvellously incoherent and inarticulate, he had thought to perpetuate in terms of experience—had become merely consecrations to their own posterity. Isabelle, Clara, Rosalind, Eleanor were all removed by their very beauty, around which men had swarmed, from the possibility of contributing anything but a sick heart and a page of puzzled words to write.

Amory based his loss of faith in help from others on several sweeping syllogisms. Granted that his generation, however bruised and decimated from this Victorian war, were the heirs of progress. Waving aside petty differences of conclusions which, although they might occasionally cause the deaths of several millions of young men, might be explained away—supposing that after all Bernard Shaw and Bernhardi, Bonar Law and Bethmann-Hollweg were mutual heirs of progress if only in agreeing against the ducking of witches—waiving the antitheses and approaching individually these men who seemed to be the leaders, he was repelled by the discrepancies and contradictions in the men themselves.

There was, for example, Thorton Hancock, respected by half the intellectual world as an authority on life, a man who had verified and believed the code he lived by, an educator of educators, an adviser to Presidents—yet Amory knew that this man had, in his heart, leaned on the priest of another religion.

And Monsignor, upon whom a cardinal rested, had moments of

strange and horrible insecurity—inexplicable in a religion that explained even disbelief in terms of its own faith: if you doubted the devil it was the devil that made you doubt him. Amory had seen Monsignor go to the houses of stolid philistines, read popular novels furiously, saturate himself in routine, to escape from that horror.

And this priest, a little wiser, somewhat purer, had been, Amory knew, not essentially older than he.

Amory was alone—he had escaped from a small enclosure into a great labyrinth. He was where Goethe was when he began "Faust"; he was where Conrad was when he wrote "Almayer's Folly."

Amory said to himself that there were essentially two sorts of people who through natural clarity or disillusion left the enclosure and sought the labyrinth. There were men like Wells and Plato, who had, half unconsciously, a strange, hidden orthodoxy, who would accept for themselves only what could be accepted for all men—incurable romanticists who never, for all their efforts, could enter the labyrinth as stark souls; there were on the other hand sword-like pioneering personalities, Samuel Butler, Renan, Voltaire, who progressed much slower, yet eventually much further, not in the direct pessimistic line of speculative philosophy but concerned in the eternal attempt to attach a positive value to life. . . .

Amory stopped. He began for the first time in his life to have a strong distrust of all generalities and epigrams. They were too easy, too dangerous to the public mind. Yet all thought usually reached the public after thirty years in some such form: Benson and Chesterton had popularized Huysmans and Newman; Shaw had sugar-coated Nietzche and Ibsen and Schopenhauer. The man in the street heard the conclusions of dead genius through some one else's clever paradoxes and didactic epigrams.

Life was a damned muddle . . . a football game with every one off-side and the referee gotten rid of—every one claiming the referee would have been on his side. . . .

Progress was a labyrinth . . . people plunging blindly in and then rushing wildly back, shouting that they had found it . . . the invisible king—the *élan vital*—the principle of evolution . . . writing a book, starting a war, founding a school. . . .

Amory, even had he not been a selfish man, would have started all inquiries with himself. He was his own best example—sitting in the rain, a human creature of sex and pride, foiled by chance and his own temperament of the balm of love and children, preserved to help in building up the living consciousness of the race.

In self-reproach and loneliness and disillusion he came to the entrance of the labyrinth.

* * *

Another dawn flung itself across the river; a belated taxi hurried along the street, its lamps still shining like burning eyes in a face white from a night's carouse. A melancholy siren sounded far down the river.

MONSIGNOR

Amory kept thinking how Monsignor would have enjoyed his own funeral. It was magnificently Catholic and liturgical. Cardinal O'Neil sang solemn high mass and the cardinal gave the final absolutions. Thorton Hancock, Mrs. Lawrence, the British and Italian ambassadors, the papal delegate, and a host of friends and priests were there — yet the inexorable shears had cut through all these threads that Monsignor had gathered into his hands. To Amory it was a haunting grief to see him lying in his coffin, with closed hands upon his purple vestments. His face had not changed, and, as he never knew he was dying, it showed no pain or fear. It was Amory's dear old friend, his and the others' — for the church was full of people with daft, staring faces, the most exalted seeming the most stricken.

The cardinal, like an archangel in cope and mitre, sprinkled the holy water; the organ broke into sound; the choir began to sing the "Requiem Eternam."

All these people grieved because they had to some extent depended upon Monsignor. Their grief was more than sentiment for the "crack in his voice or a certain break in his walk," as Wells put it. These people had leaned on Monsignor's faith, his way of finding cheer, of making religion a thing of lights and shadows, making all light and shadow merely aspects of God. People felt safe when he was near.

Of Amory's attempted sacrifice had been born merely the full realization of his disillusion, but of Monsignor's funeral was born the romantic elf who was to enter the labyrinth with him. He found something that he wanted, had always wanted and always would want — not to be admired, as he had feared; not to be loved, as he had made himself believe; but to be necessary to people, to be indispensable; he remembered the sense of security he had found in Burne.

Life opened up in one of its amazing bursts of radiance and Amory suddenly and permanently rejected an old epigram that had been playing listlessly in his mind: "Very few things matter and nothing matters very much."

On the contrary, Amory felt an immense desire to give people a sense of security.

THE BIG MAN WITH GOGGLES

On the day that Amory started on his walk to Princeton the sky was a colorless vault, cool, high and barren of the threat of rain. It was a gray day, that least fleshly of all weathers; a day of dreams and far hopes and clear visions. It was a day easily associated with those abstract truths and purities that dissolve in the sunshine or fade out in mocking laughter by the light of the moon. The trees and clouds were carved in classical severity; the sounds of the countryside had harmonized to a monotone, metallic as a trumpet, breathless as the Grecian urn.

The day had put Amory in such a contemplative mood that he caused much annoyance to several motorists who were forced to slow up considerably or else run him down. So engrossed in his thoughts was he that he was scarcely surprised at that strange phenomenon — cordiality manifested within fifty miles of Manhattan — when a passing car slowed down beside him and a voice hailed him. He looked up and saw a magnificent Locomobile in which sat two middle-aged men, one of them small and anxious looking, apparently an artificial growth on the other who was large and begoggled and imposing.

"Do you want a lift?" asked the apparently artificial growth, glancing from the corner of his eye at the imposing man as if for some habitual, silent corroboration.

"You bet I do. Thanks."

The chauffeur swung open the door, and, climbing in, Amory settled himself in the middle of the back seat. He took in his companions curiously. The chief characteristic of the big man seemed to be a great confidence in himself set off against a tremendous boredom with everything around him. That part of his face which protruded under the goggles was what is generally termed "strong"; rolls of not undignified fat had collected near his chin; somewhere above was a wide thin mouth and the rough model for a Roman nose, and, below, his shoulders collapsed without a struggle into the powerful bulk of his chest and belly. He was excellently and quietly dressed. Amory noticed that he was inclined to stare straight at the back of the chauffeur's head is if speculating steadily but hopelessly some baffling hirsute problem.

The smaller man was remarkable only for his complete submersion in the personality of the other. He was of that lower secretarial type who at forty have engraved upon their business cards: "Assistant to the President," and without a sigh consecrate the rest of their lives to second-hand mannerisms.

"Going far?" asked the smaller man in a pleasant disinterested way.

"Quite a stretch."

"Hiking for exercise?"

"No," responded Amory succinctly, "I'm walking because I can't afford to ride."

"Oh."

Then again:

"Are you looking for work? Because there's lots of work," he continued rather testily. "All this talk of lack of work. The West is especially short of labor." He expressed the West with a sweeping, lateral gesture. Amory nodded politely.

"Have you a trade?"

No—Amory had no trade.

"Clerk, eh?"

No—Amory was not a clerk.

"Whatever your line is," said the little man, seeming to agree wisely with something Amory had said, "now is the time of opportunity and business openings." He glanced again toward the big man, as a lawyer grilling a witness glances involuntarily at the jury.

Amory decided that he must say something and for the life of him could think of only one thing to say.

"Of course I want a great deal of money——"

The little man laughed mirthlessly but conscientiously.

"That's what every one wants nowadays, but they don't want to work for it."

"A very natural, healthy desire. Almost all normal people want to be rich without great effort—except the financiers in problems plays, who want to 'crash their way through.' Don't you want easy money?"

"Of course not," said the secretary indignantly.

"But," continued Amory disregarding him, "being very poor at present I am contemplating socialism as possibly my forte."

Both men glanced at him curiously.

"These bomb throwers—" The little man ceased as words lurched ponderously from the big man's chest.

"If I thought you were a bomb thrower I'd run you over to the Newark jail. That's what I think of Socialists."

Amory laughed.

"What are you," asked the big man, "one of these parlor Bolsheviks, one of these idealists? I must say I fail to see the difference. The idealists loaf around and write the stuff that stirs up the poor immigrants."

"Well," said Amory, "if being an idealist is both safe and lucrative, I might try it."

"What's your difficulty? Lost your job?"

"Not exactly, but—well, call it that."

"What was it?"

"Writing copy for an advertising agency."

"Lots of money in advertising."

Amory smiled discreetly.

"Oh, I'll admit there's money in it eventually. Talent doesn't starve any more. Even art gets enough to eat these days. Artists draw your magazine covers, write your advertisements, hash out rag-time for your theatres. By the great commercializing of printing you've found a harmless, polite occupation for every genius who might have carved his own niche. But beware the artist who's an intellectual also. The artist who doesn't fit—the Rousseau, the Tolstoi, the Samuel Butler, the Amory Blaine——"

"Who's he?" demanded the little man suspiciously.

"Well," said Amory, "he's a—he's an intellectual personage not very well known at present."

The little man laughed his conscientious laugh, and stopped rather suddenly as Amory's burning eyes turned on him.

"What are you laughing at?"

"These *intellectual* people——"

"Do you know what it means?"

The little man's eyes twitched nervously.

"Why, it *usually* means——"

"It *always* means brainy and well-educated," interrupted Amory. "It means having an active knowledge of the race's experience." Amory decided to be very rude. He turned to the big man. "The young man," he indicated the secretary with his thumb, and said young man as one says bell-boy, with no implication of youth, "has the usual muddled connotation of all popular words."

"You object to the fact that capital controls printing?" said the big man, fixing him with his goggles.

"Yes—and I object to doing their mental work for them. It seemed to me that the root of all the business I saw around me consisted in overworking and underpaying a bunch of dubs who submitted to it."

"Here now," said the big man, "you'll have to admit that the laboring man is certainly highly paid—five and six hour days—it's ridiculous. You can't buy an honest day's work from a man in the trade-unions."

"You've brought it on yourselves," insisted Amory. "You people never make concessions until they're wrung out of you."

"What people?"

"Your class; the class I belonged to until recently; those who by inheritance or industry or brains or dishonesty have become the moneyed class."

"Do you imagine that if that road-mender over there had the money he'd be any more willing to give it up?"

"No, but what's that got to do with it?"

The older man considered.

"No, I'll admit it hasn't. It rather sounds as if it had though."

"In fact," continued Amory, "he'd be worse. The lower classes are narrower, less pleasant and personally more selfish—certainly more stupid. But all that has nothing to do with the question."

"Just exactly what is the question?"

Here Amory had to pause to consider exactly what the question was.

AMORY COINS A PHRASE

"When life gets hold of a brainy man of fair education," began Amory slowly, "that is, when he marries he becomes, nine times out of ten, a conservative as far as existing social conditions are concerned. He may be unselfish, kind-hearted, even just in his own way, but his first job is to provide and to hold fast. His wife shoos him on, from ten thousand a year to twenty thousand a year, on and on, in an enclosed treadmill that hasn't any windows. He's done! Life's got him! He's no help! He's a spiritually married man."

Amory paused and decided that it wasn't such a bad phrase.

"Some men," he continued, "escape the grip. Maybe their wives have no social ambitions; maybe they've hit a sentence or two in a 'dangerous book' that pleased them; maybe they started on the tread-mill as I did and were knocked off. Anyway, they're the congressmen you can't bribe, the Presidents who aren't politicians, the writers, speakers, scientists, statesmen who aren't just popular grab-bags for a half-dozen women and children."

"He's the natural radical?"

"Yes," said Amory. "He may vary from the disillusioned critic like old Thorton Hancock, all the way to Trotsky. Now this spiritually unmarried man hasn't direct power, for unfortunately the spiritually married man, as a by-product of his money chase, has garnered in the great newspaper, the popular magazine, the influential weekly—so that Mrs. Newspaper, Mrs. Magazine, Mrs. Weekly can have a better limousine than those oil people across the street or those cement people 'round the corner."

"Why not?"

"It makes wealthy men the keepers of the world's intellectual conscience and, of course, a man who has money under one set of social institutions quite naturally can't risk his family's happiness by letting the clamor for another appear in his newspaper."

"But it appears," said the big man.

"Where?—in the discredited mediums. Rotten cheap-papered weeklies."

"All right—go on."

"Well, my first point is that through a mixture of conditions of which the family is the first, there are these two sorts of brains. One sort takes human nature as it finds it, uses its timidity, its weakness, and its strength for its own ends. Opposed is the man who, being spiritually unmarried, continually seeks for new systems that will control or counteract human nature. His problem is harder. It is not life that's complicated, it's the struggle to guide and control life. That is his struggle. He is a part of progress—the spiritually married man is not."

The big man produced three big cigars, and proffered them on his huge palm. The little man took one, Amory shook his head and reached for a cigarette.

"Go on talking," said the big man. "I've been wanting to hear one of you fellows."

GOING FASTER

"Modern life," began Amory again, "changes no longer century by century, but year by year, ten times faster than it ever has before— populations doubling, civilizations unified more closely with other civilizations, economic interdependence, racial questions, and—we're *dawdling* along. My idea is that we've got to go very much faster." He slightly emphasized the last words and the chauffeur unconsciously increased the speed of the car. Amory and the big man laughed; the little man laughed, too, after a pause.

"Every child," said Amory, "should have an equal start. If his father can endow him with a good physique and his mother with some common sense in his early education, that should be his heritage. If the father can't give him a good physique, if the mother has spent in chasing men the years in which she should have been preparing herself to educate her children, so much the worse for the child. He shouldn't be artificially bolstered up with money, sent to these horrible tutoring schools, dragged through college . . . Every boy ought to have an equal start."

"All right," said the big man, his goggles indicating neither approval nor objection.

"Next I'd have a fair trial of government ownership of all industries."

"That's been proven a failure."

"No—it merely failed. If we had government ownership we'd have the best analytical business minds in the government working for something besides themselves. We'd have Mackays instead of Burlesons; we'd have Morgans in the Treasury Department; we'd have Hills running interstate commerce. We'd have the best lawyers in the Senate."

"They wouldn't give their best efforts for nothing. McAdoo——"

"No," said Amory, shaking his head. "Money isn't the only stimulus that brings out the best that's in a man, even in America."

"You said a while ago that it was."

"It is, right now. But if it were made illegal to have more than a certain amount the best men would all flock for the one other reward which attracts humanity—honor."

The big man made a sound that was very like *boo*.

"That's the silliest thing you've said yet."

"No, it isn't silly. It's quite plausible. If you'd gone to college you'd have been struck by the fact that the men there would work twice as hard for any one of a hundred petty honors as those other men did who were earning their way through."

"Kids—child's play!" scoffed his antagonist.

"Not by a darned sight—unless we're all children. Did you ever see a grown man when he's trying for a secret society—or a rising family whose name is up at some club? They'll jump when they hear the sound of the word. The idea that to make a man work you've got to hold gold in front of his eyes is a growth, not an axiom. We've done that for so long that we've forgotten there's any other way. We've made a world where that's necessary. Let me tell you"—Amory became emphatic—"if there were ten men insured against either wealth or starvation, and offered a green ribbon for five hours' work a day and a blue ribbon for ten hours' work a day, nine out of ten of them would be trying for the blue ribbon. That competitive instinct only wants a badge. If the size of their house is the badge they'll sweat their heads off for that. If it's only a blue ribbon, I damn near believe they'll work just as hard. They have in other ages."

"I don't agree with you."

"I know it," said Amory nodding sadly. "It doesn't matter any more though. I think these people are going to come and take what they want pretty soon."

A fierce hiss came from the little man.

"Machine-guns!"

"Ah, but you've taught them their use."

The big man shook his head.

"In this country there are enough property owners not to permit that sort of thing."

Amory wished he knew the statistics of property owners and non-property owners; he decided to change the subject.

But the big man was aroused.

"When you talk of 'taking things away,' you're on dangerous ground."

"How can they get it without taking it? For years people have been stalled off with promises. Socialism may not be progress, but the threat of the red flag is certainly the inspiring force of all reform. You've got to be sensational to get attention."

"Russia is your example of a beneficent violence, I suppose?"

"Quite possibly," admitted Amory. "Of course, it's overflowing just as the French Revolution did, but I've no doubt that it's really a great experiment and well worth while."

"Don't you believe in moderation?"

"You won't listen to the moderates, and it's almost too late. The truth is that the public has done one of those startling and amazing things that they do about once in a hundred years. They've seized an idea."

"What is it?"

"That however the brains and abilities of men may differ, their stomachs are essentially the same."

THE LITTLE MAN GETS HIS

"If you took all the money in the world," said the little man with much profundity, "and divided it up in equ— —"

"Oh, shut up!" said Amory briskly and, paying no attention to the little man's enraged stare, he went on with his argument.

"The human stomach—" he began; but the big man interrupted rather impatiently.

"I'm letting you talk, you know," he said, "but please avoid stomachs. I've been feeling mine all day. Anyway, I don't agree with one-half you've said. Government ownership is the basis of your whole argument, and it's invariably a beehive of corruption. Men won't work for blue ribbons, that's all rot."

When he ceased the little man spoke up with a determined nod, as if resolved this time to have his say out.

"There are certain things which are human nature," he asserted with an owl-like look, "which always have been and always will be, which can't be changed."

Amory looked from the small man to the big man helplessly.

"Listen to that! *That's* what makes me discouraged with progress.

Listen to that! I can name offhand over one hundred natural phenomena that have been changed by the will of man—a hundred instincts in man that have been wiped out or are now held in check by civilization. What this man here just said has been for thousands of years the last refuge of the associated muttonheads of the world. It negates the efforts of every scientist, statesman, physician, inventor, and philosopher that ever gave his life to humanity's service. It's a flat impeachment of all that's worth while in human nature. Every person over twenty-five years old who makes that statement in cold blood ought to be deprived of the franchise."

The little man leaned back against the seat, his face purple with rage. Amory continued, addressing his remarks to the big man.

"These quarter-educated, stale-minded men such as your friend here, who *think* they think, every question that comes up, you'll find his type in the usual ghastly muddle. One minute it's 'the brutality and inhumanity of these Prussians'—the next it's 'we ought to exterminate the whole German people.' They always believe that 'things are in a bad way now,' but they 'haven't any faith in these idealists.' One minute they call Wilson 'just a dreamer, not practical'—a year later they rail at him for making his dreams realities. They haven't clear logical ideas on one single subject except a sturdy, stolid opposition to all change. They don't think uneducated people should be highly paid, but they won't see that if they don't pay the uneducated people their children are going to be uneducated too, and we're going round and round in a circle. That—is the great middle class!"

The big man with a broad grin on his face leaned over and smiled at the little man.

"You're catching it pretty heavy, Garvin; how do you feel?"

The little man made an attempt to smile and act as if the whole matter were so ridiculous as to be beneath notice. But Amory was not through.

"The theory that people are fit to govern themselves rests on this man. If he can be educated to think clearly, concisely, and logically, freed of his habit of taking refuge in platitudes and prejudices and sentimentalisms, then I'm a militant Socialist. If he can't, then I don't think it matters much what happens to man or his systems, now or hereafter."

"I am both interested and amused," said the big man. "You are very young."

"Which may only mean that I have neither been corrupted nor made timid by contemporary experience. I possess the most valuable experience, the experience of the race, for in spite of going to college I've managed to pick up a good education."

"You talk glibly."

"It's not all rubbish," cried Amory passionately. "This is the first time in my life I've argued Socialism. It's the only panacea I know. I'm restless. My whole generation is restless. I'm sick of a system where the richest man gets the most beautiful girl if he wants her, where the artist without an income has to sell his talents to a button manufacturer. Even if I had no talents I'd not be content to work ten years, condemned either to celibacy or a furtive indulgence, to give some man's son an automobile."

"But, if you're not sure ——"

"That doesn't matter," exclaimed Amory. "My position couldn't be worse. A social revolution might land me on top. Of course I'm selfish. It seems to me I've been a fish out of water in too many outworn systems. I was probably one of the two dozen men in my class at college who got a decent education; still they'd let any well-tutored flathead play football and *I* was ineligible, because some silly old men thought we should *all* profit by conic sections. I loathed the army. I loathed business. I'm in love with change and I've killed my conscience ——"

"So you'll go along crying that we must go faster."

"That, at least, is true," Amory insisted. "Reform won't catch up to the needs of civilization unless it's made to. A laissez-faire policy is like spoiling a child by saying he'll turn out all right in the end. He will—if he's made to."

"But you don't believe all this Socialist patter you talk."

"I don't know. Until I talked to you I hadn't thought seriously about it. I wasn't sure of half of what I said."

"You puzzle me," said the big man, "but you're all alike. They say Bernard Shaw, in spite of his doctrines, is the most exacting of all dramatists about his royalties. To the last farthing."

"Well," said Amory, "I simply state that I'm a product of a versatile mind in a restless generation—with every reason to throw my mind and pen in with the radicals. Even if, deep in my heart, I thought we were all blind atoms in a world as limited as a stroke of a pendulum, I and my sort would struggle against tradition; try, at least, to displace old cants with new ones. I've thought I was right about life at various times, but faith is difficult. One thing I know. If living isn't a seeking for the grail it may be a damned amusing game."

For a minute neither spoke and then the big man asked:

"What was your university?"

"Princeton."

The big man became suddenly interested; the expression of his goggles altered slightly.

"I sent my son to Princeton."

"Did you?"

"Perhaps you knew him. His name was Jesse Ferrenby. He was killed last year in France."

"I knew him very well. In fact, he was one of my particular friends."

"He was—a—quite a fine boy. We were very close."

Amory began to perceive a resemblance between the father and the dead son and he told himself that there had been all along a sense of familiarity. Jesse Ferrenby, the man who in college had borne off the crown that he had aspired to. It was all so far away. What little boys they had been, working for blue ribbons——

The car slowed up at the entrance to a great estate, ringed around by a huge hedge and a tall iron fence.

"Won't you come in for lunch?"

Amory shook his head.

"Thank you, Mr. Ferrenby, but I've got to get on."

The big man held out his hand. Amory saw that the fact that he had known Jesse more than outweighed any disfavor he had created by his opinions. What ghosts were people with which to work! Even the little man insisted on shaking hands.

"Good-by!" shouted Mr. Ferrenby, as the car turned the corner and started up the drive. "Good luck to you and bad luck to your theories."

"Same to you, sir," cried Amory, smiling and waving his hand.

"OUT OF THE FIRE, OUT OF THE LITTLE ROOM"

Eight hours from Princeton Amory sat down by the Jersey road-side and looked at the frost-bitten country. Nature as a rather coarse phenomenon composed largely of flowers that, when closely inspected, appeared motheaten, and of ants that endlessly traversed blades of grass, was always disillusioning; nature represented by skies and waters and far horizons was more likable. Frost and the promise of winter thrilled him now, made him think of a wild battle between St. Regis' and Groton, ages ago, seven years ago—and of an autumn day in France twelve months before when he had lain in tall grass, his platoon flattened down close around him, waiting to tap the shoulders of a Lewis gunner. He saw the two pictures together with somewhat the same primitive exaltation—two games he had played, differing in quality of acerbity, linked in a way that differed them from Rosalind or the subject of labyrinths which were, after all, the business of life.

"I am selfish," he thought.

"This is not a quality that will change when I 'see human suffering' or 'lose my parents' or 'help others.'

"This selfishness is not only part of me. It is the most living part.

"It is by somehow transcending rather than by avoiding that self-ishness that I can bring poise and balance into my life.

"There is no virtue of unselfishness that I cannot use. I can make sacrifices, be charitable, give to a friend, endure for a friend, lay down my life for a friend—all because these things may be the best possible expression of myself; yet I have not one drop of the milk of human kindness."

The problem of evil had solidified for Amory into the problem of sex. He was beginning to identify evil with the strong phallic worship in Brooke and the early Wells. Inseparably linked with evil was beauty—beauty, still a constant rising tumult; soft in Eleanor's voice, in an old song at night, rioting deliriously through life like superimposed waterfalls, half rhythm, half darkness. Amory knew that every time he had reached toward it longingly it had leered out at him with the grotesque face of evil. Beauty of great art, beauty of all joy, most of all the beauty of women.

After all, it had too many associations with license and indulgence. Weak things were often beautiful, weak things were never good. And in this new loneliness of his that had been selected for what greatness he might achieve, beauty must be relative or, itself a harmony, it would make only a discord.

In a sense this gradual renunciation of beauty was the second step after his disillusion had been made complete. He felt that he was leaving behind him his chance of being a certain type of artist. It seemed so much more important to be a certain sort of man.

His mind turned a corner suddenly and he found himself thinking of the Catholic Church. The idea was strong in him that there was a certain intrinsic lack in those to whom orthodox religion was necessary, and religion to Amory meant the Church of Rome. Quite conceivably it was an empty ritual but it was seemingly the only assimilative, traditionary bulwark against the decay of morals. Until the great mobs could be educated into a moral sense some one must cry: "Thou shalt not!" Yet any acceptance was, for the present, impossible. He wanted time and the absence of ulterior pressure. He wanted to keep the tree without ornaments, realize fully the direction and momentum of this new start.

The afternoon waned from the purging good of three o'clock to the golden beauty of four. Afterward he walked through the dull ache of a setting sun when even the clouds seemed bleeding and at twilight he came to a graveyard. There was a dusky, dreamy smell of flowers and the ghost of a new moon in the sky and shadows everywhere. On an impulse he considered trying to open the door of a rusty iron vault built into the side of a hill; a vault washed clean and covered with late-blooming, weepy watery-blue flowers that might have grown from dead eyes, sticky to the touch with a sickening odor.

Amory wanted to *feel* "William Dayfield, 1864."

He wondered that graves ever made people consider life in vain. Somehow he could find nothing hopeless in having lived. All the broken columns and clasped hands and doves and angels meant romances. He fancied that in a hundred years he would like having young people speculate as to whether his eyes were brown or blue, and he hoped quite passionately that his grave would have about it an air of many, many years ago. It seemed strange that out of a row of Union soldiers two or three made him think of dead loves and dead lovers, when they were exactly like the rest, even to the yellowish moss.

Long after midnight the towers and spires of Princeton were visible, with here and there a late-burning light—and suddenly out of the clear darkness the sound of bells. As an endless dream it went on; the spirit of the past brooding over a new generation, the chosen youth from the muddled, unchastened world, still fed romantically on the mistakes and half-forgotten dreams of dead statesmen and poets. Here was a new generation, shouting the old cries, learning the old creeds, through a revery of long days and nights; destined finally to go out into that dirty gray turmoil to follow love and pride; a new generation dedicated more than the last to the fear of poverty and the worship of success; grown up to find all Gods dead, all wars fought, all faiths in man shaken. . . .

Amory, sorry for them, was still not sorry for himself—art, politics, religion, whatever his medium should be, he knew he was safe now, free from all hysteria—he could accept what was acceptable, roam, grow, rebel, sleep deep through many nights. . . .

There was no God in his heart, he knew; his ideas were still in riot; there was ever the pain of memory; the regret for his lost youth—yet the waters of disillusion had left a deposit on his soul, responsibility and a love of life, the faint stirring of old ambitions and unrealized dreams. But—oh, Rosalind! Rosalind! . . .

"It's all a poor substitute at best," he said sadly.

And he could not tell why the struggle was worth while, why he had determined to use to the utmost himself and his heritage from the personalities he had passed. . . .

He stretched out his arms to the crystalline, radiant sky.

"I know myself," he cried, "but that is all."

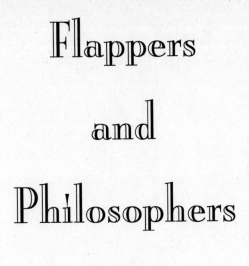

Flappers

and

Philosophers

To Zelda

Contents

The

Offshore

Pirate

THIS UNLIKELY STORY BEGINS ON A SEA THAT
was a blue dream, as colorful as blue-silk stockings, and beneath a
sky as blue as the irises of children's eyes. From the western half of the
sky the sun was shying little golden disks at the sea—if you gazed
intently enough you could see them skip from wave tip to wave tip
until they joined a broad collar of golden coin that was collecting half a
mile out and would eventually be a dazzling sunset. About half-way
between the Florida shore and the golden collar a white steam-yacht,
very young and graceful, was riding at anchor and under a blue-and-
white awning aft a yellow-haired girl reclined in a wicker settee reading "The Revolt of the Angels," by Anatole France.

She was about nineteen, slender and supple, with a spoiled alluring
mouth and quick gray eyes full of a radiant curiosity. Her feet, stock-

ingless, and adorned rather than clad in blue-satin slippers which swung nonchalantly from her toes, were perched on the arm of a settee adjoining the one she occupied. And as she read she intermittently regaled herself by a faint application to her tongue of a half-lemon that she held in her hand. The other half, sucked dry, lay on the deck at her feet and rocked very gently to and fro at the almost imperceptible motion of the tide.

The second half-lemon was well-nigh pulpless and the golden collar had grown astonishing in width, when suddenly the drowsy silence which enveloped the yacht was broken by the sound of heavy footsteps and an elderly man topped with orderly gray hair and clad in a white-flannel suit appeared at the head of the companionway. There he paused for a moment until his eyes became accustomed to the sun, and then seeing the girl under the awning he uttered a long even grunt of disapproval.

If he had intended thereby to obtain a rise of any sort he was doomed to disappointment. The girl calmly turned over two pages, turned back one, raised the lemon mechanically to tasting distance, and then very faintly but quite unmistakably yawned.

"Ardita!" said the gray-haired man sternly.

Ardita uttered a small sound indicating nothing.

"Ardita!" he repeated. "Ardita!"

Ardita raised the lemon languidly, allowing three words to slip out before it reached her tongue.

"Oh, shut up."

"Ardita!"

"What?"

"Will you listen to me—or will I have to get a servant to hold you while I talk to you?"

The lemon descended slowly and scornfully.

"Put it in writing."

"Will you have the decency to close that abominable book and discard that damn lemon for two minutes?"

"Oh, can't you lemme alone for a second?"

"Ardita, I have just received a telephone message from the shore——"

"Telephone?" She showed for the first time a faint interest.

"Yes, it was——"

"Do you mean to say," she interrupted wonderingly, "'at they let you run a wire out here?"

"Yes, and just now——"

"Won't other boats bump into it?"

"No. It's run along the bottom. Five min——"

"Well, I'll be darned! Gosh! Science is golden or something—isn't it?"

"Will you let me say what I started to?"

"Shoot!"

"Well, it seems—well, I am up here—" He paused and swallowed several times distractedly. "Oh, yes. Young woman, Colonel Moreland has called up again to ask me to be sure to bring you in to dinner. His son Toby has come all the way from New York to meet you and he's invited several other young people. For the last time, will you——"

"No," said Ardita shortly, "I won't. I came along on this darn cruise with the one idea of going to Palm Beach, and you knew it, and I absolutely refuse to meet any darn old colonel or any darn young Tobey or any darn old young people or to set foot in any other darn old town in this crazy state. So you either take me to Palm Beach or else shut up and go away."

"Very well. This is the last straw. In your infatuation for this man—a man who is notorious for his excesses, a man your father would not have allowed to so much as mention your name—you have reflected the demi-monde rather than the circles in which you have presumably grown up. From now on——"

"I know," interrupted Ardita ironically, "from now on you go your way and I go mine. I've heard that story before. You know I'd like nothing better."

"From now on," he announced grandiloquently, "you are no niece of mine. I——"

"O-o-o-oh!" The cry was wrung from Ardita with the agony of a lost soul. "Will you stop boring me! Will you go 'way! Will you jump overboard and drown! Do you want me to throw this book at you!"

"If you dare do any——"

Smack! "The Revolt of the Angels" sailed through the air, missed its target by the length of a short nose, and bumped cheerfully down the companionway.

The gray-haired man made an instinctive step backward and then two cautious steps forward. Ardita jumped to her five feet four and stared at him defiantly, her gray eyes blazing.

"Keep off!"

"How dare you!" he cried.

"Because I darn please!"

"You've grown unbearable! Your disposition——"

"You've made me that way! No child ever has a bad disposition unless it's her family's fault! Whatever I am, you did it."

Muttering something under his breath her uncle turned and, walking forward, called in a loud voice for the launch. Then he returned to the awning, where Ardita had again seated herself and resumed her attention to the lemon.

"I am going ashore," he said slowly. "I will be out again at nine o'clock to-night. When I return we will start back to New York, where I shall turn you over to your aunt for the rest of your natural, or rather unnatural, life."

He paused and looked at her, and then all at once something in the utter childishness of her beauty seemed to puncture his anger like an inflated tire and render him helpless, uncertain, utterly fatuous.

"Ardita," he said not unkindly, "I'm no fool. I've been round. I know men. And, child, confirmed libertines don't reform until they're tired—and then they're not themselves—they're husks of themselves." He looked at her as if expecting agreement, but receiving no sight or sound of it he continued. "Perhaps the man loves you—that's possible. He's loved many women and he'll love many more. Less than a month ago, one month, Ardita, he was involved in a notorious affair with that red-haired woman, Mimi Merril; promised to give her the diamond bracelet that the Czar of Russia gave his mother. You know—you read the papers."

"Thrilling scandals by an anxious uncle," yawned Ardita. "Have it filmed. Wicked clubman making eyes at virtuous flapper. Virtuous flapper conclusively vamped by his lurid past. Plans to meet him at Palm Beach. Foiled by anxious uncle."

"Will you tell me why the devil you want to marry him?"

"I'm sure I couldn't say," said Ardita shortly. "Maybe because he's the only man I know, good or bad, who has an imagination and the courage of his convictions. Maybe it's to get away from the young fools that spend their vacuous hours pursuing me around the country. But as for the famous Russian bracelet, you can set your mind at rest on that score. He's going to give it to me at Palm Beach—if you'll show a little intelligence."

"How about the—red-haired woman?"

"He hasn't seen her for six months," she said angrily. "Don't you suppose I have enough pride to see to that? Don't you know by this time that I can do any darn thing with any darn man I want to?"

She put her chin in the air like the statue of France Aroused, and then spoiled the pose somewhat by raising the lemon for action.

"Is it the Russian bracelet that fascinates you?"

"No, I'm merely trying to give you the sort of argument that would appeal to your intelligence. And I wish you'd go 'way," she said, her temper rising again. "You know I never change my mind. You've been boring me for three days until I'm about to go crazy. I won't go ashore! Won't! Do you hear? Won't!"

"Very well," he said, "and you won't go to Palm Beach either. Of all the selfish, spoiled, uncontrolled, disagreeable, impossible girls I have — —"

Splush! The half-lemon caught him in the neck. Simultaneously came a hail from over the side.

"The launch is ready, Mr. Farnam."

Too full of words and rage to speak, Mr. Farnam cast one utterly condemning glance at his niece and, turning, ran swiftly down the ladder.

II

Five o'clock rolled down from the sun and plumped soundlessly into the sea. The golden collar widened into a glittering island; and a faint breeze that had been playing with the edges of the awning and swaying one of the dangling blue slippers became suddenly freighted with song. It was a chorus of men in close harmony and in perfect rhythm to an accompanying sound of oars cleaving the blue waters. Ardita lifted her head and listened.

> "Carrots and peas,
>   Beans on their knees,
>   Pigs in the seas,
>   Lucky fellows!
>   Blow us a breeze,
>   Blow us a breeze,
>   Blow us a breeze,
>   With your bellows."

Ardita's brow wrinkled in astonishment. Sitting very still she listened eagerly as the chorus took up a second verse.

> "Onions and beans,
>   Marshalls and Deans,
>   Goldbergs and Greens
>   And Costellos.
>   Blow us a breeze,
>   Blow us a breeze,
>   Blow us a breeze,
>   With your bellows."

With an exclamation she tossed her book to the desk, where it sprawled at a straddle, and hurried to the rail. Fifty feet away a large rowboat was approaching containing seven men, six of them rowing and one standing up in the stern keeping time to their song with an orchestra leader's baton.

> "Oysters and rocks,
> Sawdust and socks,
> Who could make clocks
> Out of cellos? —"

The leader's eyes suddenly rested on Ardita, who was leaning over the rail spellbound with curiosity. He made a quick movement with his baton and the singing instantly ceased. She saw that he was the only white man in the boat—the six rowers were Negroes.

"Narcissus ahoy!" he called politely.

"What's the idea of all the discord?" demanded Ardita cheerfully. "Is this the varsity crew from the county nut farm?"

By this time the boat was scraping the side of the yacht and a great hulking Negro in the bow turned round and grasped the ladder. Thereupon the leader left his position in the stern and before Ardita had realized his intention he ran up the ladder and stood breathless before her on the deck.

"The women and children will be spared!" he said briskly. "All crying babies will be immediately drowned and all males put in double irons!"

Digging her hands excitedly down into the pockets of her dress Ardita stared at him, speechless with astonishment.

He was a young man with a scornful mouth and the bright blue eyes of a healthy baby set in a dark sensitive face. His hair was pitch black, damp and curly—the hair of a Grecian statue gone brunette. He was trimly built, trimly dressed, and graceful as an agile quarter-back.

"Well, I'll be a son of a gun!" she said dazedly.

They eyed each other coolly.

"Do you surrender the ship?"

"Is this an outburst of wit?" demanded Ardita. "Are you an idiot— or just being initiated to some fraternity?"

"I asked if you surrendered the ship."

"I thought the country was dry," said Ardita disdainfully. "Have you been drinking finger-nail enamel? You better get off this yacht!"

"What?" The young man's voice expressed incredulity.

"Get off the yacht! You heard me!"

He looked at her for a moment as if considering what she had said.

"No," said his scornful mouth slowly, "no, I won't get off the yacht. You can get off if you wish."

Going to the rail he gave a curt command and immediately the crew of the rowboat scrambled up the ladder and ranged themselves in line before him, a coal-black and burly darky at one end and a miniature mulatto of four feet nine at the other. They seemed to be uniformly dressed in some sort of blue costume ornamented with dust, mud, and tatters; over the shoulder of each was slung a small, heavy-looking white sack, and under their arms they carried large black cases apparently containing musical instruments.

"'Ten-*shun!*" commanded the young man, snapping his own heels together crisply. "Right *driss!* Front! Step out here, Babe!"

The smallest Negro took a quick step forward and saluted.

"Yas-suh!"

"Take command, go down below, catch the crew and tie 'em up—all except the engineer. Bring him up to me. Oh, and pile those bags by the rail there."

"Yas-suh!"

Babe saluted again and wheeling about motioned for the five others to gather about him. Then after a short whispered consultation they all filed noiselessly down the companionway.

"Now," said the young man cheerfully to Ardita, who had witnessed this last scene in withering silence, "if you will swear on your honor as a flapper—which probably isn't worth much—that you'll keep that spoiled little mouth of yours tight shut for forty-eight hours, you can row yourself ashore in our rowboat."

"Otherwise what?"

"Otherwise you're going to sea in a ship."

With a little sigh as for a crisis well passed, the young man sank into the settee Ardita had lately vacated and stretched his arms lazily. The corners of his mouth relaxed appreciatively as he looked round at the rich striped awning, the polished brass, and the luxurious fittings of the deck. His eye fell on the book, and then on the exhausted lemon.

"Hm," he said, "Stonewall Jackson claimed that lemon-juice cleared his head. Your head feel pretty clear?"

Ardita disdained to answer.

"Because inside of five minutes you'll have to make a clear decision whether it's go or stay."

He picked up the book and opened it curiously.

"'The Revolt of the Angels.' Sounds pretty good. French, eh?" He stared at her with new interest. "You French?"

"No."

"What's your name?"

"Farnam."

"Farnam what?"

"Ardita Farnam."

"Well, Ardita, no use standing up there and chewing out the insides of your mouth. You ought to break those nervous habits while you're young. Come over here and sit down."

Ardita took a carved jade case from her pocket, extracted a cigarette and lit it with a conscious coolness, though she knew her hand was trembling a little; then she crossed over with her supple, swinging walk, and sitting down in the other settee blew a mouthful of smoke at the awning.

"You can't get me off this yacht," she said steadily, "and you haven't got very much sense if you think you'll get far with it. My uncle'll have wirelesses zigzagging all over this ocean by half past six."

"Hm."

She looked quickly at his face, caught anxiety stamped there plainly in the faintest depression of the mouth's corners.

"It's all the same to me," she said, shrugging her shoulders. "'Tisn't my yacht. I don't mind going for a coupla hours' cruise. I'll even lend you that book so you'll have something to read on the revenue boat that takes you up to Sing Sing."

He laughed scornfully.

"If that's advice you needn't bother. This is part of a plan arranged before I ever knew this yacht existed. If it hadn't been this one it'd have been the next one we passed anchored along the coast."

"Who are you?" demanded Ardita suddenly. "And what are you?"

"You've decided not to go ashore?"

"I never even faintly considered it."

"We're generally known," he said, "all seven of us, as Curtis Carlyle and his Six Black Buddies, late of the Winter Garden and the Midnight Frolic."

"You're singers?"

"We were until to-day. At present, due to those white bags you see there, we're fugitives from justice, and if the reward offered for our capture hasn't by this time reached twenty thousand dollars I miss my guess."

"What's in the bags?" asked Ardita curiously.

"Well," he said, "for the present we'll call it—mud—Florida mud."

III

Within ten minutes after Curtis Carlyle's interview with a very frightened engineer, the yacht Narcissus was under way, steaming south through a balmy tropical twilight. The little mulatto, Babe, who seemed to have Carlyle's implicit confidence, took full command of the situation. Mr. Farnam's valet and the chef, the only members of the crew on board except the engineer, having shown fight, were now reconsidering, strapped securely to their bunks below. Trombone Mose, the biggest Negro, was set busy with a can of paint obliterating the name Narcissus from the bow, and substituting the name Hula Hula, and the others congregated aft and became intently involved in a game of craps.

Having given orders for a meal to be prepared and served on deck at seven-thirty, Carlyle rejoined Ardita, and, sinking back into his settee, half closed his eyes and fell into a state of profound abstraction.

Ardita scrutinized him carefully—and classed him immediately as a romantic figure. He gave the effect of towering self-confidence erected on a slight foundation—just under the surface of each of his decisions she discerned a hesitancy that was in decided contrast to the arrogant curl of his lips.

"He's not like me," she thought. "There's a difference somewhere."

Being a supreme egotist Ardita frequently thought about herself; never having had her egotism disputed she did it entirely naturally and with no detraction from her unquestioned charm. Though she was nineteen she gave the effect of a high-spirited, precocious child, and in the present glow of her youth and beauty all the men and women she had known were but driftwood on the ripples of her temperament. She had met other egotists—in fact she found that selfish people bored her rather less than unselfish people—but as yet there had not been one she had not eventually defeated and brought to her feet.

But though she recognized an egotist in the settee next to her, she felt none of that usual shutting of doors in her mind which meant clearing ship for action; on the contrary her instinct told her that this man was somehow completely pregnable and quite defenseless. When Ardita defied convention—and of late it had been her chief amusement—it was from an intense desire to be herself, and she felt that this man, on the contrary, was preoccupied with his own defiance.

She was much more interested in him than she was in her own situation, which affected her as the prospect of a matinée might affect a

ten-year-old child. She had implicit confidence in her ability to take
care of herself under any and all circumstances.

The night deepened. A pale new moon smiled misty-eyed upon the
sea, and as the shore faded dimly out and dark clouds were blown like
leaves along the far horizon a great haze of moonshine suddenly
bathed the yacht and spread an avenue of glittering mail in her swift
path. From time to time there was the bright flare of a match as one of
them lighted a cigarette, but except for the low undertone of the throb-
bing engines and the even wash of the waves about the stern, the yacht
was quiet as a dream boat star-bound through the heavens. Round
them flowed the smell of the night sea, bringing with it an infinite
languor.

Carlyle broke the silence at last.

"Lucky girl," he sighed, "I've always wanted to be rich—and buy
all this beauty."

Ardita yawned.

"I'd rather be you," she said frankly.

"You would—for about a day. But you do seem to possess a lot of
nerve for a flapper."

"I wish you wouldn't call me that."

"Beg your pardon."

"As to nerve," she continued slowly, "it's my one redeeming fea-
ture. I'm not afraid of anything in heaven or earth."

"Hm, I am."

"To be afraid," said Ardita, "a person has either to be very great
and strong—or else a coward. I'm neither." She paused for a moment,
and eagerness crept into her tone. "But I want to talk about you. What
on earth have you done—and how did you do it?"

"Why?" he demanded cynically. "Going to write a movie about
me?"

"Go on," she urged. "Lie to me by the moonlight. Do a fabulous
story."

A Negro appeared, switched on a string of small lights under the
awning, and began setting the wicker table for supper. And while they
ate cold sliced chicken, salad, artichokes, and strawberry jam from the
plentiful larder below, Carlyle began to talk, hesitantly at first, but
eagerly as he saw she was interested. Ardita scarcely touched her food
as she watched his dark young face—handsome, ironic, faintly ineffectual.

He began life as a poor kid in a Tennessee town, he said, so poor
that his people were the only white family in their street. He never
remembered any white children—but there were inevitably a dozen
pickaninnies streaming in his trail, passionate admirers whom he kept

in tow by the vividness of his imagination and the amount of trouble he was always getting them in and out of. And it seemed that this association diverted a rather unusual musical gift into a strange channel.

There had been a colored woman named Belle Pope Calhoun who played the piano at parties given for white children—nice white children that would have passed Curtis Carlyle with a sniff. But the ragged little "poh white" used to sit beside her piano by the hour and try to get in an alto with one of those kazoos that boys hum through. Before he was thirteen he was picking up a living teasing ragtime out of a battered violin in little cafés round Nashville. Eight years later the ragtime craze hit the country, and he took six darkies on the Orpheum circuit. Five of them were boys he had grown up with; the other was the little mulatto, Babe Divine, who was a wharf nigger round New York, and long before that a plantation hand in Bermuda, until he stuck an eight-inch stiletto in his master's back. Almost before Carlyle realized his good fortune he was on Broadway, with offers of engagements on all sides, and more money than he had ever dreamed of.

It was about then that a change began in his whole attitude, a rather curious, embittering change. It was when he realized that he was spending the golden years of his life gibbering round a stage with a lot of black men. His act was good of its kind—three trombones, three saxophones, and Carlyle's flute—and it was his own peculiar sense of rhythm that made all the difference; but he began to grow strangely sensitive about it, began to hate the thought of appearing, dreaded it from day to day.

They were making money—each contract he signed called for more—but when he went to managers and told them that he wanted to separate from his sextet and go on as a regular pianist, they laughed at him and told him he was crazy—it would be an artistic suicide. He used to laugh afterward at the phrase "artistic suicide." They all used it.

Half a dozen times they played at private dances at three thousand dollars a night, and it seemed as if these crystallized all his distaste for his mode of livelihood. They took place in clubs and houses that he couldn't have gone into in the daytime. After all, he was merely playing the role of the eternal monkey, a sort of sublimated chorus man. He was sick of the very smell of the theatre, of powder and rouge and the chatter of the greenroom, and the patronizing approval of the boxes. He couldn't put his heart into it any more. The idea of a slow approach to the luxury of leisure drove him wild. He was, of course, progressing toward it, but, like a child, eating his ice-cream so slowly that he couldn't taste it at all.

He wanted to have a lot of money and time, and opportunity to read and play, and the sort of men and women round him that he could never have—the kind who, if they thought of him at all, would have considered him rather contemptible; in short he wanted all those things which he was beginning to lump under the general head of aristocracy, an aristocracy which it seemed almost any money could buy except money made as he was making it. He was twenty-five then, without family or education or any promise that he would succeed in a business career. He began speculating wildly, and within three weeks he had lost every cent he had saved.

Then the war came. He went to Plattsburg, and even there his profession followed him. A brigadier-general called him up to head-quarters and told him he could serve the country better as a band leader—so he spent the war entertaining celebrities behind the line with a headquarters band. It was not so bad—except that when the infantry came limping back from the trenches he wanted to be one of them. The sweat and mud they wore seemed only one of those ineffable symbols of aristocracy that were forever eluding him.

"It was the private dances that did it. After I came back from the war the old routine started. We had an offer from a syndicate of Florida hotels. It was only a question of time then."

He broke off and Ardita looked at him expectantly, but he shook his head.

"No," he said, "I'm not going to tell you about it. I'm enjoying it too much, and I'm afraid I'd lose a little of that enjoyment if I shared it with any one else. I want to hang on to those few breathless, heroic moments when I stood out before them all and let them know I was more than a damn bobbing, squawking clown."

From up forward came suddenly the low sound of singing. The Negroes had gathered together on the deck and their voices rose together in a haunting melody that soared in poignant harmonics toward the moon. And Ardita listened in enchantment.

> "Oh down—
>   Oh down,
> Mammy wanna take me downa milky way,
> Oh down—
>   Oh down,
> Pappy say to-morra-a-a-ah!
> But mammy say to-day,
> Yes—mammy say to-day!"

Carlyle sighed and was silent for a moment, looking up at the gathered host of stars blinking like arclights in the warm sky. The

Negroes' song had died away to a plaintive humming, and it seemed as if minute by minute the brightness and the great silence were increasing until he could almost hear the midnight toilet of the mermaids as they combed their silver dripping curls under the moon and gossiped to each other of the fine wrecks they lived in on the green opalescent avenues below.

"You see," said Carlyle softly, "this is the beauty I want. Beauty has got to be astonishing, astounding—it's got to burst in on you like a dream, like the exquisite eyes of a girl."

He turned to her, but she was silent.

"You see, don't you, Anita—I mean, Ardita?"

Again she made no answer. She had been sound asleep for some time.

IV

In the dense sun-flooded noon of next day a spot in the sea before them resolved casually into a green-and-gray islet, apparently composed of a great granite cliff at its northern end which slanted south through a mile of vivid coppice and grass to a sandy beach melting lazily into the surf. When Ardita, reading in her favorite seat, came to the last page of "The Revolt of the Angels" and, slamming the book shut, looked up and saw it, she gave a little cry of delight and called to Carlyle, who was standing moodily by the rail.

"Is this it? Is this where you're going?"

Carlyle shrugged his shoulders carelessly.

"You've got me." He raised his voice and called up to the acting skipper: "Oh, Babe, is this your island?"

The mulatto's miniature head appeared from round the corner of the deck-house.

"Yas-suh! This yeah's it."

Carlyle joined Ardita.

"Looks sort of sporting, doesn't it?"

"Yes," she agreed, "but it doesn't look big enough to be much of a hiding-place."

"You still putting your faith in those wirelesses your uncle was going to have zigzagging round?"

"No," said Ardita frankly. "I'm all for you. I'd really like to see you make a get-away."

He laughed.

"You're our Lady Luck. Guess we'll have to keep you with us as a mascot—for the present, anyway."

"You couldn't very well ask me to swim back," she said coolly. "If you do I'm going to start writing dime novels founded on that interminable history of your life you gave me last night."

He flushed and stiffened slightly.

"I'm very sorry I bored you."

"Oh, you didn't—until just at the end with some story about how furious you were because you couldn't dance with the ladies you played music for."

He rose angrily.

"You have got a darn mean little tongue."

"Excuse me," she said, melting into laughter, "but I'm not used to having men regale me with the story of their life ambitions—especially if they've lived such deathly platonic lives."

"Why? What do men usually regale you with?"

"Oh, they talk about me," she yawned. "They tell me I'm the spirit of youth and beauty."

"What do you tell them?"

"Oh, I agree quietly."

"Does every man you meet tell you he loves you?"

Ardita nodded.

"Why shouldn't he? All life is just a progression toward, and then a recession from, one phrase—'I love you.'"

Carlyle laughed and sat down.

"That's very true. That's—that's not bad. Did you make that up?"

"Yes—or rather I found it out. It doesn't mean anything especially. It's just clever."

"It's the sort of remark," he said gravely, "that's typical of your class."

"Oh," she interrupted impatiently, "don't start that lecture on aristocracy again! I distrust people who can be intense at this hour in the morning. It's a mild form of insanity—a sort of breakfast-food jag. Morning's the time to sleep, swim, and be careless."

Ten minutes later they had swung round in a wide circle as if to approach the island from the north.

"There's a trick somewhere," commented Ardita thoughtfully. "He can't mean just to anchor up against this cliff."

They were heading straight in now toward the solid rock, which must have been well over a hundred feet tall, and not until they were within fifty yards of it did Ardita see their objective. Then she clapped her hands in delight. There was a break in the cliff entirely hidden by a curious overlapping of rock, and through this break the yacht entered and very slowly traversed a narrow channel of crystal-clear water between high gray walls. Then they were riding at anchor in a miniature world of green and gold, a gilded bay smooth as glass and set round with tiny palms, the whole resembling the mirror lakes and twig trees that children set up in sand piles.

"Not so darned bad!" said Carlyle excitedly. "I guess that little coon knows his way round this corner of the Atlantic."

His exuberance was contagious, and Ardita became quite jubilant.

"It's an absolutely sure-fire hiding-place!"

"Lordy, yes! It's the sort of island you read about."

The rowboat was lowered into the golden lake and they pulled ashore.

"Come on," said Carlyle as they landed in the slushy sand, "we'll go exploring."

The fringe of palms was in turn ringed in by a round mile of flat, sandy country. They followed it south and brushing through a farther rim of tropical vegetation came out on a pearl-gray virgin beach where Ardita kicked off her brown golf shoes—she seemed to have permanently abandoned stockings—and went wading. Then they sauntered back to the yacht, where the indefatigable Babe had luncheon ready for them. He had posted a lookout on the high cliff to the north to watch the sea on both sides, though he doubted if the entrance to the cliff was generally known—he had never even seen a map on which the island was marked.

"What's its name," asked Ardita—"the island, I mean?"

"No name 'tall," chuckled Babe. "Reckin she jus' island, 'at's all."

In the late afternoon they sat with their backs against great boulders on the highest part of the cliff and Carlyle sketched for her his vague plans. He was sure they were hot after him by this time. The total proceeds of the coup he had pulled off, and concerning which he still refused to enlighten her, he estimated as just under a million dollars. He counted on lying up here several weeks and then setting off southward, keeping well outside the usual channels of travel, rounding the Horn and heading for Callao, in Peru. The details of coaling and provisioning he was leaving entirely to Babe, who, it seemed, had sailed these seas in every capacity from cabin-boy aboard a coffee trader to virtual first mate on a Brazilian pirate craft, whose skipper had long since been hung.

"If he'd been white he'd have been king of South America long ago," said Carlyle emphatically. "When it comes to intelligence he makes Booker T. Washington look like a moron. He's got the guile of every race and nationality whose blood is in his veins, and that's half a dozen or I'm a liar. He worships me because I'm the only man in the world who can play better ragtime than he can. We used to sit together on the wharfs down on the New York water-front, he with a bassoon and me with an oboe, and we'd blend minor keys in African harmonics a thousand years old until the rats would crawl up the posts and sit round groaning and squeaking like dogs will in front of a phonograph."

Ardita roared.

"How you can tell 'em!"

Carlyle grinned.

"I swear that's the gos——"

"What you going to do when you get to Callao?" she interrupted.

"Take ship for India. I want to be a rajah. I mean it. My idea is to go up into Afghanistan somewhere, buy up a palace and a reputation, and then after about five years appear in England with a foreign accent and a mysterious past. But India first. Do you know, they say that all the gold in the world drifts very gradually back to India. Something fascinating about that to me. And I want leisure to read—an immense amount."

"How about after that?"

"Then," he answered defiantly, "comes aristocracy. Laugh if you want to—but at least you'll have to admit that I know what I want—which I imagine is more than you do."

"On the contrary," contradicted Ardita, reaching in her pocket for her cigarette case, "when I met you I was in the midst of a great uproar of all my friends and relatives because I did know what I wanted."

"What was it?"

"A man."

He started.

"You mean you were engaged?"

"After a fashion. If you hadn't come aboard I had every intention of slipping ashore yesterday evening—how long ago it seems—and meeting him in Palm Beach. He's waiting there for me with a bracelet that once belonged to Catharine of Russia. Now don't mutter anything about aristocracy," she put in quickly. "I liked him simply because he had had an imagination and the utter courage of his convictions."

"But your family disapproved, eh?"

"What there is of it—only a silly uncle and a sillier aunt. It seems he got into some scandal with a red-haired woman named Mimi something—it was frightfully exaggerated, he said, and men don't lie to me—and anyway I didn't care what he'd done; it was the future that counted. And I'd see to that. When a man's in love with me he doesn't care for other amusements. I told him to drop her like a hot cake, and he did."

"I feel rather jealous," said Carlyle, frowning—and then he laughed. "I guess I'll just keep you along with us until we get to Callao.

Then I'll lend you enough money to get back to the States. By that time you'll have had a chance to think that gentleman over a little more."

"Don't talk to me like that!" fired up Ardita. "I won't tolerate the parental attitude from anybody! Do you understand me?"

He chuckled and then stopped, rather abashed, as her cold anger seemed to fold him about and chill him.

"I'm sorry," he offered uncertainly.

"Oh, don't apologize! I can't stand men who say 'I'm sorry' in that manly, reserved tone. Just shut up!"

A pause ensued, a pause which Carlyle found rather awkward, but which Ardita seemed not to notice at all as she sat contentedly enjoying her cigarette and gazing out at the shining sea. After a minute she crawled out on the rock and lay with her face over the edge looking down. Carlyle, watching her, reflected how it seemed impossible for her to assume an ungraceful attitude.

"Oh, look!" she cried. "There's a lot of sort of ledges down there. Wide ones of all different heights."

He joined her and together they gazed down the dizzy height.

"We'll go swimming to-night!" she said excitedly. "By moonlight."

"Wouldn't you rather go in at the beach on the other end?"

"Not a chance. I like to dive. You can use my uncle's bathing-suit, only it'll fit you like a gunny sack, because he's a very flabby man. I've got a one-piece affair that's shocked the natives all along the Atlantic coast from Biddeford Pool to St. Augustine."

"I suppose you're a shark."

"Yes, I'm pretty good. And I look cute too. A sculptor up at Rye last summer told me my calves were worth five hundred dollars."

There didn't seem to be any answer to this, so Carlyle was silent, permitting himself only a discreet interior smile.

V

When the night crept down in shadowy blue and silver, they threaded the shimmering channel in the rowboat and, tying it to a jutting rock, began climbing the cliff together. The first shelf was ten feet up, wide, and furnishing a natural diving platform. There they sat down in the bright moonlight and watched the faint incessant surge of the waters, almost stilled now as the tide set seaward.

"Are you happy?" he asked suddenly.

She nodded.

"Always happy near the sea. You know," she went on, "I've been thinking all day that you and I are somewhat alike. We're both rebels—only for different reasons. Two years ago, when I was just eighteen, and you were——"

"Twenty-five."

"—well, we were both conventional successes. I was an utterly devastating débutante and you were a prosperous musician just commissioned in the army——"

"Gentleman by act of Congress," he put in ironically.

"Well, at any rate, we both fitted. If our corners were not rubbed off they were at least pulled in. But deep in us both was something that made us require more for happiness. I didn't know what I wanted. I went from man to man, restless, impatient, month by month getting less acquiescent and more dissatisfied. I used to sit sometimes chewing at the insides of my mouth and thinking I was going crazy—I had a frightful sense of transiency. I wanted things now—now—now! Here I was—beautiful—I am, aren't I?"

"Yes," agreed Carlyle tentatively.

Ardita rose suddenly.

"Wait a second. I want to try this delightful-looking sea."

She walked to the end of the ledge and shot out over the sea, doubling up in mid-air and then straightening out and entering the water straight as a blade in a perfect jack-knife dive.

In a minute her voice floated up to him.

"You see, I used to read all day and most of the night. I began to resent society——"

"Come on up here," he interrupted. "What on earth are you doing?"

"Just floating round on my back. I'll be up in a minute. Let me tell you. The only thing I enjoyed was shocking people; wearing something quite impossible and quite charming to a fancy-dress party, going round with the fastest men in New York, and getting into some of the most hellish scrapes imaginable."

The sounds of splashing mingled with her words, and then he heard her hurried breathing as she began climbing up the side of the ledge.

"Go on in!" she called.

Obediently he rose and dived. When he emerged, dripping, and made the climb, he found that she was no longer on the ledge, but after a frightened second he heard her light laughter from another shelf ten feet up. There he joined her and they both sat quietly for a moment, their arms clasped round their knees, panting a little from the climb.

"The family were wild," she said suddenly. "They tried to marry me off. And then when I'd begun to feel that after all life was scarcely

worth living I found something"—her eyes went skyward exultantly—
"I found something!"

Carlyle waited and her words came with a rush.

"Courage—just that; courage as a rule of life, and something to
cling to always. I began to build up this enormous faith in myself. I
began to see that in all my idols in the past some manifestation of
courage had unconsciously been the thing that attracted me. I began
separating courage from the other things of life. All sorts of courage—
the beaten, bloody prize-fighter coming up for more—I used to make
men take me to prize-fights; the déclassé woman sailing through a nest
of cats and looking at them as if they were mud under her feet; the
liking what you like always; the utter disregard for other people's opinions—just to live as I liked always and to die in my own way—Did you
bring up the cigarettes?"

He handed one over and held a match for her silently.

"Still," Ardita continued, "the men kept gathering—old men and
young men, my mental and physical inferiors, most of them, but all
intensely desiring to have me—to own this rather magnificent proud
tradition I'd built up round me. Do you see?"

"Sort of. You never were beaten and you never apologized."

"Never!"

She sprang to the edge, poised for a moment like a crucified figure
against the sky; then describing a dark parabola, plunked without a
slash between two silver ripples twenty feet below.

Her voice floated up to him again.

"And courage to me meant ploughing through that dull gray mist
that comes down on life—not only overriding people and circumstances but overriding the bleakness of living. A sort of insistence on
the value of life and the worth of transient things."

She was climbing up now, and at her last words her head, with the
damp yellow hair slicked symmetrically back, appeared on his level.

"All very well," objected Carlyle. "You can call it courage, but your
courage is really built, after all, on a pride of birth. You were bred to
that defiant attitude. On my gray days even courage is one of the
things that's gray and lifeless."

She was sitting near the edge, hugging her knees and gazing abstractedly at the white moon; he was farther back, crammed like a
grotesque god into a niche in the rock.

"I don't want to sound like Pollyanna," she began, "but you haven't
grasped me yet. My courage is faith—faith in the eternal resilience of
me—that joy'll come back, and hope and spontaneity. And I feel that
till it does I've got to keep my lips shut and my chin high, and my eyes
wide—not necessarily any silly smiling. Oh, I've been through hell

without a whine quite often—and the female hell is deadlier than the male."

"But supposing," suggested Carlyle, "that before joy and hope and all that came back the curtain was drawn on you for good?"

Ardita rose, and going to the wall climbed with some difficulty to the next ledge, another ten or fifteen feet above.

"Why," she called back, "then I'd have won!"

He edged out till he could see her.

"Better not dive from there! You'll break your back," he said quickly.

She laughed.

"Not I!"

Slowly she spread her arms and stood there swan-like, radiating a pride in her young perfection that lit a warm glow in Carlyle's heart.

"We're going through the black air with our arms wide," she called, "and our feet straight out behind like a dolphin's tail, and we're going to think we'll never hit the silver down there till suddenly it'll be all warm round us and full of little kissing, caressing waves."

Then she was in the air, and Carlyle involuntarily held his breath. He had not realized that the dive was nearly forty feet. It seemed an eternity before he heard the swift compact sound as she reached the sea.

And it was with his glad sigh of relief when her light watery laughter curled up the side of the cliff and into his anxious ears that he knew he loved her.

VI

Time, having no axe to grind, showered down upon them three days of afternoons. When the sun cleared the port-hole of Ardita's cabin an hour after dawn she rose cheerily, donned her bathing-suit, and went up on deck. The Negroes would leave their work when they saw her, and crowd, chuckling and chattering, to the rail as she floated, an agile minnow, on and under the surface of the clear water. Again in the cool of the afternoon she would swim—and loll and smoke with Carlyle upon the cliff; or else they would lie on their sides in the sands of the southern beach, talking little but watching the day fade colorfully and tragically into the infinite languor of a tropical evening.

And with the long, sunny hours Ardita's idea of the episode as incidental, madcap, a sprig of romance in a desert of reality, gradually left her. She dreaded the time when he would strike off southward; she dreaded all the eventualities that presented themselves to her; thoughts were suddenly troublesome and decisions odious. Had prayers found place in the pagan rituals of her soul she would have asked of life only to be unmolested for a while, lazily acquiescent to the ready, naïve flow of Carlyle's ideas, his vivid boyish imagination, and the vein of monomania that seemed to run crosswise through his temperament and colored his every action.

But this is not a story of two on an island, nor concerned primarily with love bred of isolation. It is merely the presentation of two personalities, and its idyllic setting among the palms of the Gulf Stream is quite incidental. Most of us are content to exist and breed and fight for the right to do both, and the dominant idea, the foredoomed attempt to control one's destiny, is reserved for the fortunate or unfortunate few. To me the interesting thing about Ardita is the courage that will tarnish with her beauty and youth.

"Take me with you," she said late one night as they sat lazily in the grass under the shadowy spreading palms. The Negroes had brought ashore their musical instruments, and the sound of weird ragtime was drifting softly over on the warm breath of the night. "I'd love to reappear in ten years as a fabulously wealthy high-caste Indian lady," she continued.

Carlyle looked at her quickly.

"You can, you know."

She laughed.

"Is it a proposal of marriage? Extra! Ardita Farnam becomes pirate's bride. Society girl kidnapped by ragtime bank robber."

"It wasn't a bank."

"What was it? Why won't you tell me?"

"I don't want to break down your illusions."

"My dear man, I have no illusions about you."

"I mean your illusions about yourself."

She looked up in surprise.

"About myself! What on earth have I got to do with whatever stray felonies you've committed?"

"That remains to be seen."

She reached over and patted his hand.

"Dear Mr. Curtis Carlyle," she said softly, "are you in love with me?"

"As if it mattered."

"But it does—because I think I'm in love with you."

He looked at her ironically.

"Thus swelling your January total to half a dozen," he suggested. "Suppose I call your bluff and ask you to come to India with me?"

"Shall I?"

He shrugged his shoulders.

"We can get married in Callao."

"What sort of life can you offer me? I don't mean that unkindly, but seriously; what would become of me if the people who want that twenty-thousand-dollar reward ever catch up with you?"

"I thought you weren't afraid."

"I never am—but I won't throw my life away just to show one man I'm not."

"I wish you'd been poor. Just a little poor girl dreaming over a fence in a warm cow country."

"Wouldn't it have been nice?"

"I'd have enjoyed astonishing you—watching your eyes open on things. If you only wanted things! Don't you see?"

"I know—like girls who stare into the windows of jewelry-stores."

"Yes—and want the big oblong watch that's platinum and has diamonds all round the edge. Only you'd decide it was too expensive and choose one of white gold for a hundred dollars. Then I'd say: 'Expensive? I should say not!' And we'd go into the store and pretty soon the platinum one would be gleaming on your wrist."

"That sounds so nice and vulgar—and fun, doesn't it?" murmured Ardita.

"Doesn't it? Can't you see us travelling round and spending money right and left, and being worshipped by bell-boys and waiters? Oh, blessed are the simple rich, for they inherit the earth!"

"I honestly wish we were that way."

"I love you, Ardita," he said gently.

Her face lost its childish look for a moment and became oddly grave.

"I love to be with you," she said, "more than with any man I've ever met. And I like your looks and your dark old hair, and the way you go over the side of the rail when we come ashore. In fact, Curtis Carlyle, I like all the things you do when you're perfectly natural. I think you've got nerve, and you know how I feel about that. Sometimes when you're around I've been tempted to kiss you suddenly and tell you that you were just an idealistic boy with a lot of caste nonsense in his head. Perhaps if I were just a little bit older and a little more bored I'd go with you. As it is, I think I'll go back and marry—that other man."

Over across the silver lake the figures of the Negroes writhed and squirmed in the moonlight, like acrobats who, having been too long inactive, must go through their tricks from sheer surplus energy. In single file they marched, weaving in concentric circles, now with their heads thrown back, now bent over their instruments like piping fauns.

And from trombone and saxophone ceaselessly whined a blended melody, sometimes riotous and jubilant, sometimes haunting and plaintive as a death-dance from the Congo's heart.

"Let's dance!" cried Ardita. "I can't sit still with that perfect jazz going on."

Taking her hand he led her out into a broad stretch of hard sandy soil that the moon flooded with great splendor. They floated out like drifting moths under the rich hazy light, and as the fantastic symphony wept and exulted and wavered and despaired, Ardita's last sense of reality dropped away, and she abandoned her imagination to the dreamy summer scents of tropical flowers and the infinite starry spaces overhead, feeling that if she opened her eyes it would be to find herself dancing with a ghost in a land created by her own fancy.

"This is what I should call an exclusive private dance," he whispered.

"I feel quite mad—but delightfully mad!"

"We're enchanted. The shades of unnumbered generations of cannibals are watching us from high up on the side of the cliff there."

"And I'll bet the cannibal women are saying that we dance too close, and that it was immodest of me to come without my nosering."

They both laughed softly—and then their laughter died as over across the lake they heard the trombone stop in the middle of a bar, and the saxophones give a startled moan and fade out.

"What's the matter?" called Carlyle.

After a moment's silence they made out the dark figure of a man rounding the silver lake at a run. As he came closer they saw it was Babe in a state of unusual excitement. He drew up before them and gasped out his news in a breath.

"Ship stan'in' off sho' 'bout half a mile, suh. Mose, he uz on watch, he say look's if she's done ancho'd."

"A ship—what kind of a ship?" demanded Carlyle anxiously.

Dismay was in his voice, and Ardita's heart gave a sudden wrench as she saw his whole face suddenly droop.

"He say he don't know, suh."

"Are they landing a boat?"

"No, suh."

"We'll go up," said Carlyle.

They ascended the hill in silence, Ardita's hand still resting in Carlyle's as it had when they finished dancing. She felt it clinch nervously from time to time as though he were unaware of the contact, but though he hurt her she made no attempt to remove it. It seemed an hour's climb before they reached the top and crept cautiously across the silhouetted plateau to the edge of the cliff. After one short look

Carlyle involuntarily gave a little cry. It was a revenue boat with six-inch guns mounted fore and aft.

"They know!" he said with a short intake of breath. "They know! They picked up the trail somewhere."

"Are you sure they know about the channel? They may be only standing by to take a look at the island in the morning. From where they are they couldn't see the opening in the cliff."

"They could with field-glasses," he said hopelessly. He looked at his wrist-watch. "It's nearly two now. They won't do anything until dawn, that's certain. Of course there's always the faint possibility that they're waiting for some other ship to join; or for a coaler."

"I suppose we may as well stay right here."

The hours passed and they lay there side by side, very silently, their chins in their hands like dreaming children. In back of them squatted the Negroes, patient, resigned, acquiescent, announcing now and then with sonorous snores that not even the presence of danger could subdue their unconquerable African craving for sleep.

Just before five o'clock Babe approached Carlyle. There were half a dozen rifles aboard the Narcissus he said. Had it been decided to offer no resistance? A pretty good fight might be made, he thought, if they worked out some plan.

Carlyle laughed and shook his head.

"That isn't a Spic army out there, Babe. That's a revenue boat. It'd be like a bow and arrow trying to fight a machine-gun. If you want to bury those bags somewhere and take a chance on recovering them later, go on and do it. But it won't work—they'd dig this island over from one end to the other. It's a lost battle all round, Babe."

Babe inclined his head silently and turned away, and Carlyle's voice was husky as he turned to Ardita.

"There's the best friend I ever had. He'd die for me, and be proud to, if I'd let him."

"You've given up?"

"I've no choice. Of course there's always one way out—the sure way—but that can wait. I wouldn't miss my trial for anything—it'll be an interesting experiment in notoriety. 'Miss Farnam testifies that the pirate's attitude to her was at all times that of a gentleman'."

"Don't!" she said. "I'm awfully sorry."

When the color faded from the sky and lustreless blue changed to leaden gray a commotion was visible on the ship's deck, and they made out a group of officers clad in white duck, gathered near the rail. They had field-glasses in their hands and were attentively examining the islet.

"It's all up," said Carlyle grimly.

"Damn!" whispered Ardita. She felt tears gathering in her eyes.

"We'll go back to the yacht," he said. "I prefer that to being hunted out up here like a 'possum."

Leaving the plateau they descended the hill, and reaching the lake were rowed out to the yacht by the silent Negroes. Then, pale and weary, they sank into the settees and waited.

Half an hour later, in the dim gray light, the nose of the revenue boat appeared in the channel and stopped, evidently fearing that the bay might be too shallow. From the peaceful look of the yacht, the man and the girl in the settees, and the Negroes lounging curiously against the rail, they evidently judged that there would be no resistance, for two boats were lowered casually over the side, one containing an officer and six bluejackets, and the other, four rowers and, in the stern, two gray-haired men in yachting flannels. Ardita and Carlyle stood up, and half unconsciously started toward each other. Then he paused and putting his hand suddenly into his pocket he pulled out a round, glittering object and held it out to her.

"What is it?" she asked wonderingly.

"I'm not positive, but I think from the Russian inscription inside that it's your promised bracelet."

"Where—where on earth——"

"It came out of one of those bags. You see, Curtis Carlyle and his Six Black Buddies, in the middle of their performance in the tearoom of the hotel at Palm Beach, suddenly changed their instruments for automatics and held up the crowd. I took this bracelet from a pretty, overrouged woman with red hair."

Ardita frowned and then smiled.

"So that's what you did! You *have* got nerve!"

He bowed.

"A well-known bourgeois quality," he said.

And then dawn slanted dynamically across the deck and flung the shadows reeling into gray corners. The dew rose and turned to golden mist, thin as a dream, enveloping them until they seemed gossamer relics of the late night, infinitely transient and already fading. For a moment sea and sky were breathless, and dawn held a pink hand over the young mouth of life—then from out in the lake came the complaint of a rowboat and the swish of oars.

Suddenly against the golden furnace low in the east their two graceful figures melted into one, and he was kissing her spoiled young mouth.

"It's a sort of glory," he murmured after a second.

She smiled up at him.

"Happy, are you?"

Her sigh was a benediction—an ecstatic surety that she was youth and beauty now as much as she would ever know. For another instant life was radiant and time a phantom and their strength eternal—then there was a bumping, scraping sound as the rowboat scraped alongside.

Up the ladder scrambled the two gray-haired men, the officer and two of the sailors with their hands on their revolvers. Mr. Farnam folded his arms and stood looking at his niece.

"So," he said, nodding his head slowly.

With a sigh her arms unwound from Carlyle's neck, and her eyes, transfigured and far away, fell upon the boarding party. Her uncle saw her upper lip slowly swell into that arrogant pout he knew so well.

"So," he repeated savagely. "So this is your idea of—of romance. A runaway affair, with a high-seas pirate."

Ardita glanced at him carelessly.

"What an old fool you are!" she said quietly.

"Is that the best you can say for yourself?"

"No," she said, as if considering. "No, there's something else. There's that well-known phrase with which I have ended most of our conversations for the past few years—'Shut up!'"

And with that she turned, included the two old men, the officer, and the two sailors in a curt glance of contempt, and walked proudly down the companionway.

But had she waited an instant longer she would have heard a sound from her uncle quite unfamiliar in most of their interviews. He gave vent to a whole-hearted amused chuckle, in which the second old man joined.

The latter turned briskly to Carlyle, who had been regarding this scene with an air of cryptic amusement.

"Well, Toby," he said genially, "you incurable, hare-brained, romantic chaser of rainbows, did you find that she was the person you wanted?"

Carlyle smiled confidently.

"Why—naturally," he said. "I've been perfectly sure ever since I first heard tell of her wild career. That's why I had Babe send up the rocket last night."

"I'm glad you did," said Colonel Moreland gravely. "We've been keeping pretty close to you in case you should have trouble with those six strange niggers. And we hoped we'd find you two in some such compromising position," he sighed. "Well, set a crank to catch a crank!"

"Your father and I sat up all night hoping for the best—or perhaps it's the worst. Lord knows you're welcome to her, my boy. She's run me crazy. Did you give her the Russian bracelet my detective got from that Mimi woman?"

Carlyle nodded.

"Sh!" he said. "She's coming on deck."

Ardita appeared at the head of the companionway and gave a quick involuntary glance at Carlyle's wrists. A puzzled look passed across her face. Back aft the Negroes had begun to sing, and the cool lake, fresh with dawn, echoed serenely to their low voices.

"Ardita," said Carlyle unsteadily.

She swayed a step toward him.

"Ardita," he repeated breathlessly, "I've got to tell you the—the truth. It was all a plant, Ardita. My name isn't Carlyle. It's Moreland, Toby Moreland. The story was invented, Ardita, invented out of thin Florida air."

She stared at him, bewildered amazement, disbelief, and anger flowing in quick waves across her face. The three men held their breaths. Moreland, Senior, took a step toward her; Mr. Farnam's mouth dropped a little open as he waited, panic-stricken, for the expected crash.

But it did not come. Ardita's face became suddenly radiant, and with a little laugh she went swiftly to young Moreland and looked up at him without a trace of wrath in her gray eyes.

"Will you swear," she said quietly, "that it was entirely a product of your own brain?"

"I swear," said young Moreland eagerly.

She drew his head down and kissed him gently.

"What an imagination!" she said softly and almost enviously. "I want you to lie to me just as sweetly as you know how for the rest of my life."

The Negroes' voices floated drowsily back, mingled in an air that she had heard them sing before.

> "Time is a thief;
> Gladness and grief
> Cling to the leaf
> As it yellows——"

"What was in the bags?" she asked softly.

"Florida mud," he answered. "That was one of the two true things I told you."

"Perhaps I can guess the other one," she said; and reaching up on her tiptoes she kissed him softly in the illustration.

The Ice

Palace

THE SUNLIGHT DRIPPED OVER THE HOUSE LIKE golden paint over an art jar, and the freckling shadows here and there only intensified the rigor of the bath of light. The Butterworth and Larkin houses flanking were intrenched behind great stodgy trees; only the Happer house took the full sun, and all day long faced the dusty road-street with a tolerant kindly patience. This was the city of Tarleton in southernmost Georgia, September afternoon.

Up in her bedroom window Sally Carrol Happer rested her nineteen-year-old chin on a fifty-two-year-old sill and watched Clark Darrow's ancient Ford turn the corner. The car was hot—being partly metallic it retained all the heat it absorbed or evolved—and Clark Darrow sitting bolt upright at the wheel wore a pained, strained ex-

pression as though he considered himself a spare part, and rather likely
to break. He laboriously crossed two dust ruts, the wheels squeaking
indignantly at the encounter, and then with a terrifying expression he
gave the steering-gear a final wrench and deposited self and car approximately in front of the Happer steps. There was a plaintive heav-
ing sound, a death-rattle, followed by a short silence; and then the air
was rent by a startling whistle.

Sally Carrol gazed down sleepily. She started to yawn, but finding
this quite impossible unless she raised her chin from the windowsill,
changed her mind and continued silently to regard the car, whose
owner sat brilliantly if perfunctorily at attention as he waited for an
answer to his signal. After a moment the whistle once more split the
dusty air.

"Good mawnin'."

With difficulty Clark twisted his tall body round and bent a distorted glance on the window.

"'Tain't mawnin', Sally Carrol."

"Isn't it, sure enough?"

"What you doin'?"

"Eatin' 'n apple."

"Come on go swimmin'—want to?"

"Reckon so."

"How 'bout hurrin' up?"

"Sure enough."

Sally Carrol sighed voluminously and raised herself with profound
inertia from the floor, where she had been occupied in alternately
destroying parts of a green apple and painting paper dolls for her
younger sister. She approached a mirror, regarded her expression with
a pleased and pleasant languor, dabbed two spots of rouge on her lips
and a grain of powder on her nose, and covered her bobbed corn-
colored hair with a rose-littered sunbonnet. Then she kicked over the
painting water, said, "Oh, damn!"—but let it lay—and left the room.

"How you, Clark?" she inquired a minute later as she slipped nim-
bly over the side of the car.

"Mighty fine, Sally Carrol."

"Where we go swimmin'?"

"Out to Walley's Pool. Told Marylyn we'd call by an' get her an'
Joe Ewing."

Clark was dark and lean, and when on foot was rather inclined to
stoop. His eyes were ominous and his expression somewhat petulant
except when startlingly illuminated by one of his frequent smiles. Clark
had "a income"—just enough to keep himself in ease and his car in

gasolene—and he had spent the two years since he graduated from
Georgia Tech in dozing round the lazy streets of his home town,
discussing how he could best invest his capital for an immediate fortune.

Hanging round he found not at all difficult; a crowd of little girls
had grown up beautifully, the amazing Sally Carrol foremost among
them; and they enjoyed being swum with and danced with and made
love to in the flower-filled summery evenings—and they all liked Clark
immensely. When feminine company palled there were half a dozen
other youths who were always just about to do something, and meanwhile were quite willing to join him in a few holes of golf, or a game of
billiards, or the consumption of a quart of "hard yella licker." Every
once in a while one of these contemporaries made a farewell round of
calls before going up to New York or Philadelphia or Pittsburgh to go
into business, but mostly they just stayed round in this languid paradise of dreamy skies and firefly evenings and noisy niggery street
fairs—and especially of gracious, soft-voiced girls, who were brought
up on memories instead of money.

The Ford having been excited into a sort of restless, resentful life,
Clark and Sally Carroll rolled and rattled down Valley Avenue into
Jefferson Street, where the dust road became a pavement; along opiate
Millicent Place, where there were half a dozen prosperous, substantial
mansions; and on into the down-town section. Driving was perilous
here, for it was shopping time; the population idled casually across the
streets and a drove of low-moaning oxen were being urged along in
front of a placid street-car; even the shops seemed only yawning their
doors and blinking their windows in the sunshine before retiring into a
state of utter and finite coma.

"Sally Carrol," said Clark suddenly, "it a fact that you're engaged?"

She looked at him quickly.

"Where'd you hear that?"

"Sure enough, you engaged?"

"'At's a nice question!"

"Girl told me you were engaged to a Yankee you met up in Asheville last summer."

Sally Carrol sighed.

"Never saw such an old town for rumors."

"Don't marry a Yankee, Sally Carrol. We need you round here."

Sally Carrol was silent a moment.

"Clark," she demanded suddenly, "who on earth shall I marry?"

"I offer my services."

"Honey, you couldn't support a wife," she answered cheerfully. "Anyway, I know you too well to fall in love with you."

"'At doesn't mean you ought to marry a Yankee," he persisted.

"S'pose I love him?"

He shook his head.

"You couldn't. He'd be a lot different from us, every way."

He broke off as he halted the car in front of a rambling, dilapidated house. Marylyn Wade and Joe Ewing appeared in the doorway.

"'Lo, Sally Carrol."

"Hi!"

"How you-all?"

"Sally Carrol," demanded Marylyn as they started off again, "you engaged?"

"Lawdy, where'd all this start? Can't I look at a man 'thout everybody in town engagin' me to him?"

Clark stared straight in front of him at a bolt on the clattering wind-shield.

"Sally Carrol," he said with a curious intensity, "don't you like us?"

"What?"

"Us down here?"

"Why, Clark, you know I do. I adore all you boys."

"Then why you gettin' engaged to a Yankee?"

"Clark, I don't know. I'm not sure what I'll do, but—well, I want to go places and see people. I want my mind to grow. I want to live where things happen on a big scale."

"What you mean?"

"Oh, Clark, I love you, and I love Joe here, and Ben Arrot, and you-all, but you'll—you'll——"

"We'll all be failures?"

"Yes. I don't mean only money failures, but just sort of—of ineffectual and sad, and—oh, how can I tell you?"

"You mean because we stay here in Tarleton?"

"Yes, Clark; and because you like it and never want to change things or think or go ahead."

He nodded and she reached over and pressed his hand.

"Clark," she said softly, "I wouldn't change you for the world. You're sweet the way you are. The things that'll make you fail I'll love always—the living in the past, the lazy days and nights you have, and all your carelessness and generosity."

"But you're goin' away?"

"Yes—because I couldn't ever marry you. You've a place in my heart no one else ever could have, but tied down here I'd get restless.

I'd feel I was—wastin' myself. There's two sides to me, you see. There's the sleepy old side you love; an' there's a sort of energy—the feelin' that makes me do wild things. That's the part of me that may be useful somewhere, that'll last when I'm not beautiful any more."

She broke off with characteristic suddenness and sighed, "Oh, sweet cooky!" as her mood changed.

Half closing her eyes and tipping back her head till it rested on the seat-back she let the savory breeze fan her eyes and ripple the fluffy curls of her bobbed hair. They were in the country now, hurrying between tangled growths of bright-green coppice and grass and tall trees that sent sprays of foliage to hang a cool welcome over the road. Here and there they passed a battered Negro cabin, its oldest white-haired inhabitant smoking a corncob pipe beside the door, and half a dozen scantily clothed pickaninnies parading tattered dolls on the wild-grown grass in front. Farther out were lazy cotton-fields, where even the workers seemed intangible shadows lent by the sun to the earth, not for toil, but to while away some age-old tradition in the golden September fields. And round the drowsy picturesqueness, over the trees and shacks and muddy rivers, flowed the heat, never hostile, only comforting, like a great warm nourishing bosom for the infant earth.

"Sally Carrol, we're here!"

"Poor chile's soun' asleep."

"Honey, you dead at last outa sheer laziness?"

"Water, Sally Carrol! Cool water waitin' for you!"

Her eyes opened sleepily.

"Hi!" she murmured, smiling.

II

In November Harry Bellamy, tall, broad, and brisk, came down from his Northern city to spend four days. His intention was to settle a matter that had been hanging fire since he and Sally Carrol had met in Asheville, North Carolina, in midsummer. The settlement took only a quiet afternoon and an evening in front of a glowing open fire, for Harry Bellamy had everything she wanted; and, besides, she loved him—loved him with that side of her she kept especially for loving. Sally Carrol had several rather clearly defined sides.

On his last afternoon they walked, and she found their steps tending half-unconsciously toward one of her favorite haunts, the cemetery. When it came in sight, gray-white and golden-green under the cheerful late sun, she paused, irresolute, by the iron gate.

"Are you mournful by nature, Harry?" she asked with a faint smile.

"Mournful? Not I."

"Then let's go in here. It depresses some folks, but I like it."

They passed through the gateway and followed a path that led through a wavy valley of graves—dusty-gray and mouldly for the fifties; quaintly carved with flowers and jars for the seventies; ornate and hideous for the nineties, with fat marble cherubs lying in sodden sleep on stone pillows, and great impossible growths of nameless granite flowers. Occasionally they saw a kneeling figure with tributary flowers, but over most of the graves lay silence and withered leaves with only the fragrance that their own shadowy memories could waken in living minds.

They reached the top of a hill where they were fronted by a tall, round head-stone, freckled with dark spots of damp and half grown over with vines.

"Margery Lee," she read, "1844-1873. Wasn't she nice? She died when she was twenty-nine. Dear Margery Lee," she added softly. "Can't you see her, Harry?"

"Yes, Sally Carrol."

He felt a little hand insert itself into his.

"She was dark, I think; and she always wore her hair with a ribbon in it, and gorgeous hoopskirts of Alice blue and old rose."

"Yes."

"Oh, she was sweet, Harry! And she was the sort of girl born to stand on a wide, pillared porch and welcome folks in. I think perhaps a lot of men went away to war meanin' to come back to her; but maybe none of 'em ever did."

He stooped down close to the stone, hunting for any record of marriage.

"There's nothing here to show."

"Of course not. How could there be anything there better than just 'Margery Lee,' and that eloquent date?"

She drew close to him and an unexpected lump came into his throat as her yellow hair brushed his cheek.

"You see how she was, don't you, Harry?"

"I see," he agreed gently. "I see through your precious eyes. You're beautiful now, so I know she must have been."

Silent and close they stood, and he could feel her shoulders trembling a little. An ambling breeze swept up the hill and stirred the brim of her floppity hat.

"Let's go down there!"

She was pointing to a flat stretch on the other side of the hill where along the green turf were a thousand grayish-white crosses stretching in endless, ordered rows like the stacked arms of a battalion.

"Those are the Confederate dead," said Sally Carrol simply.

They walked along and read the inscriptions, always only a name and a date, sometimes quite indecipherable.

"The last row is the saddest—see, 'way over there. Every cross has just a date on it, and the word 'Unknown.'"

She looked at him and her eyes brimmed with tears.

"I can't tell you how real it is to me, darling—if you don't know."

"How you feel about it is beautiful to me."

"No, no, it's not me, it's them—that old time that I've tried to have live in me. These were just men, unimportant evidently or they wouldn't have been 'unknown'; but they died for the most beautiful thing in the world—the dead South. You see," she continued, her voice still husky, her eyes glistening with tears, "people have these dreams they fasten onto things, and I've always grown up with that dream. It was so easy because it was all dead and there weren't any disillusions comin' to me. I've tried in a way to live up to those past standards of noblesse oblige—there's just the last remnants of it, you know, like the roses of an old garden dying all round us—streaks of strange courtliness and chivalry in some of these boys an' stories I used to hear from a Confederate soldier who lived next door, and a few old darkies. Oh, Harry, there was something, there was something! I couldn't ever make you understand, but it was there."

"I understand," he assured her again quietly.

Sally Carrol smiled and dried her eyes on the tip of a handkerchief protruding from his breast pocket.

"You don't feel depressed, do you, lover? Even when I cry I'm happy here, and I get a sort of strength from it."

Hand in hand they turned and walked slowly away. Finding soft grass she drew him down to a seat beside her with their backs against the remnants of a low broken wall.

"Wish those three old women would clear out," he complained. "I want to kiss you, Sally Carrol."

"Me, too."

They waited impatiently for the three bent figures to move off, and then she kissed him until the sky seemed to fade out and all her smiles and tears to vanish in an ecstasy of eternal seconds.

Afterward they walked slowly back together, while on the corners twilight played at somnolent black-and-white checkers with the end of day.

"You'll be up about mid-January," he said, "and you've got to stay a month at least. It'll be slick. There's a winter carnival on, and if you've never really seen snow it'll be like fairy-land to you. There'll be skating and skiing and tobogganing and sleigh-riding, and all sorts of torchlight parades on snow-shoes. They haven't had one for years, so they're going to make it a knock-out."

"Will I be cold, Harry?" she asked suddenly.

"You certainly won't. You may freeze your nose, but you won't be shivery cold. It's hard and dry, you know."

"I guess I'm a summer child. I don't like any cold I've ever seen." She broke off, and they were both silent for a minute.

"Sally Carrol," he said very slowly, "what do you say to—March?"

"I say I love you."

"March?"

"March, Harry."

III

All night in the Pullman it was very cold. She rang for the porter to ask for another blanket, and when he couldn't give her one she tried vainly, by squeezing down into the bottom of her berth and doubling back the bedclothes, to snatch a few hours' sleep. She wanted to look her best in the morning.

She rose at six and sliding uncomfortably into her clothes stumbled up to the diner for a cup of coffee. The snow had filtered into the vestibules and covered the floor with a slippery coating. It was intriguing, this cold, it crept in everywhere. Her breath was quite visible and she blew into the air with a naïve enjoyment. Seated in the diner she stared out the window at white hills and valleys and scattered pines whose every branch was a green platter for a cold feast of snow. Sometimes a solitary farmhouse would fly by, ugly and bleak and lone on the white waste; and with each one she had an instant of chill compassion for the souls shut in there waiting for spring.

As she left the diner and swayed back into the Pullman she experienced a surging rush of energy and wondered if she was feeling the bracing air of which Harry had spoken. This was the North, the North—her land now!

> "Then blow, ye winds, heigho!
> A-roving I will go,"

she chanted exultantly to herself.

"What's 'at?" inquired the porter politely.

"I said: 'Brush me off.'"

The long wires of the telegraph-poles doubled; two tracks ran up beside the train—three—four; came a succession of white-roofed houses, a glimpse of a trolley-car with frosted windows, streets—more streets—the city.

She stood for a dazed moment in the frosty station before she saw three fur-bundled figures descending upon her.

"There she is!"

"Oh, Sally Carrol!"

Sally Carrol dropped her bag.

"Hi!"

A faintly familiar icy-cold face kissed her, and then she was in a group of faces all apparently emitting great clouds of heavy smoke; she was shaking hands. There were Gordon, a short, eager man of thirty who looked like an amateur knocked-about model for Harry, and his wife, Myra, a listless lady with flaxen hair under a fur automobile cap. Almost immediately Sally Carrol thought of her as vaguely Scandinavian. A cheerful chauffeur adopted her bag, and amid ricochets of half-phrases, exclamations, and perfunctory listless "my dears" from Myra, they swept each other from the station.

Then they were in a sedan bound through a crooked succession of snowy streets where dozens of little boys were hitching sleds behind grocery wagons and automobiles.

"Oh," cried Sally Carrol, "I want to do that! Can we, Harry?"

"That's for kids. But we might——"

"It looks like such a circus!" she said regretfully.

Home was a rambling frame house set on a white lap of snow, and there she met a big, gray-haired man of whom she approved, and a lady who was like an egg, and who kissed her—these were Harry's parents. There was a breathless, indescribable hour crammed full of half-sentences, hot water, bacon and eggs and confusion; and after that she was alone with Harry in the library, asking him if she dared smoke.

It was a large room with a Madonna over the fireplace and rows upon rows of books in covers of light gold and dark gold and shiny red. All the chairs had little lace squares where one's head should rest, the couch was just comfortable, the books looked as if they had been read—some—and Sally Carrol had an instantaneous vision of the battered old library at home, with her father's huge medical books, and the oil-paintings of her three great-uncles, and the old couch that had been mended up for forty-five years and was still luxurious to dream in. This room struck her as being neither attractive nor particularly otherwise. It was simply a room with a lot of fairly expensive things in it that all looked about fifteen years old.

"What do you think of it up here?" demanded Harry eagerly. "Does it surprise you? Is it what you expected, I mean?"

"You are, Harry," she said quietly, and reached out her arms to him.

But after a brief kiss he seemed anxious to extort enthusiasm from her.

"The town, I mean. Do you like it? Can you feel the pep in the air?"

"Oh, Harry," she laughed, "you'll have to give me time. You can't just fling questions at me."

She puffed at her cigarette with a sigh of contentment.

"One thing I want to ask you," he began rather apologetically "You Southerners put quite an emphasis on family, and all that—not that it isn't quite all right, but you'll find it a little different here. I mean— you'll notice a lot of things that'll seem to you sort of vulgar display at first, Sally Carrol; but just remember that this is a three-generation town. Everybody has a father, and about half of us have grandfathers. Back of that we don't go."

"Of course," she murmured.

"Our grandfathers, you see, founded the place, and a lot of them had to take some pretty queer jobs while they were doing the founding. For instance, there's one woman who at present is about the social model for the town; well, her father was the first public ash man— things like that."

"Why," said Sally Carrol, puzzled, "did you s'pose I was goin' to make remarks about people?"

"Not at all," interrupted Harry, "and I'm not apologizing for any one either. It's just that—well, a Southern girl came up here last summer and said some unfortunate things, and—oh, I just thought I'd tell you."

Sally Carrol felt suddenly indignant—as though she had been unjustly spanked—but Harry evidently considered the subject closed, for he went on with a great surge of enthusiasm.

"It's carnival time, you know. First in ten years. And there's an ice palace they're building now that's the first they've had since eighty-five. Built out of blocks of the clearest ice they could find—on a tremendous scale."

She rose and walking to the window pushed aside the heavy Turkish portières and looked out.

"Oh!" she cried suddenly. "There's two little boys makin' a snow man! Harry, do you reckon I can go out an' help 'em?"

"You dream! Come here and kiss me."

She left the window rather reluctantly.

"I don't guess this is a very kissable climate, is it? I mean, it makes you so you don't want to sit round, doesn't it?"

"We're not going to. I've got a vacation for the first week you're here, and there's a dinner-dance to-night."

"Oh, Harry," she confessed, subsiding in a heap, half in his lap, half in the pillows, "I sure do feel confused. I haven't got an idea whether I'll like it or not, an' I don't know what people expect, or anythin'. You'll have to tell me, honey."

"I'll tell you," he said softly, "if you'll just tell me you're glad to be here."

"Glad—just awful glad!" she whispered, insinuating herself into his arms in her own peculiar way. "Where you are is home for me, Harry."

And as she said this she had the feeling for almost the first time in her life that she was acting a part.

That night, amid the gleaming candles of a dinner-party, where the men seemed to do most of the talking while the girls sat in a haughty and expensive aloofness, even Harry's presence on her left failed to make her feel at home.

"They're a good-looking crowd, don't you think?" he demanded. "Just look round. There's Spud Hubbard, tackle at Princeton last year, and Junie Morton—he and the red-haired fellow next to him were both Yale hockey captains; Junie was in my class. Why, the best athletes in the world come from these states round here. This is a man's country, I tell you. Look at John J. Fishburn!"

"Who's he?" asked Sally Carrol innocently.

"Don't you know?"

"I've heard the name."

"Greatest wheat man in the Northwest, and one of the greatest financiers in the country."

She turned suddenly to a voice on her right.

"I guess they forgot to introduce us. My name's Roger Patton."

"My name is Sally Carrol Happer," she said graciously.

"Yes, I know. Harry told me you were coming."

"You a relative?"

"No, I'm a professor."

"Oh," she laughed.

"At the university. You're from the South, aren't you?"

"Yes; Tarleton, Georgia."

She liked him immediately—a reddish-brown mustache under watery blue eyes that had something in them that these other eyes lacked, some quality of appreciation. They exchanged stray sentences through dinner, and she made up her mind to see him again.

After coffee she was introduced to numerous good-looking young men who danced with conscious precision and seemed to take it for granted that she wanted to talk about nothing except Harry.

'Heavens,' she thought, 'they talk as if my being engaged made me older than they are—as if I'd tell their mothers on them!'

In the South an engaged girl, even a young married woman, expected the same amount of half-affectionate badinage and flattery that would be accorded a débutante, but here all that seemed banned. One young man, after getting well started on the subject of Sally Carrol's eyes, and how they had allured him ever since she entered the room, went into a violent confusion when he found she was visiting the Bellamys—was Harry's fiancée. He seemed to feel as though he had made some risqué and inexcusable blunder, became immediately formal, and left her at the first opportunity.

She was rather glad when Roger Patton cut in on her and suggested that they sit out a while.

"Well," he inquired, blinking cheerily, "how's Carmen from the South?"

"Mighty fine. How's—how's Dangerous Dan McGrew? Sorry, but he's the only Northerner I know much about."

He seemed to enjoy that.

"Of course," he confessed, "as a professor of literature I'm not supposed to have read 'Dangerous Dan McGrew.' "

"Are you a native?"

"No, I'm a Philadelphian. Imported from Harvard to teach French. But I've been here ten years."

"Nine years, three hundred an' sixty-four days longer than me."

"Like it here?"

"Uh-huh. Sure do!"

"Really?"

"Well, why not? Don't I look as if I were havin' a good time?"

"I saw you look out the window a minute ago—and shiver."

"Just my imagination," laughed Sally Carrol. "I'm used to havin' everythin' quiet outside, an' sometimes I look out an' see a flurry of snow, an' it's just as if somethin' dead was movin'."

He nodded appreciatively.

"Ever been North before?"

"Spent two Julys in Asheville, North Carolina."

"Nice-looking crowd, aren't they?" suggested Patton, indicating the swirling floor.

Sally Carrol started. This had been Harry's remark.

"Sure are! They're—canine."

"What?"

She flushed.

"I'm sorry; that sounded worse than I meant it. You see, I always think of people as feline or canine, irrespective of sex."

"Which are you?"

"I'm feline. So are you. So are most Southern men an' most of these girls here."

"What's Harry?"

"Harry's canine distinctly. All the men I've met to-night seem to be canine."

"What does 'canine' imply? A certain conscious masculinity as opposed to subtlety?"

"Reckon so. I never analyzed it—only I just look at people an' say 'canine' or 'feline' right off. It's right absurd, I guess."

"Not at all. I'm interested. I used to have a theory about these people. I think they're freezing up."

"What?"

"I think they're growing like Swedes—Ibsenesque, you know. Very gradually getting gloomy and melancholy. It's these long winters. Ever read any Ibsen?"

She shook her head.

"Well, you find in his characters a certain brooding rigidity. They're righteous, narrow, and cheerless, without infinite possibilities for great sorrow or joy."

"Without smiles or tears?"

"Exactly. That's my theory. You see there are thousands of Swedes up here. They come, I imagine, because the climate is very much like their own, and there's been a gradual mingling. There're probably not half a dozen here to-night, but—we've had four Swedish governors. Am I boring you?"

"I'm mighty interested."

"Your future sister-in-law is half Swedish. Personally I like her, but my theory is that Swedes react rather badly on us as a whole. Scandinavians, you know, have the largest suicide rate in the world."

"Why do you live here if it's so depressing?"

"Oh, it doesn't get me. I'm pretty well cloistered, and I suppose books mean more than people to me anyway."

"But writers all speak about the South being tragic. You know— Spanish señoritas, black hair and daggers an' haunting music."

He shook his head.

"No, the Northern races are the tragic races—they don't indulge in the cheering luxury of tears."

Sally Carrol thought of her graveyard. She supposed that that was vaguely what she had meant when she said it didn't depress her.

"The Italians are about the gayest people in the world—but it's a dull subject," he broke off. "Anyway, I want to tell you you're marrying a pretty fine man."

Sally Carrol was moved by an impulse of confidence.

"I know. I'm the sort of person who wants to be taken care of after a certain point, and I feel sure I will be."

"Shall we dance? You know," he continued as they rose, "it's encouraging to find a girl who knows what she's marrying for. Nine-tenths of them think of it as a sort of walking into a moving-picture sunset."

She laughed, and liked him immensely.

Two hours later on the way home she nestled near Harry in the back seat.

"Oh, Harry," she whispered, "it's so co-old!"

"But it's warm in here, darling girl."

"But outside it's cold; and oh, that howling wind!"

She buried her face deep in his fur coat and trembled involuntarily as his cold lips kissed the tip of her ear.

IV

The first week of her visit passed in a whirl. She had her promised toboggan-ride at the back of an automobile through a chill January twilight. Swathed in furs she put in a morning tobogganing on the country-club hill; even tried skiing, to sail through the air for a glorious moment and then land in a tangle laughing bundle on a soft snowdrift. She liked all the winter sports, except an afternoon spent snow-shoeing over a glaring plain under pale yellow sunshine, but she soon realized that these things were for children—that she was being humored and that the enjoyment round her was only a reflection of her own.

At first the Bellamy family puzzled her. The men were reliable and she liked them; to Mr. Bellamy especially, with his iron-gray hair and energetic dignity, she took an immediate fancy, once she found that he was born in Kentucky; this made of him a link between the old life and the new. But toward the women she felt a definite hostility. Myra, her future sister-in-law, seemed the essence of spiritless conventionality. Her conversation was so utterly devoid of personality that Sally Carrol, who came from a country where a certain amount of charm and assurance could be taken for granted in the women, was inclined to despise her.

"If those women aren't beautiful," she thought, "they're nothing. They just fade out when you look at them. They're glorified domestics. Men are the centre of every mixed group."

Lastly there was Mrs. Bellamy, whom Sally Carrol detested. The first day's impression of an egg had been confirmed—an egg with a cracked, veiny voice and such an ungracious dumpiness of carriage that Sally Carrol felt that if she once fell she would surely scramble. In addition, Mrs. Bellamy seemed to typify the town in being innately hostile to strangers. She called Sally Carrol "Sally," and could not be persuaded that the double name was anything more than a tedious, ridiculous nickname. To Sally Carrol this shortening of her name was like presenting her to the public half clothed. She loved "Sally Carrol"; she loathed "Sally." She knew also that Harry's mother disapproved of her bobbed hair; and she had never dared smoke down-stairs after that first day when Mrs. Bellamy had come into the library sniffing violently.

Of all the men she met she preferred Roger Patton, who was a frequent visitor at the house. He never again alluded to the Ibsenesque tendency of the populace, but when he came in one day and found her curled upon the sofa bent over "Peer Gynt," he laughed and told her to forget what he'd said—that it was all rot.

And then one afternoon in her second week she and Harry hovered on the edge of a dangerously steep quarrel. She considered that he precipitated it entirely, though the Serbia in the case was an unknown man who had not had his trousers pressed.

They had been walking homeward between mounds of high-piled snow and under a sun which Sally Carrol scarcely recognized. They passed a little girl done up in gray wool until she resembled a small Teddy bear, and Sally Carrol could not resist a gasp of maternal appreciation.

"Look! Harry!"

"What?"

"That little girl—did you see her face?"

"Yes, why?"

"It was red as a little strawberry. Oh, she was cute!"

"Why, your own face is almost as red as that already! Everybody's healthy here. We're out in the cold as soon as we're old enough to walk. Wonderful climate!"

She looked at him and had to agree. He was mightily healthy-looking; so was his brother. And she had noticed the new red in her own cheeks that very morning.

Suddenly their glances were caught and held, and they stared for a moment at the street-corner ahead of them. A man was standing there, his knees bent, his eyes gazing upward with a tense expression as though he were about to make a leap toward the chilly sky. And then they both exploded into a shout of laughter, for coming closer they discovered it had been a ludicrous momentary illusion produced by the extreme bagginess of the man's trousers.

"Reckon that's one on us," she laughed.

"He must be a Southerner, judging by those trousers," suggested Harry mischievously.

"Why, Harry!"

Her surprised look must have irritated him.

"Those damn Southerners!"

Sally Carrol's eyes flashed.

"Don't call 'em that!"

"I'm sorry, dear," said Harry, malignantly apologetic, "but you know what I think of them. They're sort of—sort of degenerates—not at all like the old Southerners. They've lived so long down there with all the colored people that they've gotten lazy and shiftless."

"Hush your mouth, Harry!" she cried angrily. "They're not! They may be lazy—anybody would be in that climate—but they're my best friends, an' I don't want to hear 'em criticised in any such sweepin' way. Some of 'em are the finest men in the world."

"Oh, I know. They're all right when they come North to college, but of all the hangdog, ill-dressed, slovenly lot I ever saw, a bunch of small-town Southerners are the worst!"

Sally Carrol was clenching her gloved hands and biting her lip furiously.

"Why," continued Harry, "there was one in my class at New Haven, and we all thought that at last we'd found the true type of Southern aristocrat, but it turned out that he wasn't an aristocrat at all—just the son of a Northern carpetbagger who owned about all the cotton round Mobile."

"A Southerner wouldn't talk the way you're talking now," she said evenly.

"They haven't the energy!"

"Or the somethin' else."

"I'm sorry, Sally Carrol, but I've heard you say yourself that you'd never marry——"

"That's quite different. I told you I wouldn't want to tie my life to any of the boys that are round Tarleton now, but I never made any sweepin' generalities."

They walked along in silence.

"I probably spread it on a bit thick, Sally Carrol. I'm sorry."

She nodded but made no answer. Five minutes later as they stood in the hallway she suddenly threw her arms round him.

"Oh, Harry," she cried, her eyes brimming with tears, "let's get married next week. I'm afraid of having fusses like that. I'm afraid, Harry. It wouldn't be that way if we were married."

But Harry, being in the wrong, was still irritated.

"That'd be idiotic. We decided on March."

The tears in Sally Carrol's eyes faded; her expression hardened slightly.

"Very well—I suppose I shouldn't have said that."

Harry melted.

"Dear little nut!" he cried. "Come and kiss me and let's forget."

That very night at the end of a vaudeville performance the orchestra played "Dixie," and Sally Carrol felt something stronger and more enduring than her tears and smiles of the day brim up inside her. She leaned forward gripping the arms of her chair until her face grew crimson.

"Sort of get you, dear?" whispered Harry.

But she did not hear him. To the spirited throb of the violins and the inspiring beat of the kettledrums her own old ghosts were marching by and on into the darkness, and as fifes whistled and sighed in the low encore they seemed so nearly out of sight that she could have waved good-by.

> "Away, Away,
>   Away down South in Dixie!
> Away, away,
>   Away down South in Dixie!"

V

It was a particularly cold night. A sudden thaw had nearly cleared the streets the day before, but now they were traversed again with a powdery wraith of loose snow that travelled in wavy lines before the feet of the wind, and filled the lower air with a fine-particled mist. There was no sky—only a dark, ominous tent that draped in the tops of the streets and was in reality a vast approaching army of snow-flakes—while over it all, chilling away the comfort from the brown-and-green glow of lighted windows and muffling the steady trot of the horse pulling their sleigh, interminably washed the north wind. It was a dismal town after all, she thought—dismal.

Sometimes at night it had seemed to her as though no one lived here—they had all gone long ago—leaving lighted houses to be covered in time by tombing heaps of sleet. Oh, if there should be snow on her grave! To be beneath great piles of it all winter long, where even her headstone would be a light shadow against light shadows. Her grave—a grave that should be flower-strewn and washed with sun and rain.

She thought again of those isolated country houses that her train had passed, and of the life there the long winter through—the ceaseless glare through the windows, the crust forming on the soft drifts of snow, finally the slow, cheerless melting, and the harsh spring of which Roger Patton had told her. Her spring—to lose it forever—with its lilacs and the lazy sweetness it stirred in her heart. She was laying away that spring—afterward she would lay away that sweetness.

With a gradual insistence the storm broke. Sally Carrol felt a film of flakes melt quickly on her eyelashes, and Harry reached over a furry arm and drew down her complicated flannel cap. Then the small flakes came in skirmish-line, and the horse bent his neck patiently as a transparency of white appeared momentarily on his coat.

"Oh, he's cold, Harry," she said quickly.

"Who? The horse? Oh, no, he isn't. He likes it!"

After another ten minutes they turned a corner and came in sight of their destination. On a tall hill, outlined in vivid glaring green against the wintry sky, stood the ice palace. It was three stories in the air, with battlements and embrasures and narrow icicled windows, and the innumerable electric lights inside made a gorgeous transparency of the great central hall. Sally Carrol clutched Harry's hand under the fur robe.

"It's beautiful!" he cried excitedly. "My golly, it's beautiful, isn't it! They haven't had one here since eighty-five!"

Somehow the notion of there not having been one since eighty-five oppressed her. Ice was a ghost, and this mansion of it was surely peopled by those shades of the eighties, with pale faces and blurred snow-filled hair.

"Come on, dear," said Harry.

She followed him out of the sleigh and waited while he hitched the horse. A party of four—Gordon, Myra, Roger Patton, and another girl—drew up beside them with a mighty jingle of bells. There was quite a crowd already, bundled in fur or sheepskin, shouting and calling to each other as they moved through the snow, which was now so thick that people could scarcely be distinguished a few yards away.

"It's a hundred and seventy feet tall," Harry was saying to a muffled figure beside him as they trudged toward the entrance, "covers six thousand square yards."

She caught snatches of conversation: "One main hall"—"walls twenty to forty inches thick"—"and the ice cave has almost a mile of—"—"this Canuck who built it——"

They found their way inside, and dazed by the magic of the great crystal walls Sally Carrol found herself repeating over and over two lines from "Kubla Khan":

It was a miracle of rare device,
A sunny pleasure-dome with caves of ice!

In the great glittering cavern with the dark shut out she took a seat on a wooden bench, and the evening's oppression lifted. Harry was right—it was beautiful; and her gaze travelled the smooth surface of the walls, the blocks for which had been selected for their purity and clearness to obtain this opalescent, translucent effect.

"Look! Here we go—oh, boy!" cried Harry.

A band in a far corner struck up "Hail, Hail, the Gang's All Here!" which echoed over to them in wild muddled acoustics, and then the lights suddenly went out; silence seemed to flow down the icy sides and sweep over them. Sally Carrol could still see her white breath in the darkness, and a dim row of pale faces over on the other side.

The music eased to a sighing complaint, and from outside drifted in the full-throated resonant chant of the marching clubs. It grew louder like some pæan of a viking tribe traversing an ancient wild; it swelled—they were coming nearer; then a row of torches appeared, and another and another, and keeping time with their moccasined feet a long column of gray-mackinawed figures swept in, snowshoes slung at their shoulders, torches soaring and flickering as their voices rose along the great walls.

The gray column ended and another followed, the light streaming luridly this time over red toboggan caps and flaming crimson mackinaws, and as they entered they took up the refrain; then came a long platoon of blue and white, of green, of white, of brown and yellow.

"Those white ones are the Wacouta Club," whispered Harry eagerly. "Those are the men you've met round at dances."

The volume of the voices grew; the great cavern was a phantasmagoria of torches waving in great banks of fire, of colors and the rhythm of soft-leather steps. The leading column turned and halted, platoon deployed in front of platoon until the whole procession made a solid flag of flame, and then from thousands of voices burst a mighty shout that filled the air like a crash of thunder, and sent the torches wavering. It was magnificent, it was tremendous! To Sally Carrol it was the North offering sacrifice on some mighty altar to the gray pagan God of Snow. As the shout died the band struck up again and there came more singing, and then long reverberating cheers by each club. She sat very quiet, listening while the staccato cries rent the stillness; and then she started, for there was a volley of explosion, and great clouds of smoke went up here and there through the cavern—the flash-light photographers at work—and the council was over. With the band at their head the clubs formed in column once more, took up their chant, and began to march out.

"Come on!" shouted Harry. "We want to see the labyrinths downstairs before they turn the lights off!"

They all rose and started toward the chute—Harry and Sally Carrol in the lead, her little mitten buried in his big fur gantlet. At the bottom of the chute was a long empty room of ice, with the ceiling so low that they had to stoop—and their hands were parted. Before she realized what he intended Harry had darted down one of the half-dozen glittering passages that opened into the room and was only a vague receding blot against the green shimmer.

"Harry!" she called.

"Come on!" he cried back.

She looked round the empty chamber; the rest of the party had evidently decided to go home, were already outside somewhere in the blundering snow. She hesitated and then darted in after Harry.

"Harry!" she shouted.

She had reached a turning-point thirty feet down; she heard a faint muffled answer far to the left, and with a touch of panic fled toward it. She passed another turning, two more yawning alleys.

"Harry!"

No answer. She started to run straight forward, and then turned like lightning and sped back the way she had come, enveloped in a sudden icy terror.

She reached a turn—was it here?—took the left and came to what should have been the outlet into the long, low room, but it was only another glittering passage with darkness at the end. She called again, but the walls gave back a flat, lifeless echo with no reverberations. Retracing her steps she turned another corner, this time following a wide passage. It was like the green lane between the parted waters of the Red Sea, like a damp vault connecting empty tombs.

She slipped a little now as she walked, for ice had formed on the bottom of her overshoes; she had to run her gloves along the half-slippery, half-sticky walls to keep her balance.

"Harry!"

Still no answer. The sound she made bounced mockingly down to the end of the passage.

Then on an instant the lights went out, and she was in complete darkness. She gave a small, frightened cry, and sank down into a cold little heap on the ice. She felt her left knee do something as she fell, but she scarcely noticed it as some deep terror far greater than any fear of being lost settled upon her. She was alone with this presence that came out of the North, the dreary loneliness that rose from ice-bound whalers in the Arctic seas, from smokeless, trackless wastes where were strewn the whitened bones of adventure. It was an icy breath of death; it was rolling down low across the land to clutch at her.

With a furious, despairing energy she rose again and started blindly down the darkness. She must get out. She might be lost in here for days, freeze to death and lie embedded in the ice like corpses she had read of, kept perfectly preserved until the melting of a glacier. Harry probably thought she had left with the others—he had gone by now; no one would know until late next day. She reached pitifully for the wall. Forty inches thick, they had said—forty inches thick!

"Oh!"

On both sides of her along the walls she felt things creeping, damp souls that haunted this palace, this town, this North.

"Oh, send somebody—send somebody!" she cried aloud.

Clark Darrow—he would understand; or Joe Ewing; she couldn't be left here to wander forever—to be frozen, heart, body, and soul. This her—this Sally Carrol! Why, she was a happy thing. She was a happy little girl. She liked warmth and summer and Dixie. These things were foreign—foreign.

"You're not crying," something said aloud. "You'll never cry any more. Your tears would just freeze; all tears freeze up here!"

She sprawled full length on the ice.

"Oh, God!" she faltered.

A long single file of minutes went by, and with a great weariness she felt her eyes closing. Then some one seemed to sit down near her and take her face in warm, soft hands. She looked up gratefully.

"Why, it's Margery Lee," she crooned softly to herself. "I knew you'd come." It really was Margery Lee, and she was just as Sally Carrol had known she would be, with a young, white brow, and wide, welcoming eyes, and a hoop-skirt of some soft material that was quite comforting to rest on.

"Margery Lee."

It was getting darker now and darker—all those tombstones ought to be repainted, sure enough, only that would spoil 'em, of course. Still, you ought to be able to see 'em.

Then after a succession of moments that went fast and then slow, but seemed to be ultimately resolving themselves into a multitude of blurred rays converging toward a pale-yellow sun, she heard a great cracking noise break her new-found stillness.

It was the sun, it was a light; a torch, and a torch beyond that, and another one, and voices; a face took flesh below the torch, heavy arms raised her, and she felt something on her cheek—it felt wet. Some one had seized her and was rubbing her face with snow. How ridiculous — with snow!

"Sally Carrol! Sally Carrol!"

It was Dangerous Dan McGrew; and two other faces she didn't know.

"Child, child! We've been looking for you two hours! Harry's half-crazy!"

Things came rushing back into place — the singing, the torches, the great shout of the marching clubs. She squirmed in Patton's arms and gave a long, low cry.

"Oh, I want to get out of here! I'm going back home. Take me home" — her voice rose to a scream that sent a chill to Harry's heart as he came racing down the next passage — "to-morrow!" she cried with delirious, unrestrained passion — "To-morrow! To-morrow! To-morrow!"

VI

The wealth of golden sunlight poured a quite enervating yet oddly comforting heat over the house where day long it faced the dusty stretch of road. Two birds were making a great to-do in a cool spot found among the branches of a tree next door, and down the street a colored woman was announcing herself melodiously as a purveyor of strawberries. It was April afternoon.

Sally Carrol Happer, resting her chin on her arm, and her arm on an old window-seat, gazed sleepily down over the spangled dust whence the heat waves were rising for the first time this spring. She was watching a very ancient Ford turn a perilous corner and rattle and groan to a jolting stop at the end of the walk. She made no sound, and in a minute a strident familiar whistle rent the air. Sally Carrol smiled and blinked.

"Good mawnin'."

A head appeared tortuously from under the cartop below.

"'Tain't mawnin', Sally Carrol."

"Sure enough!" she said in affected surprise. "I guess maybe not."

"What you doin'?"

"Eatin' green peach. 'Spect to die any minute."

Clark twisted himself a last impossible notch to get a view of her face.

"Water's warm as a kettla steam, Sally Carrol. Wanta go swimmin'?"

"Hate to move," sighed Sally Carrol lazily, "but I reckon so."

Head and

Shoulders

IN 1915 HORACE TARBOX WAS THIRTEEN YEARS
old. In that year he took the examinations for entrance to Princeton
University and received the Grade A—excellent—in Caesar, Cicero,
Vergil, Xenophon, Homer, Algebra, Plane Geometry, Solid Geometry,
and Chemistry.

Two years later, while George M. Cohan was composing "Over
There," Horace was leading the sophomore class by several lengths
and digging out theses on "The Syllogism as an Obsolete Scholastic
Form," and during the battle of Château-Thierry he was sitting at his
desk deciding whether or not to wait until his seventeenth birthday
before beginning his series of essays on "The Pragmatic Bias of the
New Realists."

After a while some newsboy told him that the war was over, and he was glad, because it meant that Peat Brothers, publishers, would get out their new edition of "Spinoza's Improvement of the Understanding." Wars were all very well in their way, made young men self-reliant or something, but Horace felt that he could never forgive the President for allowing a brass band to play under his window on the night of the false armistice, causing him to leave three important sentences out of his thesis on "German Idealism."

The next year he went up to Yale to take his degree as Master of Arts.

He was seventeen then, tall and slender, with near-sighted gray eyes and an air of keeping himself utterly detached from the mere words he let drop.

"I never feel as though I'm talking to him," expostulated Professor Dillinger to a sympathetic colleague. "He makes me feel as though I were talking to his representative. I always expect him to say: 'Well, I'll ask myself and find out.'"

And then, just as nonchalantly as though Horace Tarbox had been Mr. Beef the butcher or Mr. Hat the haberdasher, life reached in, seized him, handled him, stretched him, and unrolled him like a piece of Irish lace on a Saturday-afternoon bargain-counter.

To move in the literary fashion I should say that this was all because when way back in colonial days the hardy pioneers had come to a bald place in Connecticut and asked of each other, "Now, what shall we build here?" the hardiest one among 'em had answered: "Let's build a town where theatrical managers can try out musical comedies!" How afterward they founded Yale College there, to try the musical comedies on, is a story every one knows. At any rate one December, "Home James" opened at the Shubert, and all the students encored Marcia Meadow, who sang a song about the Blundering Blimp in the first act and did a shaky, shivery, celebrated dance in the last.

Marcia was nineteen. She didn't have wings, but audiences agreed generally that she didn't need them. She was a blonde by natural pigment, and she wore no paint on the streets at high noon. Outside of that she was no better than most women.

It was Charlie Moon who promised her five thousand Pall Malls if she would pay a call on Horace Tarbox, prodigy extraordinary. Charlie was a senior in Sheffield, and he and Horace were first cousins. They liked and pitied each other.

Horace had been particularly busy that night. The failure of the Frenchman Laurier to appreciate the significance of the new realists was preying on his mind. In fact, his only reaction to a low, clearcut rap at his study was to make him speculate as to whether any rap would have actual existence without an ear there to hear it. He fancied he was verging more and more toward pragmatism. But at that moment, though he did not know it, he was verging with astounding rapidity toward something quite different.

The rap sounded—three seconds leaked by—the rap sounded.

"Come in," muttered Horace automatically.

He heard the door open and then close, but, bent over his book in the big armchair before the fire, he did not look up.

"Leave it on the bed in the other room," he said absently.

"Leave what on the bed in the other room?"

Marcia Meadow had to talk her songs, but her speaking voice was like byplay on a harp.

"The laundry."

"I can't."

Horace stirred impatiently in his chair.

"Why can't you?"

"Why, because I haven't got it."

"Hm!" he replied testily. "Suppose you go back and get it."

Across the fire from Horace was another easychair. He was accustomed to change to it in the course of an evening by way of exercise and variety. One chair he called Berkeley, the other he called Hume. He suddenly heard a sound as of a rustling, diaphanous form sinking into Hume. He glanced up.

"Well," said Marcia with the sweet smile she used in Act Two ("Oh, so the Duke liked my dancing!"), "Well, Omar Khayyam, here I am beside you singing in the wilderness."

Horace stared at her dazedly. The momentary suspicion came to him that she existed there only as a phantom of his imagination. Women didn't come into men's rooms and sink into men's Humes. Women brought laundry and took your seat in the street-car and married you later on when you were old enough to know fetters.

This woman had clearly materialized out of Hume. The very froth of her brown gauzy dress was an emanation from Hume's leather arm there! If he looked long enough he would see Hume right through her and then he would be alone again in the room. He passed his fist across his eyes. He really must take up those trapeze exercises again.

"For Pete's sake, don't look so critical!" objected the emanation pleasantly. "I feel as if you were going to wish me away with that patent dome of yours. And then there wouldn't be anything left of me except my shadow in your eyes."

Horace coughed. Coughing was one of his two gestures. When he talked you forgot he had a body at all. It was like hearing a phonograph record by a singer who had been dead a long time.

"What do you want?" he asked.

"I want them letters," whined Marcia melodramatically—"them letters of mine you bought from my grandsire in 1881."

Horace considered.

"I haven't got your letters," he said evenly. "I am only seventeen years old. My father was not born until March 3, 1879. You evidently have me confused with some one else."

"You're only seventeen?" repeated Marcia suspiciously.

"Only seventeen."

"I knew a girl," said Marcia reminiscently, "who went on the ten-twenty-thirty when she was sixteen. She was so stuck on herself that she could never say 'sixteen' without putting the 'only' before it. We got to calling her 'Only Jessie.' And she's just where she was when she started—only worse. 'Only' is a bad habit, Omar—it sounds like an alibi."

"My name is not Omar."

"I know," agreed Marcia, nodding—"your name's Horace. I just call you Omar because you remind me of a smoked cigarette."

"And I haven't your letters. I doubt if I've ever met your grandfather. In fact, I think it very improbable that you yourself were alive in 1881."

Marcia stared at him in wonder.

"Me—1881? Why sure! I was second-line stuff when the Florodora Sextette was still in the convent. I was the original nurse to Mrs. Sol Smith's Juliette. Why, Omar, I was a canteen singer during the War of 1812."

Horace's mind made a sudden successful leap, and he grinned.

"Did Charlie Moon put you up to this?"

Marcia regarded him inscrutably.

"Who's Charlie Moon?"

"Small—wide nostrils—big ears."

She grew several inches and sniffed.

"I'm not in the habit of noticing my friends' nostrils."

"Then it was Charlie?"

Marcia bit her lip—and then yawned.

"Oh, let's change the subject, Omar. I'll pull a snore in this chair in a minute."

"Yes," replied Horace gravely, 'Hume has often been considered soporific."

"Who's your friend—and will he die?"

Then of a sudden Horace Tarbox rose slenderly and began to pace the room with his hands in his pockets. This was his other gesture.

"I don't care for this," he said, as if he were talking to himself—"at all. Not that I mind your being here—I don't. You're quite a pretty little thing, but I don't like Charlie Moon's sending you up here. Am I a laboratory experiment on which the janitors as well as the chemists can make experiments? Is my intellectual development humorous in any way? Do I look like the pictures of the little Boston boy in the comic magazines? Has that callow ass, Moon, with his eternal tales about his week in Paris, any right to— —"

"No," interrupted Marcia emphatically. "And you're a sweet boy. Come here and kiss me."

Horace stopped quickly in front of her.

"Why do you want me to kiss you?" he asked intently. "Do you just go round kissing people?"

"Why, yes," admitted Marcia, unruffled. "'At's all life is. Just going round kissing people."

"Well," replied Horace emphatically, "I must say your ideas are horribly garbled! In the first place life isn't just that, and in the second place I won't kiss you. It might get to be a habit and I can't get rid of habits. This year I've got in the habit of lolling in bed until seven-thirty."

Marcia nodded understandingly.

"Do you ever have any fun?" she asked.

"What do you mean by fun?"

"See here," said Marcia sternly, "I like you, Omar, but I wish you'd talk as if you had a line on what you were saying. You sound as if you were gargling a lot of words in your mouth and lost a bet every time you spilled a few. I asked you if you ever had any fun."

Horace shook his head.

"Later, perhaps," he answered. "You see I'm a plan. I'm an experiment. I don't say that I don't get tired of it sometimes—I do. Yet—oh, I can't explain! But what you and Charlie Moon call fun wouldn't be fun to me."

"Please explain."

Horace stared at her, started to speak and then, changing his mind, resumed his walk. After an unsuccessful attempt to determine whether or not he was looking at her Marcia smiled at him.

"Please explain."

Horace turned.

"If I do, will you promise to tell Charlie Moon that I wasn't in?"

"Uh-uh."

"Very well, then. Here's my history: I was a 'why' child. I wanted to see the wheels go round. My father was a young economics professor at Princeton. He brought me up on the system of answering every question I asked him to the best of his ability. My response to that gave him the idea of making an experiment in precocity. To aid in the massacre I had ear trouble—seven operations between the ages of nine and twelve. Of course this kept me apart from other boys and made me ripe for forcing. Anyway, while my generation was laboring through 'Uncle Remus' I was honestly enjoying Catullus in the original.

"I passed off my college examinations when I was thirteen because I couldn't help it. My chief associates were professors, and I took a tremendous pride in knowing that I had a fine intelligence, for though I was unusually gifted I was not abnormal in other ways. When I was sixteen I got tired of being a freak; I decided that some one had made a bad mistake. Still as I'd gone that far I concluded to finish it up by taking my degree of Master of Arts. My chief interest in life is the study of modern philosophy. I am a realist of the School of Anton Laurier—with Bergsonian trimmings—and I'll be eighteen years old in two months. That's all."

"Whew!" exclaimed Marcia. "That's enough! You do a neat job with the parts of speech."

"Satisfied?"

"No, you haven't kissed me."

"It's not in my programme," demurred Horace. "Understand that I don't pretend to be above physical things. They have their place, but——"

"Oh, don't be so darned reasonable!"

"I can't help it."

"I hate these slot-machine people."

"I assure you I—" began Horace.

"Oh, shut up!"

"My own rationality——"

"I didn't say anything about your nationality. You're an Amuricun, ar'n't you?"

"Yes."

"Well, that's O. K. with me. I got a notion I want to see you do something that isn't in your highbrow programme. I want to see if a what-ch-call-em with Brazilian trimmings—that thing you said you were—can be a little human."

Horace shook his head again.

"I won't kiss you."

"My life is blighted," muttered Marcia tragically. "I'm a beaten woman. I'll go through life without ever having a kiss with Brazilian trimmings." She sighed. "Anyways, Omar, will you come and see my show?"

"What show?"

"I'm a wicked actress from 'Home James'!"

"Light opera?"

"Yes—at a stretch. One of the characters is a Brazilian rice-planter. That might interest you."

"I saw 'The Bohemian Girl' once," reflected Horace aloud. "I enjoyed it—to some extent."

"Then you'll come?"

"Well, I'm—I'm——"

"Oh, I know—you've got to run down to Brazil for the weekend."

"Not at all. I'd be delighted to come."

Marcia clapped her hands.

"Goodyforyou! I'll mail you a ticket—Thursday night?"

"Why, I——"

"Good! Thursday night it is."

She stood up and walking close to him laid both hands on his shoulders.

"I like you, Omar. I'm sorry I tried to kid you. I thought you'd be sort of frozen, but you're a nice boy."

He eyed her sardonically.

"I'm several thousand generations older than you are."

"You carry your age well."

They shook hands gravely.

"My name's Marcia Meadow," she said emphatically. "'Member it—Marcia Meadow. And I won't tell Charlie Moon you were in."

An instant later, as she was skimming down the last flight of stairs three at a time, she heard a voice call over the upper banister: "Oh, say——"

She stopped and looked up—made out a vague form leaning over.

"Oh, say!" called the prodigy again. "Can you hear me?"

"Here's your connection, Omar."

"I hope I haven't given you the impression that I consider kissing intrinsically irrational."

"Impression? Why, you didn't even give me the kiss—Never fret—so long."

Two doors near her opened curiously at the sound of a feminine voice. A tentative cough sounded from above. Gathering her skirts, Marcia dived wildly down the last flight and was swallowed up in the murky Connecticut air outside.

Up-stairs Horace paced the floor of his study. From time to time he glanced toward Berkeley waiting there in suave dark-red respectability, an open book lying suggestively on his cushions. And then he found that his circuit of the floor was bringing him each time nearer to Hume. There was something about Hume that was strangely and inexpressibly different. The diaphanous form still seemed hovering near, and had Horace sat there he would have felt as if he were sitting on a lady's lap. And though Horace couldn't have named the quality of difference, there was such a quality—quite intangible to the speculative mind, but real, nevertheless. Hume was radiating something that in all the two hundred years of his influence he had never radiated before.

Hume was radiating attar of roses.

II

On Thursday night Horace Tarbox sat in an aisle seat in the fifth row and witnessed "Home James." Oddly enough he found that he was enjoying himself. The cynical students near him were annoyed at his audible appreciation of time-honored jokes in the Hammerstein tradition. But Horace was waiting with anxiety for Marcia Meadow singing her song about a Jazz-bound Blundering Blimp. When she did appear, radiant under a floppity flower-faced hat, a warm glow settled over him, and when the song was over he did not join in the storm of applause. He felt somewhat numb.

In the intermission after the second act an usher materialized beside him, demanded to know if he were Mr. Tarbox, and then handed him a note written in a round adolescent hand. Horace read it in some confusion, while the usher lingered with withering patience in the aisle.

Dear Omar: After the show I always grow an awful hunger. If you want to satisfy it for me in the Taft Grill just communicate your answer to the big-timber guide that brought this and oblige.

Your friend,
Marcia Meadow.

"Tell her"—he coughed—"tell her that it will be quite all right. I'll meet her in front of the theatre."

The big-timber guide smiled arrogantly.

"I giss she meant for you to come roun' t' the stage door."

"Where—where is it?"

"Ou'side. Tunayulef. Down ee alley."

"What?"

"Ou'side. Turn to y' left! Down ee alley!"

The arrogant person withdrew. A freshman behind Horace snickered.

Then half an hour later, sitting in the Taft Grill opposite the hair that was yellow by natural pigment, the prodigy was saying an odd thing.

"Do you have to do that dance in the last act?" he was asking earnestly—"I mean, would they dismiss you if you refused to do it?"

Marcia grinned.

"It's fun to do it. I like to do it."

And then Horace came out with a *faux pas*.

"I should think you'd detest it," he remarked succinctly. "The people behind me were making remarks about your bosom."

Marcia blushed fiery red.

"I can't help that," she said quickly. "The dance to me is only a sort of acrobatic stunt. Lord, it's hard enough to do! I rub liniment into my shoulders for an hour every night."

"Do you have—fun while you're on the stage?"

"Uh-huh—sure! I got in the habit of having people look at me, Omar, and I like it."

"Hm!" Horace sank into a brownish study.

"How's the Brazilian trimmings?"

"Hm!" repeated Horace, and then after a pause: "Where does the play go from here?"

"New York."

"For how long?"

"All depends. Winter—maybe."

"Oh!"

"Coming up to lay eyes on me, Omar, or aren't you int'rested? Not as nice here, is it, as it was up in your room? I wish we was there now."

"I feel idiotic in this place," confessed Horace, looking around him nervously.

"Too bad! We got along pretty well."

At this he looked suddenly so melancholy that she changed her tone, and reaching over patted his hand.

"Ever take an actress out to supper before?"

"No," said Horace miserably, "and I never will again. I don't know why I came to-night. Here under all these lights and with all these people laughing and chattering I feel completely out of my sphere. I don't know what to talk to you about."

"We'll talk about me. We talked about you last time."

"Very well."

"Well, my name really is Meadow, but my first name isn't Marcia—it's Veronica. I'm nineteen. Question—how did the girl make her leap to the footlights? Answer—she was born in Passaic, New Jersey, and up to a year ago she got the right to breathe by pushing Nabiscoes in Marcel's tea-room in Trenton. She started going with a guy named Robbins, a singer in the Trent House cabaret, and he got her to try a song and dance with him one evening. In a month we were filling the supper-room every night. Then we went to New York with meet-my-friend letters thick as a pile of napkins.

"In two days we'd landed a job at Divinerries', and I learned to shimmy from a kid at the Palais Royal. We stayed at Divinerries' six months until one night Peter Boyce Wendell, the columnist, ate his milk-toast there. Next morning a poem about Marvellous Marcia came out in his newspaper, and within two days I had three vaudeville offers and a chance at the Midnight Frolic. I wrote Wendell a thank-you letter, and he printed it in his column—said that the style was like Carlyle's, only more rugged, and that I ought to quit dancing and do North American literature. This got me a coupla more vaudeville offers and a chance as an ingénue in a regular show. I took it—and here I am, Omar."

When she finished they sat for a moment in silence, she draping the last skeins of a Welsh rabbit on her fork and waiting for him to speak.

"Let's get out of here," he said suddenly.

Marcia's eyes hardened.

"What's the idea? Am I making you sick?"

"No, but I don't like it here. I don't like to be sitting here with you."

Without another word Marcia signalled for the waiter.

"What's the check?" she demanded briskly. "My part—the rabbit and the ginger ale."

Horace watched blankly as the waiter figured it.

"See here," he began, "I intended to pay for yours too. You're my guest."

With a half-sigh Marcia rose from the table and walked from the room. Horace, his face a document in bewilderment, laid a bill down and followed her out, up the stairs and into the lobby. He overtook her in front of the elevator and they faced each other.

"See here," he repeated, "you're my guest. Have I said something to offend you?"

After an instant of wonder Marcia's eyes softened.

"You're a rude fella," she said slowly. "Don't you know you're rude?"

"I can't help it," said Horace with a directness she found quite disarming. "You know I like you."

"You said you didn't like being with me."

"I didn't like it."

"Why not?"

Fire blazed suddenly from the gray forests of his eyes.

"Because I didn't. I've formed the habit of liking you. I've been thinking of nothing much else for two days."

"Well, if you——"

"Wait a minute," he interrupted. "I've got something to say. It's this: in six weeks I'll be eighteen years old. When I'm eighteen years old I'm coming up to New York to see you. Is there some place in New York where we can go and not have a lot of people in the room?"

"Sure!" smiled Marcia. "You can come up to my 'partment. Sleep on the couch, if you want to."

"I can't sleep on couches," he said shortly. "But I want to talk to you."

"Why, sure," repeated Marcia—"in my 'partment."

In his excitement Horace put his hands in his pockets.

"All right—just so I can see you alone. I want to talk to you as we talked up in my room."

"Honey boy," cried Marcia, laughing, "is it that you want to kiss me?"

"Yes," Horace almost shouted. "I'll kiss you if you want me to."

The elevator man was looking at them reproachfully. Marcia edged toward the grated door.

"I'll drop you a post-card," she said.

Horace's eyes were quite wild.

"Send me a post-card! I'll come up any time after January first. I'll be eighteen then."

And as she stepped into the elevator he coughed enigmatically, yet with a vague challenge, at the ceiling, and walked quickly away.

III

He was there again. She saw him when she took her first glance at the restless Manhattan audience—down in the front row with his head bent a bit forward and his gray eyes fixed on her. And she knew that to him they were alone together in a world where the high-rouged row of ballet faces and the massed whines of the violins were as imperceivable as powder on a marble Venus. An instinctive defiance rose within her.

"Silly boy!" she said to herself hurriedly, and she didn't take her encore.

"What do they expect for a hundred a week—perpetual motion?" she grumbled to herself in the wings.

"What's the trouble, Marcia?"

"Guy I don't like down in front."

During the last act, as she waited for her specialty, she had an odd attack of stage fright. She had never sent Horace the promised post-card. Last night she had pretended not to see him—had hurried from the theatre immediately after her dance to pass a sleepless night in her apartment, thinking—as she had so often in the last month—of his pale, rather intent face, his slim, boyish figure, the merciless, unworldly abstraction that made him charming to her.

And now that he had come she felt vaguely sorry—as though an unwonted responsibility was being forced on her.

"Infant prodigy!" she said aloud.

"What?" demanded the Negro comedian standing beside her.

"Nothing—just talking about myself."

On the stage she felt better. This was her dance—and she always felt that the way she did it wasn't suggestive any more than to some men every pretty girl is suggestive. She made it a stunt.

"Uptown, downtown, jelly on a spoon,
After sundown shiver by the moon."

He was not watching her now. She saw that clearly. He was look-ing very deliberately at a castle on the back drop, wearing that expres-sion he had worn in the Taft Grill. A wave of exasperation swept over her—he was criticising her.

"That's the vibration that thr-ills me,
Funny how affection fi-lls me,
Uptown, downtown— —"

Unconquerable revulsion seized her. She was suddenly and horri-bly conscious of her audience as she had never been since her first appearance. Was that a leer on a pallid face in the front row, a droop of disgust on one young girl's mouth? These shoulders of hers—these shoulders shaking—were they hers? Were they real? Surely shoulders weren't made for this!

"Then—you'll see at a glance
I'll need some funeral ushers with St. Vitus dance
At the end of the world I'll— —"

The bassoon and two cellos crashed into a final chord. She paused and poised a moment on her toes with every muscle tense, her young face looking out dully at the audience in what one young girl afterward called "such a curious, puzzled look," and then without bowing rushed from the stage. Into the dressing-room she sped, kicked out of one dress and into another, and caught a taxi outside.

Her apartment was very warm — small, it was, with a row of professional pictures and sets of Kipling and O. Henry which she had bought once from a blue-eyed agent and read occasionally. And there were several chairs which matched, but were none of them comfortable, and a pink-shaded lamp with blackbirds painted on it and an atmosphere of rather stifled pink throughout. There were nice things in it — nice things unrelentingly hostile to each other, offsprings of a vicarious, impatient taste acting in stray moments. The worst was typified by a great picture framed in oak bark of Passaic as seen from the Erie Railroad — altogether a frantic, oddly extravagant, oddly penurious attempt to make a cheerful room. Marcia knew it was a failure.

Into this room came the prodigy and took her two hands awkwardly.

"I followed you this time," he said.

"Oh!"

"I want you to marry me," he said.

Her arms went out to him. She kissed his mouth with a sort of passionate wholesomeness.

"There!"

"I love you," he said.

She kissed him again and then with a little sigh flung herself into an armchair and half lay there, shaken with absurd laughter.

"Why, you infant prodigy!" she cried.

"Very well, call me that if you want to. I once told you that I was ten thousand years older than you — I am."

She laughed again.

"I don't like to be disapproved of."

"No one's ever going to disapprove of you again."

"Omar," she asked, "why do you want to marry me?"

The prodigy rose and put his hands in his pockets.

"Because I love you, Marcia Meadow."

And then she stopped calling him Omar.

"Dear boy," she said, "you know I sort of love you. There's something about you — I can't tell what — that just puts my heart through the wringer every time I'm round you. But, honey—" She paused.

"But what?"

"But lots of things. But you're only just eighteen, and I'm nearly twenty."

"Nonsense!" he interrupted. "Put it this way — that I'm in my nineteenth year and you're nineteen. That makes us pretty close — without counting that other ten thousand years I mentioned."

Marcia laughed.

"But there are some more 'buts.' Your people——"

"My people!" exclaimed the prodigy ferociously. "My people tried to make a monstrosity out of me." His face grew quite crimson at the enormity of what he was going to say. "My people can go way back and sit down!"

"My heavens!" cried Marcia in alarm. "All that? On tacks, I suppose."

"Tacks—yes," he agreed wildly—"on anything. The more I think of how they allowed me to become a little dried-up mummy——"

"What makes you think you're that?" asked Marcia quietly—"me?"

"Yes. Every person I've met on the streets since I met you has made me jealous because they knew what love was before I did. I used to call it the 'sex impulse.' Heavens!"

"There's more 'buts,' " said Marcia.

"What are they?"

"How could we live?"

"I'll make a living."

"You're in college."

"Do you think I care anything about taking a Master of Arts degree?"

"You want to be Master of Me, hey?"

"Yes! What? I mean, no!"

Marcia laughed, and crossing swiftly over sat in his lap. He put his arm round her wildly and implanted the vestige of a kiss somewhere near her neck.

"There's something white about you," mused Marcia, "but it doesn't sound very logical."

"Oh, don't be so darned reasonable!"

"I can't help it," said Marcia.

"I hate these slot-machine people!"

"But we——"

"Oh, shut up!"

And as Marcia couldn't talk through her ears she had to.

IV

Horace and Marcia were married early in February. The sensation in academic circles both at Yale and Princeton was tremendous. Horace Tarbox, who at fourteen had been played up in the Sunday magazine sections of metropolitan newspapers, was throwing over his career, his chance of being a world authority on American philosophy, by marrying a chorus girl—they made Marcia a chorus girl. But like all modern stories it was a four-and-a-half-day wonder.

They took a flat in Harlem. After two weeks' search, during which his idea of the value of academic knowledge faded unmercifully, Horace took a position as clerk with a South American export company— some one had told him that exporting was the coming thing. Marcia was to stay in her show for a few months—anyway until he got on his feet. He was getting a hundred and twenty-five to start with, and though of course they told him it was only a question of months until he would be earning double that, Marcia refused even to consider giving up the hundred and fifty a week that she was getting at the time.

"We'll call ourselves Head and Shoulders, dear," she said softly, "and the shoulders'll have to keep shaking a little longer until the old head gets started."

"I hate it," he objected gloomily.

"Well," she replied emphatically, "your salary wouldn't keep us in a tenement. Don't think I want to be public—I don't. I want to be yours. But I'd be a half-wit to sit in one room and count the sunflowers on the wall-paper while I waited for you. When you pull down three hundred a month I'll quit."

And much as it hurt his pride, Horace had to admit that hers was the wiser course.

March mellowed into April. May read a gorgeous riot act to the parks and waters of Manhattan, and they were very happy. Horace, who had no habits whatsoever—he had never had time to form any— proved the most adaptable of husbands, and as Marcia entirely lacked opinions on the subjects that engrossed him there were very few joltings and bumpings. Their minds moved in different spheres. Marcia acted as practical factotum, and Horace lived either in his old world of abstract ideas or in a sort of triumphantly earthy worship and adoration of his wife. She was a continual source of astonishment to him— the freshness and originality of her mind, her dynamic, clear-headed energy, and her unfailing good humor.

And Marcia's co-workers in the nine-o'clock show, whither she had transferred her talents, were impressed with her tremendous pride in her husband's mental powers. Horace they knew only as a very slim, tight-lipped, and immature-looking young man, who waited every night to take her home.

"Horace," said Marcia one evening when she met him as usual at eleven, "you looked like a ghost standing there against the street lights. You losing weight?"

He shook his head vaguely.

"I don't know. They raised me to a hundred and thirty-five dollars to-day, and — —"

"I don't care," said Marcia severely. "You're killing yourself working at night. You read those big books on economy — —"

"Economics," corrected Horace.

"Well, you read 'em every night long after I'm asleep. And you're getting all stooped over like you were before we were married."

"But, Marcia, I've got to — —"

"No, you haven't, dear. I guess I'm running this shop for the present, and I won't let my fella ruin his health and eyes. You got to get some exercise."

"I do. Every morning I — —"

"Oh, I know! But those dumb-bells of yours wouldn't give a consumptive two degrees of fever. I mean real exercise. You've got to join a gymnasium. 'Member you told me you were such a trick gymnast once that they tried to get you out for the team in college and they couldn't because you had a standing date with Herb Spencer?"

"I used to enjoy it," mused Horace, "but it would take up too much time now."

"All right," said Marcia. "I'll make a bargain with you. You join a gym and I'll read one of those books from the brown row of 'em."

" 'Pepy's Diary'? Why, that ought to be enjoyable. He's very light."

"Not for me — he isn't. It'll be like digesting plate glass. But you been telling me how much it'd broaden my lookout. Well, you go to a gym three nights a week and I'll take one big dose of Sammy."

Horace hesitated.

"Well — —"

"Come on, now! You do some giant swings for me and I'll chase some culture for you."

So Horace finally consented, and all through a baking summer he spent three and sometimes four evenings a week experimenting on the trapeze in Skipper's Gymnasium. And in August he admitted to Marcia that it made him capable of more mental work during the day.

" 'Mens sana in corpore sano,' " he said.

"Don't believe in it," replied Marcia. "I tried one of those patent medicines once and they're all bunk. You stick to gymnastics."

One night in early September, while he was going through one of his contortions on the rings in the nearly deserted room, he was addressed by a meditative fat man whom he had noticed watching him for several nights.

"Say, lad, do that stunt you were doin' last night."

Horace grinned at him from his perch.

"I invented it," he said. "I got the idea from the fourth proposition of Euclid."

"What circus he with?"

"He's dead."

"Well, he must of broke his neck doin' that stunt. I set here last night thinkin' sure you was goin' to break yours."

"Like this!" said Horace, and swinging onto the trapeze he did his stunt.

"Don't it kill your neck an' shoulder muscles?"

"It did at first, but inside of a week I wrote the *quod erat demonstrandum* on it."

"Hm!"

Horace swung idly on the trapeze.

"Ever think of takin' it up professionally?" asked the fat man.

"Not I."

"Good money in it if you're willin' to do stunts like 'at an' can get away with it."

"Here's another," chirped Horace eagerly, and the fat man's mouth dropped suddenly agape as he watched this pink-jerseyed Prometheus again defy the gods and Isaac Newton.

The night following this encounter Horace got home from work to find a rather pale Marcia stretched out on the sofa waiting for him.

"I fainted twice to-day," she began without preliminaries.

"What?"

"Yep. You see baby's due in four months now. Doctor says I ought to have quit dancing two weeks ago."

Horace sat down and thought it over.

"I'm glad, of course," he said pensively—"I mean glad that we're going to have a baby. But this means a lot of expense."

"I've got two hundred and fifty in the bank," said Marcia hopefully, "and two weeks' pay coming."

Horace computed quickly.

"Including my salary, that'll give us nearly fourteen hundred for the next six months."

Marcia looked blue.

"That all? Course I can get a job singing somewhere this month. And I can go to work again in March."

"Of course nothing!" said Horace gruffly. "You'll stay right here. Let's see now—there'll be doctor's bills and a nurse, besides the maid. We've got to have some more money."

"Well," said Marcia wearily, "I don't know where it's coming from. It's up to the old head now. Shoulders is out of business."

Horace rose and pulled on his coat.

"Where are you going?"

"I've got an idea," he answered. "I'll be right back."

Ten minutes later, as he headed down the street toward Skipper's Gymnasium, he felt a placid wonder, quite unmixed with humor, at what he was going to do. How he would have gaped at himself a year before! How every one would have gaped! But when you opened your door at the rap of life you let in many things.

The gymnasium was brightly lit, and when his eyes became accustomed to the glare he found the meditative fat man seated on a pile of canvas mats smoking a big cigar.

"Say," began Horace directly, "were you in earnest last night when you said I could make money on my trapeze stunts?"

"Why, yes," said the fat man in surprise.

"Well, I've been thinking it over, and I believe I'd like to try it. I could work at night and on Saturday afternoons—and regularly if the pay is high enough."

The fat man looked at his watch.

"Well," he said. "Charlie Paulson's the man to see. He'll book you inside of four days, once he sees you work out. He won't be in now, but I'll get hold of him for to-morrow night."

The fat man was as good as his word. Charlie Paulson arrived next night and put in a wondrous hour watching the prodigy swoop through the air in amazing parabolas, and on the night following he brought two large men with him who looked as though they had been born smoking black cigars and talking about money in low, passionate voices. Then on the succeeding Saturday Horace Tarbox's torso made its first professional appearance in a gymnastic exhibition at the Coleman Street Gardens. But though the audience numbered nearly five thousand people, Horace felt no nervousness. From his childhood he had read papers to audiences—learned that trick of detaching himself.

"Marcia," he said cheerfully later that same night, "I think we're out of the woods. Paulson thinks he can get me an opening at the Hippodrome, and that means an all-winter engagement. The Hippodrome, you know, is a big——"

"Yes, I believe I've heard of it," interrupted Marcia, "but I want to know about this stunt you're doing. It isn't any spectacular suicide, is it?"

"It's nothing," said Horace quietly. "But if you can think of any nicer way of a man killing himself than taking a risk for you, why that's the way I want to die."

Marcia reached up and wound both arms tightly round his neck.

"Kiss me," she whispered, "and call me 'dear heart.' I love to hear you say 'dear heart.' And bring me a book to read to-morrow. No more Sam Pepys, but something trick and trashy. I've been wild for something to do all day. I felt like writing letters, but I didn't have anybody to write to."

"Write to me," said Horace. "I'll read them."

"I wish I could," breathed Marcia. "If I knew words enough I could write you the longest love-letter in the world—and never get tired."

But after two more months Marcia grew very tired indeed, and for a row of nights it was a very anxious, weary-looking young athlete who walked out before the Hippodrome crowd. Then there were two days when his place was taken by a young man who wore pale blue instead of white, and got very little applause. But after the two days Horace appeared again, and those who sat close to the stage remarked an expression of beatific happiness on that young acrobat's face, even when he was twisting breathlessly in the air in the middle of his amazing and original shoulder swing. After that performance he laughed at the elevator man and dashed up the stairs to the flat five steps at a time—and then tiptoed very carefully into a quiet room.

"Marcia," he whispered.

"Hello!" She smiled up at him wanly. "Horace, there's something I want you to do. Look in my top bureau drawer and you'll find a big stack of paper. It's a book—sort of—Horace. I wrote it down in these last three months while I've been laid up. I wish you'd take it to that Peter Boyce Wendell who put my letter in his paper. He could tell you whether it'd be a good book. I wrote it just the way I talk, just the way I wrote that letter to him. It's just a story about a lot of things that happened to me. Will you take it to him, Horace?"

"Yes, darling."

He leaned over the bed until his head was beside her on the pillow, and began stroking back her yellow hair.

"Dearest Marcia," he said softly.

"No," she murmured, "call me what I told you to call me."

"Dear heart," he whispered passionately—"dearest, dearest heart."

"What'll we call her?"

They rested a minute in happy, drowsy content, while Horace considered.

"We'll call her Marcia Hume Tarbox," he said at length.

"Why the Hume?"

"Because he's the fellow who first introduced us."

"That so?" she murmured, sleepily surprised. "I thought his name was Moon."

Her eyes closed, and after a moment the slow, lengthening surge of the bedclothes over her breast showed that she was asleep.

Horace tiptoed over to the bureau and opening the top drawer found a heap of closely scrawled, lead-smeared pages. He looked at the first sheet:

SANDRA PEPYS, SYNCOPATED
BY MARCIA TARBOX

He smiled. So Samuel Pepys had made an impression on her after all. He turned a page and began to read. His smile deepened—he read on. Half an hour passed and he became aware that Marcia had waked and was watching him from the bed.

"Honey," came in a whisper.

"What, Marcia?"

"Do you like it?"

Horace coughed.

"I seem to be reading on. It's bright."

"Take it to Peter Boyce Wendell. Tell him you got the highest marks in Princeton once and that you ought to know when a book's good. Tell him this one's a world beater."

"All right, Marcia," said Horace gently.

Her eyes closed again and Horace crossing over kissed her forehead—stood there for a moment with a look of tender pity. Then he left the room.

All that night the sprawly writing on the pages, the constant mistakes in spelling and grammar, and the weird punctuation danced before his eyes. He woke several times in the night, each time full of a welling chaotic sympathy for this desire of Marcia's soul to express itself in words. To him there was something infinitely pathetic about it, and for the first time in months he began to turn over in his mind his own half-forgotten dreams.

He had meant to write a series of books, to popularize the new realism as Schopenhauer had popularized pessimism and William James pragmatism.

But life hadn't come that way. Life took hold of people and forced them into flying rings. He laughed to think of that rap at his door, the diaphanous shadow in Hume, Marcia's threatened kiss.

"And it's still me," he said aloud in wonder as he lay awake in the darkness. "I'm the man who sat in Berkeley with temerity to wonder if that rap would have had actual existence had my ear not been there to hear it. I'm still that man. I could be electrocuted for the crimes he committed.

"Poor gauzy souls trying to express ourselves in something tangible. Marcia with her written book; I with my unwritten ones. Trying to choose our mediums and then taking what we get—and being glad."

V

"Sandra Pepys, Syncopated," with an introduction by Peter Boyce Wendell, the columnist, appeared serially in *Jordan's Magazine*, and came out in book form in March. From its first published instalment it attracted attention far and wide. A trite enough subject—a girl from a small New Jersey town coming to New York to go on the stage—treated simply, with a peculiar vividness of phrasing and a haunting undertone of sadness in the very inadequacy of its vocabulary, it made an irresistible appeal.

Peter Boyce Wendell, who happened at that time to be advocating the enrichment of the American language by the immediate adoption of expressive vernacular words, stood as its sponsor and thundered his indorsement over the placid bromides of the conventional reviewers.

Marcia received three hundred dollars an instalment for the serial publication, which came at an opportune time, for though Horace's monthly salary at the Hippodrome was now more than Marcia's had ever been, young Marcia was emitting shrill cries which they interpreted as a demand for country air. So early April found them installed in a bungalow in Westchester County, with a place for a lawn, a place for a garage, and a place for everything, including a sound-proof impregnable study, in which Marcia faithfully promised Mr. Jordan she would shut herself up when her daughter's demands began to be abated, and compose immortally illiterate literature.

"It's not half bad," thought Horace one night as he was on his way from the station to his house. He was considering several prospects that had opened up, a four months' vaudeville offer in five figures, a chance to go back to Princeton in charge of all gymnasium work. Odd! He had once intended to go back there in charge of all philosophic work, and now he had not even been stirred by the arrival in New York of Anton Laurier, his old idol.

The gravel crunched raucously under his heel. He saw the lights of his sitting-room gleaming and noticed a big car standing in the drive. Probably Mr. Jordan again, come to persuade Marcia to settle down to work.

She had heard the sound of his approach and her form was silhouetted against the lighted door as she came out to meet him.

"There's some Frenchman here," she whispered nervously. "I can't pronounce his name, but he sounds awful deep. You'll have to jaw with him."

"What Frenchman?"

"You can't prove it by me. He drove up an hour ago with Mr. Jordan and said he wanted to meet Sandra Pepys, and all that sort of thing.

Two men rose from chairs as they went inside.

"Hello, Tarbox," said Jordan. "I've just been bringing together two celebrities. I've brought M'sieur Laurier out with me. M'sieur Laurier, let me present Mr. Tarbox, Mrs. Tarbox's husband."

"Not Anton Laurier!" exclaimed Horace.

"But, yes. I must come. I have to come. I have read the book of Madame, and I have been charmed"—he fumbled in his pocket—"ah, I have read of you too. In this newspaper which I read to-day it has your name."

He finally produced a clipping from a magazine.

"Read it!" he said eagerly. "It has about you too."

Horace's eye skipped down the page.

"A distinct contribution to American dialect literature," it said. "No attempt at literary tone; the book derives its very quality from this fact, as did 'Huckleberry Finn.' "

Horace's eyes caught a passage lower down; he became suddenly aghast—read on hurriedly:

"Marcia Tarbox's connection with the stage is not only as a spectator but as the wife of a performer. She was married last year to Horace Tarbox, who every evening delights the children at the Hippodrome with his wondrous flying-ring performance. It is said that the young couple have dubbed themselves Head and Shoulders, referring doubtless to the fact that Mrs. Tarbox supplies the literary and mental qualities, while the supple and agile shoulders of her husband contribute their share to the family fortunes.

"Mrs. Tarbox seems to merit that much-abused title—'prodigy.' Only twenty——"

Horace stopped reading, and with a very odd expression in his eyes gazed intently at Anton Laurier.

"I want to advise you—" he began hoarsely.

"What?"

"About raps. Don't answer them! Let them alone—have a padded door."

The
Cut-Glass
Bowl

THERE WAS A ROUGH STONE AGE AND A smooth stone age and a bronze age, and many years afterward a cut-glass age. In the cut-glass age, when young ladies had persuaded young men with long, curly mustaches to marry them, they sat down several months afterward and wrote thank-you notes for all sorts of cut-glass presents—punch-bowls, finger-bowls, dinner-glasses, wine-glasses, ice-cream dishes, bonbon dishes, decanters, and vases—for, though cut glass was nothing new in the nineties, it was then especially busy reflecting the dazzling light of fashion from the Back Bay to the fastnesses of the Middle West.

After the wedding the punch-bowls were arranged on the side-board with the big bowl in the centre; the glasses were set up in the china-closet; the candlesticks were put at both ends of things—and then the struggle for existence began. The bonbon dish lost its little handle and became a pin-tray upstairs; a promenading cat knocked the little bowl off the sideboard, and the hired girl chipped the middle-sized one with the sugar-dish; then the wine-glasses succumbed to leg fractures, and even the dinner-glasses disappeared one by one like the ten little niggers, the last one ending up, scarred and maimed, as a tooth-brush holder among other shabby genteels on the bathroom shelf. But by the time all this had happened the cut-glass age was over, anyway.

It was well past its first glory on the day the curious Mrs. Roger Fairboalt came to see the beautiful Mrs. Harold Piper.

"My *dear*," said the curious Mrs. Roger Fairboalt, "I *love* your house. I think it's *quite* artistic."

"I'm *so* glad," said the beautiful Mrs. Harold Piper, lights appearing in her young, dark eyes; "and you *must* come often. I'm almost *always* alone in the afternoon."

Mrs. Fairboalt would have liked to remark that she didn't believe this at all and couldn't see how she'd be expected to—it was all over town that Mr. Freddy Gedney had been dropping in on Mrs. Piper five afternoons a week for the past six months. Mrs. Fairboalt was at that ripe age where she distrusted all beautiful women— —

"I love the dining-room *most*," she said, "all that *marvellous* china, and that *huge* cut-glass bowl."

Mrs. Piper laughed, so prettily that Mrs. Fairboalt's lingering reservations about the Freddy Gedney story quite vanished.

"Oh, that big bowl!" Mrs. Piper's mouth forming the words was a vivid rose petal. "There's a story about that bowl— —"

"Oh— —"

"You remember young Carleton Canby? Well, he was very attentive at one time, and the night I told him I was going to marry Harold, seven years ago, in ninety-two, he drew himself way up and said: 'Evylyn, I'm going to give a present that's as hard as you are and as beautiful and as empty and as easy to see through.' He frightened me a little—his eyes were so black. I thought he was going to deed me a haunted house or something that would explode when you opened it. That bowl came, and of course it's beautiful. Its diameter or circumference or something is two and a half feet—or perhaps it's three and a half. Anyway, the sideboard is really too small for it; it sticks way out."

"My *dear*, wasn't that *odd!* And he left town about then, didn't he?" Mrs. Fairboalt was scribbling italicized notes on her memory—"*Hard, Beautiful, Empty,* and *Easy to see through.*"

"Yes, he went West—or South—or somewhere," answered Mrs. Piper, radiating that divine vagueness that helps to lift beauty out of time.

Mrs. Fairboalt drew on her gloves, approving the effect of largeness given by the open sweep from the spacious music-room through the library, disclosing a part of the dining-room beyond. It was really the nicest smaller house in town, and Mrs. Piper had talked of moving to a larger one on Devereaux Avenue. Harold Piper must be *coining* money.

As she turned into the sidewalk under the gathering autumn dusk she assumed that disapproving, faintly unpleasant expression that almost all successful women of forty wear on the street.

If *I* were Harold Piper, she thought, I'd spend a *little* less time on business and a *little* more time at home. Some *friend* should speak to him.

But if Mrs. Fairboalt had considered it a successful afternoon she would have named it a triumph had she waited two minutes longer. For while she was still a black receding figure a hundred yards down the street, a very good-looking distraught young man turned up the walk to the Piper house. Mrs. Piper answered the door-bell herself, and with a rather dismayed expression led him quickly into the library.

"I had to see you," he began wildly; "your note played the devil with me. Did Harold frighten you into this?"

She shook her head.

"I'm through, Fred," she said slowly, and her lips had never looked to him so much like tearings from a rose. "He came home last night sick with it. Jessie Piper's sense of duty was too much for her, so she went down to his office and told him. He was hurt and—oh, I can't help seeing it his way, Fred. He says we've been club gossip all summer and he didn't know it, and now he understands snatches of conversation he's caught and veiled hints people have dropped about me. He's mighty angry, Fred, and he loves me and I love him—rather."

Gedney nodded slowly and half closed his eyes.

"Yes," he said, "yes, my trouble's like yours. I can see other people's points of view too plainly." His gray eyes met her dark ones frankly. "The blessed thing's over. My God, Evylyn, I've been sitting down at the office all day looking at the outside of your letter, and looking at it and looking at it——"

"You've got to go, Fred," she said steadily, and the slight emphasis of hurry in her voice was a new thrust for him. "I gave him my word of honor I wouldn't see you. I know just how far I can go with Harold, and being here with you this evening is one of the things I can't do."

They were still standing, and as she spoke she made a little movement toward the door. Gedney looked at her miserably, trying, here at the end, to treasure up a last picture of her—and then suddenly both of them were stiffened into marble at the sound of steps on the walk outside. Instantly her arm reached out grasping the lapel of his coat— half urged, half swung him through the big door into the dark dining-room.

"I'll make him go up-stairs," she whispered close to his ear. "Don't move till you hear him on the stairs. Then go out the front way."

Then he was alone listening as she greeted her husband in the hall.

Harold Piper was thirty-six, nine years older than his wife. He was handsome—with marginal notes: these being eyes that were too close together, and a certain woodenness when his face was in repose. His attitude toward this Gedney matter was typical of all his attitudes. He had told Evylyn that he considered the subject closed and would never reproach her nor allude to it in any form; and he told himself that this was rather a big way of looking at it—that she was not a little impressed. Yet, like all men who are preoccupied with their own broadness, he was exceptionally narrow.

He greeted Evylyn with emphasized cordiality this evening.

"You'll have to hurry and dress, Harold," she said eagerly. "We're going to the Bronsons'."

He nodded.

"It doesn't take me long to dress, dear," and, his words trailing off, he walked on into the library. Evylyn's heart clattered loudly.

"Harold—" she began, with a little catch in her voice, and followed him in. He was lighting a cigarette. "You'll have to hurry, Harold," she finished, standing in the doorway.

"Why?" he asked, a trifle impatiently. "You're not dressed yourself yet, Evie."

He stretched out in a Morris chair and unfolded a newspaper. With a sinking sensation Evylyn saw that this meant at least ten minutes— and Gedney was standing breathless in the next room. Supposing Harold decided that before he went upstairs he wanted a drink from the decanter on the sideboard. Then it occurred to her to forestall this contingency by bringing him the decanter and a glass. She dreaded calling his attention to the dining-room in any way, but she couldn't risk the other chance.

But at the same moment Harold rose and, throwing his paper down, came toward her.

"Evie, dear," he said, bending and putting his arms about her, "I hope you're not thinking about last night—" She moved close to him, trembling. "I know," he continued, "it was just an imprudent friendship on your part. We all make mistakes."

Evylyn hardly heard him. She was wondering if by sheer clinging to him she could draw him out and up the stairs. She thought of playing sick, asking to be carried up—unfortunately, she knew he would lay her on the couch and bring her whiskey.

Suddenly her nervous tension moved up a last impossible notch. She had heard a very faint but quite unmistakable creak from the floor of the dining-room. Fred was trying to get out the back way.

Then her heart took a flying leap as a hollow ringing note like a gong echoed and re-echoed through the house. Gedney's arm had struck the big cut-glass bowl.

"What's that!" cried Harold. "Who's there?"

She clung to him but he broke away, and the room seemed to crash about her ears. She heard the pantry-door swing open, a scuffle, the rattle of a tin pan, and in wild despair she rushed into the kitchen and pulled up the gas. Her husband's arm slowly unwound from Gedney's neck, and he stood there very still, first in amazement, then with pain dawning in his face.

"My golly!" he said in bewilderment, and then repeated: "My golly!"

He turned as if to jump again at Gedney, stopped, his muscles visibly relaxed, and he gave a bitter little laugh.

"You people—you people—" Evylyn's arms were around him and her eyes were pleading with him frantically, but he pushed her away and sank dazed into a kitchen chair, his face like procelain. "You've been doing things to me, Evylyn. Why, you little devil! You little *devil!*"

She had never felt so sorry for him; she had never loved him so much.

"It wasn't her fault," said Gedney rather humbly. "I just came." But Piper shook his head, and his expression when he stared up was as if some physical accident had jarred his mind into a temporary inability to function. His eyes, grown suddenly pitiful, struck a deep, un-sounded chord in Evylyn—and simultaneously a furious anger surged in her. She felt her eyelids burning; she stamped her foot violently; her hands scurried nervously over the table as if searching for a weapon, and then she flung herself wildly at Gedney.

"Get out!" she screamed, dark eyes blazing, little fists beating help-lessly on his outstretched arm. "You did this! Get out of here—get out—get *out! Get out!*"

II

Concerning Mrs. Harold Piper at thirty-five, opinion was divided—women said she was still handsome; men said she was pretty no longer. And this was probably because the qualities in her beauty that women had feared and men had followed had vanished. Her eyes were still as large and as dark and as sad, but the mystery had departed; their sadness was no longer eternal, only human, and she had developed a habit, when she was startled or annoyed, of twitching her brows together and blinking several times. Her mouth also had lost: the red had receded and the faint down-turning of its corners when she smiled, that had added to the sadness of the eyes and been vaguely mocking and beautiful, was quite gone. When she smiled now the corners of her lips turned up. Back in the days when she revelled in her own beauty Evylyn had enjoyed that smile of hers—she had accentuated it. When she stopped accentuating it, it faded out and the last of her mystery with it.

Evylyn had ceased accentuating her smile within a month after the Freddy Gedney affair. Externally things had gone on very much as they had before. But in those few minutes during which she had discovered how much she loved her husband, Evylyn had realized how indelibly she had hurt him. For a month she struggled against aching silences, wild reproaches and accusations—she pled with him, made quiet, pitiful little love to him, and he laughed at her bitterly—and then she, too, slipped gradually into silence and a shadowy, unpenetrable barrier dropped between them. The surge of love that had risen in her she lavished on Donald, her little boy, realizing him almost wonderingly as a part of her life.

The next year a piling up of mutual interests and responsibilities and some stray flicker from the past brought husband and wife together again—but after a rather pathetic flood of passion Evylyn realized that her great opportunity was gone. There simply wasn't anything left. She might have been youth and love for both—but that time of silence had slowly dried up the springs of affection and her own desire to drink again of them was dead.

She began for the first time to seek women friends, to prefer books she had read before, to sew a little where she could watch her two children to whom she was devoted. She worried about little things—if she saw crumbs on the dinner-table her mind drifted off the conversation: she was receding gradually into middle age.

Her thirty-fifth birthday had been an exceptionally busy one, for they were entertaining on short notice that night, and as she stood in her bedroom window in the late afternoon she discovered that she was quite tired. Ten years before she would have lain down and slept, but now she had a feeling that things needed watching: maids were cleaning down-stairs, bric-a-brac was all over the floor, and there were sure to be grocery-men that had to be talked to imperatively—and then there was a letter to write Donald, who was fourteen and in his first year away at school.

She had nearly decided to lie down, nevertheless, when she heard a sudden familiar signal from little Julie down-stairs. She compressed her lips, her brows twitched together, and she blinked.

"Julie!" she called.

"Ah-h-h-ow!" prolonged Julie plaintively. Then the voice of Hilda, the second maid, floated up the stairs.

"She cut herself a little, Mis' Piper."

Evylyn flew to her sewing-basket, rummaged until she found a torn handkerchief, and hurried down-stairs. In a moment Julie was crying in her arms as she searched for the cut, faint, disparaging evidences of which appeared on Julie's dress!

"My *thu*-mb!" explained Julie. "Oh-h-h-h, t'urts."

"It was the bowl here, the he'y one," said Hilda apologetically. "It was waitin' on the floor while I polished the sideboard, and Julie came along an' went to foolin' with it. She yust scratch herself."

Evylyn frowned heavily at Hilda, and twisting Julie decisively in her lap, began tearing strips off the handkerchief.

"Now—let's see it, dear."

Julie held it up and Evylyn pounced.

"There!"

Julie surveyed her swatched thumb doubtfully. She crooked it; it waggled. A pleased, interested look appeared in her tear-stained face. She sniffled and waggled it again.

"You *precious!*" cried Evylyn and kissed her, but before she left the room she levelled another frown at Hilda. Careless! Servants all that way nowadays. If she could get a good Irishwoman—but you couldn't any more—and these Swedes——

At five o'clock Harold arrived and, coming up to her room, threatened in a suspiciously jovial tone to kiss her thirty-five times for her birthday. Evylyn resisted.

"You've been drinking," she said shortly, and then added qualitatively, "a little. You know I loathe the smell of it."

"Evie," he said, after a pause, seating himself in a chair by the window, "I can tell you something now. I guess you've known things haven't been going quite right down-town."

She was standing at the window combing her hair, but at these words she turned and looked at him.

"How do you mean? You've always said there was room for more than one wholesale hardware house in town." Her voice expressed some alarm.

"There *was*," said Harold significantly, "but this Clarence Ahearn is a smart man."

"I was surprised when you said he was coming to dinner."

"Evie," he went on, with another slap at his knee, "after January first 'The Clarence Ahearn Company' becomes 'The Ahearn, Piper Company'—and 'Piper Brothers' as a company ceases to exist."

Evylyn was startled. The sound of his name in second place was somehow hostile to her; still he appeared jubilant.

"I don't understand, Harold."

"Well, Evie, Ahearn had been fooling around with Marx. If those two had combined we'd have been the little fellow, struggling along, picking up smaller orders, hanging back on risks. It's a question of capital, Evie, and 'Ahearn and Marx' would have had the business just like 'Ahearn and Piper' is going to now." He paused and coughed and a little cloud of whiskey floated up to her nostrils. "Tell you the truth, Evie, I've suspected that Ahearn's wife had something to do with it. Ambitious little lady, I'm told. Guess she knew the Marxes couldn't help her much here."

"Is she—common?" asked Evie.

"Never met her, I'm sure—but I don't doubt it. Clarence Ahearn's name's been up at the Country Club five months—no action taken." He waved his hand disparagingly. "Ahearn and I had lunch together to-day and just about clinched it, so I thought it'd be nice to have him and his wife up to-night—just have nine, mostly family. After all, it's a big thing for me, and of course we'll have to see something of them, Evie."

"Yes," said Evie thoughtfully, "I suppose we will."

Evylyn was not disturbed over the social end of it—but the idea of "Piper Brothers" becoming "The Ahearn, Piper Company" startled her. It seemed like going down in the world.

Half an hour later, as she began to dress for dinner, she heard his voice from down-stairs.

"Oh, Evie, come down!"

She went out into the hall and called over the banister: "What is it?"

"I want you to help me make some of that punch before dinner."

Hurriedly rehooking her dress, she descended the stairs and found him grouping the essentials on the dining-room table. She went to the sideboard and, lifting one of the bowls, carried it over.

"Oh, no," he protested, "let's use the big one. There'll be Ahearn and his wife and you and I and Milton, that's five, and Tom and Jessie, that's seven, and your sister and Joe Ambler, that's nine. You don't know how quick that stuff goes when *you* make it."

"We'll use this bowl," she insisted. "It'll hold plenty. You know how Tom is."

Tom Lowrie, husband to Jessie, Harold's first cousin, was rather inclined to finish anything in a liquid way that he began.

Harold shook his head.

"Don't be foolish. That one holds only about three quarts and there's nine of us, and the servants'll want some—and it isn't very strong punch. It's so much more cheerful to have a lot, Evie; we don't have to drink all of it."

"I say the small one."

Again he shook his head obstinately.

"No; be reasonable."

"I *am* reasonable," she said shortly. "I don't want any drunken men in the house."

"Who said you did?"

"Then use the small bowl."

"Now, Evie——"

He grasped the smaller bowl to lift it back. Instantly her hands were on it, holding it down. There was a momentary struggle, and then, with a little exasperated grunt, he raised his side, slipped it from her fingers, and carried it to the sideboard.

She looked at him and tried to make her expression contemptuous, but he only laughed. Acknowledging her defeat but disclaiming all future interest in the punch, she left the room.

III

At seven-thirty, her cheeks glowing and her high-piled hair gleaming with a suspicion of brilliantine, Evylyn descended the stairs. Mrs. Ahearn, a little woman concealing a slight nervousness under red hair and an extreme Empire gown, greeted her volubly. Evylyn disliked her on the spot, but the husband she rather approved of. He had keen blue eyes and a natural gift of pleasing people that might have made him, socially, had he not so obviously committed the blunder of marrying too early in his career.

"I'm glad to know Piper's wife," he said simply. "It looks as though your husband and I are going to see a lot of each other in the future."

She bowed, smiled graciously, and turned to greet the others: Milton Piper, Harold's quiet, unassertive younger brother; the two Lowries, Jessie and Tom; Irene, her own unmarried sister; and finally Joe Ambler, a confirmed bachelor and Irene's perennial beau.

Harold led the way into dinner.

"We're having a punch evening," he announced jovially—Evylyn saw that he had already sampled his concoction—"so there won't be any cocktails except the punch. It's m' wife's greatest achievement, Mrs. Ahearn; she'll give you the recipe if you want it; but owing to a slight"—he caught his wife's eye and paused—"to a slight indisposition, I'm responsible for this batch. Here's how!"

All through dinner there was punch, and Evylyn, noticing that Ahearn and Milton Piper and all the women were shaking their heads negatively at the maid, knew she had been right about the bowl; it was still half full. She resolved to caution Harold directly afterward, but when the women left the table Mrs. Ahearn cornered her, and she found herself talking cities and dressmakers with a polite show of interest.

"We've moved around a lot," chattered Mrs. Ahearn, her red hair nodding violently. "Oh, yes, we've never stayed so long in a town before—but I do hope we're here for good. I like it here; don't you?"

"Well, you see, I've always lived here, so naturally——"

"Oh, that's true," said Mrs. Ahearn and laughed. "Clarence always used to tell me he had to have a wife he could come home to and say: 'Well, we're going to Chicago to-morrow to live, so pack up.' I got so I never expected to live *any*where." She laughed her little laugh again; Evylyn suspected that it was her society laugh.

"Your husband is a very able man, I imagine."

"Oh, yes," Mrs. Ahearn assured her eagerly. "He's brainy, Clarence is. Ideas and enthusiasm, you know. Finds out what he wants and then goes and gets it."

Evylyn nodded. She was wondering if the men were still drinking punch back in the dining-room. Mrs. Ahearn's history kept unfolding jerkily, but Evylyn had ceased to listen. The first odor of massed cigars began to drift in. It wasn't really a large house, she reflected; on an evening like this the library sometimes grew blue with smoke, and next day one had to leave the windows open for hours to air the heavy staleness out of the curtains. Perhaps this partnership might . . . she began to speculate on a new house . . .

Mrs. Ahearn's voice drifted in on her:

"I really would like the recipe if you have it written down some-where — —"

Then there was a sound of chairs in the dining-room and the men strolled in. Evylyn saw at once that her worst fears were realized. Harold's face was flushed and his words ran together at the ends of sentences, while Tom Lowrie lurched when he walked and narrowly missed Irene's lap when he tried to sink onto the couch beside her. He sat there blinking dazedly at the company. Evylyn found herself blinking back at him, but she saw no humor in it. Joe Ambler was smiling contentedly and purring on his cigar. Only Ahearn and Milton Piper seemed unaffected.

"It's a pretty fine town, Ahearn," said Ambler, "you'll find that."

"I've found it so," said Ahearn pleasantly.

"You find it more, Ahearn," said Harold, nodding emphatically, "'f I've an'thin' do 'th it."

He soared into a eulogy of the city, and Evylyn wondered uncomfortably if it bored every one as it bored her. Apparently not. They were all listening attentively. Evylyn broke in at the first gap.

"Where've you been living, Mr. Ahearn?" she asked interestedly. Then she remembered that Mrs. Ahearn had told her, but it didn't matter. Harold mustn't talk so much. He was such an *ass* when he'd been drinking. But he plopped directly back in.

"Tell you, Ahearn. Firs' you wanna get a house up here on the hill. Get Stearne house or Ridgeway house. Wanna have it so people say: 'There's Ahearn house.' Solid, you know, tha's effec' it gives."

Evylyn flushed. This didn't sound right at all. Still Ahearn didn't seem to notice anything amiss, only nodded gravely.

"Have you been looking—" But her words trailed off unheard as Harold's voice boomed on.

"Get house—tha's start. Then you get know people. Snobbish town first toward outsider, but not long—not after know you. People like you"—he indicated Ahearn and his wife with a sweeping gesture—"all right. Cordial as an'thin' once get by first barrer-bar-barrer—" He swallowed, and then said "barrier," repeated it masterfully.

Evylyn looked appealingly at her brother-in-law, but before he could intercede a thick mumble had come crowding out of Tom Lowrie, hindered by the dead cigar which he gripped firmly with his teeth.

"Huma uma ho huma ahdy um — —"

"What?" demanded Harold earnestly.

Resignedly and with difficulty Tom removed the cigar—that is, he removed part of it, and then blew the remainder with a *whut* sound across the room, where it landed liquidly and limply in Mrs. Ahearn's lap.

"Beg pardon," he mumbled, and rose with the vague intention of going after it. Milton's hand on his coat collapsed him in time, and Mrs. Ahearn not ungracefully flounced the tobacco from her skirt to the floor, never once looking at it.

"I was sayin'," continued Tom thickly, "'fore 'at happened"—he waved his hand apologetically toward Mrs. Ahearn—"I was sayin' I heard all truth that Country Club matter."

Milton leaned and whispered something to him.

"Lemme 'lone," he said petulantly, "know what I'm doin'. 'At's what they came for."

Evylyn sat there in a panic, trying to make her mouth form words. She saw her sister's sardonic expression and Mrs. Ahearn's face turning a vivid red. Ahearn was looking down at his watchchain, fingering it.

"I heard who's been keepin' y' out, an' he's not a bit better'n you. I can fix whole damn thing up. Would've before, but I didn't know you. Harol' tol' me you felt bad about the thing— —"

Milton Piper rose suddenly and awkwardly to his feet. In a second every one was standing tensely and Milton was saying something very hurriedly about having to go early, and the Ahearns were listening with eager intentness. Then Mrs. Ahearn swallowed and turned with a forced smile toward Jessie. Evylyn saw Tom lurch forward and put his hand on Ahearn's shoulder—and suddenly she was listening to a new, anxious voice at her elbow, and, turning, found Hilda, the second maid.

"Please, Mis' Piper, I tank Yulie got her hand poisoned. It's all swole up and her cheeks is hot and she's moanin' an' groanin'— —"

"Julie is?" Evylyn asked sharply. The party suddenly receded. She turned quickly, sought with her eyes for Mrs. Ahearn, slipped toward her.

"If you'll excuse me, Mrs.— " She had momentarily forgotten the name, but she went right on: "My little girl's been taken sick. I'll be down when I can." She turned and ran quickly up the stairs, retaining a confused picture of rays of cigar smoke and a loud discussion in the centre of the room that seemed to be developing into an argument.

Switching on the light in the nursery, she found Julie tossing feverishly and giving out odd little cries. She put her hand against the cheeks. They were burning. With an exclamation she followed the arm down under the cover until she found the hand. Hilda was right. The whole thumb was swollen to the wrist and in the centre was a little inflamed sore. Blood-poisoning! her mind cried in terror. The bandage had come off the cut and she'd gotten something in it. She'd cut it at three o'clock—it was now nearly eleven. Eight hours. Blood-poisoning couldn't possibly develop so soon. She rushed to the 'phone.

Doctor Martin across the street was out. Doctor Foulke, their family physician, didn't answer. She racked her brains and in desperation called her throat specialist, and bit her lip furiously while he looked up the numbers of two physicians. During that interminable moment she thought she heard loud voices down-stairs—but she seemed to be in another world now. After fifteen minutes she located a physician who sounded angry and sulky at being called out of bed. She ran back to the nursery and, looking at the hand, found it was somewhat more swollen.

"Oh, God!" she cried, and kneeling beside the bed began smoothing back Julie's hair over and over. With a vague idea of getting some hot water, she rose and started toward the door, but the lace of her dress caught in the bed-rail and she fell forward on her hands and knees. She struggled up and jerked frantically at the lace. The bed moved and Julie groaned. Then more quietly but with suddenly fumbling fingers she found the pleat in front, tore the whole pannier completely off, and rushed from the room.

Out in the hall she heard a single loud, insistent voice, but as she reached the head of the stairs it ceased and an outer door banged.

The music-room came into view. Only Harold and Milton were there, the former leaning against a chair, his face very pale, his collar open, and his mouth moving loosely.

"What's the matter?"

Milton looked at her anxiously.

"There was a little trouble——"

Then Harold saw her and, straightening up with an effort, began to speak.

"'Sult m'own cousin m'own house. God damn common nouveau rish. 'Sult m'own cousin——"

"Tom had trouble with Ahearn and Harold interfered," said Milton.

"My Lord, Milton," cried Evylyn, "couldn't you have done something?"

"I tried; I——"

"Julie's sick," she interrupted; "she's poisoned herself. Get him to bed if you can."

Harold looked up.

"Julie sick?"

Paying no attention, Evylyn brushed by through the dining-room, catching sight, with a burst of horror, of the big punch-bowl still on the table, the liquid from melted ice in its bottom. She heard steps on the front stairs—it was Milton helping Harold up—and then a mumble: "Why, Julie's a'righ'."

"Don't let him go into the nursery!" she shouted.

The hours blurred into a nightmare. The doctor arrived just before midnight and within a half-hour had lanced the wound. He left at two after giving her the addresses of two nurses to call up and promising to return at half past six. It was blood-poisoning.

At four, leaving Hilda by the bedside, she went to her room, and slipping with a shudder out of her evening dress, kicked it into a corner. She put on a house dress and returned to the nursery while Hilda went to make coffee.

Not until noon could she bring herself to look into Harold's room, but when she did it was to find him awake and staring very miserably at the ceiling. He turned blood-shot hollow eyes upon her. For a minute she hated him, couldn't speak. A husky voice came from the bed.

"What time is it?"

"Noon."

"I made a damn fool— —"

"It doesn't matter," she said sharply. "Julie's got blood-poisoning. They may"—she choked over the words—"they think she'll have to lose her hand."

"What?"

"She cut herself on that—that bowl."

"Last night?"

"Oh, what does it matter?" she cried. "She's got blood-poisoning. Can't you hear?"

He looked at her bewildered—sat half-way up in bed.

"I'll get dressed," he said.

Her anger subsided and a great wave of weariness and pity for him rolled over her. After all, it was his trouble, too.

"Yes," she answered listlessly, "I suppose you'd better."

IV

If Evylyn's beauty had hesitated in her early thirties it came to an abrupt decision just afterward and completely left her. A tentative outlay of wrinkles on her face suddenly deepened and flesh collected rapidly on her legs and hips and arms. Her mannerism of drawing her brows together had become an expression—it was habitual when she was reading or speaking and even while she slept. She was forty-six.

As in most families whose fortunes have gone down rather than up, she and Harold had drifted into a colorless antagonism. In repose they looked at each other with the toleration they might have felt for broken old chairs; Evylyn worried a little when he was sick and did her best to be cheerful under the wearying depression of living with a disappointed man.

Family bridge was over for the evening and she sighed with relief. She had made more mistakes than usual this evening and she didn't care. Irene shouldn't have made that remark about the infantry being particularly dangerous. There had been no letter for three weeks now, and, while this was nothing out of the ordinary, it never failed to make her nervous; naturally she hadn't known how many clubs were out.

Harold had gone up-stairs, so she stepped out on the porch for a breath of fresh air. There was a bright glamour of moonlight diffusing on the sidewalks and lawns, and with a little half yawn, half laugh, she remembered one long moonlight affair of her youth. It was astonishing to think that life had once been the sum of her current love-affairs. It was now the sum of her current problems.

There was the problem of Julie—Julie was thirteen, and lately she was growing more and more sensitive about her deformity and preferred to stay always in her room reading. A few years before she had been frighened at the idea of going to school, and Evylyn could not bring herself to send her, so she grew up in her mother's shadow, a pitiful little figure with the artificial hand that she made no attempt to use but kept forlornly in her pocket. Lately she had been taking lessons in using it because Evylyn had feared she would cease to lift the arm altogether, but after the lessons, unless she made a move with it in listless obedience to her mother, the little hand would creep back to the pocket of her dress. For a while her dresses were made without pockets, but Julie had moped around the house so miserably at a loss all one month that Evylyn weakened and never tried the experiment again.

The problem of Donald had been different from the start. She had attempted vainly to keep him near her as she had tried to teach Julie to lean less on her—lately the problem of Donald had been snatched out of her hands; his division had been abroad for three months.

She yawned again—life was a thing for youth. What a happy youth she must have had! She remembered her pony, Bijou, and the trip to Europe with her mother when she was eighteen——

"Very, very complicated," she said aloud and severely to the moon, and, stepping inside, was about to close the door when she heard a noise in the library and started.

It was Martha, the middle-aged servant: they kept only one now.

"Why, Martha!" she said in surprise.

Martha turned quickly.

"Oh, I thought you was up-stairs. I was jist— —"

"Is anything the matter?"

Martha hesitated.

"No; I—" She stood there fidgeting. "It was a letter, Mrs. Piper, that I put somewhere."

"A letter? Your own letter?" asked Evylyn, switching on the light.

"No, it was to you. 'Twas this afternoon, Mrs. Piper, in the last mail. The postman give it to me and then the back door-bell rang. I had it in my hand, so I must have stuck it somewhere. I thought I'd just slip in now and find it."

"What sort of a letter? From Mr. Donald?"

"No, it was an advertisement, maybe, or a business letter. It was a long, narrow one, I remember."

They began a search through the music-room, looking on trays and mantelpieces, and then through the library, feeling on the tops of rows of books. Martha paused in despair.

"I can't think where. I went straight to the kitchen. The dining-room, maybe." She started hopefully for the dining-room, but turned suddenly at the sound of a gasp behind her. Evylyn had sat down heavily in a Morris chair, her brows drawn very close together, eyes blinking furiously.

"Are you sick?"

For a minute there was no answer. Evylyn sat there very still and Martha could see the very quick rise and fall of her bosom.

"Are you sick?" she repeated.

"No," said Evylyn slowly, "but I know where the letter is. Go 'way, Martha. I know."

Wonderingly, Martha withdrew, and still Evylyn sat there, only the muscles around her eyes moving—contracting and relaxing and contracting again. She knew now where the letter was—she knew as well as if she had put it there herself. And she felt instinctively and unquestionably what the letter was. It was long and narrow like an advertisement, but up in the corner in large letters it said "War Department" and, in smaller letters below, "Official Business." She knew it lay there in the big bowl with her name in ink on the outside and her soul's death within.

Rising uncertainly, she walked toward the dining-room, feeling her way along the bookcases and through the doorway. After a moment she found the light and switched it on.

There was the bowl, reflecting the electric light in crimson squares edged with black and yellow squares edged with blue, ponderous and glittering, grotesquely and triumphantly ominous. She took a step forward and paused again; another step and she would see over the top and into the inside—another step and she would see an edge of white—another step—her hands fell on the rough, cold surface— —

In a moment she was tearing it open, fumbling with an obstinate fold, holding it before her while the typewritten page glared out and struck at her. Then it fluttered like a bird to the floor. The house that had seemed whirring, buzzing a moment since, was suddenly very quiet; a breath of air crept in through the open front door carrying the noise of a passing motor; she heard faint sounds from up-stairs and then a grinding racket in the pipe behind the bookcases—her husband turning off a water-tap— —

And in that instant it was as if this were not, after all, Donald's hour except in so far as he was a marker in the insidious contest that had gone on in sudden surges and long, listless interludes between Evylyn and this cold, malignant thing of beauty, a gift of enmity from a man whose face she had long since forgotten. With its massive, brooding passivity it lay there in the centre of her house as it had lain for years, throwing out the ice-like beams of a thousand eyes, perverse glitterings merging each into each, never aging, never changing.

Evylyn sat down on the edge of the table and stared at it fascinated. It seemed to be smiling now, a very cruel smile, as if to say:

"You see, this time I didn't have to hurt you directly. I didn't bother. You know it was I who took your son away. You know how cold I am and how hard and how beautiful, because once you were just as cold and hard and beautiful."

The bowl seemed suddenly to turn itself over and then to distend and swell until it became a great canopy that glittered and trembled over the room, over the house, and, as the walls melted slowly into mist, Evylyn saw that it was still moving out, out and far away from her, shutting off far horizons and suns and moons and stars except as inky blots seen faintly through it. And under it walked all the people, and the light that came through to them was refracted and twisted until shadow seemed light and light seemed shadow—until the whole panorama of the world became changed and distorted under the twinkling heaven of the bowl.

Then there came a far-away, booming voice like a low, clear bell. It came from the centre of the bowl and down the great sides to the ground and then bounced toward her eagerly.

"You see, I am fate," it shouted, "and stronger than your puny plans; and I am how-things-turn-out and I am different from your little dreams, and I am the flight of time and the end of beauty and unfulfilled desire; all the accidents and imperceptions and the little minutes that shape the crucial hours are mine. I am the exception that proves no rules, the limits of your control, the condiment in the dish of life."

The booming sound stopped; the echoes rolled away over the wide land to the edge of the bowl that bounded the world and up the great sides and back to the centre where they hummed for a moment and died. Then the great walls began slowly to bear down upon her, growing smaller and smaller, coming closer and closer as if to crush her; and as she clinched her hands and waited for the swift bruise of the cold glass, the bowl gave a sudden wrench and turned over—and lay there on the sideboard, shining and inscrutable, reflecting in a hundred prisms myriad, many-colored glints and gleams and crossings and interlacings of light.

The cold wind blew in again through the front door, and with a desperate, frantic energy Evylyn stretched both her arms around the bowl. She must be quick—she must be strong. She tightened her arms until they ached, tauted the thin strips of muscle under her soft flesh, and with a mighty effort raised it and held it. She felt the wind blow cold on her back where her dress had come apart from the strain of her effort, and as she felt it she turned toward it and staggered under the great weight out through the library and on toward the front door. She must be quick—she must be strong. The blood in her arms throbbed dully and her knees kept giving way under her, but the feel of the cool glass was good.

Out the front door she tottered and over to the stone steps, and there, summoning every fibre of her soul and body for a last effort, swung herself half around—for a second, as she tried to loose her hold, her numb fingers clung to the rough surface, and in that second she slipped, and losing balance, toppled forward with a despairing cry, her arms still around the bowl . . . down . . .

Over the way lights went on; far down the block the crash was heard, and pedestrians rushed up wonderingly; up-stairs a tired man awoke from the edge of sleep and a little girl whimpered in a haunted doze. And all over the moonlit sidewalk around the still, black form, hundreds of prisms and cubes and splinters of glass reflected the light in little gleams of blue, and black edged with yellow, and yellow, and crimson edged with black.

Bernice Bobs
Her Hair

AFTER DARK ON SATURDAY NIGHT ONE COULD
stand on the first tee of the golf-course and see the country-club
windows as a yellow expanse over a very black and wavy ocean. The
waves of this ocean, so to speak, were the heads of many curious
caddies, a few of the more ingenious chauffeurs, the golf professional's
deaf sister—and there were usually several stray, diffident waves who
might have rolled inside had they so desired. This was the gallery.

The balcony was inside. It consisted of the circle of wicker chairs
that lined the wall of the combination clubroom and ballroom. At these
Saturday-night dances it was largely feminine; a great babble of middle-aged ladies with sharp eyes and icy hearts behind lorgnettes and
large bosoms. The main function of the balcony was critical. It occasionally showed grudging admiration, but never approval, for it is well

known among ladies over thirty-five that when the younger set dance in the summer-time it is with the very worst intentions in the world, and if they are not bombarded with stony eyes, stray couples will dance weird barbaric interludes in the corners, and the more popular, more dangerous girls will sometimes be kissed in the parked limousines of unsuspecting dowagers.

But, after all, this critical circle is not close enough to the stage to see the actors' faces and catch the subtler byplay. It can only frown and lean, ask questions and make satisfactory deductions from its set of postulates, such as the one which states that every young man with a large income leads the life of a hunted partridge. It never really appreciates the drama of the shifting, semicruel world of adolescence. No; boxes, orchestra-circle, principals, and chorus are represented by the medley of faces and voices that sway to the plaintive African rhythm of Dyer's dance orchestra.

From sixteen-year-old Otis Ormonde, who has two more years at Hill School, to G. Reese Stoddard, over whose bureau at home hangs a Harvard law diploma; from little Madeleine Hogue, whose hair still feels strange and uncomfortable on top of her head, to Bessie MacRae, who has been the life of the party a little too long—more than ten years—the medley is not only the centre of the stage but contains the only people capable of getting an unobstructed view of it.

With a flourish and a bang the music stops. The couples exchange artificial, effortless smiles, facetiously repeat *"la-de-ðað-ða* dum-*ðum,"* and then the clatter of young feminine voices soars over the burst of clapping.

A few disappointed stags caught in midfloor as they had been about to cut in subsided listlessly back to the walls, because this was not like the riotous Christmas dances—these summer hops were considered just pleasantly warm and exciting, where even the younger marrieds rose and performed ancient waltzes and terrifying fox trots to the tolerant amusement of their younger brothers and sisters.

Warren McIntyre, who casually attended Yale, being one of the unfortunate stags, felt in his dinner-coat pocket for a cigarette and strolled out onto the wide, semidark veranda, where couples were scattered at tables, filling the lantern-hung night with vague words and hazy laughter. He nodded here and there at the less absorbed and as he passed each couple some half-forgotten fragment of a story played in his mind, for it was not a large city and every one was Who's Who to every one else's past. There, for example, were Jim Strain and Ethel Demorest, who had been privately engaged for three years. Every one knew that as soon as Jim managed to hold a job for more than two months she would marry him. Yet how bored they both looked, and how wearily Ethel regarded Jim sometimes, as if she wondered why she had trained the vines of her affection on such a wind-shaken poplar.

Warren was nineteen and rather pitying with those of his friends who had gone East to college. But, like most boys, he bragged tremendously about the girls of his city when he was away from it. There was Genevieve Ormonde, who regularly made the rounds of dances, house-parties, and football games at Princeton, Yale, Williams, and Cornell; there was black-eyed Roberta Dillon, who was quite as famous to her own generation as Hiram Johnson or Ty Cobb; and, of course, there was Marjorie Harvey, who besides having a fairylike face and a dazzling, bewildering tongue was already justly celebrated for having turned five cart-wheels in succession during the last pump-and-slipper dance at New Haven.

Warren, who had grown up across the street from Marjorie, had long been "crazy about her." Sometimes she seemed to reciprocate his feeling with a faint gratitude, but she had tried him by her infallible test and informed him gravely that she did not love him. Her test was that when she was away from him she forgot him and had affairs with other boys. Warren found this discouraging, especially as Marjorie had been making little trips all summer, and for the first two or three days after each arrival home he saw great heaps of mail on the Harveys' hall table addressed to her in various masculine handwritings. To make matters worse, all during the month of August she had been visited by her cousin Bernice from Eau Claire, and it seemed impossible to see her alone. It was always necessary to hunt round and find some one to take care of Bernice. As August waned this was becoming more and more difficult.

Much as Warren worshipped Marjorie, he had to admit that Cousin Bernice was sorta dopeless. She was pretty, with dark hair and high color, but she was no fun on a party. Every Saturday night he danced a long arduous duty dance with her to please Marjorie, but he had never been anything but bored in her company.

"Warren"—a soft voice at his elbow broke in upon his thoughts, and he turned to see Marjorie, flushed and radiant as usual. She laid a hand on his shoulder and a glow settled almost imperceptibly over him.

"Warren," she whispered, "do something for me—dance with Bernice. She's been stuck with little Otis Ormonde for almost an hour."

Warren's glow faded.

"Why—sure," he answered half-heartedly.

"You don't mind, do you? I'll see that you don't get stuck."

"'Sall right."

Marjorie smiled—that smile that was thanks enough.

"You're an angel, and I'm obliged loads."

With a sigh the angel glanced round the veranda, but Bernice and Otis were not in sight. He wandered back inside, and there in front of the women's dressing-room he found Otis in the center of a group of young men who were convulsed with laughter. Otis was branishing a piece of timber he had picked up, and discoursing volubly.

"She's gone in to fix her hair," he announced wildly. "I'm waiting to dance another hour with her."

Their laughter was renewed.

"Why don't some of you cut in?" cried Otis resentfully. "She likes more variety."

"Why, Otis," suggested a friend, "you've just barely got used to her."

"Why the two-by-four, Otis?" inquired Warren, smiling.

"The two-by-four? Oh, this? This is a club. When she comes out I'll hit her on the head and knock her in again."

Warren collapsed on a settee and howled with glee.

"Never mind, Otis," he articulated finally. "I'm relieving you this time."

Otis simulated a sudden fainting attack and handed the stick to Warren.

"If you need it, old man," he said hoarsely.

No matter how beautiful or brilliant a girl may be, the reputation of not being frequently cut in on makes her position at a dance unfortunate. Perhaps boys prefer her company to that of the butterflies with whom they dance a dozen times an evening, but youth in this jazz-nourished generation is temperamentally restless, and the idea of fox-trotting more than one full fox trot with the same girl is distasteful, not to say odious. When it comes to several dances and the intermissions between she can be quite sure that a young man, once relieved, will never tread on her wayward toes again.

Warren danced the next full dance with Bernice, and finally, thankful for the intermission, he led her to a table on the veranda. There was a moment's silence while she did unimpressive things with her fan.

"It's hotter here than in Eau Claire," she said.

Warren stifled a sigh and nodded. It might be for all he knew or cared. He wondered idly whether she was a poor conversationalist because she got no attention or got no attention because she was a poor conversationalist.

"You going to be here much longer?" he asked, and then turned rather red. She might suspect his reasons for asking.

"Another week," she answered, and stared at him as if to lunge at his next remark when it left his lips.

Warren fidgeted. Then with a sudden charitable impulse he decided to try part of his line on her. He turned and looked at her eyes.

"You've got an awfully kissable mouth," he began quietly.

This was a remark that he sometimes made to girls at college proms
when they were talking in just such half-dark as this. Bernice distinctly
jumped. She turned an ungraceful red and became clumsy with her
fan. No one had ever made such a remark to her before.

"Fresh!"—the word had slipped out before she realized it, and she
bit her lip. Too late she decided to be amused, and offered him a
flustered smile.

Warren was annoyed. Though not accustomed to have that remark
taken seriously, still it usually provoked a laugh or a paragraph of
sentimental banter. And he hated to be called fresh, except in a joking
way. His charitable impulse died and he switched the topic.

"Jim Strain and Ethel Demorest sitting out as usual," he commented.

This was more in Bernice's line, but a faint regret mingled with her
relief as the subject changed. Men did not talk to her about kissable
mouths, but she knew that they talked in some such way to other girls.

"Oh, yes," she said, and laughed. "I hear they've been mooning
round for years without a red penny. Isn't it silly?"

Warren's disgust increased. Jim Strain was a close friend of his
brother's, and anyway he considered it bad form to sneer at people for
not having money. But Bernice had had no intention of sneering. She
was merely nervous.

II

When Marjorie and Bernice reached home at half after midnight
they said good night at the top of the stairs. Though cousins, they were
not intimates. As a matter of fact Marjorie had no female intimates—
she considered girls stupid. Bernice on the contrary all through this
parent-arranged visit had rather longed to exchange those confidences
flavored with giggles and tears that she considered an indispensable
factor in all feminine intercourse. But in this respect she found
Marjorie rather cold; felt somehow the same difficulty in talking to her
that she had in talking to men. Marjorie never giggled, was never
frightened, seldom embarrassed, and in fact had very few of the qualities which Bernice considered appropriately and blessedly feminine.

As Bernice busied herself with toothbrush and paste this night she
wondered for the hundredth time why she never had any attention
when she was away from home. That her family were the wealthiest in

Eau Claire, that her mother entertained tremendously, gave little dinners for her daughter before all dances and bought her a car of her own to drive round in, never occurred to her as factors in her hometown social success. Like most girls she had been brought up on the warm milk prepared by Annie Fellows Johnston and on novels in which the female was beloved because of certain mysterious womanly qualities, always mentioned but never displayed.

Bernice felt a vague pain that she was not at present engaged in being popular. She did not know that had it not been for Marjorie's campaigning she would have danced the entire evening with one man; but she knew that even in Eau Claire other girls with less position and less pulchritude were given a much bigger rush. She attributed this to something subtly unscrupulous in those girls. It had never worried her, and if it had her mother would have assured her that the other girls cheapened themselves and that men really respected girls like Bernice.

She turned out the light in her bathroom, and on an impulse decided to go in and chat for a moment with her aunt Josephine, whose light was still on. Her soft slippers bore her noiselessly down the carpeted hall, but hearing voices inside she stopped near the partly opened door. Then she caught her own name, and without any definite intention of eavesdropping lingered—and the thread of the conversation going on inside pierced her consciousness sharply as if it had been drawn through with a needle.

"She's absolutely hopeless!" It was Marjorie's voice. "Oh, I know what you're going to say! So many people have told you how pretty and sweet she is, and how she can cook! What of it? She has a bum time. Men don't like her."

"What's a little cheap popularity?"

Mrs. Harvey sounded annoyed.

"It's everything when you're eighteen," said Marjorie emphatically. "I've done my best. I've been polite and I've made men dance with her, but they just won't stand being bored. When I think of that gorgeous coloring wasted on such a ninny, and think what Martha Carey could do with it—oh!"

"There's no courtesy these days."

Mrs. Harvey's voice implied that modern situations were too much for her. When she was a girl all young ladies who belonged to nice families had glorious times.

"Well," said Marjorie, "no girl can permanently bolster up a lame-duck visitor, because these days it's every girl for herself. I've even tried to drop her hints about clothes and things, and she's been furious—given me the funniest looks. She's sensitive enough to know she's not getting away with much, but I'll bet she consoles herself by thinking that she's very virtuous and that I'm too gay and fickle and will come to a bad end. All unpopular girls think that way. Sour grapes! Sarah Hopkins refers to Genevieve and Roberta and me as gardenia girls! I'll bet she'd give ten years of her life and her European education to be a gardenia girl and have three or four men in love with her and be cut in on every few feet at dances."

"It seems to me," interrupted Mrs. Harvey rather wearily, "that you ought to be able to do something for Bernice. I know she's not very vivacious."

Marjorie groaned.

"Vivacious! Good grief! I've never heard her say anything to a boy except that it's hot or the floor's crowded or that she's going to school in New York next year. Sometimes she asks them what kind of car they have and tells them the kind she has. Thrilling!"

There was a short silence, and then Mrs. Harvey took up her refrain: "All I know is that other girls not half so sweet and attractive get partners. Martha Carey, for instance, is stout and loud, and her mother is distinctly common. Roberta Dillon is so thin this year that she looks as though Arizona were the place for her. She's dancing herself to death."

"But, mother," objected Marjorie impatiently, "Martha is cheerful and awfully witty and an awfully slick girl, and Roberta's a marvellous dancer. She's been popular for ages!"

Mrs. Harvey yawned.

"I think it's that crazy Indian blood in Bernice," continued Marjorie. "Maybe she's a reversion to type. Indian women all just sat round and never said anything."

"Go to bed, you silly child," laughed Mrs. Harvey. "I wouldn't have told you that if I'd thought you were going to remember it. And I think most of your ideas are perfectly idiotic," she finished sleepily.

There was another silence, while Marjorie considered whether or not convincing her mother was worth the trouble. People over forty can seldom be permanently convinced of anything. At eighteen our convictions are hills from which we look; at forty-five they are caves in which we hide.

Having decided this, Marjorie said good night. When she came out into the hall it was quite empty.

III

While Marjorie was breakfasting late next day Bernice came into the room with a rather formal good morning, sat down opposite, stared intently over and slightly moistened her lips.

"What's on your mind?" inquired Marjorie, rather puzzled.

Bernice paused before she threw her hand-grenade.

"I heard what you said about me to your mother last night."

Marjorie was startled, but she showed only a faintly heightened color and her voice was quite even when she spoke.

"Where were you?"

"In the hall. I didn't mean to listen—at first."

After an involuntary look of contempt Marjorie dropped her eyes and became very interested in balancing a stray corn-flake on her finger.

"I guess I'd better go back to Eau Claire—if I'm such a nuisance." Bernice's lower lip was trembling violently and she continued on a wavering note: "I've tried to be nice, and—and I've been first neglected and then insulted. No one ever visited me and got such treatment."

Marjorie was silent.

"But I'm in the way, I see. I'm a drag on you. Your friends don't like me." She paused, and then remembered another one of her grievances. "Of course I was furious last week when you tried to hint to me that that dress was unbecoming. Don't you think I know how to dress myself?"

"No," murmured Marjorie less than half-aloud.

"What?"

"I didn't hint anything," said Marjorie succinctly. "I said, as I remember, that it was better to wear a becoming dress three times straight than to alternate it with two frights."

"Do you think that was a very nice thing to say?"

"I wasn't trying to be nice." Then after a pause: "When do you want to go?"

Bernice drew in her breath sharply.

"Oh!" It was a little half-cry.

Marjorie looked up in surprise.

"Didn't you say you were going?"

"Yes, but——"

"Oh, you were only bluffing!"

They stared at each other across the breakfast-table for a moment.

Misty waves were passing before Bernice's eyes, while Marjorie's face wore that rather hard expression that she used when slightly intoxicated undergraduates were making love to her.

"So you were bluffing," she repeated as if it were what she might have expected.

Bernice admitted it by bursting into tears. Marjorie's eyes showed boredom.

"You're my cousin," sobbed Bernice. "I'm v-v-visiting you. I was to stay a month, and if I go home my mother will know and she'll wah-wonder— —"

Marjorie waited until the shower of broken words collapsed into little sniffles.

"I'll give you my month's allowance," she said coldly, "and you can spend this last week anywhere you want. There's a very nice hotel— —"

Bernice's sobs rose to a flute note, and rising of a sudden she fled from the room.

An hour later, while Marjorie was in the library absorbed in composing one of those non-committal, marvellously elusive letters that only a young girl can write, Bernice reappeared, very red-eyed and consciously calm. She cast no glance at Marjorie but took a book at random from the shelf and sat down as if to read. Marjorie seemed absorbed in her letter and continued writing. When the clock showed noon Bernice closed her book with a snap.

"I suppose I'd better get my railroad ticket."

This was not the beginning of the speech she had rehearsed upstairs, but as Marjorie was not getting her cues—wasn't urging her to be reasonable; it's all a mistake—it was the best opening she could muster.

"Just wait till I finish this letter," said Marjorie without looking round. "I want to get it off in the next mail."

After another minute, during which her pen scratched busily, she turned round and relaxed with an air of "at your service." Again Bernice had to speak.

"Do you want me to go home?"

"Well," said Marjorie, considering, "I suppose if you're not having a good time you'd better go. No use being miserable."

"Don't you think common kindness— —"

"Oh, please don't quote 'Little Women'!" cried Marjorie impatiently. "That's out of style."

"You think so?"

"Heavens, yes! What modern girl could live like those inane females?"

"They were the models for our mothers."

Marjorie laughed.

"Yes, they were—not! Besides, our mothers were all very well in their way, but they know very little about their daughters' problems."

Bernice drew herself up.

"Please don't talk about my mother."

Marjorie laughed.

"I don't think I mentioned her."

Bernice felt that she was being led away from her subject.

"Do you think you've treated me very well?"

"I've done my best. You're rather hard material to work with."

The lids of Bernice's eyes reddened.

"I think you're hard and selfish, and you haven't a feminine quality in you."

"Oh, my Lord!" cried Marjorie in desperation. "You little nut! Girls like you are responsible for all the tiresome colorless marriages; all those ghastly inefficiencies that pass as feminine qualities. What a blow it must be when a man with imagination marries the beautiful bundle of clothes that he's been building ideals around, and finds that she's just a weak, whining, cowardly mass of affectations!"

Bernice's mouth had slipped half open.

"The womanly woman!" continued Marjorie. "Her whole early life is occupied in whining criticisms of girls like me who really do have a good time."

Bernice's jaw descended farther as Marjorie's voice rose.

"There's some excuse for an ugly girl whining. If I'd been irretrievably ugly I'd never have forgiven my parents for bringing me into the world. But you're starting life without any handicap—" Marjorie's little fist clenched. "If you expect me to weep with you you'll be disappointed. Go or stay, just as you like." And picking up her letters she left the room.

Bernice claimed a headache and failed to appear at luncheon. They had a matinée date for the afternoon, but the headache persisting, Marjorie made explanation to a not very downcast boy. But when she returned late in the afternoon she found Bernice with a strangely set face waiting for her in her bedroom.

"I've decided," began Bernice without preliminaries, "that maybe you're right about things—possibly not. But if you'll tell me why your friends aren't—aren't interested in me I'll see if I can do what you want me to."

Marjorie was at the mirror shaking down her hair.

"Do you mean it?"

"Yes."

"Without reservations? Will you do exactly what I say?"

"Well, I— —"

"Well nothing! Will you do exactly as I say?"

"If they're sensible things."

"They're not! You're no case for sensible things."

"Are you going to make—to recommend— —"

"Yes, everything. If I tell you to take boxing-lessons you'll have to do it. Write home and tell your mother you're going to stay another two weeks."

"If you'll tell me— —"

"All right—I'll just give you a few examples now. First, you have no ease of manner. Why? Because you're never sure about your personal appearance. When a girl feels that she's perfectly groomed and dressed she can forget that part of her. That's charm. The more parts of yourself you can afford to forget the more charm you have."

"Don't I look all right?"

"No; for instance, you never take care of your eyebrows. They're black and lustrous, but by leaving them straggly they're a blemish. They'd be beautiful if you'd take care of them in one-tenth the time you take doing nothing. You're going to brush them so that they'll grow straight."

Bernice raised the brows in question.

"Do you mean to say that men notice eyebrows?"

"Yes—subconsciously. And when you go home you ought to have your teeth straightened a little. It's almost imperceptible, still— —"

"But I thought," interrupted Bernice in bewilderment, "that you despised little dainty feminine things like that."

"I hate dainty minds," answered Marjorie. "But a girl has to be dainty in person. If she looks like a million dollars she can talk about Russia, ping-pong, or the League of Nations and get away with it."

"What else?"

"Oh, I'm just beginning! There's your dancing."

"Don't I dance all right?"

"No, you don't—you lean on a man; yes, you do—ever so slightly. I noticed it when we were dancing together yesterday. And you dance standing up straight instead of bending over a little. Probably some old lady on the side-line once told you that you looked so dignified that way. But except with a very small girl it's much harder on the man, and he's the one that counts."

"Go on." Bernice's brain was reeling.

"Well, you've got to learn to be nice to men who are sad birds. You look as if you'd been insulted whenever you're thrown with any except the most popular boys. Why, Bernice, I'm cut in on every few feet—

and who does most of it? Why, those very sad birds. No girl can afford to neglect them. They're the big part of any crowd. Young boys too shy to talk are the very best conversational practice. Clumsy boys are the best dancing practice. If you can follow them and yet look graceful you can follow a baby tank across a barb-wire sky-scraper."

Bernice sighed profoundly, but Marjorie was not through.

"If you go to a dance and really amuse, say, three sad birds that dance with you; if you talk so well to them that they forget they're stuck with you, you've done something. They'll come back next time, and gradually so many sad birds will dance with you that the attractive boys will see there's no danger of being stuck—then they'll dance with you."

"Yes," agreed Bernice faintly. "I think I begin to see."

"And finally," concluded Marjorie, "poise and charm will just come. You'll wake up some morning knowing you've attained it, and men will know it too."

Bernice rose.

"It's been awfully kind of you—but nobody's ever talked to me like this before, and I feel sort of startled."

Marjorie made no answer but gazed pensively at her own image in the mirror.

"You're a peach to help me," continued Bernice.

Still Marjorie did not answer, and Bernice thought she had seemed too grateful.

"I know you don't like sentiment," she said timidly.

Marjorie turned to her quickly.

"Oh, I wasn't thinking about that. I was considering whether we hadn't better bob your hair."

Bernice collapsed backward upon the bed.

IV

On the following Wednesday evening there was a dinner-dance at the country club. When the guests strolled in Bernice found her place-card with a slight feeling of irritation. Though at her right sat G. Reece Stoddard, a most desirable and distinguished young bachelor, the all-important left held only Charley Paulson. Charley lacked height, beauty, and social shrewdness, and in her new enlightenment Bernice decided that his only qualification to be her partner was that he had never been stuck with her. But this feeling of irritation left with the last of the soup-plates, and Marjorie's specific instruction came to her. Swallowing her pride she turned to Charley Paulson and plunged.

"Do you think I ought to bob my hair, Mr. Charley Paulson?"
Charley looked up in surprise.

"Why?"

"Because I'm considering it. It's such a sure and easy way of attracting attention."

Charley smiled pleasantly. He could not know this had been rehearsed. He replied that he didn't know much about bobbed hair. But Bernice was there to tell him.

"I want to be a society vampire, you see," she announced coolly, and went on to inform him that bobbed hair was the necessary prelude. She added that she wanted to ask his advice, because she had heard he was so critical about girls.

Charley, who knew as much about the psychology of women as he did of the mental states of Buddhist contemplatives, felt vaguely flattered.

"So I've decided," she continued, her voice rising slightly, "that early next week I'm going down to the Sevier Hotel barber-shop, sit in the first chair, and get my hair bobbed." She faltered, noticing that the people near her had paused in their conversation and were listening; but after a confused second Marjorie's coaching told, and she finished her paragraph to the vicinity at large. "Of course I'm charging admission, but if you'll all come down and encourage me I'll issue passes for the inside seats."

There was a ripple of appreciative laughter, and under cover of it G. Reece Stoddard leaned over quickly and said close to her ear: "I'll take a box right now."

She met his eyes and smiled as if he had said something surpassingly brilliant.

"Do you believe in bobbed hair?" asked G. Reece in the same undertone.

"I think it's unmoral," affirmed Bernice gravely. "But, of course, you've either got to amuse people or feed 'em or shock 'em." Marjorie had culled this from Oscar Wilde. It was greeted with a ripple of laughter from the men and a series of quick, intent looks from the girls. And then as though she had said nothing of wit or moment Bernice turned again to Charley and spoke confidentially in his ear.

"I want to ask you your opinion of several people. I imagine you're a wonderful judge of character."

Charley thrilled faintly—paid her a subtle compliment by overturning her water.

Two hours later, while Warren McIntyre was standing passively in the stag line abstractedly watching the dancers and wondering whither and with whom Marjorie had disappeared, an unrelated perception began to creep slowly upon him—a perception that Bernice, cousin to Marjorie, had been cut in on several times in the past five minutes. He closed his eyes, opened them and looked again. Several minutes back she had been dancing with a visiting boy, a matter easily accounted for; a visiting boy would know no better. But now she was dancing with some one else, and there was Charley Paulson headed for her with enthusiastic determination in his eye. Funny—Charley seldom danced with more than three girls an evening.

Warren was distinctly surprised when—the exchange having been effected—the man relieved proved to be none other than G. Reece Stoddard himself. And G. Reece seemed not at all jubilant at being relieved. Next time Bernice danced near, Warren regarded her intently. Yes, she was pretty, distinctly pretty; and to-night her face seemed really vivacious. She had that look that no woman, however histrionically proficient, can successfully counterfeit—she looked as if she were having a good time. He liked the way she had her hair arranged, wondered if it was brilliantine that made it glisten so. And that dress was becoming—a dark red that set off her shadowy eyes and high coloring. He remembered that he had thought her pretty when she first came to town, before he had realized that she was dull. Too bad she was dull—dull girls unbearable—certainly pretty though.

His thoughts zigzagged back to Marjorie. This disappearance would be like other disappearances. When she reappeared he would demand where she had been—would be told emphatically that it was none of his business. What a pity she was so sure of him! She basked in the knowledge that no other girl in town interested him; she defied him to fall in love with Genevieve or Roberta.

Warren sighed. The way to Marjorie's affections was a labyrinth indeed. He looked up. Bernice was again dancing with the visiting boy. Half unconsciously he took a step out from the stag line in her direction, and hesitated. Then he said to himself that it was charity. He walked toward her—collided suddenly with G. Reece Stoddard.

"Pardon me," said Warren.

But G. Reece had not stopped to apologize. He had again cut in on Bernice.

That night at one o'clock Marjorie, with one hand on the electric-light switch in the hall, turned to take a last look at Bernice's sparkling eyes.

"So it worked?"

"Oh, Marjorie, yes!" cried Bernice.

"I saw you were having a gay time."

"I did! The only trouble was that about midnight I ran short of talk. I had to repeat myself—with different men of course. I hope they won't compare notes."

"Men don't," said Marjorie, yawning, "and it wouldn't matter if they did—they'd think you were even trickier."

She snapped out the light, and as they started up the stairs Bernice grasped the banister thankfully. For the first time in her life she had been danced tired.

"You see," said Marjorie at the top of the stairs, "one man sees another man cut in and he thinks there must be something there. Well, we'll fix up some new stuff to-morrow. Good night."

"Good night."

As Bernice took down her hair she passed the evening before her in review. She had followed instructions exactly. Even when Charley Paulson cut in for the eighth time she had simulated delight and had apparently been both interested and flattered. She had not talked about the weather or Eau Claire or automobiles or her school, but had confined her conversation to me, you, and us.

But a few minutes before she fell asleep a rebellious thought was churning drowsily in her brain—after all, it was she who had done it. Marjorie, to be sure, had given her her conversation, but then Marjorie got much of her conversation out of things she read. Bernice had bought the red dress, though she had never valued it highly before Marjorie dug it out of her trunk—and her own voice had said the words, her own lips had smiled, her own feet had danced. Marjorie nice girl—vain, though—nice evening—nice boys—like Warren— Warren—Warren—what's-his-name—Warren— —

She fell asleep.

V

To Bernice the next week was a revelation. With the feeling that people really enjoyed looking at her and listening to her came the foundation of self-confidence. Of course there were numerous mistakes at first. She did not know, for instance, that Draycott Deyo was study-ing for the ministry; she was unaware that he had cut in on her because he thought she was a quiet, reserved girl. Had she known these things she would not have treated him to the line which began "Hello, Shell Shock!" and continued with the bathtub story—"It takes a frightful lot of energy to fix my hair in the summer—there's so much of it—so I always fix it first and powder my face and put on my hat; then I get into the bathtub, and dress afterward. Don't you think that's the best plan?"

Though Draycott Deyo was in the throes of difficulties concerning baptism by immersion and might possibly have seen a connection, it must be admitted that he did not. He considered feminine bathing an immoral subject, and gave her some of his ideas on the depravity of modern society.

But to offset that unfortunate occurrence Bernice had several signal successes to her credit. Little Otis Ormonde pleaded off from a trip East and elected instead to follow her with a puppylike devotion, to the amusement of his crowd and to the irritation of G. Reece Stoddard, several of whose afternoon calls Otis completely ruined by the disgusting tenderness of the glances he bent on Bernice. He even told her the story of the two-by-four and the dressing-room to show her how frightfully mistaken he and every one else had been in their first judgment of her. Bernice laughed off that incident with a slight sinking sensation.

Of all Bernice's conversation perhaps the best known and most universally approved was the line about the bobbing of her hair.

"Oh, Bernice, when you goin' to get the hair bobbed?"

"Day after to-morrow maybe," she would reply, laughing. "Will you come and see me? Because I'm counting on you, you know."

"Will we? You know! But you better hurry up."

Bernice, whose tonsorial intentions were strictly dishonorable, would laugh again.

"Pretty soon now. You'd be surprised."

But perhaps the most significant symbol of her success was the gray car of the hypercritical Warren McIntyre, parked daily in front of the Harvey house. At first the parlor-maid was distinctly startled when he asked for Bernice instead of Marjorie; after a week of it she told the cook that Miss Bernice had gotta holda Miss Marjorie's best fella.

And Miss Bernice had. Perhaps it began with Warren's desire to rouse jealousy in Marjorie; perhaps it was the familiar though unrecognized strain of Marjorie in Bernice's conversation; perhaps it was both of these and something of sincere attraction besides. But somehow the collective mind of the younger set knew within a week that Marjorie's most reliable beau had made an amazing face-about and was giving an indisputable rush to Marjorie's guest. The question of the moment was how Marjorie would take it. Warren called Bernice on the 'phone twice a day, sent her notes, and they were frequently seen together in his roadster, obviously engrossed in one of those tense, significant conversations as to whether or not he was sincere.

Marjorie on being twitted only laughed. She said she was mighty glad that Warren had at last found some one who appreciated him. So the younger set laughed, too, and guessed that Marjorie didn't care and let it go at that.

One afternoon, when there were only three days left of her visit, Bernice was waiting in the hall for Warren, with whom she was going to a bridge party. She was in rather a blissful mood, and when Marjorie—also bound for the party—appeared beside her and began casually to adjust her hat in the mirror, Bernice was utterly unprepared for anything in the nature of a clash. Marjorie did her work very coldly and succinctly in three sentences.

"You may as well get Warren out of your head," she said coldly.

"What?" Bernice was utterly astounded.

"You may as well stop making a fool of yourself over Warren McIntyre. He doesn't care a snap of his fingers about you."

For a tense moment they regarded each other—Marjorie scornful, aloof; Bernice astounded, half-angry, half-afraid. Then two cars drove up in front of the house and there was a riotous honking. Both of them gasped faintly, turned, and side by side hurried out.

All through the bridge party Bernice strove in vain to master a rising uneasiness. She had offended Marjorie, the sphinx of sphinxes. With the most wholesome and innocent intentions in the world she had stolen Marjorie's property. She felt suddenly and horribly guilty. After the bridge game, when they sat in an informal circle and the conversation became general, the storm gradually broke. Little Otis Ormonde inadvertently precipitated it.

"When you going back to kindergarten, Otis?" some one had asked.

"Me? Day Bernice gets her hair bobbed."

"Then your education's over," said Marjorie quickly. "That's only a bluff of hers. I should think you'd have realized."

"That a fact?" demanded Otis, giving Bernice a reproachful glance.

Bernice's ears burned as she tried to think up an effectual comeback. In the face of this direct attack her imagination was paralyzed.

"There's a lot of bluffs in the world," continued Marjorie quite pleasantly. "I should think you'd be young enough to know that, Otis."

"Well," said Otis, "maybe so. But gee! With a line like Bernice's——"

"Really?" yawned Marjorie. "What's her latest bon mot?"

No one seemed to know. In fact, Bernice, having trifled with her muse's beau, had said nothing memorable of late.

"Was that really all a line?" asked Roberta curiously.

Bernice hesitated. She felt that wit in some form was demanded of her, but under her cousin's suddenly frigid eyes she was completely incapacitated.

"I don't know," she stalled.

"Splush!" said Marjorie. "Admit it!"

Bernice saw that Warren's eyes had left a ukulele he had been tinkering with and were fixed on her questioningly.

"Oh, I don't know!" she repeated steadily. Her cheeks were glowing.

"Splush!" remarked Marjorie again.

"Come through, Bernice," urged Otis. "Tell her where to get off."

Bernice looked round again—she seemed unable to get away from Warren's eyes.

"I like bobbed hair," she said hurriedly, as if he had asked her a question, "and I intend to bob mine."

"When?" demanded Marjorie.

"Any time."

"No time like the present," suggested Roberta.

Otis jumped to his feet.

"Good stuff!" he cried. "We'll have a summer bobbing party. Sevier Hotel barber-shop, I think you said."

In an instant all were on their feet. Bernice's heart throbbed violently.

"What?" she gasped.

Out of the group came Marjorie's voice, very clear and contemptuous.

"Don't worry—she'll back out!"

"Come on, Bernice!" cried Otis, starting toward the door.

Four eyes—Warren's and Marjorie's—stared at her, challenged her, defied her. For another second she wavered wildly.

"All right," she said swiftly, "I don't care if I do."

An eternity of minutes later, riding down-town through the late afternoon beside Warren, the others following in Roberta's car close behind, Bernice had all the sensations of Marie Antoinette bound for the guillotine in a tumbrel. Vaguely she wondered why she did not cry out that it was all a mistake. It was all she could do to keep from clutching her hair with both hands to protect it from the suddenly hostile world. Yet she did neither. Even the thought of her mother was no deterrent now. This was the test supreme of her sportsmanship, her right to walk unchallenged in the starry heaven of popular girls.

Warren was moodily silent, and when they came to the hotel he drew up at the curb and nodded to Bernice to precede him out. Roberta's car emptied a laughing crowd into the shop, which presented two bold plate-glass windows to the street.

Bernice stood on the curb and looked at the sign, Sevier Barber-Shop. It was a guillotine indeed, and the hangman was the first barber, who, attired in a white coat and smoking a cigarette, leaned nonchalantly against the first chair. He must have heard of her; he must have been waiting all week, smoking eternal cigarettes beside that portentous, too-often-mentioned first chair. Would they blindfold her? No, but they would tie a white cloth round her neck lest any of her blood—nonsense—hair—should get on her clothes.

"All right, Bernice," said Warren quickly.

With her chin in the air she crossed the sidewalk, pushed open the swinging screen-door, and giving not a glance to the uproarious, riotous row that occupied the waiting bench, went up to the first barber.

"I want you to bob my hair."

The first barber's mouth slid somewhat open. His cigarette dropped to the floor.

"Huh?"

"My hair—bob it!"

Refusing further preliminaries, Bernice took her seat on high. A man in the chair next to her turned on his side and gave her a glance, half lather, half amazement. One barber started and spoiled little Willy Schuneman's monthly haircut. Mr. O'Reilly in the last chair grunted and swore musically in ancient Gaelic as a razor bit into his cheek. Two bootblacks became wide-eyed and rushed for her feet. No, Bernice didn't care for a shine.

Outside a passer-by stopped and stared; a couple joined him; half a dozen small boys' noses sprang into life, flattened against the glass; and snatches of conversation borne on the summer breeze drifted in through the screen-door.

"Lookada long hair on a kid!"

"Where'd yuh get 'at stuff? 'At's a bearded lady he just finished shavin'."

But Bernice saw nothing, heard nothing. Her only living sense told her that this man in the white coat had removed one tortoiseshell comb and then another; that his fingers were fumbling clumsily with unfamiliar hairpins; that this hair, this wonderful hair of hers, was going—she would never again feel its long voluptuous pull as it hung in a dark-brown glory down her back. For a second she was near breaking down, and then the picture before her swam mechanically into her vision—Marjorie's mouth curling in a faint ironic smile as if to say: "Give up and get down! You tried to buck me and I called your bluff. You see you haven't got a prayer."

And some last energy rose up in Bernice, for she clenched her hands under the white cloth, and there was a curious narrowing of her eyes that Marjorie remarked on to some one long afterward.

Twenty minutes later the barber swung her round to face the mirror, and she flinched at the full extent of the damage that had been wrought. Her hair was not curly, and now it lay in lank lifeless blocks on both sides of her suddenly pale face. It was ugly as sin—she had known it would be ugly as sin. Her face's chief charm had been a Madonna-like simplicity. Now that was gone and she was—well, frightfully mediocre—not stagy; only ridiculous, like a Greenwich Villager who had left her spectacles at home.

As she climbed down from the chair she tried to smile—failed miserably. She saw two of the girls exchange glances; noticed Marjorie's mouth curved in attenuated mockery—and that Warren's eyes were suddenly very cold.

"You see"—her words fell into an awkward pause—"I've done it."

"Yes, you've—done it," admitted Warren.

"Do you like it?"

There was a half-hearted "Sure" from two or three voices, another awkward pause, and then Marjorie turned swiftly and with serpentlike intensity to Warren.

"Would you mind running me down to the cleaners?" she asked. "I've simply got to get a dress there before supper. Roberta's driving right home and she can take the others."

Warren stared abstractedly at some infinite speck out the window. Then for an instant his eyes rested coldly on Bernice before they turned to Marjorie.

"Be glad to," he said slowly.

VI

Bernice did not fully realize the outrageous trap that had been set for her until she met her aunt's amazed glance just before dinner.

"Why, Bernice!"

"I've bobbed it, Aunt Josephine."

"Why, child!"

"Do you like it?"

"Why, Ber-nice!"

"I suppose I've shocked you."

"No, but what'll Mrs. Deyo think to-morrow night? Bernice, you should have waited until after the Deyos' dance—you should have waited if you wanted to do that."

"It was sudden, Aunt Josephine. Anyway, why does it matter to Mrs. Deyo particularly?"

"Why, child," cried Mrs. Harvey, "in her paper on 'The Foibles of the Younger Generation' that she read at the last meeting of the Thursday Club she devoted fifteen minutes to bobbed hair. It's her pet abomination. And the dance is for you and Marjorie!"

"I'm sorry."

"Oh, Bernice, what'll your mother say? She'll think I let you do it."

"I'm sorry."

Dinner was an agony. She had made a hasty attempt with a curling-iron, and burned her finger and much hair. She could see that her aunt was both worried and grieved, and her uncle kept saying, "Well, I'll be darned!" over and over in a hurt and faintly hostile tone. And Marjorie sat very quietly, intrenched behind a faint smile, a faintly mocking smile.

Somehow she got through the evening. Three boys called; Marjorie disappeared with one of them, and Bernice made a listless unsuccessful attempt to entertain the two others—sighed thankfully as she climbed the stairs to her room at half past ten. What a day!

When she had undressed for the night the door opened and Marjorie came in.

"Bernice," she said, "I'm awfully sorry about the Deyo dance. I'll give you my word of honor I'd forgotten all about it."

"'Sall right," said Bernice shortly. Standing before the mirror she passed her comb slowly through her short hair.

"I'll take you down-town to-morrow," continued Marjorie, "and the hairdresser'll fix it so you'll look slick. I didn't imagine you'd go through with it. I'm really mighty sorry."

"Oh, 'sall right!"

"Still it's your last night, so I suppose it won't matter much."

Then Bernice winced as Marjorie tossed her own hair over her shoulders and began to twist it slowly into two long blond braids until in her cream-colored negligée she looked like a delicate painting of some Saxon princess. Fascinated, Bernice watched the braids grow. Heavy and luxurious they were, moving under the supple fingers like restive snakes—and to Bernice remained this relic and the curling-iron and a to-morrow full of eyes. She could see G. Reece Stoddard, who liked her, assuming his Harvard manner and telling his dinner partner that Bernice shouldn't have been allowed to go to the movies so much; she could see Draycott Deyo exchanging glances with his mother and then being conscientiously charitable to her. But then perhaps by to-morrow Mrs. Deyo would have heard the news; would send round an icy little note requesting that she fail to appear—and behind her back they would all laugh and know that Marjorie had made a fool of her; that her chance at beauty had been sacrificed to the jealous whim of a selfish girl. She sat down suddenly before the mirror, biting the inside of her cheek.

"I like it," she said with an effort. "I think it'll be becoming."

Marjorie smiled.

"It looks all right. For heaven's sake, don't let it worry you!"

"I won't."

"Good night, Bernice."

But as the door closed something snapped within Bernice. She sprang dynamically to her feet, clenching her hands, then swiftly and noiselessly crossed over to her bed and from underneath it dragged out her suitcase. Into it she tossed toilet articles and a change of clothing. Then she turned to her trunk and quickly dumped in two drawerfuls of lingerie and summer dresses. She moved quietly, but with deadly efficiency, and in three-quarters of an hour her trunk was locked and strapped and she was fully dressed in a becoming new travelling suit that Marjorie had helped her pick out.

Sitting down at her desk she wrote a short note to Mrs. Harvey, in which she briefly outlined her reasons for going. She sealed it, addressed it, and laid it on her pillow. She glanced at her watch. The train left at one, and she knew that if she walked down to the Marborough Hotel two blocks away she could easily get a taxicab.

Suddenly she drew in her breath sharply and an expression flashed into her eyes that a practised character reader might have connected vaguely with the set look she had worn in the barber's chair—somehow a development of it. It was quite a new look for Bernice—and it carried consequences.

She went stealthily to the bureau, picked up an article that lay there, and turning out all the lights stood quietly until her eyes became accustomed to the darkness. Softly she pushed open the door to Marjorie's room. She heard the quiet, even breathing of an untroubled conscience asleep.

She was by the bedside now, very deliberate and calm. She acted swiftly. Bending over she found one of the braids of Marjorie's hair, followed it up with her hand to the point nearest the head, and then holding it a little slack so that the sleeper would feel no pull, she reached down with the shears and severed it. With the pigtail in her hand she held her breath. Marjorie had muttered something in her sleep. Bernice deftly amputated the other braid, paused for an instant, and then flitted swiftly and silently back to her own room.

Down-stairs she opened the big front door, closed it carefully behind her, and feeling oddly happy and exuberant stepped off the porch into the moonlight, swinging her heavy grip like a shopping-bag. After a minute's brisk walk she discovered that her left hand still held the two blond braids. She laughed unexpectedly—had to shut her mouth hard to keep from emitting an absolute peal. She was passing Warren's house now, and on the impulse she set down her baggage, and swinging the braids like pieces of rope flung them at the wooden porch, where they landed with a slight thud. She laughed again, no longer restraining herself.

"Huh!" she giggled wildly. "Scalp the selfish thing!"

Then picking up her suitcase she set off at a half-run down the moonlit street.

Benediction

THE BALTIMORE STATION WAS HOT AND crowded, so Lois was forced to stand by the telegraph desk for interminable, sticky seconds while a clerk with big front teeth counted and recounted a large lady's day message, to determine whether it contained the innocuous forty-nine words or the fatal fifty-one.

Lois, waiting, decided she wasn't quite sure of the address, so she took the letter out of her bag and ran over it again.

Darling:—it began—*I understand and I'm happier than life ever meant me to be. If I could give you the things you've always been in tune with—but I can't, Lois; we can't marry and we can't lose each other and let all this glorious love end in nothing.*

Until your letter came, dear, I'd been sitting here in the half dark thinking and thinking where I could go and ever forget you; abroad, perhaps, to drift through Italy or Spain and dream away the pain of having lost you where the crumbling ruins of older, mellower civilizations would mirror only the desolation of my heart—and then your letter came.

Sweetest, bravest girl, if you'll wire me I'll meet you in Wilmington— till then I'll be here just waiting and hoping for every long dream of you to come true.

Howard.

She had read the letter so many times that she knew it word by word, yet it still startled her. In it she found many faint reflections of the man who wrote it—the mingled sweetness and sadness in his dark eyes, the furtive, restless excitement she felt sometimes when he talked to her, his dreamy sensuousness that lulled her mind to sleep. Lois was nineteen and very romantic and curious and courageous.

The large lady and the clerk having compromised on fifty words, Lois took a blank and wrote her telegram. And there were no over-tones to the finality of her decision.

It's just destiny—she thought—it's just the way things work out in this damn world. If cowardice is all that's been holding me back there won't be any more holding back. So we'll just let things take their course, and never be sorry.

The clerk scanned her telegram:

Arrived Baltimore today spend day with my brother meet me Wilming-ton three P.M. Wednesday Love

Lois.

"Fifty-four cents," said the clerk admiringly.
And never be sorry—thought Lois—and never be sorry——

II

Trees filtering light onto dappled grass. Trees like tall, languid la-dies with feather fans coquetting airily with the ugly roof of the monas-tery. Trees like butlers, bending courteously over placid walks and paths. Trees, trees over the hills on either side and scattering out in clumps and lines and woods all through eastern Maryland, delicate lace on the hems of many yellow fields, dark opaque backgrounds for flowered bushes or wild climbing gardens.

Some of the trees were very gay and young, but the monastery trees were older than the monastery which, by true monastic standards, wasn't very old at all. And, as a matter of fact, it wasn't technically called a monastery, but only a seminary; nevertheless it shall be a monastery here despite its Victorian architecture or its Edward VII additions, or even its Woodrow Wilsonian, patented, last-a-century roofing.

Out behind was the farm where half a dozen lay brothers were sweating lustily as they moved with deadly efficiency around the vegetable-gardens. To the left, behind a row of elms, was an informal baseball diamond where three novices were being batted out by a fourth, amid great chasings and puffings and blowings. And in front, as a great mellow bell boomed the half-hour, a swarm of black, human leaves were blown over the checker-board of paths under the courteous trees.

Some of these black leaves were very old with cheeks furrowed like the first ripples of a splashed pool. Then there was a scattering of middle-aged leaves whose forms when viewed in profile in their revealing gowns were beginning to be faintly unsymmetrical. These carried thick volumes of Thomas Aquinas and Henry James and Cardinal Mercier and Immanuel Kant and many bulging notebooks filled with lecture data.

But most numerous were the young leaves; blond boys of nineteen with very stern, conscientious expressions; men in the late twenties with a keen self-assurance from having taught out in the world for five years—several hundreds of them, from city and town and country in Maryland and Pennsylvania and Virginia and West Virginia and Delaware.

There were many Americans and some Irish and some tough Irish and a few French, and several Italians and Poles, and they walked informally arm in arm with each other in twos and threes or in long rows, almost universally distinguished by the straight mouth and the considerable chin—for this was the Society of Jesus, founded in Spain five hundred years before by a tough-minded soldier who trained men to hold a breach or a salon, preach a sermon or write a treaty, and do it and not argue . . .

Lois got out of a bus into the sunshine down by the outer gate. She was nineteen with yellow hair and eyes that people were tactful enough not to call green. When men of talent saw her in a streetcar they often furtively produced little stub-pencils and backs of envelopes and tried to sum up that profile or the thing that the eyebrows did to her eyes. Later they looked at their results and usually tore them up with wondering sighs.

Though Lois was very jauntily attired in an expensively appropriate travelling affair, she did not linger to pat out the dust which covered her clothes, but started up the central walk with curious glances at either side. Her face was very eager and expectant, yet she hadn't at all that glorified expression that girls wear when they arrive for a Senior Prom at Princeton or New Haven; still, as there were no senior proms here, perhaps it didn't matter.

She was wondering what he would look like, whether she'd possibly know him from his picture. In the picture, which hung over her mother's bureau at home, he seemed very young and hollow-cheeked and rather pitiful, with only a well-developed mouth and an ill-fitting probationer's gown to show that he had already made a momentous decision about his life. Of course he had been only nineteen then and now he was thirty-six—didn't look like that at all; in recent snap-shots he was much broader and his hair had grown a little thin—but the impression of her brother she had always retained was that of the big picture. And so she had always been a little sorry for him. What a life for a man! Seventeen years of preparation and he wasn't even a priest yet—wouldn't be for another year.

Lois had an idea that this was all going to be rather solemn if she let it be. But she was going to give her very best imitation of undiluted sunshine, the imitation she could give even when her head was splitting or when her mother had a nervous breakdown or when she was particularly romantic and curious and courageous. This brother of hers undoubtedly needed cheering up, and he was going to be cheered up, whether he liked it or not.

As she drew near the great, homely front door she saw a man break suddenly away from a group and, pulling up the skirts of his gown, run toward her. He was smiling, she noticed, and he looked very big and—and reliable. She stopped and waited, knew that her heart was beating unusually fast.

"Lois!" he cried, and in a second she was in his arms. She was suddenly trembling.

"Lois!" he cried again, "why, this is wonderful! I can't tell you, Lois, how *much* I've looked forward to this. Why, Lois, you're beautiful!"

Lois gasped.

His voice, though restrained, was vibrant with energy and that odd sort of enveloping personality she had thought that she only of the family possessed.

"I'm mighty glad, too—Kieth."

She flushed, but not unhappily, at this first use of his name.

"Lois—Lois—Lois," he repeated in wonder. "Child, we'll go in here a minute, because I want you to meet the rector, and then we'll walk around. I have a thousand things to talk to you about."

His voice became graver. "How's mother?"

She looked at him for a moment and then said something that she had not intended to say at all, the very sort of thing she had resolved to avoid.

"Oh, Kieth—she's—she's getting worse all the time, every way."

He nodded slowly as if he understood.

"Nervous, well—you can tell me about that later. Now——"

She was in a small study with a large desk, saying something to a little, jovial, white-haired priest who retained her hand for some seconds.

"So this is Lois!"

He said it as if he had heard of her for years.

He entreated her to sit down.

Two other priests arrived enthusiastically and shook hands with her and addressed her as "Kieth's little sister," which she found she didn't mind a bit.

How assured they seemed; she had expected a certain shyness, reserve at least. There were several jokes unintelligible to her, which seemed to delight every one, and the little Father Rector referred to the trio of them as "dim old monks," which she appreciated, because of course they weren't monks at all. She had a lightning impression that they were especially fond of Kieth—the Father Rector had called him "Kieth" and one of the others had kept a hand on his shoulder all through the conversation. Then she was shaking hands again and promising to come back a little later for some ice-cream, and smiling and smiling and being rather absurdly happy . . . she told herself that it was because Kieth was so delighted in showing her off.

Then she and Kieth were strolling along a path, arm in arm, and he was informing her what an absolute jewel the Father Rector was.

"Lois," he broke off suddenly, "I want to tell you before we go any farther how much it means to me to have you come up here. I think it was—mighty sweet of you. I know what a gay time you've been having."

Lois gasped. She was not prepared for this. At first when she had conceived the plan of taking the hot journey down to Baltimore, staying the night with a friend and then coming out to see her brother, she had felt rather consciously virtuous, hoped he wouldn't be priggish or resentful about her not having come before—but walking here with him under the trees seemed such a little thing, and surprisingly a happy thing.

"Why, Kieth," she said quickly, "you know I couldn't have waited a day longer. I saw you when I was five, but of course I didn't remember, and how could I have gone on without practically ever having seen my only brother?"

"It was mighty sweet of you, Lois," he repeated.

Lois blushed—he *did* have personality.

"I want you to tell me all about yourself," he said after a pause. "Of course I have a general idea what you and mother did in Europe those fourteen years, and then we were all so worried, Lois, when you had pneumonia and couldn't come down with mother—let's see, that was two years ago—and then, well, I've seen your name in the papers, but it's all been so unsatisfactory. I haven't known you, Lois."

She found herself analyzing his personality as she analyzed the personality of every man she met. She wondered if the effect of—of intimacy that he gave was bred by his constant repetition of her name. He said it as if he loved the word, as if it had an inherent meaning to him.

"Then you were at school," he continued.

"Yes, at Farmington. Mother wanted me to go to a convent—but I didn't want to."

She cast a side glance at him to see if he would resent this.

But he only nodded slowly.

"Had enough convents abroad, eh?"

"Yes—and Kieth, convents are different there anyway. Here even in the nicest ones there are so many *common* girls."

He nodded again.

"Yes," he agreed, "I suppose there are, and I know how you feel about it. It grated on me here, at first, Lois, though I wouldn't say that to any one but you; we're rather sensitive, you and I, to things like this."

"You mean the men here?"

"Yes, some of them of course were fine, the sort of men I'd always been thrown with, but there were others; a man named Regan, for instance—I hated the fellow, and now he's about the best friend I have. A wonderful character, Lois; you'll meet him later. Sort of man you'd like to have with you in a fight."

Lois was thinking that Kieth was the sort of man she'd like to have with *her* in a fight.

"How did you—how did you first happen to do it?" she asked, rather shyly, "to come here, I mean. Of course mother told me the story about the Pullman car."

"Oh, that—" He looked rather annoyed.

"Tell me that. I'd like to hear you tell it."

"Oh, it's nothing, except what you probably know. It was evening and I'd been riding all day and thinking about—about a hundred things, Lois, and then suddenly I had a sense that some one was sitting across from me, felt that he'd been there for some time, and had a vague idea that he was another traveller. All at once he leaned over toward me and I heard a voice say: 'I want you to be a priest, that's what I want.' Well, I jumped up and cried out, 'Oh, my God, not that!'—made an idiot of myself before about twenty people; you see there wasn't any one sitting there at all. A week after that I went to the Jesuit College in Philadelphia and crawled up the last flight of stairs to the rector's office on my hands and knees."

There was another silence and Lois saw that her brother's eyes wore a far-away look, that he was staring unseeingly out over the sunny fields. She was stirred by the modulations of his voice and the sudden silence that seemed to flow about him when he finished speaking.

She noticed now that his eyes were of the same fibre as hers, with the green left out, and that his mouth was much gentler, really, than in the picture—or was it that the face had grown up to it lately? He was getting a little bald just on top of his head. She wondered if that was from wearing a hat so much. It seemed awful for a man to grow bald and no one to care about it.

"Were you—pious when you were young, Kieth?" she asked. "You know what I mean. Were you religious? If you don't mind these personal questions."

"Yes," he said with his eyes still far away—and she felt that his intense abstraction was as much a part of his personality as his attention. "Yes, I suppose I was, when I was—sober."

Lois thrilled slightly.

"Did you drink?"

He nodded.

"I was on the way to making a bad hash of things." He smiled and, turning his gray eyes on her, changed the subject.

"Child, tell me about mother. I know it's been awfully hard for you there, lately. I know you've had to sacrifice a lot and put up with a great deal, and I want you to know how fine of you I think it is. I feel, Lois, that you're sort of taking the place of both of us there."

Lois thought quickly how little she had sacrificed; how lately she had constantly avoided her nervous, half-invalid mother.

"Youth shouldn't be sacrificed to age, Kieth," she said steadily.

"I know," he sighed, "and you oughtn't to have the weight on your shoulders, child. I wish I were there to help you."

She saw how quickly he had turned her remark and instantly she knew what this quality was that he gave off. He was *sweet*. Her thoughts went off on a side-track and then she broke the silence with an odd remark.

"Sweetness is hard," she said suddenly.

"What?"

"Nothing," she denied in confusion. "I didn't mean to speak aloud. I was thinking of something—of a conversation with a man named Freddy Kebble."

"Maury Kebble's brother?"

"Yes," she said, rather surprised to think of him having known Maury Kebble. Still there was nothing strange about it. "Well, he and I were talking about sweetness a few weeks ago. Oh, I don't know—I said that a man named Howard—that a man I knew was sweet, and he didn't agree with me, and we began talking about what sweetness in a man was. He kept telling me I meant a sort of soppy softness, but I knew I didn't—yet I didn't know exactly how to put it. I see now. I meant just the opposite. I suppose real sweetness is a sort of hardness—and strength."

Kieth nodded.

"I see what you mean. I've known old priests who had it."

"I'm talking about young men," she said, rather defiantly.

"Oh!"

They had reached the now deserted baseball diamond and, pointing her to a wooden bench, he sprawled full length on the grass.

"Are these *young* men happy here, Kieth?"

"Don't they look happy, Lois?"

"I suppose so, but those *young* ones, those two we just passed— have they—are they——"

"Are they signed up?" he laughed. "No, but they will be next month."

"Permanently?"

"Yes—unless they break down mentally or physically. Of course in a discipline like ours a lot drop out."

"But those *boys*. Are they giving up fine chances outside—like you did?"

He nodded.

"Some of them."

"But, Kieth, they don't know what they're doing. They haven't had any experience of what they're missing."

"No, I suppose not."

"It doesn't seem fair. Life has just sort of scared them at first. Do they all come in so *young*?"

"No, some of them have knocked around, led pretty wild lives—Regan, for instance."

"I should think that sort would be better," she said meditatively, "men that had *seen* life."

"No," said Kieth earnestly, "I'm not sure that knocking about gives a man the sort of experience he can communicate to others. Some of the broadest men I've known have been absolutely rigid about themselves. And reformed libertines are a notoriously intolerant class. Don't you think so, Lois?"

She nodded, still meditative, and he continued:

"It seems to me that when one weak person goes to another, it isn't help they want; it's a sort of companionship in guilt, Lois. After you were born, when mother began to get nervous she used to go and weep with a certain Mrs. Comstock. Lord, it used to make me shiver. She said it comforted her, poor old mother. No, I don't think that to help others you've got to show yourself at all. Real help comes from a stronger person whom you respect. And their sympathy is all the bigger because it's impersonal."

"But people want human sympathy," objected Lois. "They want to feel the other person's been tempted."

"Lois, in their hearts they want to feel that the other person's been weak. That's what they mean by human.

"Here in this old monkery, Lois," he continued with a smile, "they try to get all that self-pity and pride in our own wills out of us right at the first. They put us to scrubbing floors—and other things. It's like that idea of saving your life by losing it. You see we sort of feel that the less human a man is, in your sense of human, the better servant he can be to humanity. We carry it out to the end, too. When one of us dies his family can't even have him then. He's buried here under a plain wooden cross with a thousand others."

His tone changed suddenly and he looked at her with a great brightness in his gray eyes.

"But way back in a man's heart there are some things he can't get rid of—and one of them is that I'm awfully in love with my little sister."

With a sudden impulse she knelt beside him in the grass and, leaning over, kissed his forehead.

"You're hard, Kieth," she said, "and I love you for it—and you're sweet."

III

Back in the reception-room Lois met a half-dozen more of Kieth's particular friends; there was a young man named Jarvis, rather pale and delicate-looking, who, she knew, must be a grandson of old Mrs. Jarvis at home, and she mentally compared this ascetic with a brace of his riotous uncles.

And there was Regan with a scarred face and piercing intent eyes that followed her about the room and often rested on Kieth with something very like worship. She knew then what Kieth had meant about "a good man to have with you in a fight."

He's the missionary type—she thought vaguely—China or something.

"I want Kieth's sister to show us what the shimmy is," demanded one young man with a broad grin.

Lois laughed.

"I'm afraid the Father Rector would send me shimmying out the gate. Besides, I'm not an expert."

"I'm sure it wouldn't be best for Jimmy's soul anyway," said Kieth solemnly. "He's inclined to brood about things like shimmys. They were just starting to do the—maxixe, wasn't it, Jimmy?—when he became a monk, and it haunted him his whole first year. You'd see him when he was peeling potatoes, putting his arm around the bucket and making irreligious motions with his feet."

There was a general laugh in which Lois joined.

"An old lady who comes here to Mass sent Kieth this ice-cream," whispered Jarvis under cover of the laugh, "because she'd heard you were coming. It's pretty good, isn't it?"

There were tears trembling in Lois' eyes.

IV

Then half an hour later over in the chapel things suddenly went all wrong. It was several years since Lois had been at Benediction and at first she was thrilled by the gleaming monstrance with its central spot of white, the air rich and heavy with incense, and the sun shining through the stained-glass window of St. Francis Xavier overhead and falling in warm red tracery on the cassock of the man in front of her, but at the first notes of the *"O Salutaris Hostia"* a heavy weight seemed to descend upon her soul. Kieth was on her right and young Jarvis on her left, and she stole uneasy glances at both of them.

What's the matter with me? she thought impatiently.

She looked again. Was there a certain coldness in both their profiles that she had not noticed before—a pallor about the mouth and a curious set expression in their eyes? She shivered slightly: they were like dead men.

She felt her soul recede suddenly from Kieth's. This was her brother—this, this unnatural person. She caught herself in the act of a little laugh.

"What is the matter with me?"

She passed her hand over her eyes and the weight increased. The incense sickened her and a stray, ragged note from one of the tenors in the choir grated on her ear like the shriek of a slate-pencil. She fidgeted, and raising her hand to her hair touched her forehead, found moisture on it.

"It's hot in here, hot as the deuce."

Again she repressed a faint laugh, and then in an instant the weight upon her heart suddenly diffused into cold fear. . . . It was that candle on the altar. It was all wrong—wrong. Why didn't somebody see it? There was something *in* it. There was something coming out of it, taking form and shape above it.

She tried to fight down her rising panic, told herself it was the wick. If the wick wasn't straight, candles did something—but they didn't do this! With incalculable rapidity a force was gathering within her, a tremendous, assimilative force, drawing from every sense, every corner of her brain, and as it surged up inside her she felt an enormous, terrified repulsion. She drew her arms in close to her side, away from Kieth and Jarvis.

Something in that candle . . . she was leaning forward—in another moment she felt she would go forward toward it—didn't any one see it? . . . anyone?

"Ugh!"

She felt a space beside her and something told her that Jarvis had gasped and sat down very suddenly . . . then she was kneeling and as the flaming monstrance slowly left the altar in the hands of the priest, she heard a great rushing noise in her ears—the crash of the bells was like hammer-blows . . . and then in a moment that seemed eternal a great torrent rolled over her heart—there was a shouting there and a lashing as of waves . . .

. . . She was calling, felt herself calling for Kieth, her lips mouthing the words that would not come:

"Kieth! Oh, my God! *Kieth!*"

Suddenly she became aware of a new presence, something external, in front of her, consummated and expressed in warm red tracery. Then she knew. It was the window of St. Francis Xavier. Her mind gripped at it, clung to it finally, and she felt herself calling again endlessly, impotently—Kieth—Kieth!

Then out of a great stillness came a voice:

"Blessed be God."

With a gradual rumble sounded the response rolling heavily through the chapel:

"Blessed be God."

The words sang instantly in her heart; the incense lay mystically and sweetly peaceful upon the air, and *the candle on the altar went out.*

"Blessed be His Holy Name."

"Blessed be His Holy Name."

Every thing blurred into a swinging mist. With a sound half-gasp, half-cry she rocked on her feet and reeled backward into Kieth's suddenly outstretched arms.

V

"Lie still, child."

She closed her eyes again. She was on the grass outside, pillowed on Kieth's arm, and Regan was dabbing her head with a cold towel.

"I'm all right," she said quietly.

"I know, but just lie still a minute longer. It was too hot in there. Jarvis felt it, too."

She laughed as Regan again touched her gingerly with the towel.

"I'm all right," she repeated.

But though a warm peace was filling her mind and heart she felt oddly broken and chastened, as if some one had held her stripped soul up and laughed.

VI

Half an hour later she walked leaning on Kieth's arm down the long central path toward the gate.

"It's been such a short afternoon," he sighed, "and I'm so sorry you were sick, Lois."

"Kieth, I'm feeling fine now, really; I wish you wouldn't worry."

"Poor old child. I didn't realize that Benediction'd be a long service for you after your hot trip out here and all."

She laughed cheerfully.

"I guess the truth is I'm not much used to Benediction. Mass is the limit of my religious exertions."

She paused and then continued quickly:

"I don't want to shock you, Kieth, but I can't tell you how—how *inconvenient* being a Catholic is. It really doesn't seem to apply any more. As far as morals go, some of the wildest boys I know are Catholics. And the brightest boys—I mean the ones who think and read a lot, don't seem to believe in much of anything any more."

"Tell me about it. The bus won't be here for another half-hour."

They sat down on a bench by the path.

"For instance, Gerald Carter, he's published a novel. He absolutely roars when people mention immortality. And then Howa—well, another man I've known well, lately, who was Phi Beta Kappa at Harvard, says that no intelligent person can believe in Supernatural Christianity. He says Christ was a great socialist, though. Am I shocking you?"

She broke off suddenly.

Kieth smiled.

"You can't shock a monk. He's a professional shock-absorber."

"Well," she continued, "that's about all. It seems so—so *narrow*. Church schools, for instance. There's more freedom about things that Catholic people can't see—like birth control."

Kieth winced, almost imperceptibly, but Lois saw it.

"Oh," she said quickly, "everybody talks about everything now."

"It's probably better that way."

"Oh, yes, much better. Well, that's all, Kieth. I just wanted to tell you why I'm a little—lukewarm, at present."

"I'm not shocked, Lois. I understand better than you think. We all go through those times. But I know it'll come out all right, child. There's that gift of faith that we have, you and I, that'll carry us past the bad spots."

He rose as he spoke and they started again down the path.

"I want you to pray for me sometimes, Lois. I think your prayers would be about what I need. Because we've come very close in these few hours, I think."

Her eyes were suddenly shining.

"Oh, we have, we have!" she cried. "I feel closer to you now than to any one in the world."

He stopped suddenly and indicated the side of the path.

"We might—just a minute——"

It was a pietà, a life-size statue of the Blessed Virgin set within a semicircle of rocks.

Feeling a little self-conscious she dropped on her knees beside him and made an unsuccessful attempt at prayer.

She was only half through when he rose. He took her arm again.

"I wanted to thank Her for letting us have this day together," he said simply.

Lois felt a sudden lump in her throat and she wanted to say something that would tell him how much it had meant to her, too. But she found no words.

"I'll always remember this," he continued, his voice trembling a little—"this summer day with you. It's been just what I expected. You're just what I expected, Lois."

"I'm awfully glad, Kieth."

"You see, when you were little they kept sending me snap-shots of you, first as a baby and then as a child in socks playing on the beach with a pail and shovel, and then suddenly as a wistful little girl with wondering, pure eyes—and I used to build dreams about you. A man has to have something living to cling to. I think, Lois, it was your little white soul I tried to keep near me—even when life was at its loudest and every intellectual idea of God seemed the sheerest mockery, and desire and love and a million things came up to me and said: 'Look here at me! See, I'm Life. You're turning your back on it!' All the way through that shadow, Lois, I could always see your baby soul flitting on ahead of me, very frail and clear and wonderful."

Lois was crying softly. They had reached the gate and she rested her elbow on it and dabbed furiously at her eyes.

"And then later, child, when you were sick I knelt all one night and asked God to spare you for me—for I knew then that I wanted more; He had taught me to want more. I wanted to know you moved and breathed in the same world with me. I saw you growing up, that white innocence of yours changing to a flame and burning to give light to other weaker souls. And then I wanted some day to take your children on my knee and hear them call the crabbed old monk Uncle Kieth."

He seemed to be laughing now as he talked.

"Oh, Lois, Lois, I was asking God for more then. I wanted the letters you'd write me and the place I'd have at your table. I wanted an awful lot, Lois, dear."

"You've got me, Kieth," she sobbed, "you know it, say you know it. Oh, I'm acting like a baby but I didn't think you'd be this way, and I—oh, Kieth—Kieth——"

He took her hand and patted it softly.

"Here's the bus. You'll come again, won't you?"

She put her hands on his cheeks, and drawing his head down, pressed her tear-wet face against his.

"Oh, Kieth, brother, some day I'll tell you something——"

He helped her in, saw her take down her handkerchief and smile bravely at him, as the driver flicked his whip and the bus rolled off. Then a thick cloud of dust rose around it and she was gone.

For a few minutes he stood there on the road, his hand on the gatepost, his lips half parted in a smile.

"Lois," he said aloud in a sort of wonder, "Lois, Lois."

Later, some probationers passing noticed him kneeling before the pietà, and coming back after a time found him still there. And he was there until twilight came down and the courteous trees grew garrulous overhead and the crickets took up their burden of song in the dusky grass.

VII

The first clerk in the telegraph booth in the Baltimore Station whistled through his buck teeth at the second clerk.

"S'matter?"

"See that girl—no, the pretty one with the big black dots on her veil. Too late—she's gone. You missed somep'n."

"What about her?"

"Nothing. 'Cept she's damn good-looking. Came in here yesterday and sent a wire to some guy to meet her somewhere. Then a minute ago she came in with a telegram all written out and was standin' there goin' to give it to me when she changed her mind or somep'n and all of a sudden tore it up."

"Hm."

The first clerk came around the counter and picking up the two pieces of paper from the floor put them together idly. The second clerk read them over his shoulder and subconsciously counted the words as he read. There were just thirteen.

This is in the way of a permanent goodbye. I should suggest Italy.

Lois.

"Tore it up, eh?" said the second clerk.

Dalyrimple

Goes Wrong

In the millennium an educational genius will write a book to be given to every young man on the date of his disillusion. This work will have the flavor of Montaigne's essays and Samuel Butler's notebooks—and a little of Tolstoi and Marcus Aurelius. It will be neither cheerful nor pleasant but will contain numerous passages of striking humor. Since first-class minds never believe anything very strongly until they've experienced it, its value will be purely relative . . . all people over thirty will refer to it as "depressing."

This prelude belongs to the story of a young man who lived, as you and I do, before the book.

II

The generation which numbered Bryan Dalyrimple drifted out of adolescence to a mighty fanfare of trumpets. Bryan played the star in an affair which included a Lewis gun and a nine-day romp behind the retreating German lines, so luck triumphant or sentiment rampant awarded him a row of medals and on his arrival in the States he was told that he was second in importance only to General Pershing and Sergeant York. This was a lot of fun. The governor of his State, a stray congressman, and a citizens' committee gave him enormous smiles and "By God, Sirs," on the dock at Hoboken; there were newspaper reporters and photographers who said "would you mind" and "if you could just"; and back in his home town there were old ladies, the rims of whose eyes grew red as they talked to him, and girls who hadn't remembered him so well since his father's business went blah! in nineteen-twelve.

But when the shouting died he realized that for a month he had been the house guest of the mayor, that he had only fourteen dollars in the world, and that "the name that will live forever in the annals and legends of this State" was already living there very quietly and obscurely.

One morning he lay late in bed and just outside his door he heard the up-stairs maid talking to the cook. The up-stairs maid said that Mrs. Hawkins, the mayor's wife, had been trying for a week to hint Dalyrimple out of the house. He left at eleven o'clock in intolerable confusion, asking that his trunk be sent to Mrs. Beebe's boarding-house.

Dalyrimple was twenty-three and he had never worked. His father had given him two years at the State University and passed away about the time of his son's nine-day romp, leaving behind him some mid-Victorian furniture and a thin packet of folded papers that turned out to be grocery bills. Young Dalyrimple had very keen gray eyes, a mind that delighted the army psychological examiners, a trick of having read it—whatever it was—some time before, and a cool hand in a hot situation. But these things did not save him a final unresigned sigh when he realized that he had to go to work—right away.

It was early afternoon when he walked into the office of Theron G. Macy, who owned the largest wholesale grocery house in town. Plump, prosperous, wearing a pleasant but quite unhumorous smile, Theron G. Macy greeted him warmly.

"Well—how do, Bryan? What's on your mind?"

To Dalyrimple, straining with his admission, his own words, when they came, sounded like an Arab beggar's whine for alms.

"Why—this question of a job." ("This question of a job" seemed somehow more clothed than just "a job.")

"A job?" An almost imperceptible breeze blew across Mr. Macy's expression.

"You see, Mr. Macy," continued Dalyrimple, "I feel I'm wasting time. I want to get started at something. I had several chances about a month ago but they all seem to have—gone——"

"Let's see," interrupted Mr. Macy. "What were they?"

"Well, just at the first the governor said something about a vacancy on his staff. I was sort of counting on that for a while, but I hear he's given it to Allen Gregg, you know, son of G. P. Gregg. He sort of forgot what he said to me—just talking, I guess."

"You ought to push those things."

"Then there was that engineering expedition, but they decided they'd have to have a man who knew hydraulics, so they couldn't use me unless I paid my own way."

"You had just a year at the university?"

"Two. But I didn't take any science or mathematics. Well, the day the battalion paraded, Mr. Peter Jordan said something about a vacancy in his store. I went around there to-day and I found he meant a sort of floor-walker—and then you said something one day"—he paused and waited for the older man to take him up, but noting only a minute wince continued—"about a position, so I thought I'd come and see you."

"There was a position," confessed Mr. Macy reluctantly, "but since then we've filled it." He cleared his throat again. "You've waited quite a while."

"Yes, I suppose I did. Everybody told me there was no hurry—and I'd had these various offers."

Mr. Macy delivered a paragraph on present-day opportunities which Dalyrimple's mind completely skipped.

"Have you had any business experience?"

"I worked on a ranch two summers as a rider."

"Oh, well," Mr. Macy disparaged this neatly, and then continued: "What do you think you're worth?"

"I don't know."

"Well, Bryan, I tell you, I'm willing to strain a point and give you a chance."

Dalyrimple nodded.

"Your salary won't be much. You'll start by learning the stock.

Then you'll come in the office for a while. Then you'll go on the road. When could you begin?"

"How about to-morrow?"

"All right. Report to Mr. Hanson in the stock-room. He'll start you off."

He continued to regard Dalyrimple steadily until the latter, realizing that the interview was over, rose awkwardly.

"Well, Mr. Macy, I'm certainly much obliged."

"That's all right. Glad to help you, Bryan."

After an irresolute moment, Dalyrimple found himself in the hall. His forehead was covered with perspiration, and the room had not been hot.

"Why the devil did I thank the son of a gun?" he muttered.

III

Next morning Mr. Hanson informed him coldly of the necessity of punching the time-clock at seven every morning, and delivered him for instruction into the hands of a fellow worker, one Charley Moore.

Charley was twenty-six, with that faint musk of weakness hanging about him that is often mistaken for the scent of evil. It took no psychological examiner to decide that he had drifted into indulgence and laziness as casually as he had drifted into life, and was to drift out. He was pale and his clothes stank of smoke; he enjoyed burlesque shows, billiards, and Robert Service, and was always looking back upon his last intrigue or forward to his next one. In his youth his taste had run to loud ties, but now it seemed to have faded, like his vitality, and was expressed in pale-lilac four-in-hands and indeterminate gray collars. Charley was listlessly struggling that losing struggle against mental, moral, and physical anæmia that takes place ceaselessly on the lower fringe of the middle classes.

The first morning he stretched himself on a row of cereal cartons and carefully went over the limitations of the Theron G. Macy Company.

"It's a piker organization. My gosh! Lookit what they give me. I'm quittin' in a coupla months. Hell! Me stay with this bunch!"

The Charley Moores are always going to change jobs next month. They do, once or twice in their careers, after which they sit around comparing their last job with the present one, to the infinite disparagement of the latter.

"What do you get?" asked Dalyrimple curiously.

"Me? I get sixty." This rather defiantly.

"Did you start at sixty?"

"Me? No, I started at thirty-five. He told me he'd put me on the road after I learned the stock. That's what he tells 'em all!"

"How long've you been here?" asked Dalyrimple with a sinking sensation.

"Me? Four years. My last year, too, you bet your boots."

Dalyrimple rather resented the presence of the store detective as he resented the time-clock, and he came into contact with him almost immediately through the rule against smoking. This rule was a thorn in his side. He was accustomed to his three or four cigarettes in a morning, and after three days without it he followed Charley Moore by a circuitous route up a flight of back stairs to a little balcony where they indulged in peace. But this was not for long. One day in his second week the detective met him in a nook of the stairs, on his descent, and told him sternly that next time he'd be reported to Mr. Macy. Dalyrimple felt like an errant school-boy.

Unpleasant facts came to his knowledge. There were "cave-dwellers" in the basement who had worked there for ten or fifteen years at sixty dollars a month, rolling barrels and carrying boxes through damp, cement-walled corridors, lost in that echoing half-darkness between seven and five-thirty and, like himself, compelled several times a month to work until nine at night.

At the end of a month he stood in line and received forty dollars. He pawned a cigarette-case and a pair of field-glasses and managed to live—to eat, sleep, and smoke. It was, however, a narrow scrape; as the ways and means of economy were a closed book to him and the second month brought no increase, he voiced his alarm.

"If you've got a drag with old Macy, maybe he'll raise you," was Charley's disheartening reply. "But he didn't raise *me* 'till I'd been here nearly two years."

"I've got to live," said Dalyrimple simply. "I could get more pay as a laborer on the railroad but, golly, I want to feel I'm where there's a chance to get ahead."

Charles shook his head sceptically and Mr. Macy's answer next day was equally unsatisfactory.

Dalyrimple had gone to the office just before closing time.

"Mr. Macy, I'd like to speak to you."

"Why—yes." The unhumorous smile appeared. The voice was faintly resentful.

"I want to speak to you in regard to more salary."

Mr. Macy nodded.

"Well," he said doubtfully, "I don't know exactly what you're doing. I'll speak to Mr. Hanson."

He knew exactly what Dalyrimple was doing, and Dalyrimple knew he knew.

"I'm in the stock-room—and, sir, while I'm here I'd like to ask you how much longer I'll have to stay there."

"Why—I'm not sure exactly. Of course it takes some time to learn the stock."

"You told me two months when I started."

"Yes. Well, I'll speak to Mr. Hanson."

Dalyrimple paused, irresolute.

"Thank you, sir."

Two days later he again appeared in the office with the result of a count that had been asked for by Mr. Hesse, the bookkeeper. Mr. Hesse was engaged and Dalyrimple, waiting, began idly fingering a ledger on the stenographer's desk.

Half unconsciously he turned a page—he caught sight of his name—it was a salary list:

Dalyrimple
Demming
Donahoe
Everett

His eyes stopped— —

Everett $60

So Tom Everett, Macy's weak-chinned nephew, had started at sixty—and in three weeks he had been out of the packing-room and into the office.

So that was it! He was to sit and see man after man pushed over him: sons, cousins, sons of friends, irrespective of their capabilities, while *he* was cast for a pawn, with "going on the road" dangled before his eyes—put off with the stock remark: "I'll see; I'll look into it." At forty, perhaps, he would be a bookkeeper like old Hesse, tired, listless Hesse with dull routine for his stint and a dull background of boarding-house conversation.

This was a moment when a genii should have pressed into his hand the book for disillusioned young men. But the book has not been written.

A great protest swelling into revolt surged up in him. Ideas half forgotten, chaotically perceived and assimilated, filled his mind. Get on—that was the rule of life—and that was all. How he did it, didn't matter—but to be Hesse or Charley Moore.

"I won't!" he cried aloud.

The bookkeeper and the stenographers looked up in surprise.

"What?"

For a second Dalyrimple stared—then walked up to the desk.

"Here's that data," he said brusquely. "I can't wait any longer."

Mr. Hesse's face expressed surprise.

It didn't matter what he did—just so he got out of this rut. In a dream he stepped from the elevator into the stock-room, and walking to an unused aisle, sat down on a box, covering his face with his hands.

His brain was whirring with the frightful jar of discovering a platitude for himself.

"I've got to get out of this," he said aloud and then repeated, "I've got to get out"—and he didn't mean only out of Macy's wholesale house.

When he left at five-thirty it was pouring rain, but he struck off in the opposite direction from his boarding-house, feeling, in the first cool moisture that oozed soggily through his old suit, an odd exultation and freshness. He wanted a world that was like walking through rain, even though he could not see far ahead of him, but fate had put him in the world of Mr. Macy's fetid storerooms and corridors. At first merely the overwhelming need of change took him, then half-plans began to formulate in his imagination.

"I'll go East—to a big city—meet people—bigger people—people who'll help me. Interesting work somewhere. My God, there *must* be."

With sickening truth it occurred to him that his facility for meeting people was limited. Of all places it was here in his own town that he should be known, was known—famous—before the waters of oblivion had rolled over him.

You had to cut corners, that was all. Pull—relationship—wealthy marriages——

For several miles the continued reiteration of this preoccupied him and then he perceived that the rain had become thicker and more opaque in the heavy gray of twilight and that the houses were falling away. The district of full blocks, then of big houses, then of scattering little ones, passed and great sweeps of misty country opened out on both sides. It was hard walking here. The sidewalk had given place to a dirt road, streaked with furious brown rivulets that splashed and squashed around his shoes.

Cutting corners—the words began to fall apart, forming curious

phrasings—little illuminated pieces of themselves. They resolved into
sentences, each of which had a strangely familiar ring.

Cutting corners meant rejecting the old childhood principles that
success came from faithfulness to duty, that evil was necessarily pun-
ished or virtue necessarily rewarded—that honest poverty was happier
than corrupt riches.

It meant being hard.

This phrase appealed to him and he repeated it over and over. It
had to do somehow with Mr. Macy and Charley Moore—the attitudes,
the methods of each of them.

He stopped and felt his clothes. He was drenched to the skin. He
looked about him and, selecting a place in the fence where a tree
sheltered it, perched himself there.

In my credulous years—he thought—they told me that evil was a
sort of dirty hue, just as definite as a soiled collar, but it seems to me
that evil is only a manner of hard luck, or heredity-and-environment,
or "being found out." It hides in the vacillations of dubs like Charley
Moore as certainly as it does in the intolerance of Macy, and if it ever
gets much more tangible it becomes merely an arbitrary label to paste
on the unpleasant things in other people's lives.

In fact—he concluded—it isn't worth worrying over what's evil
and what isn't. Good and evil aren't any standard to me—and they can
be a devil of a bad hindrance when I want something. When I want
something bad enough, common sense tells me to go and take it—and
not get caught.

And then suddenly Dalyrimple knew what he wanted first. He
wanted fifteen dollars to pay his overdue board bill.

With a furious energy he jumped from the fence, whipped off his
coat, and from its black lining cut with his knife a piece about five
inches square. He made two holes near its edge and then fixed it on his
face, pulling his hat down to hold it in place. It flapped grotesquely and
then dampened and clung to his forehead and cheeks.

Now. . . . The twilight had merged to dripping dusk . . . black
as pitch. He began to walk quickly back toward town, not waiting to
remove the mask but watching the road with difficulty through the
jagged eye-holes. He was not conscious of any nervousness . . . the
only tension was caused by a desire to do the thing as soon as possible.

He reached the first sidewalk, continued on until he saw a hedge
far from any lamp-post, and turned in behind it. Within a minute he
heard several series of footsteps—he waited—it was a woman and he
held his breath until she passed . . . and then a man, a laborer. The
next passer, he felt, would be what he wanted . . . the laborer's foot-

falls died far up the drenched street . . . other steps grew near, grew suddenly louder.

Dalyrimple braced himself.

"Put up your hands!"

The man stopped, uttered an absurd little grunt, and thrust pudgy arms skyward.

Dalyrimple went through the waistcoat.

"Now, you shrimp," he said, setting his hand suggestively to his own hip pocket, "you run, and stamp—loud! If I hear your feet stop I'll put a shot after you!"

Then he stood there in sudden uncontrollable laughter as audibly frightened footsteps scurried away into the night.

After a moment he thrust the roll of bills into his pocket, snatched off his mask, and running quickly across the street, darted down an alley.

IV

Yet, however Dalyrimple justified himself intellectually, he had many bad moments in the weeks immediately following his decision. The tremendous pressure of sentiment and inherited tradition kept raising riot with his attitude. He felt morally lonely.

The noon after his first venture he ate in a little lunch-room with Charley Moore and, watching him unspread the paper, waited for a remark about the hold-up of the day before. But either the hold-up was not mentioned or Charley wasn't interested. He turned listlessly to the sporting sheet, read Doctor Crane's crop of seasoned bromides, took in an editorial on ambition with his mouth slightly ajar, and then skipped to Mutt and Jeff.

Poor Charley—with his faint aura of evil and his mind that refused to focus, playing a lifeless solitaire with cast-off mischief.

Yet Charley belonged on the other side of the fence. In him could be stirred up all the flamings and denunciations of righteousness; he would weep at a stage heroine's lost virtue, he could become lofty and contemptuous at the idea of dishonor.

On my side, thought Dalyrimple, there aren't any resting-places; a man who's a strong criminal is after the weak criminals as well, so it's all guerilla warfare over here.

What will it all do to me? he thought, with a persistent weariness. Will it take the color out of life with the honor? Will it scatter my courage and dull my mind?—despiritualize me completely—does it mean eventual barrenness, eventual remorse, failure?

With a great surge of anger, he would fling his mind upon the barrier—and stand there with the flashing bayonet of his pride. Other men who broke the laws of justice and charity lied to all the world. He at any rate would not lie to himself. He was more than Byronic now: not the spiritual rebel, Don Juan; not the philosophical rebel, Faust; but a new psychological rebel of his own century—defying the sentimental a priori forms of his own mind— —

Happiness was what he wanted—a slowly rising scale of gratifications of the normal appetites—and he had a strong conviction that the materials, if not the inspiration of happiness, could be bought with money.

V

The night came that drew him out upon his second venture, and as he walked the dark street he felt in himself a great resemblance to a cat—a certain supple, swinging litheness. His muscles were rippling smoothly and sleekly under his spare, healthy flesh—he had an absurd desire to bound along the street, to run dodging among trees, to turn "cart-wheels" over soft grass.

It was not crisp, but in the air lay a faint suggestion of acerbity, inspirational rather than chilling.

"The moon is down—I have not heard the clock!"

He laughed in delight at the line which an early memory had endowed with a hushed, awesome beauty.

He passed a man, and then another a quarter of a mile afterward.

He was on Philmore Street now and it was very dark. He blessed the city council for not having put in new lamp-posts as a recent budget had recommended. Here was the red-brick Sterner residence which marked the beginning of the avenue; here was the Jordon house, the Eisenhaurs', the Dents', the Markhams', the Frasers'; the Hawkins', where he had been a guest; the Willoughbys', the Everetts', colonial and ornate; the little cottage where lived the Watts old maids between the imposing fronts of the Macys' and the Krupstadts'; the Craigs'— —

Ah . . . *there!* He paused, wavered violently—far up the street was a blot, a man walking, possibly a policeman. After an eternal second he found himself following the vague, ragged shadow of a lamp-post across a lawn, running bent very low. Then he was standing tense, without breath or need of it, in the shadow of his limestone prey.

Interminably he listened—a mile off a cat howled, a hundred yards away another took up the hymn in a demoniacal snarl, and he felt his heart dip and swoop, acting as shock-absorber for his mind. There were other sounds; the faintest fragment of song far away; strident, gossiping laughter from a back porch diagonally across the alley; and crickets, crickets singing in the patched, patterned, moonlit grass of the yard. Within the house there seemed to lie an ominous silence. He was glad he did not know who lived here.

His slight shiver hardened to steel; the steel softened and his nerves became pliable as leather; gripping his hands he gratefully found them supple, and taking out knife and pliers he went to work on the screen.

So sure was he that he was unobserved that, from the dining-room where in a minute he found himself, he leaned out and carefully pulled the screen up into position, balancing it so it would neither fall by chance nor be a serious obstacle to a sudden exit.

Then he put the open knife in his coat pocket, took out his pocket-flash, and tiptoed around the room.

There was nothing here he could use — the dining-room had never been included in his plans, for the town was too small to permit disposing of silver.

As a matter of fact his plans were of the vaguest. He had found that with a mind like his, lucrative in intelligence, intuition, and lightning decision, it was best to have but the skeleton of a campaign. The machine-gun episode had taught him that. And he was afraid that a method preconceived would give him two points of view in a crisis — and two points of view meant wavering.

He stumbled slightly on a chair, held his breath, listened, went on, found the hall, found the stairs, started up; the seventh stair creaked at his step, the ninth, the fourteenth. He was counting them automatically. At the third creak he paused again for over a minute — and in that minute he felt more alone than he had ever felt before. Between the lines on patrol, even when alone, he had had behind him the moral support of half a billion people; now he was alone, pitted against that same moral pressure — a bandit. He had never felt this fear, yet he had never felt this exultation.

The stairs came to an end, a doorway approached; he went in and listened to regular breathing. His feet were economical of steps and his body swayed sometimes at stretching as he felt over the bureau, pocketing all articles which held promise — he could not have enumerated them ten seconds afterward. He felt on a chair for possible trousers, found soft garments, women's lingerie. The corners of his mouth smiled mechanically.

Another room . . . the same breathing, enlivened by one ghastly snort that sent his heart again on its tour of his breast. Round object — watch; chain; roll of bills; stick-pins; two rings — he remembered that he had got rings from the other bureau. He started out, winced as a faint glow flashed in front of him, facing him. God!—it was the glow of his own wrist-watch on his outstretched arm.

Down the stairs. He skipped two creaking steps but found another. He was all right now, practically safe; as he neared the bottom he felt a slight boredom. He reached the dining-room—considered the silver—again decided against it.

Back in his room at the boarding-house he examined the additions to his personal property:

Sixty-five dollars in bills.

A platinum ring with three medium diamonds, worth, probably, about seven hundred dollars. Diamonds were going up.

A cheap gold-plated ring with the initials O. S. and the date inside—'03—probably a class-ring from school. Worth a few dollars. Unsalable.

A red-cloth case containing a set of false teeth.

A silver watch.

A gold chain worth more than the watch.

An empty ring-box.

A little ivory Chinese god—probably a desk ornament.

A dollar and sixty-two cents in small change.

He put the money under his pillow and the other things in the toe of an infantry boot, stuffing a stocking in on top of them. Then for two hours his mind raced like a high-power engine here and there through his life, past and future, through fear and laughter. With a vague, inopportune wish that he were married, he fell into a deep sleep about half past five.

VI

Though the newspaper account of the burglary failed to mention the false teeth, they worried him considerably. The picture of a human waking in the cool dawn and groping for them in vain, of a soft, toothless breakfast, of a strange, hollow, lisping voice calling the police station, of weary, dispirited visits to the dentist, roused a great fatherly pity in him.

Trying to ascertain whether they belonged to a man or a woman, he took them carefully out of the case and held them up near his mouth. He moved his own jaws experimentally; he measured with his fingers; but he failed to decide: they might belong either to a large-mouthed woman or a small-mouthed man.

On a warm impulse he wrapped them in brown paper from the

bottom of his army trunk, and printed FALSE TEETH on the package in clumsy pencil letters. Then, the next night, he walked down Philmore Street, and shied the package onto the lawn so that it would be near the door. Next day the paper announced that the police had a clew — they knew that the burglar was in town. However, they didn't mention what the clew was.

VII

At the end of a month "Burglar Bill of the Silver District" was the nurse-girl's standby for frightening children. Five burglaries were attributed to him, but though Dalyrimple had only committed three, he considered that majority had it and appropriated the title to himself. He had once been seen — "a large bloated creature with the meanest face you ever laid eyes on." Mrs. Henry Coleman, awaking at two o'clock at the beam of an electric torch flashed in her eye, could not have been expected to recognize Bryan Dalyrimple at whom she had waved flags last Fourth of July, and whom she had described as "not at all the daredevil type, do you think?"

When Dalyrimple kept his imagination at white heat he managed to glorify his own attitude, his emancipation from petty scruples and remorses — but let him once allow his thought to rove unarmored, great unexpected horrors and depressions would overtake him. Then for reassurance he had to go back to think out the whole thing over again. He found that it was on the whole better to give up considering himself as a rebel. It was more consoling to think of every one else as a fool.

His attitude toward Mr. Macy underwent a change. He no longer felt a dim animosity and inferiority in his presence. As his fourth month in the store ended he found himself regarding his employer in a manner that was almost fraternal. He had a vague but very assured conviction that Mr. Macy's innermost soul would have abetted and approved. He no longer worried about his future. He had the intention of accumulating several thousand dollars and then clearing out — going east, back to France, down to South America. Half a dozen times in the last two months he had been about to stop work, but a fear of attracting attention to his being in funds prevented him. So he worked on, no longer in listlessness, but with contemptuous amusement.

VIII

Then with astounding suddenness something happened that changed his plans and put an end to his burglaries.

Mr. Macy sent for him one afternoon and with a great show of jovial mystery asked him if he had an engagement that night. If he hadn't, would he please call on Mr. Alfred J. Fraser at eight o'clock. Dalyrimple's wonder was mingled with uncertainty. He debated with himself whether it were not his cue to take the first train out of town. But an hour's consideration decided him that his fears were unfounded and at eight o'clock he arrived at the big Fraser house in Philmore Avenue.

Mr. Fraser was commonly supposed to be the biggest political influence in the city. His brother was Senator Fraser, his son-in-law was Congressman Demming, and his influence, though not wielded in such a way as to make him an objectionable boss, was strong nevertheless.

He had a great, huge face, deep-set eyes, and a barn-door of an upper lip, the melange approaching a worthy climax in a long professional jaw.

During his conversation with Dalyrimple his expression kept starting toward a smile, reached a cheerful optimism, and then receded back to imperturbability.

"How do you do, sir?" he said, holding out his hand. "Sit down. I suppose you're wondering why I wanted you. Sit down."

Dalyrimple sat down.

"Mr. Dalyrimple, how old are you?"

"I'm twenty-three."

"You're young. But that doesn't mean you're foolish. Mr. Dalyrimple, what I've got to say won't take long. I'm going to make you a proposition. To begin at the beginning, I've been watching you ever since last Fourth of July when you made that speech in response to the loving-cup."

Dalyrimple murmured disparagingly, but Fraser waved him to silence.

"It was a speech I've remembered. It was a brainy speech, straight from the shoulder, and it got to everybody in that crowd. I know. I've watched crowds for years." He cleared his throat, as if tempted to digress on his knowledge of crowds—then continued. "But, Mr. Dalyrimple, I've seen too many young men who promised brilliantly go to pieces, fail through want of steadiness, too many high-power ideas, and not enough willingness to work. So I waited. I wanted to see what you'd do. I wanted to see if you'd go to work, and if you'd stick to what you started."

Dalyrimple felt a glow settle over him.

"So," continued Fraser, "when Theron Macy told me you'd started down at his place, I kept watching you, and I followed your record through him. The first month I was afraid for a while. He told me you were getting restless, too good for your job, hinting around for a raise— —"

Dalyrimple started.

"—But he said after that you evidently made up you mind to shut up and stick to it. That's the stuff I like in a young man! That's the stuff that wins out. And don't think I don't understand. I know how much harder it was for you, after all that silly flattery a lot of old women had been giving you. I know what a fight it must have been— —"

"Dalyrimple's face was burning brightly. He felt young and strangely ingenuous.

"Dalyrimple, you've got brains and you've got the stuff in you— and that's what I want. I'm going to put you into the State Senate."

"The *what?*"

"The State Senate. We want a young man who has got brains, but is solid and not a loafer. And when I say State Senate I don't stop there. We're up against it here, Dalyrimple. We've got to get some young men into politics—you know the old blood that's been running on the party ticket year in and year out."

Dalyrimple licked his lips.

"You'll run me for the State Senate?"

"I'll *put* you in the State Senate."

Mr. Fraser's expression had now reached the point nearest a smile and Dalyrimple in a happy frivolity felt himself urging it mentally on— but it stopped, locked, and slid from him. The barndoor and the jaw were separated by a line straight as a nail. Dalyrimple remembered with an effort that it was a mouth, and talked to it.

"But I'm through," he said. "My notoriety's dead. People are fed up with me."

"Those things," answered Mr. Fraser, "are mechanical. Linotype is a resuscitator of reputations. Wait till you see the *Herald*, beginning next week—that is if you're with us—that is," and his voice hardened slightly, "if you haven't got too many ideas yourself about how things ought to be run."

"No," said Dalyrimple, looking him frankly in the eyes. "You'll have to give me a lot of advice at first."

"Very well. I'll take care of your reputation then. Just keep yourself on the right side of the fence."

Dalyrimple started at this repetition of a phrase he had thought of so much lately. There was a sudden ring of the door-bell.

"That's Macy now," observed Fraser, rising. "I'll go let him in. The servants have gone to bed."

He left Dalyrimple there in a dream. The world was opening up suddenly—The State Senate, the United States Senate—so life was this after all—cutting corners—cutting corners—common sense, that was the rule. No more foolish risks now unless necessity called—but it was being hard that counted— Never to let remorse or self-reproach lose him a night's sleep—let his life be a sword of courage—there was no payment—all that was drivel—drivel. He sprang to his feet with clenched hands in a sort of triumph.

"Well, Bryan," said Mr. Macy stepping through the portières.

The two older men smiled their half-smiles at him.

"Well, Bryan," said Mr. Macy again.

Dalyrimple smiled also.

"How do, Mr. Macy?"

He wondered if some telepathy between them had made this new appreciation possible—some invisible realization. . . .

Mr. Macy held out his hand.

"I'm glad we're to be associated in this scheme—I've been for you all along—especially lately. I'm glad we're to be on the same side of the fence."

"I want to thank you, sir," said Dalyrimple simply. He felt a whimsical moisture gathering back of his eyes.

The Four

Fists

AT THE PRESENT TIME NO ONE I KNOW HAS the slightest desire to hit Samuel Meredith; possibly this is because a man over fifty is liable to be rather severely cracked at the impact of a hostile fist, but, for my part, I am inclined to think that all his hitable qualities have quite vanished. But it is certain that at various times in his life hitable qualities were in his face, as surely as kissable qualities have ever lurked in a girl's lips.

I'm sure every one has met a man like that, been casually introduced, even made a friend of him, yet felt he was the sort who aroused passionate dislike—expressed by some in the involuntary clenching of fists, and in others by mutterings about "takin' a poke" and "landin' a swift smash in ee eye." In the juxtaposition of Samuel Meredith's features this quality was so strong that it influenced his entire life.

What was it? Not the shape, certainly, for he was a pleasant-looking man from earliest youth: broad-browed, with gray eyes that were frank and friendly. Yet I've heard him tell a room full of reporters angling for a "success" story that he'd be ashamed to tell them the truth, that they wouldn't believe it, that it wasn't one story but four, that the public would not want to read about a man who had been walloped into prominence.

It all started at Phillips Andover Academy when he was fourteen. He had been brought up on a diet of caviar and bell-boys' legs in half the capitals of Europe, and it was pure luck that his mother had nervous prostration and had to delegate his education to less tender, less biassed hands.

At Andover he was given a roommate named Gilly Hood. Gilly was thirteen, undersized, and rather the school pet. From the September day when Mr. Meredith's valet stowed Samuel's clothing in the best bureau and asked, on departing, "hif there was hanything helse, Master Samuel?" Gilly cried out that the faculty had played him false. He felt like an irate frog in whose bowl has been put a goldfish.

"Good gosh!" he complained to his sympathetic contemporaries, "he's a damn stuck-up Willie. He said, 'Are the crowd here gentlemen?' and I said, 'No, they're boys,' and he said age didn't matter, and I said, 'Who said it did?' Let him get fresh with me, the ole pie-face!"

For three weeks Gilly endured in silence young Samuel's comments on the clothes and habits of Gilly's personal friends, endured French phrases in conversation, endured a hundred half-feminine meannesses that show what a nervous mother can do to a boy, if she keeps close enough to him—then a storm broke in the aquarium.

Samuel was out. A crowd had gathered to hear Gilly be wrathful about his roommate's latest sins.

"He said, 'Oh, I don't like the windows open at night,' he said, 'except only a little bit,' " complained Gilly.

"Don't let him boss you."

"Boss me? You bet he won't. I open those windows, I guess, but the darn fool won't take turns shuttin' 'em in the morning."

"Make him, Gilly, why don't you?"

"I'm going to." Gilly nodded his head in fierce agreement. "Don't you worry. He needn't think I'm any ole butler."

"Le's see you make him."

At this point the darn fool entered in person and included the crowd in one of his irritating smiles. Two boys said, "'Lo, Mer'dith"; the others gave him a chilly glance and went on talking to Gilly. But Samuel seemed unsatisfied.

"Would you mind not sitting on my bed?" he suggested politely to two of Gilly's particulars who were perched very much at ease.

"Huh?"

"My bed. Can't you understand English?"

This was adding insult to injury. There were several comments on the bed's sanitary condition and the evidence within it of animal life.

"S'matter with your old bed?" demanded Gilly truculently.

"The bed's all right, but——"

Gilly interrupted this sentence by rising and walking up to Samuel. He paused several inches away and eyed him fiercely.

"You an' your crazy ole bed," he began. "You an' your crazy——"

"Go to it, Gilly," murmured some one.

"Show the darn fool—"

Samuel returned the gaze coolly.

"Well," he said finally, "it's my bed——"

He got no further, for Gilly hauled off and hit him succinctly in the nose.

"Yea! Gilly!"

"Show the big bully!"

"Just let him touch you—he'll see!"

The group closed in on them and for the first time in his life Samuel realized the insuperable inconvenience of being passionately detested. He gazed around helplessly at the glowering, violently hostile faces. He towered a head taller than his roommate, so if he hit back he'd be called a bully and have half a dozen more fights on his hands within five minutes; yet if he didn't he was a coward. For a moment he stood there facing Gilly's blazing eyes, and then, with a sudden choking sound, he forced his way through the ring and rushed from the room.

The month following bracketed the thirty most miserable days of his life. Every waking moment he was under the lashing tongues of his contemporaries; his habits and mannerisms became butts for intolerable witticisms and, of course, the sensitiveness of adolescence was a further thorn. He considered that he was a natural pariah; that the unpopularity at school would follow him through life. When he went home for the Christmas holidays he was so despondent that his father sent him to a nerve specialist. When he returned to Andover he arranged to arrive late so that he could be alone in the bus during the drive from station to school.

Of course when he had learned to keep his mouth shut every one promptly forgot all about him. The next autumn, with his realization that consideration for others was the discreet attitude, he made good use of the clean start given him by the shortness of boyhood memory. By the beginning of his senior year Samuel Meredith was one of the best-liked boys of his class—and no one was any stronger for him than his first friend and constant companion, Gilly Hood.

II

Samuel became the sort of college student who in the early nineties drove tandems and coaches and tallyhos between Princeton and Yale and New York City to show that they appreciated the social importance of football games. He believed passionately in good form—his choosing of gloves, his tying of ties, his holding of reins were imitated by impressionable freshmen. Outside of his own set he was considered rather a snob, but as his set was *the* set, it never worried him. He played football in the autumn, drank high-balls in the winter, and rowed in the spring. Samuel despised all those who were merely sportsmen without being gentlemen, or merely gentlemen without being sportsmen.

He lived in New York and often brought home several of his friends for the week-end. Those were the days of the horse-car and in case of a crush it was, of course, the proper thing for any one of Samuel's set to rise and deliver his seat to a standing lady with a formal bow. One night in Samuel's junior year he boarded a car with two of his intimates. There were three vacant seats. When Samuel sat down he noticed a heavy-eyed laboring man sitting next to him who smelt objectionably of garlic, sagged slightly against Samuel and, spreading a little as a tired man will, took up quite too much room.

The car had gone several blocks when it stopped for a quartet of young girls, and, of course, the three men of the world sprang to their feet and proffered their seats with due observance of form. Unfortunately, the laborer, being unacquainted with the code of neckties and tallyhos, failed to follow their example, and one young lady was left at an embarrassed stance. Fourteen eyes glared reproachfully at the barbarian; seven lips curled slightly; but the object of scorn stared stolidly into the foreground in sturdy unconsciousness of his despicable conduct. Samuel was the most violently affected. He was humiliated that any male should so conduct himself. He spoke aloud.

"There's a lady standing," he said sternly.

That should have been quite enough, but the object of scorn only looked up blankly. The standing girl tittered and exchanged nervous glances with her companions. But Samuel was aroused.

"There's a lady standing," he repeated, rather raspingly. The man seemed to comprehend.

"I pay my fare," he said quietly.

Samuel turned red and his hands clenched, but the conductor was looking their way, so at a warning nod from his friends he subsided into sullen gloom.

They reached their destination and left the car, but so did the laborer, who followed them, swinging his little pail. Seeing his chance, Samuel no longer resisted his aristocratic inclination. He turned around and, launching a full-featured, dime-novel sneer, made a loud remark about the right of the lower animals to ride with human beings.

In a half-second the workman had dropped his pail and let fly at him. Unprepared, Samuel took the blow neatly on the jaw and sprawled full length into the cobblestone gutter.

"Don't laugh at me!" cried his assailant. "I been workin' all day. I'm tired as hell!"

As he spoke the sudden anger died out of his eyes and the mask of weariness dropped again over his face. He turned and picked up his pail. Samuel's friends took a quick step in his direction.

"Wait!" Samuel had risen slowly and was motioning them back. Some time, somewhere, he had been struck like that before. Then he remembered—Gilly Hood. In the silence, as he dusted himself off, the whole scene in the room at Andover was before his eyes—and he knew intuitively that he had been wrong again. This man's strength, his rest, was the protection of his family. He had more use for his seat in the street-car than any young girl.

"It's all right," said Samuel gruffly. "Don't touch him. I've been a damn fool."

Of course it took more than an hour, or a week, for Samuel to rearrange his ideas on the essential importance of good form. At first he simply admitted that his wrongness had made him powerless—as it had made him powerless against Gilly—but eventually his mistake about the workman influenced his entire attitude. Snobbishness is, after all, merely good breeding grown dictatorial; so Samuel's code remained, but the necessity of imposing it upon others had faded out in a certain gutter. Within that year his class had somehow stopped referring to him as a snob.

III

After a few years Samuel's university decided that it had shone long enough in the reflected glory of his neckties, so they declaimed to him in Latin, charged him ten dollars for the paper which proved him irretrievably educated, and sent him into the turmoil with much self-confidence, a few friends, and the proper assortment of harmless bad habits.

His family had by that time started back to shirt-sleeves, through a sudden decline in the sugar-market, and it had already unbuttoned its vest, so to speak, when Samuel went to work. His mind was that exquisite *tabula rasa* that a university education sometimes leaves, but he had both energy and influence, so he used his former ability as a dodging half-back in twisting through Wall Street crowds as runner for a bank.

His diversion was—women. There were half a dozen: two or three débutantes, an actress (in a minor way), a grass-widow, and one sentimental little brunette who was married and lived in a little house in Jersey City.

They had met on a ferry-boat. Samuel was crossing from New York on business (he had been working several years by this time) and he helped her look for a package that she had dropped in the crush.

"Do you come over often?" he inquired casually.

"Just to shop," she said shyly. She had great brown eyes and the pathetic kind of little mouth. "I've only been married three months, and we find it cheaper to live over here."

"Does he—does your husband like your being alone like this?"

She laughed, a cheery young laugh.

"Oh, dear me, no. We were to meet for dinner but I must have misunderstood the place. He'll be awfully worried."

"Well," said Samuel disapprovingly, "he ought to be. If you'll allow me I'll see you home."

She accepted his offer thankfully, so they took the cable-car together. When they walked up the path to her little house they saw a light there; her husband had arrived before her.

"He's frightfully jealous," she announced, laughingly apologetic.

"Very well," answered Samuel, rather stiffly. "I'd better leave you here."

She thanked him and, waving a good night, he left her.

That would have been quite all if they hadn't met on Fifth Avenue one morning a week later. She started and blushed and seemed so glad to see him that they chatted like old friends. She was going to her dressmaker's, eat lunch alone at Taine's, shop all afternoon, and meet her husband on the ferry at five. Samuel told her that her husband was a very lucky man. She blushed again and scurried off.

Samuel whistled all the way back to his office, but about twelve o'clock he began to see that pathetic, appealing little mouth everywhere—and those brown eyes. He fidgeted when he looked at the clock; he thought of the grill down-stairs where he lunched and the heavy male conversation thereof, and opposed to that picture appeared another: a little table at Taine's with the brown eyes and the mouth a few feet away. A few minutes before twelve-thirty he dashed on his hat and rushed for the cable-car.

She was quite surprised to see him.

"Why—hello," she said. Samuel could tell that she was just pleasantly frightened.

"I thought we might lunch together. It's so dull eating with a lot of men."

She hesitated.

"Why, I suppose there's no harm in it. How could there be!"

It occurred to her that her husband should have taken lunch with her—but he was generally so hurried at noon. She told Samuel all about him: he was a little smaller than Samuel, but oh, *much* better-looking. He was a bookkeeper and not making a lot of money, but they were very happy and expected to be rich within three or four years.

Samuel's grass-window had been in a quarrelsome mood for three or four weeks, and, through contrast, he took an accentuated pleasure in this meeting; so fresh was she, and earnest, and faintly adventurous. Her name was Marjorie.

They made another engagement; in fact, for a month they lunched together two or three times a week. When she was sure that her husband would work late Samuel took her over to New Jersey on the ferry, leaving her always on the tiny front porch, after she had gone in and lit the gas to use the security of his masculine presence outside. This grew to be a ceremony—and it annoyed him. Whenever the comfortable glow fell out through the front windows, that was his *congé;* yet he never suggested coming in and Marjorie didn't invite him.

Then, when Samuel and Marjorie had reached a stage in which they sometimes touched each other's arms gently, just to show that they were very good friends, Marjorie and her husband had one of those ultrasensitive, supercritical quarrels that couples never indulge in unless they care a great deal about each other. It started with a cold mutton-chop or a leak in the gas-jet—and one day Samuel found her in Taine's, with dark shadows under her brown eyes and a terrifying pout.

By this time Samuel thought he was in love with Marjorie—so he played up the quarrel for all it was worth. He was her best friend and patted her hand—and leaned down close to her brown curls while she whispered in little sobs what her husband had said that morning; and he was a little more than her best friend when he took her over to the ferry in a hansom.

"Marjorie," he said gently, when he left her, as usual, on the porch, "if at any time you want to call on me, remember that I am always waiting, always waiting."

She nodded gravely and put both her hands in his.

"I know," she said. "I know you're my friend, by best friend."

Then she ran into the house and he watched there until the gas went on.

For the next week Samuel was in a nervous turmoil. Some persistently rational strain warned him that at bottom he and Marjorie had little in common, but in such cases there is usually so much mud in the water that one can seldom see to the bottom. Every dream and desire told him that he loved Marjorie, wanted her, had to have her.

The quarrel developed. Marjorie's husband took to staying in New York until late at night, came home several times disagreeably over-stimulated, and made her generally miserable. They must have had too much pride to talk it out—for Marjorie's husband was, after all, pretty decent—so it drifted on from one misunderstanding to another. Marjorie kept coming more and more to Samuel; when a woman can accept masculine sympathy it is much more satisfactory to her than crying to another girl. But Marjorie didn't realize how much she had begun to rely on him, how much he was part of her little cosmos.

One night, instead of turning away when Marjorie went in and lit the gas, Samuel went in, too, and they sat together on the sofa in the little parlor. He was very happy. He envied their home, and he felt that the man who neglected such a possession out of stubborn pride was a fool and unworthy of his wife. But when he kissed Marjorie for the first time she cried softly and told him to go. He sailed home on the wings of desperate excitement, quite resolved to fan this spark of romance, no matter how big the blaze or who was burned. At the time he considered that his thoughts were unselfishly of her; in a later perspective he knew that she had meant no more than the white screen in a motion picture: it was just Samuel—blind, desirous.

Next day at Taine's, when they met for lunch, Samuel dropped all pretense and made frank love to her. He had no plans, no definite intentions, except to kiss her lips again, to hold her in his arms and feel that she was very little and pathetic and lovable. . . . He took her home, and this time they kissed until both their hearts beat high—words and phrases formed on his lips.

And then suddenly there were steps on the porch—a hand tried the outside door. Marjorie turned dead-white.

"Wait!" she whispered to Samuel, in a frightened voice, but in angry impatience at the interruption he walked to the front door and threw it open.

Every one has seen such scenes on the stage—seen them so often that when they actually happen people behave very much like actors. Samuel felt that he was playing a part and the lines came quite naturally: he announced that all had a right to lead their own lives and looked at Marjorie's husband menacingly, as if daring him to doubt it. Marjorie's husband spoke of the sanctity of the home, forgetting that it hadn't seemed very holy to him lately; Samuel continued along the line of "the right to happiness"; Marjorie's husband mentioned firearms and the divorce court. Then suddenly he stopped and scrutinized both of them—Marjorie in pitiful collapse on the sofa, Samuel haranguing the furniture in a consciously heroic pose.

"Go up-stairs, Marjorie," he said, in a different tone.

"Stay where you are!" Samuel countered quickly.

Marjorie rose, wavered, and sat down, rose again and moved hesitatingly toward the stairs.

"Come outside," said her husband to Samuel. "I want to talk to you."

Samuel glanced at Marjorie, tried to get some message from her eyes; then he shut his lips and went out.

There was a bright moon and when Marjorie's husband came down the steps Samuel could see plainly that he was suffering—but he felt no pity for him.

They stood and looked at each other, a few feet apart, and the husband cleared his throat as though it were a bit husky.

"That's my wife," he said quietly, and then a wild anger surged up inside him. "Damn you!" he cried—and hit Samuel in the face with all his strength.

In that second, as Samuel slumped to the ground, it flashed to him that he had been hit like that twice before, and simultaneously the incident altered like a dream—he felt suddenly awake. Mechanically he sprang to his feet and squared off. The other man was waiting, fists up, a yard away, but Samuel knew that though physically he had him by several inches and many pounds, he wouldn't hit him. The situation had miraculously and entirely changed—a moment before Samuel had seemed to himself heroic; now he seemed the cad, the outsider, and Marjorie's husband, silhouetted against the lights of the little house, the eternal heroic figure, the defender of his home.

There was a pause and then Samuel turned quickly away and went down the path for the last time.

IV

Of course, after the third blow Samuel put in several weeks at conscientious introspection. The blow years before at Andover had landed on his personal unpleasantness; the workman of his college days had jarred the snobbishness out of his system, and Marjorie's husband had given a severe jolt to his greedy selfishness. It threw women out of his ken until a year later, when he met his future wife; for the only sort of woman worth-while seemed to be the one who could be protected as Marjorie's husband had protected her. Samuel could not imagine his grass-widow, Mrs. De Ferriac, causing any very righteous blows on her own account.

His early thirties found him well on his feet. He was associated with old Peter Carhart, who was in those days a national figure. Carhart's physique was like a rough model for a statue of Hercules, and his record was just as solid—a pile made for the pure joy of it, without cheap extortion or shady scandal. He had been a great friend of Samuel's father, but he watched the son for six years before taking him into his own office. Heaven knows how many things he controlled at that time—mines, railroads, banks, whole cities. Samuel was very close to him, knew his likes and dislikes, his prejudices, weaknesses and many strengths.

One day Carhart sent for Samuel and, closing the door of his inner office, offered him a chair and a cigar.

"Everything O. K., Samuel?" he asked.

"Why, yes."

"I've been afraid you're getting a bit stale."

"Stale?" Samuel was puzzled.

"You've done no work outside the office for nearly ten years?"

"But I've had vacations, in the Adiron——"

Carhart waved this aside.

"I mean outside work. Seeing the things move that we've always pulled the strings of here."

"No," admitted Samuel, "I haven't."

"So," he said abruptly, "I'm going to give you an outside job that'll take about a month."

Samuel didn't argue. He rather liked the idea and he made up his mind that, whatever it was, he would put it through just as Carhart wanted it. That was his employer's greatest hobby, and the men around him were as dumb under direct orders as infantry subalterns.

"You'll go to San Antonio and see Hamil," continued Carhart. "He's got a job on hand and he wants a man to take charge."

Hamil was in charge of the Carhart interests in the Southwest, a man who had grown up in the shadow of his employer, and with whom, though they had never met, Samuel had had much official correspondence.

"When do I leave?"

"You'd better go to-morrow," answered Carhart, glancing at the calendar. "That's the first of May. I'll expect your report here on the first of June."

Next morning Samuel left for Chicago, and two days later he was facing Hamil across a table in the office of the Merchants' Trust in San Antonio. It didn't take long to get the gist of the thing. It was a big deal in oil which concerned the buying up of seventeen huge adjoining ranches. This buying up had to be done in one week, and it was a pure squeeze. Forces had been set in motion that put the seventeen owners between the devil and the deep sea, and Samuel's part was simply to "handle" the matter from a little village near Pueblo. With tact and efficiency the right man could bring it off without any friction, for it was merely a question of sitting at the wheel and keeping a firm hold. Hamil, with an astuteness many times valuable to his chief, had arranged a situation that would give a much greater clear gain than any dealing in the open market. Samuel shook hands with Hamil, arranged to return in two weeks, and left for San Felipe, New Mexico.

It occurred to him, of course, that Carhart was trying him out. Hamil's report on his handling of this might be a factor in something big for him, but even without that he would have done his best to put the thing through. Ten years in New York hadn't made him sentimental, and he was quite accustomed to finish everything he began—and a little bit more.

All went well at first. There was no enthusiasm, but each one of the seventeen ranchers concerned knew Samuel's business, knew what he had behind him, and that they had as little chance of holding out as flies on a window-pane. Some of them were resigned—some of them cared like the devil, but they'd talked it over, argued it with lawyers and couldn't see any possible loophole. Five of the ranches had oil, the other twelve were part of the chance, but quite as necessary to Hamil's purpose, in any event.

Samuel soon saw that the real leader was an early settler named McIntyre, a man of perhaps fifty, gray-haired, clean-shaven, bronzed by forty New Mexico summers, and with those clear, steady eyes that Texas and New Mexico weather are apt to give. His ranch had not as yet shown oil, but it was in the pool, and if any man hated to lose his land McIntyre did. Every one had rather looked to him at first to avert the big calamity, and he had hunted all over the territory for the legal means with which to do it, but he had failed, and he knew it. He avoided Samuel assiduously, but Samuel was sure that when the day came for the signatures he would appear.

It came—a baking May day, with hot waves rising off the parched land as far as eyes could see, and as Samuel sat stewing in his little improvised office—a few chairs, a bench, and a wooden table—he was glad the thing was almost over. He wanted to get back East the worst way, and join his wife and children for a week at the seashore.

The meeting was set for four o'clock, and he was rather surprised at three-thirty when the door opened and McIntyre came in. Samuel could not help respecting the man's attitude and feeling a bit sorry for him. McIntyre seemed closely related to the prairies, and Samuel had the little flicker of envy that city people feel toward men who live in the open.

"Afternoon," said McIntyre, standing in the open doorway, with his feet apart and his hands on his hips.

"Hello, Mr. McIntyre." Samuel rose, but omitted the formality of offering his hand. He imagined the rancher cordially loathed him, and he hardly blamed him. McIntyre came in and sat down leisurely.

"You got us," he said suddenly.

This didn't seem to require any answer.

"When I heard Carhart was back of this," he continued, "I gave up."

"Mr. Carhart is—" began Samuel, but McIntyre waved him silent.

"Don't talk about the dirty sneak-thief!"

"Mr. McIntyre," said Samuel briskly, "if this half-hour is to be devoted to that sort of talk— —"

"Oh, dry up, young man," McIntyre interrupted, "you can't abuse a man who'd do a thing like this."

Samuel made no answer.

"It's simply a dirty filch. There just *are* skunks like him too big to handle."

"You're being paid liberally," offered Samuel.

"Shut up!" roared McIntyre suddenly. "I want the privilege of talking." He walked to the door and looked out across the land, the sunny, steaming pasturage that began almost at his feet and ended with the gray-green of the distant mountains. When he turned around his mouth was trembling.

"Do you fellows love Wall Street?" he said hoarsely, "or wherever you do your dirty scheming—" He paused. "I suppose you do. No critter gets so low that he doesn't sort of love the place he's worked, where he's sweated out the best he's had in him."

Samuel watched him awkwardly. McIntyre wiped his forehead with a huge blue handkerchief, and continued:

"I reckon this rotten old devil had to have another million. I reckon we're just a few of the poor beggars he's blotted out to buy a couple more carriages or something." He waved his hand toward the door. "I built a house out there when I was seventeen, with these two hands. I took a wife there at twenty-one, added two wings, and with four mangy steers I started out. Forty summers I've saw the sun come up over those mountains and drop down red as blood in the evening, before the heat drifted off and the stars came out. I been happy in that house. My boy was born there and he died there, late one spring, in the hottest part of an afternoon like this. Then the wife and I lived there alone like we'd lived before, and sort of tried to have a home, after all, not a real home but nigh it—cause the boy always seemed around close, somehow, and we expected a lot of nights to see him runnin' up the path to supper." His voice was shaking so he could hardly speak and he turned again to the door, his gray eyes contracted.

"That's my land out there," he said, stretching out his arm, "my land, by God—It's all I got in the world—and ever wanted." He dashed his sleeve across his face, and his tone changed as he turned slowly and faced Samuel. "But I suppose it's got to go when they want it—it's got to go."

Samuel had to talk. He felt that in a minute more he would lose his head. So he began, as level-voiced as he could—in the sort of tone he saved for disagreeable duties.

"It's business, Mr. McIntyre," he said. "It's inside the law. Perhaps we couldn't have bought out two or three of you at any price, but most of you did have a price. Progress demands some things——"

Never had he felt so inadequate, and it was with the greatest relief that he heard hoof-beats a few hundred yards away.

But at his words the grief in McIntyre's eyes had changed to fury.

"You and your dirty gang of crooks!" he cried. "Not one of you has got an honest love for anything on God's earth! You're a herd of money-swine!"

Samuel rose and McIntyre took a step toward him.

"You long-winded dude. You got our land—take that for Peter Carhart!"

He swung from the shoulder quick as lightning and down went Samuel in a heap. Dimly he heard steps in the doorway and knew that some one was holding McIntyre, but there was no need. The rancher had sunk down in his chair, and dropped his head in his hands.

Samuel's brain was whirring. He realized that the fourth fist had hit him, and a great flood of emotion cried out that the law that had inexorably ruled his life was in motion again. In a half-daze he got up and strode from the room.

The next ten minutes were perhaps the hardest of his life. People talk of the courage of convictions, but in actual life a man's duty to his family may make a rigid course seem a selfish indulgence of his own righteousness. Samuel thought mostly of his family, yet he never really wavered. That jolt had brought him to.

When he came back in the room there were a lot of worried faces waiting for him, but he didn't waste any time explaining.

"Gentlemen," he said, "Mr. McIntyre has been kind enough to convince me that in this matter you are absolutely right, and the Peter Carhart interests absolutely wrong. As far as I am concerned you can keep your ranches to the rest of your days."

He pushed his way through an astounded gathering, and within a half-hour he had sent two telegrams that staggered the operator into complete unfitness for business; one was to Hamil in San Antonio; one was to Peter Carhart in New York.

Samuel didn't sleep much that night. He knew that for the first time in his business career he had made a dismal, miserable failure. But some instinct in him, stronger than will, deeper than training, had forced him to do what would probably end his ambitions and his happiness. But it was done and it never occurred to him that he could have acted otherwise.

Next morning two telegrams were waiting for him. The first was from Hamil. It contained three words:

You blamed idiot!

The second was from New York:

Deal off come to New York immediately Carhart.

Within a week things had happened. Hamil quarrelled furiously and violently defended his scheme. He was summoned to New York, and spent a bad half-hour on the carpet in Peter Carhart's office. He broke with the Carhart interests in July, and in August Samuel Meredith, at thirty-five years old, was, to all intents, made Carhart's partner. The fourth fist had done its work.

I suppose that there's a caddish streak in every man that runs crosswise across his character and disposition and general outlook. With some men it's secret and we never know it's there until they strike us in the dark one night. But Samuel's showed when it was in action, and the sight of it made people see red. He was rather lucky in that, because every time his little devil came up it met a reception that sent it scurrying down below in a sickly, feeble condition. It was the same devil, the same streak that made him order Gilly's friends off the bed, that made him go inside Marjorie's house.

If you could run your hand along Samuel Meredith's jaw you'd feel a lump. He admits he's never been sure which fist left it there, but he wouldn't lose it for anything. He says there's no cad like an old cad, and that sometimes just before making a decision, it's a great help to stroke his chin. The reporters call it a nervous characteristic, but it's not that. It's so he can feel again the gorgeous clarity, the lightning sanity of those four fists.